"I DON'T NEED A FIRE," JAIME GROANED

Then his eyes flickered. "Unless I can undress you in front of it."

Diana moistened her lips. "Yes...."

She sat on the edge of the bed, watching him strike a match to the crushed newspapers under the log. The fire caught and the spiraling flames echoed her inner feelings.

As Jaime urged her to her feet, she felt suddenly shy. Slowly he eased off her sweater and jeans, his fingers lightly caressing her flesh. When she stood before him in her satin bra and briefs, he said gently, "Now...undress me."

She stared up at him. "Jaime...."

His hands guided hers, and her shyness was replaced with anticipation. At last he stood naked before her, his tall powerful figure outlined by the firelight, and something very primitive clutched at her throat.

This was what it meant to truly desire a man.

ABOUT THE AUTHOR

Research for her tenth Superromance kept Meg
Hudson fairly close to her home on Cape Cod, but
upcoming stories will take the inveterate traveler
once again to distant shores.

Books by Meg Hudson

HARLEQUIN SUPERROMANCE
  9—SWEET DAWN OF DESIRE
 36—LOVE'S SOUND IN SILENCE
 53—RETURN TO RAPTURE
 64—THOUGH HEARTS RESIST
 70—A CHARM FOR ADONIS
 79—TWO WORLDS, ONE LOVE
 94—BELOVED STRANGER
106—THE RISING ROAD
126—NOW, IN SEPTEMBER
141—CHAMPAGNE PROMISES

HARLEQUIN AMERICAN ROMANCE
25—TO LOVE A STRANGER

These books may be available at your local bookseller.

Don't miss any of our special offers.
Write to us at the following address for
information on our newest releases.

Harlequin Reader Service
P.O. Box 52040, Phoenix, AZ 85072-2040
Canadian address: P.O. Box 2800, Postal Station A,
5170 Yonge St., Willowdale, Ont. M2N 5T5

Meg Hudson

CHAMPAGNE PROMISES

Harlequin Books

TORONTO • NEW YORK • LONDON
AMSTERDAM • PARIS • SYDNEY • HAMBURG
STOCKHOLM • ATHENS • TOKYO • MILAN

Published November 1984

First printing September 1984

ISBN 0-373-70141-1

For the Wareham Wanderers and all the other great people we know across The Bridges... and most especially for the Portuguese.

PROLOGUE

LIGHTS. Through a haze formed partly by shock, partly by pain, Diana became aware of lights... lights whose blue-white brilliance stung her eyes. But even before she could protest, something happened to block out the glaring lights. Something... no, not something... someone.

She focused on the man standing next to the long, firm bed she was lying upon. No, it wasn't a bed. It was a hospital examining table.

She was in a hospital.

She heard a male voice say, "Hello, there," and then she became aware of other sounds. People talking, their tones mostly subdued. Someone crying in the distance. Something clattering. Her imagination fancied the sounds swelling out of all proportion. They began to hurt her ears.

"Hello," the man said again, and all of Diana's senses converged upon his voice. She clung to the sound of it, grasping it as if she'd been about to drown and had found a raft floating just within her reach. It was a wonderful voice, deep, mellow, and there was a tenderness in the few words he had spoken.

She tried to move her lips, but even this slight

effort was exhausting. Somehow she managed a faint, "Hello," in return.

"That's better," the man said approvingly. Though the haze was still shimmering before her eyes she became aware of the strength of his figure, which loomed in silhouette before her, and the solidity of him. Instinctively she reached out a hand, and felt it grasped by one much larger than hers. His hand was warm, his touch as wonderful as his voice.

He leaned closer, and Diana felt as if a veil had been pulled aside. His face was clear to her, and it hardly seemed possible that it was the face of a stranger, a man she'd never seen before. She felt she'd known him forever.

His face was as wonderful as his voice and hands. Diana couldn't define why everything about him affected her in such a way. She knew only that she sensed this man was her hope...her hope for the future.

She focused on his eyes. They were beautiful, like black velvet, and they told her that he cared about her. He *cared*. Nothing before had ever been quite so important.

"My face," she began. "I...I felt the blood. Cuts...."

"Yes," he said gravely, still looking down at her with those miraculously deep, dark eyes, still holding her hand. "But you mustn't worry. I mean that honestly," he assured her as she moved slightly in protest. "You're going to be all right."

His voice softened, his words a promise between the two of them. A secret vow.

"You," he told her, "are going to be just as beautiful as ever...."

CHAPTER ONE

It HAD STARTED TO SNOW during the evening. As she gently closed the front door of the house behind her, Diana remembered that someone at the party had looked out the window at one point and announced, "It's snowing." And someone else had added, "Maybe we're going to have a white Christmas yet."

Diana was not at all averse to the idea of a white Christmas, but Christmas was nearly two weeks away, and right now, standing at the top of the steps that led to the street, she was not prepared for snow or much of anything else in the way of inclement weather. There'd been moonlight when she'd started out earlier. Who had said about New England's changeable weather, "If you don't like it, wait a minute!"

She glanced ruefully at her shoes. She'd chosen to wear strappy gold sandals because they went so well with her red chiffon dress. She'd selected the dress because it was one of the most attractive outfits she owned, and she'd felt its bright color would help her get into the Christmas spirit.

Well, though the party had been pleasant enough, she hadn't gotten into the Christmas spirit at all. And now she regretted not having brought along a pair of practical boots to walk home in. The sidewalk was already becoming slippery, a fact she quickly verified with a bit of careful testing.

Fortunately "home" was only a block and a half away, along Fairhaven's Fort Street. Home? Diana smiled wryly. It was a long time since she'd lived in a place she could truly call home.

Luckily the oyster-white, quilted puff of a coat she was wearing had a practical side. It boasted a hood, which Diana now drew up over her shoulder-length honey-gold hair. This would at least prevent the snow from trickling down her neck and keep her hair dry in the bargain, though it didn't help her visibility much. It was difficult to see as she inched along. A stiff wind blowing in from Buzzard's Bay was causing the snow to swirl in front of her, and the streetlights were few and far between.

By the time she reached the walk that led to the DuBois house, she was chilled to the marrow, and her fingers were icy as she fumbled in her gold evening bag for a key.

It was pitch dark, and she chided herself for not having remembered to put the outside light on. But then, she rationalized with a slight smile, she was a city girl, accustomed to apartment living.

She found the key and, clutching it, endeavored to work it into the door lock, which was invisible at the moment because of the snow and the darkness. Her teeth were chattering and she felt frozen to the core. She shivered convulsively, and the key, which had failed to connect with the lock, slipped completely out of her grasp.

At first she was sure it must have fallen right at her feet. Tentatively she prodded around with the toe of an inadequate shoe, but she couldn't feel the key. Finally she got down on her hands and knees, despite the cold, despite the snow, and groped. Only then did she come to the dismal conclusion that the key must have fallen off the stoop into the bushes that landscaped the front of the house.

Chagrined, Diana straightened. She'd slipped out of the party early; probably they'd still be making merry at the Burroughses' house. But she had no wish to navigate back there. The snow would be blowing in her face this time, and it was already coming down thicker and faster in just these few minutes.

The Burroughses were strangers to her anyway, and she disliked the thought of bothering them. They'd invited her to the party out of the kindness of their hearts. She was renting the old DuBois house in Fairhaven, and a word undoubtedly had been spoken in her behalf by Agatha DuBois, her absentee landlady. In fact Miss DuBois had apparently "spoken" quite a few words, because everyone Diana had met so far had been more than kind to her, including Amy Howland and her husband, Phil, who lived in the house on the right. Unfortunately the Howlands were in Boston for the weekend, and the corner house on the left was vacant. Or was it?

Peering through the swirling snow, Diana was sure she saw a light in the house on the left, at the rear of the first floor. She looked again to verify this. The light cast a yellow glow across the steadily falling snow.

The thought of negotiating the wide strip of slippery lawn between the DuBois house and the neighboring house was not a particularly pleasant one, considering the footgear she was wearing. Nor did she relish the thought of approaching the house at all. Over coffee one morning Amy Howland had mentioned that the corner house had been vacant for quite a while and she'd heard a rumor it was going to be put up for sale.

"I think it might be for the best if it *was* sold," Amy had said. Then she had shuddered slightly. "I hate empty houses. There's something so spooky about them. Particularly big empty houses. And I don't think Jaime has any intention of ever coming back here to live."

Diana's curiosity had been aroused, but before she'd had a chance to delve into the matter of why "Jaime" might not want to return to Fairhaven to live, or even who he was, for that matter, Amy had gone on to a completely different subject.

There *was* something spooky about the big square house, especially under these circumstances, Diana conceded as she grimly started toward it. The thought occurred to her as she skidded along that there was a chance someone had broken into the house, in which case she might be facing more than she'd bargained for. But it was too late to worry about that. In any event, all she was about to ask for was the loan of a flashlight.

She pounded on the back door with an authority she was far from feeling, each thump leaving a hollow echo in its wake. After the fourth or fifth knock she stood back waiting for a response. But nothing happened.

Whoever had turned on the light could have done so before going out. This thought put Diana on edge. She was cold, she was miserable and she needed shelter, damn it! Resolutely she raised her hand to pound on the door once again and almost fell forward as it suddenly swung open.

A man stood in the aperture, a tall, broadshouldered man. Diana considered herself fairly tall at five foot seven, but even though she was wearing high heels this man towered above her.

Looking at him she shuddered involuntarily and felt herself shrinking back. There was something menacing about the way he was looming over her. He must have flicked a switch along the wall because the narrow hall behind him suddenly lit up. Dim light, with that same yellowish quality as the light in the window, but still bright enough that Diana could now see him clearly. She gasped. Then he spoke, and she knew that even if she hadn't seen him at all she'd have known who he was. No one else in the world had a voice like that.

"What do you want?" he demanded, plainly annoyed at having been disturbed on this snowy December night. Yet despite the note of impatience, his voice was rich, mellow. At the sound of it a wave of memory crested in Diana and for a long moment she could only stare at him, unable to answer.

Finally she managed, in little more than a whisper, "I'm sorry. I. . . ."

He stood aside and said abruptly, "Come in."

Diana hesitated, painfully aware that the last thing this man wanted was for anyone to intrude upon him. He was making that obvious. But she was too cold, too miserable, to deny the desire to seek warmth.

She stepped past him into the narrow hall. Scowling, he said, "In there." Again Diana hesitated, but then she followed him into a big, square kitchen. A large round table stood in the center of the room, and she saw that she'd interrupted a meal of sorts. There was a partially eaten sandwich on a plate and a mug half full of coffee beside it. A folded newspaper. A pen. It looked as if he'd been doing a crossword puzzle while consuming a late, solitary supper.

Diana's eyes swerved toward the wood stove in the corner of the room and it became a magnet, drawing her. She began to rub her hands together, the warmth seeping into her chilled knuckles, and she wished she could slip off her sandals and rub her feet too.

She was afraid to turn and look at the man, afraid that she'd give herself away, that he'd know she'd recognized him. For reasons she couldn't entirely analyze she felt it important that he didn't know that. Not now, anyway. Her reasons didn't solely involve him. She didn't want to get into the past herself. It was still difficult, almost impossible, to talk about the accident, even though three years had elapsed. Almost exactly three years. It had been a December night, very much like this one, though it had not been snowing very long when the accident had happened. The snow hadn't been coming down anywhere as thickly as it was outside at the moment....

His voice cut across her memory. He asked, a knife-edge to his irony, "May I know to what I owe the honor of this visit?"

"I need a flashlight," Diana said flatly, and forced herself to turn to face him.

Their eyes meshed, his as midnight black as she remembered, velvet soft. But she also noticed a great deal about him she hadn't been aware of before. That other night she'd concentrated on separate features, his eyes, his voice and his hands. Now she saw that he was an exceptionally attractive man, despite the shadows of weariness under those midnight eyes and the deep lines of utter fatigue etched on his face.

His hair was as dark as his eyes, thick and gently waving, sculpting his head as if it had been arranged by a master artist. He had a broad forehead and strong, clear-cut features, and a full sensuous mouth.

His skin was a light olive, and she could imagine that in summer he would tan to mahogany. She guessed that just now he was even paler than usual. Had he been ill, she wondered, trying not to stare at him. He looked as if he might have been, or as if he'd undergone some kind of trauma that had taken a great deal out of him. Mental or emotional trauma, perhaps, if not physical.

He had a beautiful body. His broad shoulders and chest tapered to a narrow waist cinched by a wide leather belt with an intricately patterned, dull metal buckle. The muscularity of his long legs was emphasized by snug jeans and despite his slight pallor there was a pervasive, latent strength about him. Diana found herself thinking that he'd be a powerful adversary.

She saw that he was assessing her even as she was assessing him. She must look a wreck by now. Her hair was damp—the snow had gotten under the hood—and instinctively she reached up to make sure the half bang she wore was still intact, covering her forehead, covering the scar.

There was no telling what impression she was making on him—undoubtedly not a very good one, Diana was sure—and she wasn't surprised when he frowned. "Did you say you wanted a flashlight?" he asked her.

She nodded. "Yes."

"Why?" The question was flung at her abruptly.

"I dropped my key," Diana said reluctantly. "In the snow, that is. I'm afraid it's fallen into the bushes. I...I'm living in the house next door," she finished lamely.

"The DuBois house?" he asked, the frown deepening.

"Yes. That's right."

"I understood that Agatha DuBois was in Florida. She usually goes there for the winter."

"She is in Florida," Diana said quickly. "I'm renting the house from her."

"You're renting the DuBois place?" He shook his head. "When did Agatha start renting her house?"

"I don't think she ever has before."

"How long do you plan to stay?"

Obviously the thought of her being next door didn't thrill him, but at least this was a question to which she could give him a definite answer. "I have the house for six months," she said. "Miss DuBois plans to visit friends at several points along the way north on her return trip from Florida, so she doesn't intend to get back until the first of June."

"I see." He spoke tersely, and it wasn't necessary for him to add that he didn't like what he was "seeing." The message was loud and clear.

Warmed by the heat from the wood fire, Diana moved back toward the door that led into the hall. Then, turning toward him again, she said, "I'm Diana Ashley, by the way."

He nodded. "I'm Jaime Medeiros." He pronounced his first name softly, "*Jay*-meh," with a slight "Z-ish" slur on the "J." But it was his last name—Medeiros—that sent another wave of memory sweeping over Diana.

After this man had sutured the cuts on her head, after he'd left her, an intern had come in to see how she was doing. Although his face was a blur to her, she remembered the intern because he'd had hair the color of shining copper and a light, friendly voice that held none of the deep mystery of this man's voice.

"You lucked out," the intern had told her cheerfully. "That was the maestro who took care of you."

The words had registered dully. "The maestro?" she had repeated.

"Yes. Not that we don't have some excellent plastic surgeons hereabouts, but Dr. Medeiros is the best of the best. Usually he's in Boston. I mean, he practices there. He just happened to be down here tonight visiting a relative who's a patient here in the hospital. He has staff privileges here, and when he learned we were shorthanded he stepped in and offered to help. So, as I said, you really lucked out...."

Well, she supposed she had. The only scar that was visible slanted across her forehead an inch or so from her hairline, and it was easily camouflaged by a clever hairstyle. For that matter, it had faded over the three years since the accident until, thanks to the surgeon's skill, it was little more than a narrow line, and not at all unsightly. The camouflage was really no longer necessary, but she'd become so accustomed to trying to hide the scar in the early months that she still automatically covered it.

Jaime Medeiros interrupted her thoughts. "Is there something the matter, Miss Ashley?" he asked impatiently.

"No," she replied quickly. "If I could borrow a flashlight...."

"I hope I have one that works," he said rather glumly. "If you'll excuse me."

He left her for only a couple of minutes and returned with a large metal flashlight, testing it as he walked, turning the switch on and off. He picked up a heavy wool parka, which had been hanging over the back of one of the kitchen chairs, and slipped into it before Diana realized what he was contemplating.

"There's no need for you to come with me," she said swiftly. "It's miserable out there. If you'll just lend me the flashlight I'll return it first thing in the morning."

"On the contrary," he said. "I wouldn't think of letting you go over there in the dark. Suppose you dropped the flashlight? Then where would either of us be?"

It was an attempt at humor, she supposed, but she didn't think it was very funny. She started to retort, then saw that he was staring at her feet.

"Do you usually go around in shoes like that on a night like this?" he demanded.

"No," Diana said quickly, color stinging her cheeks. "I was at a party," she started to say, then told herself there was no reason for her to offer him any explanations.

"And you left your boots behind?" he suggested. Then added, a glint of humor flickering in those dark eyes, "Or did you drop your boots, too?"

Diana's own sense of humor rallied. "Matter of fact, I was foolish enough not to believe in what I'd been told about the unpredictability of New England weather. It didn't occur to me that snow could follow moonlight quite so swiftly."

He smiled at her, a smile that tugged at one corner of his mouth creating a lopsided effect that was especially disarming. "No," he said, "I'm sure you didn't. I'm sorry, Miss Ashley. I wish I had a pair of boots to offer you, but obviously you'd swim in mine. So I suppose there's nothing to do but set out as you are."

She nodded, the smile and his tone of voice taking her back once again. He'd smiled at her that night in the emergency room too, she remembered. There'd been nothing lopsided about his smile then, but the effect had been much the same.

He started out the door into the hall and she followed him. Opening the outside door he said, "Watch it going down the steps. Here, you'd better let me go first...."

"I'm not about to fall," she told him sedately, and then very nearly slipped on the top step. A strong hand reached out to grip her, and she tensed. She would never forget the way he'd held her hand, the way he'd told her she would be all right. And she *was* all right! Sometimes the memories were still very hard to live with...but she was all right!

"Easy there," he cautioned. "Here, let me lift you down." Before she could protest he reached up and swung her into his arms, and inadvertently she clung to him. She put her arms around his neck like a trusting child, and for a long moment he made no move to release her. His strength, his warmth, seeped into Diana, and she had the crazy wish that he'd keep on holding her like this, that he'd never let her go.

But he did let her go. He set her down firmly and said, "Now take it a step at a time. Be sure you've got the first step secured before you take the second one."

The snow had already covered the footsteps Diana had made coming across from the other house. The world stretched out whitely before them, and Diana felt the snowflakes touching her cheeks and then dissolving.

To her own surprise she laughed.

"What is it?" he asked.

"It's like being in the middle of an old-fashioned paperweight," she told him. "You know...the ones you turn upside down to make it snow."

"Yes," he nodded, "I know. There used to be one in the parlor when I was growing up. I don't know what ever happened to it. Watch it! Steady, there. You nearly slipped again."

He reached out as he spoke, clasping her arm and drawing her close to his side. "I'll keep you steady on the way across."

"Honestly, I can make it," she insisted.

"Let's be sure," he retorted. "And let's hope you dropped the key right in the center of the stoop. I'm not sure we're going to be able to find it before the spring thaw if it went into the bushes.''

But the key wasn't in the center of the stoop. Jaime turned the beam of his flashlight across the porch and let the light crisscross back and forth again. Then, with a finger, he swept away the snow slowly and carefully until it was plain that there was no key hidden beneath.

"Damn!" he exclaimed, exasperated. He turned to Diana. "Go huddle in the doorway. You'll get a little protection from the weather.'' As he spoke, he was shining the beam on the bushes at the side of the house, and Diana didn't need him to tell her the situation was hopeless. The bushes were completely snow-covered now, and the twiggy branches totally interlaced. He was right, she conceded dismally. There wasn't a prayer of finding the key for quite some time to come...if ever.

She felt both foolish and frustrated, and there was no point in trying to tell herself that this was something that could have happened to anyone. What a sorry reintroduction to one of the most attractive men she'd ever seen in her life!

The thought brought her up short. Even these few minutes with Jaime Medeiros had made her very aware of him, more aware than she'd been of any man since that other December night three years ago.

She still flinched from thinking about the accident...during her conscious hours. At night, when she was asleep and her subconscious took over, it was much too easy to succumb to dreams, terrible dreams. Nightmares.

Until she'd started reliving the accident through those nightmares, she hadn't realized that in sleep the senses could be so vivid. She could actually hear, feel, smell, even taste. At least she imagined she could, which amounted to much the same thing. The terrible crash of metal upon metal— what a tearing, hideous sound! Screams ringing out into the night, the agony of sharp, sudden pain, and then the sensation of her own blood, gushing. Sirens shrieking in the darkness, blue lights and red lights flashing through the falling snow, voices with an urgency she'd never forget, and the unconsciousness, blissful unconsciousness. And when she'd come to in the hospital emergency room, this man had been there.

Behind her the front door swung open, startling Diana so she was thrown off balance, physically as well as mentally. For a second she was in danger of slipping from her perilous position close to the edge of the porch.

Again a strong arm reached out to grip her, and Jaime said impatiently, "For God's sake, woman, let's not have any more calamities!"

He was drawing her into the hall as he spoke. He had switched on the overhead crystal chandelier, and he asked abruptly, "Where's the thermostat?"

"On the wall just outside the living room," she said, then pointed. "There."

She watched him stride across to push up the indicator. "This place is cold as hell," he commented and then laughed, a short, wry laugh.

She was staring at him, perplexed. "How did you get in?"

He smiled. "Through the cellar bulkhead. Your security system leaves a lot to be desired." He came over to her and tugged at her coat. "Here," he said. "Let's get that thing off you. It's nearly soaked through. And you might do something about those ridiculous shoes."

He started toward the kitchen with her damp coat as he spoke, and it occurred to her that he seemed quite familiar with the house. Over his shoulder he called, "Got any firewood handy?"

"Yes," Diana said, bending to unstrap the sandals. Her toes felt frozen and were beginning to ache. "There's a stack of wood next to the living-room fireplace, and more in a bin at the top of the cellar stairs."

"I'll get a fire going," he said, coming back to her. "Why don't you go and slip into something warm and dry, and take off your stockings." He cast a slightly derisive glance at her wet feet. "Otherwise you're apt to slip and break your neck."

She stiffened. "Honestly, I am not accident prone."

The word rang in her ear. It struck her that this was a strange thing for her to have said to him. They'd met initially because of an accident, though obviously he had no recollection of that. She was just a face, one of the many faces he must

have attended to during the course of his career.
And she must look very different now, from that
night in the emergency room.

She saw that he was grinning at her, and he said
lightly, "You couldn't prove it by me that you're
not accident prone, Diana." There was something
disturbingly intimate about his use of her first
name. "You nearly fell down at my kitchen door,
you nearly slipped half a dozen times on the way
over here, a minute ago you came within an inch
of tumbling off the porch...."

"I'm cold," she stated abruptly. "It...it makes
it difficult to put your feet where you want them
to go."

"Especially when you're wearing shoes like
those," he teased, surveying the flimsy sandals,
which Diana was now holding, dangling them
from their straps. "Look, get your stockings off
and put something warm on while I get the fire going. I also put the teakettle on. Do you have any
rum?"

"Yes," she said weakly.

"We can both do with a couple of hot buttered
rums," he told her. "Now...get going."

She turned quickly and started up the stairs. She
had the feeling that if she didn't move he'd probably give her a push to get her on her way.

It *was* cold in the house. She should have turned
the thermostat up before going to the party, but
she hadn't realized a cold spell was setting in any
more than she'd suspected it would shortly be
snowing. Her coat had done a reasonably good

job of protecting the chiffon dress, but it still felt chilly and damp to her touch, and she was glad to shrug out of it. She slipped into a furry, deep-blue robe, and after giving her feet a brief rubbing down put on matching slippers, which were wonderfully warm.

All the while she was thinking about the man downstairs. At this moment he was building a fire in the living-room fireplace and undoubtedly being as capable about it as he seemed to be about everything else.

Even dressed casually in old jeans and a shirt that had seen plenty of wear, there was an air of authority about Jaime Medeiros. And even in the teasing way he'd told her to get along upstairs and change her clothes, there'd been the sense that he was a person used to giving orders.

She might be imagining this because she knew he was a doctor, but she didn't think so. Though he *was* a doctor, of course. A very important doctor, according to what the intern at the hospital in New Bedford had told her about him. The best in his field.

There was no reason to think he was no longer an outstanding surgeon, no logical reason for this odd feeling she had that something had happened to him over the past three years. Something overwhelming. True, he might be here in Fairhaven only because he'd wanted some vacation time. But not many people would enjoy spending the pre-Christmas season alone in an old house.

Diana stopped short. That was exactly what she

was doing, for her own very good reasons. But Jaime had seemed such a loner and clearly hadn't wanted any company, if she was to judge from his reaction when he'd answered his door.

Diana wondered what had brought him back into her life this Christmas, then realized she would probably never know.

CHAPTER TWO

THERE WAS A BLAZE CRACKLING on the hearth and Jaime was adding another log to it when Diana walked into the living room. It was a big square room, furnished in a stiff Victorian decor. Ornate chairs and sofas, velvet drapes hanging at the long narrow windows, lots of bric-a-brac. It was far too cluttered and the dark colors too oppressive for Diana's taste, yet there was a substance about it she couldn't help admiring. Everything in the room seemed to have been made with eternity in mind, a far contrast from most modern furnishings.

Jaime straightened and stepped back. The firelight cast a gold-orange glow over his figure, highlighting the planes on his face while lending a somber quality to his features. He turned to Diana and said softly, almost as if he was speaking to himself, "It's a long while since I've been in this house."

She smiled slightly. "I thought you knew your way around pretty well."

"Yes," he nodded. "That is, I used to. As I say, it's been a long time." He turned back to the fire and gave a log an experimental thrust with a poker. Momentarily the flames burned brighter.

"Incidentally," he told her, "I bolted the cellar bulkhead after me so you'd better be sure you don't lose any more keys. Otherwise we'll have to make a more forcible entry."

"I hope there *is* another key," Diana muttered.

"Probably," he said. Then he added, "Hang in there. I've got the teakettle simmering, so I'll fix our buttered rums."

She was sitting in front of the fireplace staring contemplatively into the flames when he came back. Her thoughts were focused on him, this man who was beginning to seem a mystery figure to her. She asked herself if she could possibly be mistaken about Jaime Medeiros. She'd been pretty hazy that night in the emergency room. Wasn't there a chance that the doctor who had attended her had merely *looked* like Jaime? The Medeiros surname could be a coincidence.

But somehow she felt certain there was no chance at all of coincidence.

Jaime had made the drinks in thick brown china mugs, which were warm to the touch. The buttered rum was fragrant with spices, and Diana sniffed it appreciatively. Jaime took a chair on the opposite side of the fireplace, and she smiled across at him. "It smells wonderful."

"It tastes even better," he assured her.

The warm liquid trickled down her throat, soothing and delicious.

She laughed. "I can feel it going all the way down."

"That's the way it should be," he said. "It's

guaranteed to warm the very cockles of your heart.''

The cockles of your heart. It had been a long time since she'd heard that expression, and she mused, ''I wonder what that really means.''

''Pardon?''

''The cockles of your heart. How do you suppose such an expression ever originated?''

''Cockleshells are often heart shaped,'' he said. ''They're also bivalves, so their contents are hidden from view. When someone speaks of the cockles of the heart, he's speaking of innermost feelings....''

She stared at him. ''I'm impressed.''

''Don't be,'' he advised, and she sensed that he was deliberately keeping his tone light. ''I'm a storehouse of miscellaneous information, which isn't really worth very much at all.''

''Are you a writer?'' she ventured, even though she knew better.

His astonishment was not feigned. ''No,'' he said. He seemed amused at the idea. ''I flunked English all through school. What would make you think I might be a writer?''

''Writers tend to garner storehouses of miscellaneous information,'' she told him.

''Do you speak from experience?'' he asked.

''What?''

''Are *you* a writer?''

''No.''

''But you do have a career, don't you?'' he persisted.

She was surprised at this comment. "What makes you think I might?" she countered.

"Everything about you," he said, setting the mug of rum down on a small side table as he spoke. "You're a city girl, that's pretty clear to me."

She laughed. "You're judging me entirely by my sandals."

"No, only partly by your sandals." He smiled. "There are other things about you. The way you dress...yes, I did notice the red chiffon. Something about your manner—an urban quality. And of course it didn't take a great sleuth to determine that you're not used to making your way around on freshly fallen snow. I'd say that usually by the time you venture outdoors everything has been shoveled and plowed."

"I take it back," Diana said. "You're not a writer, you're a detective."

"Wrong again," he replied. "I just like to play guessing games, that's all, and you whet my curiosity."

Diana took a gamble. "You whet my curiosity, too," she told him frankly.

Something flickered in those midnight eyes. He did have astonishingly beautiful eyes, Diana thought dreamily, and wondered if perhaps his hot buttered rum concoction was going to her head. But his eyes, long lashed, would have made a beauty out of even a plain woman. Which was not to imply that there was anything in the least feminine about Jaime Medeiros, a silent voice told her swiftly. On the contrary. He was the most masculine man she'd ever met.

Was it Jaime or the buttered rum that was making her feel as if her senses had begun to swim in a lovely way? She felt warmed and vibrant, so much aware of. . . of everything. The room, the fire, the moment, the man. The snow, visible through a slit in the draperies, was still falling thick and white, a pristine mantle that would swiftly cover ugliness. All sorts of ugliness.

He hadn't answered her comment about being as curious about him as he was about her. Waiting, Diana knew he was not going to give her any definitive answer. He didn't want to talk about himself any more than she wanted to talk about herself. Well, she could respect that.

She tried to ignore the fact that he'd grown silent and was looking at her in a speculative sort of way. He picked up his mug and sipped the rum again, and Diana knew that something had gone out of this moment between them. He'd thrust aside a sense of sharing that in retrospect surprised her. But they *had* shared a definite feeling, there'd been a time of intimacy between them. This room had become a temporary sanctuary, and she'd opened the door when she'd admitted she was curious about him. Maybe Jaime felt it natural enough for him to be curious about other people, about her, to be specific. But obviously he'd set up safeguards around himself that he did not intend to put aside.

Diana was not about to let him get off so easily.

She picked up her own mug—it was wonderful to have something to hold in her hands, something to give a little bit of stage business before she came out with what she wanted to say. She phrased the question carefully. "I'd been told that the house next door was empty."

Surprisingly, he smiled. She had already learned that his smile could have a devastating effect, and it did once again. But she could see that her question had amused him, and that piqued her slightly.

"The house next door *was* empty, Diana."

She flushed and put the mug back on the little table next to her chair. "When did you arrive?" she asked directly.

"Late this afternoon," he replied, equally direct. "I put my car in the garage because snow was threatening."

Of course, Diana thought perversely, he was able to read the weather signs more accurately than she was.

"If I hadn't done that, you would have known there was someone in residence," he said. "But I didn't see any traces of life over here, either."

"I decided to walk to the party tonight," she said. "It was just a couple of blocks up the street and I didn't know the weather was going to change quite so...dramatically."

"It has a habit of doing that in these parts," he said dryly. "Where was this party you went to?"

"At the Burroughses. Do you know them?"

He nodded. "Yes, I know Jack and Emily." He looked across at her, shaking his head and smiling ruefully. "You've caused some complications for me."

"Me?" She was startled.

"Yes, you, Diana. I'd hoped to come back here without anyone being the wiser—for the present, at least. I'd hoped to hole in for a while. It seems that was a vain hope."

"Oh?" She bristled. "I'm not interested in telling anyone whether you're here or not, if that's what's worrying you."

He studied her, and she had the crazy feeling that he was seeing into her. "It isn't worrying me, exactly. I suppose I should have had the sense to realize that Fairhaven wasn't a very good refuge for me. For that matter, I didn't even intend to make it a refuge. I just wanted a couple of days strictly to myself...."

"And I spoiled that for you." She didn't ask, she stated the fact.

He grinned. "Chivalry may be dead, but all forms of gallantry would go out the window if I admitted that! Anyway, I can't say you've really spoiled anything for me. Maybe I'm not as much of a potential hermit as I thought I was. And imagine how much more difficult life would have been for you if I hadn't been next door tonight. Who else do you think you might have found to climb through the cellar bulkhead for you in the snow?"

He held up an admonishing finger. "Don't answer that question. The answer's obvious. Any man who happened to be around, and I'm sure you could have found someone within hailing distance if I hadn't been on the scene.''

He was smiling as he spoke, his tone light and teasing. He was offering a compliment. She accepted it grudgingly. "Look," she said, "I definitely won't tell anyone you're here if you want to keep it a secret. Ordinarily, I suppose I might have said something to Amy Howland, when she gets back from Boston, or even to Emily Burroughs when I call up to thank her for the party. But I can assure you—''

"You don't have to assure me of anything, Diana," he told her. "But just to clarify things for you, I'm not a trespasser. I own the house next door.''

"You *own* the house next door?"

"Yes," he said. "Why? You seem surprised.''

"I suppose I am surprised. I understood that the house was vacant and was about to be put up for sale.''

"Well, the house has been vacant. As for putting it up for sale.... That's a decision I haven't made yet. Who told you that, Diana?''

"I don't know," she answered uncertainly. "Amy, maybe, or perhaps it was Emily. I don't know many people in Fairhaven yet.''

"Yet?" He picked up on the word. "That sounds as if you intend to enlarge your circle.''

"I hope to.''

"In Fairhaven, in the middle of winter?" He laughed. "Strange time, strange locale," he observed. Then he asked directly, "Why Fairhaven?''

Diana understood his tendency to retreat when questioned, because she shared the same trait. But she could think of no good reason not to answer his question. She wasn't skilled at making instant subterfuge sound valid.

"I'm here for professional reasons," she said rather stiffly.

"Professional reasons?" he echoed, a smile curving the corners of his mouth.

"Yes," she said, wishing they hadn't gotten onto the subject. "I'm a historian," she began, but the phrase sounded so pompous that she amended it to, "That is, I'm working for my doctorate in history."

"You're going to write a history thesis here in Fairhaven?"

She couldn't blame him for his skepticism, but it was enough to make her become slightly defensive, something she didn't want to do. "I plan to use Fairhaven as my base," she explained, "but I'll also be researching in New Bedford, Fall River and Provincetown—coastal communities where there are large Portuguese populations."

"Portuguese?" Diana flushed at his tone, well aware that his name—Medeiros—was Portuguese, that *he* was Portuguese, this arrestingly handsome man, who was now viewing her with unconcealed amusement.

It took effort for Diana to brook that amusement, but she said staunchly, "My thesis will involve the Portuguese people, their history and their part in the history of the United States. This area makes a perfect focal point. I'm sure I don't have to tell you there's an extensive Portuguese population in coastal New England. Although there are important pockets of people of Portuguese birth or descent in other sections of the country—Connecticut, New Jersey and California, for example—coastal New England offers the greatest density and the greatest opportunity for research."

"Of course," he conceded. "You're quite right about that." She sensed he was trying not to smile now, and this was even more irritating than his open amusement. "How did you happen to choose the Portuguese as your thesis subject?" he asked, then added a bit tauntingly, "Personal acquaintance?"

"No," Diana said shortly. "I suppose you could say that in the course of some basic research I found there'd been endless studies made about other ethnic groups in this country...the Polish, the Irish, the Italians, the Germans—but the Portuguese have been relatively neglected."

"And so you're going to see to it that the Portuguese get their rightful place in history's sun?"

He was teasing, she knew and she chose to ignore it. "I hope to do a comprehensive study on coastal New England's Portuguese population, yes," she retorted.

"You said that you have this place until June, when Agatha DuBois gets back from Florida? Are you telling me that for the next six months you plan to probe the local population and then write up your findings about them as if they were germs on a microscope slide?''

''I don't think that's a very good analogy,'' Diana said. ''You sound as if I'm a dentist looking for hidden cavities. I don't intend to 'probe' at all. At least that's certainly not the word I'd use for what I plan to do. I want to get to know Portuguese people here, yes. I want to understand them. I want to learn about their history as well as their customs, their traditions. I want to learn something about what they've gotten from this country and what they want from it.'' She paused. ''Sorry. I didn't mean to get carried away.''

He looked across at her quizzically, his well-shaped dark eyebrows slightly raised. ''You're going to find the Portuguese people difficult to get to know, Diana, unless you have a most unusual approach. They are clannish, family oriented, they've felt the sting of prejudice. They are deeply steeped in tradition—the older ones, that is. The younger ones usually rebel against being Portuguese at all. They don't want to be like their parents. If you've done your homework, you must know this is par for the course on the part of most younger generations in the country today, regardless of national backgrounds. Above all else they don't want to be different. Does Agatha DuBois know this is why you came here and rented her house?'' he concluded abruptly.

''Mine isn't exactly a secret mission,'' Diana retorted, offended by his tone. ''Of course Miss DuBois knows why I'm here!''

"Of course?"

"Agatha's niece Gail is one of my oldest and dearest friends," Diana replied testily, wondering why she was explaining anything to him at all. His probing was beginning to bother her. "When Gail found out what I wanted to do she told me that her aunt had a house in Fairhaven that ordinarily stands empty throughout the winter months. Gail suggested that Miss DuBois might be willing to rent it to me, she arranged for an introduction between us and Miss DuBois was enthusiastic about my project."

"I see."

"I don't think you do," she contradicted. "Naturally I knew that Fairhaven would be an ideal place to establish a base for my research—"

"Among the Portuguese?" he finished for her.

"Yes," she replied sharply. "Among the Portuguese."

"You make us sound like a bunch of aborigines," he said, but he was smiling. "You may be in for a few surprises, Diana. Anyway, that's neither here nor there at the moment." He was standing as he spoke, grasping the mug, and he polished off the last of the rum.

"I've got to get back," he said, "but I do have one suggestion to make."

Diana wasn't sure she was going to welcome his suggestion, but she asked politely, "Yes?"

"There's an old New England custom you might do well to follow," he advised. "I checked when I went out to the kitchen to put the kettle on.

There's a board with a variety of keys on it on the wall in the pantry, including one to the front door. It would be a good idea for you to go and have a few duplicates made in the morning, and then hide the door key under one of the house shingles. Just be sure of your mathematics when you do so.''

"My mathematics?''

"Yes.'' He nodded solemnly, plainly enjoying his little speech. "Be sure you count the number of shingles up from the bottom, and the number across from the edge of the door, or whatever reference point you choose. Then shove the key under that shingle, gently but firmly, and you won't risk the chance of being locked out again.''

With that he turned. "I left my parka in the kitchen. I think I'll go out the back way. It's closer. Be sure you lock the door behind me. Not that Fairhaven isn't a relatively safe community, especially in the midst of a snowstorm, but even so. . . .''

"I know,'' she told him, matching her own cynicism to his. "In this world we live in. . . .''

"Yes,'' Jaime said, looking down at her. "Yes. . . in this world we live in.''

WHEN HE'D GONE, and she'd locked the door behind him, Diana cast a long look at the teakettle and the rum bottle and wondered whether or not it would be wise to make another drink for herself.

She decided against it. Just now, discretion was the watchword. She had no wish to blot out her senses with rum or anything else. In fact, for the first time in a very long while she had no desire to escape her own thoughts. She wanted to think about tonight, and about Jaime Medeiros.

He'd irritated her, to be sure. He'd been disparaging about a project that was very important to her. But she couldn't really blame him. She'd been a bit lofty in talking about, "the Portuguese," even though she hadn't meant it the way it had probably sounded. He'd taken her the wrong way, or at least he'd teased her into thinking he had. She'd already discovered that he could be quite a tease, and for the most part, she liked his sense of humor. A sense of humor could often be a saving grace, something to come to the rescue when the going was hard. That had been one problem in dealing with Gary. Gary had not been endowed with much of a sense of humor, and he'd had no humor at all when it came to anything concerning himself.

Diana closed her eyes tightly, telling herself she was not going to think of Gary. Not tonight. No, it was better, safer, and more enjoyable to think about Jaime Medeiros, and her curiosity about him at this point was brimming over.

As she went back into the living room and sat before a fire that was slowly dying out, she gave him points for having elicited information out of her while telling her absolutely nothing about himself except that he was the owner of the house next door and really didn't know whether he was going to sell it or not. He'd sidestepped anything else very adroitly, always turning her own questions back to the subject of her.

Well, Jaime Medeiros, Diana told herself, as the last of the logs fell apart in a shower of cascading, molten gold embers, *two can play at that game. And next time it's going to be my turn!*

DIANA AWAKENED THE FOLLOWING MORNING to the sound of church bells. Sunday. The church bells pealed out the message of the Sabbath, and their lovely sound stirred something deep within Diana.

She threw back the covers and stood, stretching, then walked across to the window to look out over a solid expanse of beautifully white snow that reached all the way to the banks of the Acushnet River, which separated Fairhaven from its sister city of New Bedford. Most of the houses on this side of Fort Street had property that went straight to the river, and there was an inescapable sense of affinity with the sea, because both Fairhaven and New Bedford were major commercial fishing ports.

Nearer the house, the thickly frosted tree branches etched intricate patterns against a backdrop of unexpectedly blue sky, and Diana was sure that if she flung the window open and breathed deeply of the winter air it would be heady as wine.

From her bedroom vantage point, she had a clear view of the garage that went with this house, the garage next door, the parallel driveways, and the rear of the house next door, as well. As she watched, she saw the back door fling open. Jaime came out to stand on his back stoop, and then surefootedly he made his way down the snow-crusted steps and headed for the garage.

She watched as he opened the garage door, then lost him from sight as he went inside. But after a few minutes he backed his car out and left it standing in the driveway with the engine running while he got out, twirling a bright-red wool scarf around his throat.

Diana had never been much of a car enthusiast. A car was transportation as far as she was concerned, and she didn't care much about makes and models. But this car was clearly expensive. She was sure it was a Mercedes, silver-gray in color. It looked like a car a successful surgeon might own.

As she watched, wondering what Jaime was about to do next, he startled her by walking in the direction of her own back door. She shrank away from the window. That way, if he glanced up, he wouldn't see her ogling him!

She quickly donned her furry blue robe, thrust her feet into her slippers and gave her hair a quick brushing. There was barely enough time to get into the bathroom and splash her face before she heard him pounding at the kitchen door.

She flew down the stairs, taking an added minute to regain her breath before she continued along the hall, her hands shaking slightly as she opened the door for him.

He filled the whole aperture. He was dressed in the same parka he'd worn the night before, but now his dark hair was covered by a navy-blue knitted cap. As she looked at him, an awareness of him came over Diana, as if he'd tangibly transmitted something of himself to her. He was a potently attractive man, dangerously attractive. She knew that warning signals should be flashing in her brain, and yet they were singularly silent. Why? She didn't want to be attracted to this man. She didn't want to be attracted to anyone! She told herself this fiercely and then had to question whether or not she was really telling herself the truth.

Time had passed. Three years had passed. She remembered the psychologist she'd consulted for months after the accident. He would have been the first to applaud her interest in Jaime. He would have told her it was way past the hour to start living again. . . .

Jaime was watching her closely and she wondered how much her face was revealing. She liked to think she was capable of camouflaging her feelings, but she was rapidly discovering that with Jaime, this was not an easy thing to do.

When he spoke, though, that deep and wonderful voice was casual enough. "Hi, there," he said.

"Hi," Diana responded weakly.

"There's a convenience store open Sundays up on Route 6. I've run out of a couple of staples, and since I was going to make the trip I wondered if you needed anything."

Diana found that she wanted very much to need something—if only so he'd come back again. She wanted to see more of him, she wanted to know more about him.

Thinking rapidly, she said, "I'm almost out of

milk.'' Granted, she didn't use very much milk, but her supply was running low.

"I could use some bread, too," she added. "Or maybe some English muffins. For breakfast. But honestly, you don't have to bother...."

"No bother," he said. "I'm going anyway."

"My purse is upstairs. If you'll wait a minute, I'll go get some money."

"No problem," he said easily. "You can pay me when I deliver your groceries, ma'am. For that matter, your credit's good."

He flashed a smile at her and the full impact of his charm swept over her. She'd thought last night he had looked rather pale and somewhat haggard. There'd been shadows under his eyes and new lines in his face. If, that is, her single memory of him from that night in the emergency room was accurate. But maybe a night's sleep had done its trick. Whatever, Jaime looked virile and very much in command of himself, and he was clear-eyed as he gazed down at her. The shadows and lines seemed to have dissipated and he radiated vitality.

"Put the coffeepot on," he told her, then grinned. "I'll bring the cream and sugar."

CHAPTER THREE

DIANA DRESSED QUICKLY, slipping on black corduroy slacks, a black turtleneck and a loose velour overblouse in a gorgeous deep-rose tone that made her feel warm just to look at it. She smoothed on lip gloss that complemented the blouse, added a skim of light-blue eye shadow, and then brushed her hair until it shone, curving her half bang softly over her forehead to hide the scar.

Her pulse was thumping, and she felt as excited as if she were a teenager about to go out on her first date. Surprised at such a reaction, she stared in the mirror at her reflection. There was a glow to her face and a light in her eyes. She frowned. This was ridiculous. There was no sensible reason why a man she hardly knew should have such an effect on her.

She glanced down at her feet, then decided to leave on the furry blue slippers. They were a bit incongruous with the rest of her clothes, but at the moment she felt like settling for comfort rather than style, a feeling she suspected her neighbor would appreciate. If he even looked at her feet, that is. She hoped he'd be more concerned with some of her other attributes.... She nearly laughed aloud at such an admission. This was all so unlike her!

She had filled the teakettle before going upstairs, and it was whistling as she entered the kitchen. She took it off the burner then got out the mugs they'd used for the buttered rum the night before. They were far more suitable for Sunday morning coffee with Jaime than Agatha DuBois's fragile china teacups.

Diana told herself that she should have gone grocery shopping the day before. Since she'd been in Fairhaven she'd eaten out or subsisted on frozen TV-dinner fare, and the fridge and the cupboard were disconcertingly bare. But she did have some bacon and four eggs, and she decided to put the bacon on to fry. It could be kept warm in the oven, and later she'd scramble the eggs.

Glancing out the kitchen window as she turned the bacon, she saw that the blue sky and sunshine had vanished as suddenly as if they'd been a mirage in the first place. The sky had clouded over, and it was beginning to snow again.

It was a relief to hear a car door slam and to know that Jaime had returned safely. Ever since the accident, Diana had had an obsession about winter driving.

Jaime was carrying a large brown paper bag, which he set down on the kitchen table with a flourish. "A Sunday paper," he told her, withdrawing it. "You'll find quite a bit about the Portuguese population in the local press. Also, the milk you requested, and the bread. And—" he pulled out another package "—I bought some *bolos*. You might say they're a Portuguese version of English muffins." His grin was mischievous. "I thought you might as well start your ethnic indoctrination on a practical level."

"Excellent idea," Diana agreed, her smile matching his.

The bacon was on the verge of becoming overdone, and she hurried to its rescue, Jaime following close behind. Glancing over her shoulder, he asked, "Am I by any chance invited to breakfast?"

"Yes," she said quickly. "Of course."

He was surprising her. Last night he'd given every evidence of resenting her intrusion. He'd made it clear that he wanted to be alone. There had been a subtle change once he came across to her house with her, though. He was annoyed briefly when he discovered there was no chance of finding her door key in the snow. But once he solved that problem and went on to make hot drinks for them, a different element entered into their relationship. An easy camaraderie.

Jaime had admitted, humorously, that perhaps he wasn't the potential hermit he'd thought he was. Diana considered his comment now and came to an impromptu conclusion. Maybe it wasn't so much that he wanted to be alone as that he wanted to block out his past. Maybe he was willing to be with her because she wasn't a part of his past—as far as he knew. Inadvertently she touched her forehead, feeling the line of the scar beneath the bang. *That* was a part of his past, something she didn't want to get into for two reasons now. As it was, they were strangers. They hadn't existed for each other until yesterday, and as long as they could keep things between them in the present tense they'd both be safe.

"Want me to toast the *bolos*?" Jaime asked.

"Yes, please."

"You do have butter?"

"Yes, in the fridge."

"I'll use the broiler, if I won't get in your way. I can butter the *bolos* first, and the butter will seep down into them as they broil."

"Fine," Diana said. "When I scramble the eggs I'll put the bacon back in the oven to warm up a bit."

"Remarkable teamwork," he complimented. "By the way, do I smell coffee?"

"Yes. Do you want a cup now?"

"I'd love one," he replied. "I work much more efficiently when I have caffeine coursing through my veins."

Diana filled both mugs. Jaime had bought cream and sugar so she added a judicious amount of cream to each cup. Then, opening the box of sugar, she asked, "How much?"

"Two heaping teaspoons," he said. "Revolting, isn't it? But I like it sweet."

He was standing at the kitchen counter buttering the *bolos* as he spoke, and she took his mug of coffee over to him.

"Just put it down there," he said, indicating a

vacant space, and she did so. . .then found herself mesmerized by the sight of his hands. They were large hands, but they were beautifully formed, his fingers long and slender. He could have been a great sculptor, Diana found herself thinking, or a great cellist—or a great surgeon.

She became aware that he had stopped spreading the butter, and she glanced up to see that he was frowning slightly. "What is it?" he asked, and it occurred to her that he was a very perceptive person. Too perceptive, maybe. She'd have to be careful.

She managed a laugh. "I admire your efficiency."

He chuckled. "For a while I worked as a short-order cook in a fish-and-chips place, during the summers when I was going to college. They didn't have a machine so I cut all the potatoes by hand. I became a real whiz at it. A one-man assembly line."

He transferred the buttered muffins onto a baking sheet, then slid the sheet into the oven and set the controls. "These'll only take a minute," he told her. "You'd better start whipping up the eggs."

Diana got down to business, and soon they were sitting opposite each other at the kitchen table with plates of food in front of them.

The *bolos* were delicious. Diana savored a bite, nodded appreciatively, then asked, "Is everything Portuguese this good?"

Jaime grinned. "What a leading question!"

"Damn!" Diana said. And then she, too, smiled. "Look, there's something I need to straighten out with you."

He raised an inquiring eyebrow. "Oh?"

"I think I got off on the wrong foot with you last night when I told you about my project," she said frankly. "You seemed to feel I was being disparaging, and I wasn't. In fact, that's the last thing I want to be."

He nodded. "Okay. I'll accept that. But I admit I'm curious. Why the Portuguese, Diana?"

"What do you mean?"

"Why have you selected the Portuguese for your undivided attention?"

"I thought I explained that," she said. "Most of the major ethnic groups in America have been researched very thoroughly. That's not to say the Portuguese haven't been researched, of course, but not to the same extent."

"And that's your only reason for choosing the subject for your doctoral thesis?" he persisted.

"No," she said. "No, it isn't." She hesitated, beginning to realize that it would be impossible to get into any serious dialogues with Jaime without taking the chance of revealing more about herself than she wanted to reveal.

"Agatha DuBois's niece—my friend Gail Landers—lives on Cape Cod," she began carefully. "Her husband, Harold, is a lawyer in Hyannis. They come over here occasionally to visit Agatha. Maybe you know them?"

He shook his head. "No. At least, I don't think

so. But for the most part I've been away from Fairhaven for quite a few years.''

"Well, last summer I spent some time with Gail. I was at. . .at rather loose ends. I got my master's in history five years ago, you see, but, well, I've never really used it. Anyway, last summer I'd come to the point where I wanted to make a real decision about what to do with the rest of my life,'' she said, avoiding his eyes as she spoke. "Finally I decided that I wanted to work toward my doctorate in history so that maybe eventually I'll be able to do something really important in my field. It was about then I visited Gail, and one day she took me out to Provincetown. You know Provincetown?''

"Yes,'' he nodded.

"Well, it was a mad jumble in summer,'' she said. "There were hundreds of tourists swarming all over the place. The whole effect was absolutely kaleidoscopic, a riot of colors and impressions, but I still got the Portuguese flavor underneath it all. I discovered that despite all the frosting on the cake, Provincetown is primarily a Portuguese-American fishing village. We went to a place where we had fish done in this marvelous garlic and rosé wine sauce. . . .''

"*Vinho D'Alhos,*'' Jaime said absently. There was skepticism to his smile. "Are you telling me that eating some Portuguese-style fish made you decide on the subject for your thesis?''

"That does make me sound frivolous, doesn't it?'' she countered. "No, it wasn't the food. It was the people and the atmosphere and a lot of intangibles I can't put into words for you. For instance, the little shrines outside some of the houses on the side streets with elaborate statues in them, some golden, some with the Madonna's robes painted blue and white. And the fishermen out on MacMillan Wharf—they look as if they'd be equally at home on the Lisbon waterfront, or in the Azores. And...."

Her words trailed off, and Jaime said wryly, "You're making your point." He smiled slightly. "Funny," he observed. "What's so natural to me seems to be so foreign and intriguing to you."

"I suppose so," she admitted. Then, hesitantly, she asked, "Your family did come from Portugal, didn't they?"

His eyes zeroed in on her face. He was giving her a quick assessment, she knew, and she only wished he'd reveal what his conclusion was. Then he said, "No. My family didn't come from Portugal."

He was amused by her obvious astonishment. Laughing, he went on, "My great-grandfather came from the Azores. The island of São Miguel, to be precise—Saint Michael. They say, incidentally, that the best cooks come from São Miguel.

"The Azores," he continued, "were once bleak and barren rocky islands. They're eight hundred miles off the coast of Europe in the Atlantic. They were discovered by the Portuguese in 1427 and later colonized. I hope you'll pardon my ethnic pride when I say the Portuguese have been the greatest navigators in the history of the world. Natural seafarers...in part because they had to be. Portugal was a poor country. As her population increased, her people had to go beyond her borders in order to make a living. So they gained sovereignty of the seas and they held it through at least the seventeenth century, opening up trade routes throughout the world. Losing many, many ships in the process, I might add." Jaime stared at Diana moodily as he continued. "There was a famous Jesuit missionary who long ago summed up the whole thing when he said, 'God gave the Portuguese a small country for a cradle, but the whole world for a grave.' And there's still too much truth to that. Too many men are lost at sea every year, right off this New England coast!"

He refilled their mugs with coffee, his face still somber. "I suppose I tend to be bitter about the sea," he confessed, "because my own grandfather and so many others I've known—people close to me—have been lost in the terrible winter storms that lash New England. Even today, with all the advances in navigational equipment, putting to sea to earn one's living remains a highly dangerous occupation."

"You make me feel very ignorant," Diana said after a moment. "I know so little about the sea."

"Where do you come from, Diana?"

"New York. I was born on Manhattan Island and I've lived there most of my life. I've traveled some, mostly on vacations. But New York primarily has been my home. In a sense I've been surrounded by the sea, but it's been an abstract sort of thing to me."

She ventured another question. "What about you?" she asked him. "Have you lived next to the sea most of your life?"

Now it was his turn to hesitate. "I suppose you could say so," he said slowly. "My life, aside from some traveling, has been pretty much divided between Boston and Fairhaven, so I know what you mean about the sense of the sea being somewhat abstract in a city. I think it's a closer reality in Boston than it is in New York, if only because Boston is so much smaller. But even so. . . ."

The question came unbidden. "Have you ever been to Portugal, Jaime?"

He shook his head. "No. I've always wanted to save Portugal—and the Azores—for a very special time in my life."

"And there's never been that sort of time?"

"No," he said. "Not. . . that sort of time."

He stood and took his plate across to the sink, rinsing it off with cold water. "I've got to get going. Some family obligations later in the day," he said, with a slight grimace.

So he had family in Fairhaven, and they knew he'd come back. So much for the recluse theory, Diana thought wryly.

He picked up his parka and shrugged into it. "What are you going to do with the rest of your day?" he asked, zipping up the jacket.

"Write a few letters," Diana told him. "At least, I should. I should also get started on my research. I borrowed a few books from the Millicent Library the other day."

"Be careful if you drive anywhere," he cautioned. "The roads are slippery."

Diana hoped he didn't notice her involuntary shudder.

As she watched him, her pulse began to thud again. Seeking refuge in the trite, she said, "Don't you want to take the cream and sugar with you? Or the rest of the *bolos*?"

He shook his head. "No. You can have the *bolos* for afternoon tea." He grinned as he spoke, and before she could frame an answer he came across the room to her. Then, taking her entirely unawares, he put his arms around her and drew her close to him. A gentle finger tilted back her chin and his lips claimed hers, his kiss deep and tender, releasing a surge of feeling in Diana that left her breathless.

He stroked her hair as he held her for a moment longer, and his voice was husky as he whispered in her ear, "What are you doing to me, Diana Ashley?"

She had no ready answer to this question, nor did she have the chance to make one anyway. By the time she rallied enough to say anything, he was gone.

AMY HOWLAND CALLED AT ten o'clock Monday morning to announce that she was back from Boston, and to invite Diana over for a cup of coffee.

Diana was only too happy to accept the invitation. The balance of Sunday had dragged interminably. She had heard Jaime's car when he drove off in the early afternoon, and it was hours and hours later, long after dark, before he returned. She realized, then, that she'd had one ear cocked in the direction of his house all day.

Amy was short, plump and blond, a pleasant person with an effervescent personality. Her husband, Phil, whom Diana had met only once, was a total contrast, tall and thin and quite aloof. He was vice-president of a New Bedford bank. In line to be president shortly, Amy had confided.

The weekend in Boston had been spent visiting some of Phil's relatives and had been "a real drag," Amy said frankly. "Very proper Bostonians, all of them," she told Diana as she poured coffee into thin, flower-sprigged cups. "They bore me to distraction."

They were having their coffee in a winterized side porch, furnished with bamboo chairs and couches, bright colored upholstery, and curtains done in splashy, tropical colors. Diana felt as if she'd been transplanted to the South Sea Islands, and the snow-covered ground and frosted trees visible through the windows were decidedly out of place.

Amy kicked off her pale-green pumps and wriggled her toes. "As far as I'm concerned things are a lot more interesting right here in Fairhaven than they are in Boston at the moment. Did you know that you now have another neighbor?"

Startled, Diana automatically replied, "Who?"

"The famous Dr. Jaime Remingio Medeiros has moved back among us," Amy confided. "According to his sister-in-law he's taken up residence in his house, which is right next door to yours.''

"His sister-in-law?'' Diana repeated.

"Flor,'' Amy said. "She's married to Guilherme Medeiros, Jaime's older brother. Everyone calls him Bill. He's part owner of a fish-packing plant here in Fairhaven, and he also has a major interest in several trawlers, among other things. The Medeiros family has been involved with the sea, one way or another, for years. Except for Jaime. He was the apple of his mother's eye, and she saw to it that enough money was put aside to send him off to college and medical school. He proved her right before she died. I guess you could say that he was just about the top plastic—or reconstructive—surgeon in Boston. But now he's given that all up. He hasn't been practicing medicine for almost two years. From what Flor says, he'd dropped out of sight entirely for the better part of this year until he suddenly appeared here in Fairhaven just a couple of days ago. It is all,'' concluded Amy, "very, very strange.''

Diana stirred a spoon of sugar into her coffee, although normally she didn't take sugar at all. But she needed a bit of action to keep her hands busy while she decided whether or not she should tell Amy Howland that she'd already met Jaime Medeiros herself.

There was no reason *not* to mention their meeting. She could make it sound a lot more casual than it had been. But Amy's comment that Jaime's actions were "very, very strange'' put a new complexion on things. Diana knew that if she were to say now that she'd had any kind of encounter with Jaime it would be only natural for Amy to be brimming with questions about how he'd looked, what Diana thought of him...and on, and on, and on. And though she could not spell out to herself an explanation for her reticence about answering these questions, or about discussing Jaime with anyone, for that matter, she knew that for now she wanted to keep their first encounters private. She wanted to learn more about him without revealing that they'd already met. This seemed a safe enough approach. Only Jaime himself knew of their meeting, and she couldn't imagine him broadcasting very much—about anything.

No, the important thing right now was to find out what it was Amy considered so strange. "Why strange, Amy?" she asked her friend directly.

Amy considered the question for a long moment. Then she said, "Well...maybe I'm jumping to conclusions, Diana. My husband's always saying that I'm too impulsive. And of course the little I know comes from Flor, and she's not a very responsive person. She doesn't take too well to questions, especially about the Medeiros family. Anyway—" Amy shrugged "—I just happened to run into Flor this morning when I went into town to pick up some supplies. She was in a hurry and we didn't have much time to talk. I suppose she told me Jaime was coming back because she thought I might see lights on in the house and call the police, thinking it was still supposed to be un-inhabited.

"Of course, I *was* dying to ask Flor a million questions," she added, "but Flor's never been a person I've felt I could really relate to. I don't imagine you've met her."

"No," Diana replied. "Not unless she was at the Burroughses' party Saturday night."

Amy shook her head. "She wouldn't have been. The Burroughses and the Medeiroses don't mix much socially. Except for Jaime, I'd say. I'm sure that if Emily had known Jaime was in Fairhaven she'd have invited him to her party. But then Jaime really moved into another world when he left Fairhaven. Not just by becoming a doctor, a very eminent doctor, but by marriage."

"By marriage?" Diana echoed, and felt a sudden sharp pain in her side.

"Jaime married Cynthia Adams," Amy reported. "One of the Boston Adamses. By that time, of course, he wasn't living in Fairhaven any longer, but once he'd become established as a surgeon he bought the house here for his mother. He told Phil once—he and Phil went to Fairhaven High years ago and they're still friends—well, he told Phil once that his mother had always wanted to live on Fort Street, and he was determined that she'd do so before she died. That was the sad part of it...."

"What was?" Diana demanded impatiently, when Amy appeared to lapse into a private reverie.

"What? Oh...Mrs. Medeiros. She never lived in the house. Jaime was about to furnish it—he wanted it to be just *so* for her—when she had a stroke. She went from the hospital into a nursing home, and she never came out of the nursing home. So Jaime had the house, but it's been vacant most of the time these past few years. Cynthia had no interest in it. Jaime didn't want to rent it; he had a caretaker look after it. Once in a while he'd come down himself, but it's only partially furnished—no place anyone would want to stay in for any length of time. Now...well, I guess he's come back because he's going to sell it, though Flor doesn't seem to be so sure. Jaime had dinner with them yesterday, but he didn't say anything about putting the house up for sale. According to Flor, he didn't say much about anything."

"Has he been ill?" Diana asked abruptly.

"Ill?"

"Has Jaime Medeiros been ill?"

"I don't think so," Amy said. She looked puzzled. "What makes you ask that?"

"You said he'd given up medicine," Diana reminded her. "He must have had a reason. I know he was very well-known as a plastic surgeon," she went on. "I...I've heard the name before. So it doesn't seem likely that he would have quit in the middle of such a promising career unless for some reason he could no longer operate."

"No, it doesn't, does it," Amy agreed. "More coffee?"

"No," Diana said. "No, thank you."

"Phil and I took a long trip almost two years ago," Amy said. "Sort of a delayed honeymoon. We spent time in Hawaii and time in California. We were gone a couple of months. I think it must have been while we were away that whatever happened involving Jaime took place. By the time we got home, it had all been hushed up. I don't think whatever it was ever made the area newspapers here, so I'd say it never got into the Boston papers, or it would have filtered through. Maybe it wasn't anything that would have been newsworthy anyway. I really don't know. And I have an idea that Bill Medeiros told Flor she'd better hold her tongue about it or she'd be very, very sorry. Bill thinks the world of Jaime. He'd do anything in his power to protect him."

Amy smiled. "Well," she said brightly, "when you moved into the DuBois house you didn't know there'd be all sorts of interesting and mysterious things going on in the neighborhood, did you?"

Diana smiled. "No," she agreed. "I sure didn't." She let it go at that. Amy was a good person, but Diana suspected she was inclined to gossip. At least she wasn't malicious; in fact she'd conveyed sympathy for Jaime. But as for the "interesting and mysterious things," Diana was certain that her ebullient new acquaintance had no idea at all just how interesting and how mysterious their mutual neighbor really was. And she wasn't about to tell her.

CHAPTER FOUR

DIANA LEFT AMY HOWLAND'S with the object of accomplishing one errand in particular. She wanted to find a store that made duplicate keys, and to have three keys made that would fit the front door of the DuBois house.

During her first two weeks in Fairhaven, before the snow had created both a mental and a physical driving hazard for her, she had explored the town. She'd driven down to the end of Fort Street to the old Revolutionary War fort on the water, Fort Phoenix, but it had been too cold to get out and do much exploring. So she had satisfied herself temporarily by driving around and getting an overview of the town from her car. Fairhaven fascinated her. Admittedly, much of it had grown up rapidly before the zoning ordinance era. Marine supply and repair facilities and boat storage buildings loomed up in the middle of even the best residential areas, and it was commonplace to see boats of varying sizes "drydocked" for the winter right on their owners' side lawns. But it was Fairhaven's astonishing architecture that had impressed Diana.

The Fairhaven High School had amazed her. It

was located on Route 6, which was known locally as Huttleston Avenue and, until the construction of the nearby interstate highway a few years earlier, had been the main highway in the area. Classically Elizabethan in style, the school was huge and imposing and quite unlike any high school she'd ever seen. The magnificent church— cathedral, really—of Gothic Elizabethan architecture that dominated the center of the town was equally impressive and unusual in a town of Fairhaven's size. So was the Millicent Library, where she'd taken out a card a few days earlier, and a number of the other local buildings. There was a story behind all of this, she was sure. Maybe Jaime could tell it to her, since he had once attended Fairhaven High.

She flinched when she thought of Jaime. It had been a shock to hear that he was married, a shock that had left her with a nagging lingering ache, no matter how many times she tried to tell herself that she was being a fool. Maybe the problem was that he hadn't *seemed* married. Thinking this, she laughed at her own naiveté. She had more reason than most women to know that married men could sometimes appear extremely "single." But the memory, the feel of that one fleeting kiss was something she could not erase, any more than she could summon up a justifiable sense of righteous indignation at the thought of his having kissed her at all. The kiss, Diana brooded, had been given so freely, so lovingly, that it was difficult—impossible—to believe that the man who'd bestowed it could be committed to another woman. But there was no reason to think Amy might be wrong.

There'd been no evidence of a woman in the house next door. It had seemed obvious that Jaime was living there alone, in fact that he wanted to be alone, she told herself, remembering his initial irritation the night she'd invaded his privacy. But, Amy had said that Jaime's wife had never cared for Fairhaven, which could account for her absence, and also lend validity to his decision to sell the house.

Amy had indicated that in Jaime's mind the house was entwined with his mother. Diana wondered how long ago his mother had died? Amy hadn't mentioned that, and Diana hadn't wanted to ask. She had suppressed the many questions she would have loved to pose because she hadn't wanted to appear overly curious in Amy's eyes about their neighbor.

She couldn't help glancing at Jaime's house as she went to get her car out of the garage, but she saw no sign of anyone, which was just as well. She wasn't sure she'd be up to facing Jaime right now... after yesterday's parting kiss. She had responded to him, and she was sure he was aware of it. Knowing what she knew about him now, she didn't want to risk any repeat performances.

The roads had been well cleared, but the weekend's snow cluttered the curbs as a reminder, and it took courage to drive. Diana chose to go directly up to Route 6, where she would be less likely to come upon any icy patches, and soon she came to a large shopping plaza with a store that made duplicate keys. That task completed, she spent some time in a supermarket, going up and down the aisles until she'd gathered together a few staples with which to stock her pantry and fridge.

She stopped in a small restaurant for a bowl of steaming clam chowder, and thought about driving across the river and looking around New Bedford before going back home. The old city had a fascinating history, and she'd been wanting to visit the famous Whaling Museum and other places of interest. She found herself wishing she had someone to go with her. Someone who loved history as much as she did, who could share the wonders and the nostalgia of the past with her.

Jaime? Diana shook her head, impatient with herself. But she decided to postpone her visit to New Bedford until another day.

As she turned off the main route onto the first street before the bridge that spanned the Acushnet River, Diana made an impulsive decision. She wanted to give Jaime a small gift as a thank-you for his rescue mission the other night, and it seemed to her that a bottle of wine would be a good choice.

She stopped at a corner package store and discovered that the new Beaujolais was in—a young wine meant to be drunk within a reasonably short time. After studying the labels she bought two bottles.

Home again, Diana parked the car as close to the kitchen door as possible then trudged back and forth across the snow with her bundles. She'd taken the precaution today of wearing boots with good, firm soles and she managed not to slip once. During the course of her trips to the car she couldn't help but glance surreptitiously toward the house next door, but there was still no sign of life there.

Her purchases stashed away, Diana brewed herself a cup of tea and tried to settle down with one of the books she'd borrowed from the library. But she found it impossible to concentrate. Her thoughts kept roaming to the house next door—and its occupant.

To be living in a house that was only partially furnished and full of painful memories must be bleak, to say the least. She could imagine the sense of triumph Jaime Medeiros must have felt when he was able to afford the house on Fort Street for his mother, and then the intense sorrow that must have come when he knew she'd never be able to live in it.

Fort Street, in Diana's opinion, boasted the most beautiful houses in town, and Jaime's was one of the most impressive of all of them. A low stone wall edged his corner property, and the house itself sat well back from the street with a wide expanse of lawn in front and gardens at the rear that sloped down to the river. It must be beautiful in summer, she thought. She'd also noticed from an upstairs window in the DuBois house that a small private dock jutted into the water.

The house was part stone and part brick, and at some point over the years the bricks had been painted white. There was a large, glassed-in side porch on the opposite side from the DuBois house—Diana had spied it when driving by—and a traditional widow's walk centering the roof. It was a large house, more of a mansion really, Diana decided, and she could imagine that its interior held all sorts of potential for furnishing and decorating. Interior decorating was a hobby of hers and she'd long dreamed of the day when she might have a house of her own to turn her talents to. She'd lived in apartments most of her life, and although she'd made whatever space she was living in distinctively her own, she'd always been aware that one day she would be moving on again.

Now she sat thinking about Jaime Medeiros and his house, and what a tremendously challenging experience it would be to be given a free hand at decorating a place like that. As the daylight faded, Diana daydreamed, her book about the history of Fairhaven remaining unopened in her lap.

Only when it was almost dark did she get up and walk over to the side window. Her heart gave an odd little lurch when she saw a light in the kitchen window next door.

Diana knew she should leave well enough alone. Yet she'd bought the wine for him, after all, and there would be no harm in delivering it. She could just hand it to him at the door. Probably he wouldn't invite her in, anyway.

She put on her boots, her heavy coat, and a

mohair beret, which she could pull down snugly around her face. She'd bought a flashlight today, a big, bright one, and with the two bottles of wine secure in a shopping bag she started out.

It was only when she was partway down the steps, out of the shelter offered by the house, that she discovered the wind had picked up while she was indoors and was now blowing a regular gale. Coming directly off the water, it was icy in its fury, and Diana shuddered. She thought of the way Jaime had spoken of the men who put out to sea to make a living. She could only dimly imagine what it must be like to be out in a fishing boat on a night like this.

The wind was so strong that she had to fight to make her way against it, and by the time she'd climbed Jaime's back steps and was knocking on his door she felt as if she'd just been through a real struggle. He waited so long to answer her knock that she began to think he must have gone out— his garage door was closed. When she'd just about decided to turn back, the door swung open and once again she saw him silhouetted in the light from the hall behind him.

"Diana!" he exclaimed. "Don't tell me...."

"No," Diana said. "No, I haven't lost any more keys. I...I have a present for you. And also a favor to ask of you."

"Come in," he said, and moved back to let her enter.

Diana hesitated, but with the wind howling at her back she had no desire to start right out again, despite her previous intentions. Entering the kitchen, she saw that there was a can of beer and a newspaper on the table at the place where Jaime had evidently been sitting, and her relief was sharp. For a terrible second she'd wondered if his wife could possibly be here with him, if maybe she had come down today and joined him. But the beer and the newspaper were mute evidence that he'd been alone.

Diana turned to him, smiling, and held out the shopping bag. "Here," she said. "It's just a small thank-you. I really appreciate your coming to my rescue the other night."

He grinned. "It was my pleasure," he told her. "I don't get the chance to play the knight-in-shining-armor role very often." He put the bag on the table and pulled out first one bottle of wine and then the other. "Thanks very much. You've picked a favorite of mine. But *two* bottles...."

"It was a two-bottle rescue mission," she told him. Despite herself, she was sniffing as she spoke, aware that the most heavenly aroma permeated the kitchen.

"What is it?" she asked him.

"Soup," he replied. "Kale soup, a lot of people call it Portuguese soup. I make mine from an heirloom family recipe. Lots of linguiça in it—that's a Portuguese smoked sausage with a flavor all its own, if you're not familiar with it. Potatoes and carrots and kale and kidney beans and celery, different seasonings, wine...ambrosia, when you put all of those things together in the right proportion.''

He was tossing the empty beer can into the trash as he spoke, then he went to a kitchen cupboard and brought out two stemmed wineglasses. He foraged in a drawer for a corkscrew. ''Take off your coat, Diana,'' he urged. ''You must join me in a glass of this. It would be no fun to drink it by myself.''

It was an invitation she couldn't resist. She slipped off her coat and sat down at the kitchen table, and she experienced the crazy feeling that she'd come home. That she'd finally come home, after years of traveling through a bleak, emotional desert. There was a warmth to being here with Jaime, a wonderful sense of rapport.

He poured the wine, then took a moment to hold his glass up to the light, studying the rich ruby color of the Beaujolais. He clicked his glass with hers and said, ''*Saude*. And may your days be filled with miracles, *menina*.''

''And yours,'' she replied softly.

There was a bittersweetness to his smile, and he shook his head slightly. ''When it comes to myself,'' he said, ''I'm not much of a believer in miracles.'' Then, before she could make any comment, he added quickly, ''I'll get us some cheese to go with the wine.''

She watched him move across to the fridge, and she knew that the statement he'd just made about himself had been inadvertent, and he'd only parry any attempt of hers to get back to the subject.

Troubled, she watched him put a block of cheese on the table and pare off some thin slices before offering it to her, and again she was conscious of his hands. Visibly, at least, there was nothing wrong with his hands. Was his affliction not so easily perceptible to the eye? Some form of arthritis, maybe, that would prevent his operating?

She wondered how old Jaime was. It was difficult to estimate accurately, but she judged that he must be in his late thirties. Diana had recently passed her twenty-ninth birthday, and she guessed that he was maybe eight or nine years older than she was.

A quizzical gleam shone in his dark eyes as he said lightly, "I'd love to be able to read your thoughts."

"They're classified," Diana replied, keeping her tone equally light. She reached for another slice of cheese and munched it before asking casually, "You went to school here, didn't you, Jaime?"

The question was so unexpected that she couldn't blame him for looking surprised. "In Fairhaven? Yes, I went to elementary and high school here, if that's what you mean."

"That architectural marvel up on Route 6?" Diana persisted.

"Yes. It is quite a marvel, isn't it?"

"Like a number of the buildings here in Fairhaven," Diana said and nodded. "Who built them, Jaime?"

"They were the gift to the town of a man named

Henry Huttleston Rogers," he told her. "His was a classic American success story. He was born here in Fairhaven in 1839, and he worked as a newsboy growing up, but by the turn of the century he'd become an industrial baron. That was before the days of income tax, remember," Jaime added rather wryly. "A man could make and keep a fortune.

"Actually, Rogers gave a lot of his fortune to his native town in the form of the buildings he left as a legacy. Seems to me someone wrote an article a while back about 'Fairhaven's Fabulous Architecture,' and it is fabulous. The high school speaks for itself. The Unitarian church in the center of town was modeled after an English cathedral. Rogers built it in memory of his mother. Then there's the town hall, and the Millicent Library, and a number of other buildings. They give Fairhaven an impressive skyline."

"What an astonishing legacy," Diana said.

"Yes, it was. It is," Jaime agreed. "Henry Rogers's gift to his hometown will live on for a long, long time. He built buildings that would endure. There's a rare stability about them in this transient age we live in."

Jaime was refilling their wineglasses as he spoke, and Diana raised a protesting hand. "I'm not sure I should have another one."

He looked up. "Why?"

Again, she couldn't give him a totally honest answer. But the fact was, she felt entirely too content here in Jaime's kitchen with him. Just to be near him was euphoric. But it was a dangerous euphoria.

"Why shouldn't you have another glass of wine?" he repeated.

"It was a gift," she hedged. "I didn't mean to stay here and drink it all up. That is, I didn't intend to...to interrupt you."

"You're not interrupting me, Diana," he told her, continuing to fill her glass and then setting the wine bottle aside. "I wasn't doing a damned thing. At least I wasn't accomplishing anything. I was sitting here drinking a beer, trying to decide what I *should* do—about a lot of things. And coming to no conclusions at all. The sight of your face was a very welcome diversion. I might add," he said deliberately, "that it's a very lovely face, and it surprises me to think that a young woman of your sophistication blushes so easily!"

Diana had always blushed easily, a trait she hated. She knew her face was flooding with added color at the moment, because her cheeks actually stung.

He laughed softly and reached out a long finger, touching her cheek gently with it. "It's very becoming, *menina*."

"What does *menina* mean?" she asked him.

"Little girl," he said. "And despite that sophistication I just mentioned, you do seem like a little girl in a number of ways. How old are you, Diana?"

"Twenty-nine."

"You look younger."

"I don't know why I should," she said ruefully, and this was true enough. Life had dished up enough experience to her over the course of her twenty-nine years that she felt, if anything, she should look older.

"You don't wear any rings," he said, "but I can't believe there's no man in your life."

"There isn't."

"Have you been married?"

The question came so suddenly that it rocked her. "Yes," she said reluctantly.

"You're divorced?"

"No." She hated explaining, she hated the word. "I'm a widow."

"I'm sorry," he said quickly. "I guess I'm prying where I shouldn't pry. Forgive me, Diana. I don't like people asking me personal questions so I should have the grace not to ask them myself."

"It's all right," she replied unsteadily, and reached for the wine. Her hand was shaking as she lifted the glass to her lips, and she knew that she was giving him entirely the wrong impression. She was coming on like a grief-stricken widow, still mourning her husband, and that wasn't the case at all. Her marriage had been over by the time Gary had been killed in the horrible crash that had left her with a scar on her forehead and a badly shattered psyche. She'd been driving, and she and Gary had been arguing. She'd just made a hot and hasty retort to a caustic statement he'd thrown at her when the bus had loomed up in front of her. On the icy road there had been no way to avoid it.

She shuddered, and Jaime said, "God, Diana! I really am sorry!"

"It's all right," she repeated. "Jaime, don't look like that. You haven't done anything. I'm the one who should learn how to deal with this."

His eyes were very dark. "It hasn't been very long, has it?"

"What...?"

"Since you lost your husband," he elaborated.

"It has been three years," she said slowly.

"Three years?" She saw the flash of surprise cross his face. But then he said, "Forgive me, I'm doing it again. I don't mean to pry, Diana. Look, let's talk about your doctoral thesis."

She smiled shakily. "I have the impression that you don't especially favor my choice of a research subject."

"On the contrary. I couldn't favor it more. Matter of fact, I'd love...."

He broke off, and she asked, "What would you love to do?"

He shrugged slightly. "I was about to tell you that I'd love to teach you all about the Portuguese. But that does have its implications, doesn't it?"

His tone was teasing, but there was an underlying quality that was more than innuendo. He was telling her without telling her that he was as fully aware as she was of something very special between the two of them. It wasn't easy to define, this feeling that seemed as natural as it was wonderful. Allegorically, Diana supposed, the historian in her surfacing, some of what she was experiencing dated right back to Adam and Eve. With Jaime, she was deeply aware of the inherent differences between men and women to an extent she'd never fathomed before. Jaime intrigued her, he mystified her, he attracted her strongly, and her voice was husky as she answered a question that had been posed lightly, but wasn't light at all.

"I'm not sure," she said, trying to get some levity into her conclusion, "that you'd be the best choice of teacher!"

"Wise woman," Jaime approved, then added hastily, too hastily, "I'll get us some soup. You're going to stay and try my soup, aren't you?"

There was no way she could have refused him. "Yes," she nodded.

"There's a loaf of Portuguese bread over there on the counter," he told her. "Bring it, will you, and some butter? There's some softened butter in a dish on top of the fridge."

"Portuguese bread, yet," she teased, as she took the crusty loaf out of its wrappings and put it on a board, which she placed on the table with a sharp knife beside it for cutting.

"Yes, Portuguese bread, yet," he said. "The Portuguese make some of the best bread in the world. This white bread, then there's a *pão doce* made with a sweet dough—something like the dough the *bolos* were made of. And at Easter there's another special sweet bread called *massa sovada*. Eggs in their shell are put into little hollows in the dough as a decoration. My mother used to make *massa sovada*, and there'd be a regular riot to see which of the kids got an egg."

"How many of you were there?" Diana asked.

Jaime was ladling the fragrant, steaming soup into deep bowls. "There were four of us, originally," he said. "Guilherme, who lives here in Fairhaven, was the oldest. My sister Rose came next. She married a Californian, they've lived in San Francisco for years. After Rose, there was me, and Miguel was the youngest. Miguel was lost at sea nearly ten years ago. This time of year," he said broodingly, "in a terrible storm."

He'd told her earlier that his grandfather had been lost at sea, and a number of his friends, but he hadn't mentioned a brother. As she watched him place a bowl of soup in front of her, Diana could imagine how hard Miguel's death must have hit him. Hard enough that it was still difficult for him to talk about it even after a decade.

He put his own bowl of soup on the table then pulled up a chair and sat down. "Are you going to cut the bread or shall I?" he asked, with the obvious intention of changing the subject.

"I will," she said, and cut off two thick slices, one of which she handed to him. "Pardon my fingers."

"To receive bread from your fingers is an honor, *menina*," he said, and flashed her a smile that made her go weak all the way down to her toes. "Watch the soup. It's hot."

It was hot but it was also delicious. "This is the best thing I've ever tasted," Diana said sincerely, savoring the marvelous flavor.

"Another mark for the Portuguese." Jaime grinned. "I'd say your research is progressing very well."

"And I'd say you're laughing at me," Diana accused him lightly.

"Not at all," he assured her. "I merely want to make certain that you get started on the right track. You've taken on quite a subject, you know. I wouldn't want you to go astray in your pursuit of it."

"No," she said, playing up to him. "That would be dreadful!"

"It would be indeed." He broke off a piece of bread and buttered it. "There are a great number of facts that you must get straight at the very beginning," he told her. "Including the one that it was not the Pilgrims who were the first Europeans to set foot on the New England coast, but the Portuguese."

Diana had already touched on this information in a history course years earlier and intended to refresh her memory in her research, but hearing the information from Jaime's lips was much more enticing than reading a history book.

"Oh come on, now, Jaime," she protested teasingly.

"I'm serious. Oh, I know there's a theory that the Vikings—Leif Ericsson and some of his company—explored Cape Cod even earlier, but I've never quite credited that. However, in the early 1500s, Miguel Corte-Real did sail up the Taunton River, not far from here, where he left an inscription on a large rock."

"Really?" she asked. This fact was new to her.

"Actually, the first recorded voyage of the Portuguese to North America was that of Gaspar Corte-Real, a nobleman from the Azores who embarked on a search for the elusive western route to Asia. That had been Christopher Columbus's motive, remember? Corte-Real reached the North American coast in the year 1500. He landed first at Newfoundland, and then he went as far south as the Hudson Strait before he sailed back to Portugal. The following year he came back and this time he touched at Cape Breton. He saw Indians there wearing Venetian-style earrings, and this led him to believe he had found the fabulous Orient. He sent two of his ships back to Portugal with the word of his alleged discovery, and then continued on his own explorations. He was never heard from again."

"He was related to Miguel Corte-Real?" Diana asked.

Jaime nodded. "His brother," he said. "It was a few years later when King Emanuel commissioned Miguel to sail to North America to see if he could learn the fate of Gaspar's expedition. Miguel never came back, either, but some leading historians are certain that he left his mark on the rock in the Taunton River. Matter of fact you can see it for yourself. It's called the Dighton Rock, and it's been enshrined in a state park of the same name. It's not a very long drive from here. I'll take you over there one day, if you'd like."

"I'd love it!" Diana exclaimed.

Jaime laughed. "Your eyes are shining. Have I

told you how beautiful I find those gray, rain-water eyes.''

''Jaime. . .'' she began unsteadily.

''I find all of you very beautiful, *menina*,'' he said softly. His midnight eyes were caressing her as he spoke, and everything in Diana responded to him. Passion, long a stranger to her, sent quivering fingers of desire coursing through her, the intensity of her feeling for him staggering her. She had always thought herself a very strong person emotionally, but now she was possessed by a sweet and lovely weakness that appalled her even as it infiltrated every cell in her body. She'd never believed it possible for a person with any decent quotient of common sense to be swept off her feet. Until this moment Diana had always been in control, and knowing now that she could yield to this man as easily as she'd agreed to share his supper came as an overwhelming shock to her. Yet it was a shock from which she really didn't want to rally—not deep down inside.

She forced an all-important fact to cut across this compliancy, which was so foreign to her. Jaime Medeiros was *married*! She had to make herself remember that he wasn't free.

''What is it, *menina*?'' he asked her gently. ''Why are you looking at me like that? If I didn't know better, I'd say you were afraid of me.''

She was afraid of him. With a swift, convulsive movement Diana pushed back her chair and stood up. ''Excuse me, Jaime,'' she blurted. ''I really have to go home.''

He frowned. "What are you saying, Diana?"

"I have to go home, that's all. Thank you for the soup, it was delicious, and for the wine—"

"And for the bread and butter?" he asked grimly. "What is this, Diana? You and I both know that you don't have to go home. I think we also both know that you want to stay as much as I want you to stay. I saw it in your eyes only a moment ago. Though I said that you were a little girl in some ways, I didn't mean to imply that I consider you an adolescent. You are a woman, for God's sake! So why all of a sudden are you behaving like a scared rabbit with me?"

"Jaime...."

"What the hell just happened, Diana?" he demanded. "I don't seem to be able to figure it out by myself."

"There is nothing to figure out," she said, her voice low. "I can't stay here, that's all."

She saw his mouth tense. "I don't understand you," he said flatly. "But regardless of that, you have nothing to worry about. I don't know what turned you off so abruptly, and if you refuse to tell me, there's nothing I can do about it. But you're safe, I assure you," he added coldly. "I don't take women by force. Such a show of strength doesn't interest me. The only thing I will say to you is that you shouldn't touch a match to a candle unless you expect a flame to result. That's the kind of game only young and silly girls tend to play—or extremely foolish women. I wouldn't have put you in either category."

Diana shook her head, her emotions gone numb. Jaime was acting as if she was in the wrong, when he was the one at fault. Yet she couldn't seem to find the words to tell him so.

"Jaime," she began again, and he cut her off impatiently.

"Don't try to manufacture an explanation," he cautioned. "You've already made your point. Perhaps I was wrong, perhaps I was presumptuous, and in that case I apologize. But," he finished wearily, "it's too late. Go on home, Diana!"

CHAPTER FIVE

DIANA WENT HOME. But when she staggered and slipped on the snow this time it was because tears were blinding her eyes.

She'd left the back door open. As she pushed it open, she remembered that she'd had a favor to ask of Jaime, which she'd completely forgotten about until now. She'd intended to give him one of the house keys she'd had made and to ask him to keep it as a safeguard. Then, she was going to explain to him whimsically, she'd never again have to worry about being locked out in the cold. How wrong she'd been!

As she took off her coat and draped it over the back of a chair, Diana glanced through the window and saw a bulky silhouette dark against the kitchen light across the way. So, Jaime had watched till she'd gotten into the house safely. She supposed that should give her a sense of security, but it didn't. Instead she flinched to think of him watching her progress from his house to hers. How aware he must have been of her unsteadiness!

Impatiently she crossed to the window and pulled down the shade. But though she blotted out the image of Jaime's silhouette, it was impossible to dispense so easily with the tantalizing mental picture of the man himself.

She had acted like a child. No wonder he'd been puzzled, then annoyed, then downright angry. She'd had only one thought in mind. Escape. He was married, and the last thing in the world she wanted was a serious relationship with a married man. She'd seen too many of her friends go that route with bitterly unhappy results. And she'd also done her share of suffering as the wife of a married man who hadn't hesitated to get involved with someone else.

Jaime had been right about her response to him. He'd read her as clearly as if she was an illuminated map. They were adults; they both knew where the current that ran between them would lead if they gave it the chance to flow freely. They both wanted each other. Well, Diana told herself, she should have been honest enough to admit that to him. . .and then tell him that she knew he was married and the best thing for both of them would be to call a halt now.

Sighing, she poured herself a glass of sherry and took it into the living room. She'd kept the thermostat up during the day so the room was warm enough. But the empty fireplace seemed especially bleak when she remembered the roaring blaze she'd shared with Jaime the night before last. Night before last? It seemed much longer ago than that.

She switched on the old china lamp, its twin round domes painted with rust and yellow flowers. It was one of the many antiques scattered throughout the house, and Diana would have preferred something more contemporary. A newer lamp would give better illumination, and these old "Gone with the Wind" lamps, were becoming quite valuable. She didn't want to risk the chance of breaking any of Agatha DuBois's family heirlooms.

By the old lamp's soft light, she tried to become involved in one of the local history books she'd borrowed from the Millicent Library, but the effort was useless. Too many thoughts infringed, too many regrets.

Jaime Medeiros was the first man who'd attracted her in more years than she liked to think about. It was ironic that he should be out of her reach when, since Gary's death, there'd been so many who would have been more than willing to start a relationship with her. More than a few of them had been married, too, and even the single men, she remembered, her lips curving in a bitter smile, had followed the same game plan.

Diana had learned quickly that men tended to become interested in young widows because they assumed the women were sex starved. At first she'd been amused, and then disgusted, by these men, some she'd met for the first time, others she'd known for years, who were so willing, in such a benevolent way, to ease her trauma and help her get over her grief. She'd become a master at refusal.

In quite a different way tonight, she'd refused

Jaime Medeiros. And as a result she'd been left with an aching emptiness.

All thoughts came to a sudden halt when she heard the kitchen door close with a thud. When the sound was followed by footsteps coming along the hall, her pulse began to thud. If Jaime wasn't willing to take her poorly expressed no as an answer, she didn't know how she was going to be able to handle whatever might come next.

But it wasn't Jaime who appeared in the living-room doorway, and a kind of fear she'd never felt before crept over Diana as she faced the intruder.

Jaime had warned her to keep her doors locked, and she should have taken him more seriously. Her whole body tensing, she stood up without even realizing what she was doing and faced him. "What do you want?" she demanded.

The man standing in the doorway seemed as startled to see her as she was to see him. Man? He wasn't much more than a boy, Diana saw now. Not that it made much difference. He was about her height, slim, wiry. Strong. He was wearing heavy rubber boots—a fisherman's boots—pulled up over his faded jeans. A thick wool parka covered broad, powerful shoulders. She'd be no match for him, Diana knew, and she couldn't help but shrink back, wondering if she'd be able to make it to the front door and start hollering for help before he could overtake her.

But despite an urge to try to flee, she held her ground, staring directly into eyes that were large, dark and liquid—and hostile. She felt herself on the edge of screaming.

There was a tenseness to his swarthy face that was alarming, and it was all Diana could do to control her voice enough to phrase her question again. "What do you want?" she repeated hoarsely.

"Who are you?" he shot back by way of answer.

"Who am *I*?" Anger at his intrusion, at his nerve, came to dispel some of the fear. "Look, I don't know what you want, but I'd suggest you get out of here...*now*!"

Amazingly the hostility faded, and he flashed her a smile, his teeth glinting whitely against the dark skin. An instant before, his irregular features had seemed forbidding, but the smile altered his face, making him surprisingly attractive. "I think I must have the wrong house," he told her.

"You think you must have the wrong house?" Diana echoed, edging toward the front door.

"I'm looking for Jaime Medeiros," he said.

Diana stopped and shook her head, not certain whether to believe him or not. Then she said tautly, "The Medeiros house is next door. On the corner."

He nodded, but he made no move to leave. Finally he said slowly, "Look, I'm sorry. I scared you, I know. I'm sorry about that. I...."

"It's all right," Diana said. "Just go, that's all!"

"Miss...."

"Just *go*," she repeated, her nerves fraying.

He left with an anxious backward glance, and it wasn't until she heard the back door thud again that Diana began to breathe normally. She wasted no time in speeding out to the kitchen and locking and bolting the door, then checking the front-door lock, as well.

This incident was all she'd needed right now. Like many people who have spent most of their lives in cities she'd felt relatively safe in a smaller place, and she obviously hadn't paid as much attention to Jaime's admonition as she should have. Living in the heart of Manhattan, she'd automatically taken precautions with such things as door locks. She *was* city wise, which made this latest experience all the more of a travesty. And her intruder had been more right than he may have realized. Whether he'd come into her house innocently or not, he'd scared the hell out of her.

The telephone pealed, and Diana started at the sound of it, then told herself she was being too edgy. She forced herself to sound calm as she picked up the receiver and said, "Hello?"

"Diana?" Jaime didn't need to identify himself. No one else had a voice like that.

"Diana?" he repeated. "Are you all right?"

"Yes, I'm all right," she snapped.

"Manny says he's afraid he frightened you. Manny Ribeiro. He says he plowed into your house by mistake, the kitchen door was unlocked."

"I know," she said. "And please don't say anything to me about it."

"I wasn't about to say anything to you about it," Jaime assured her. "But just be sure you lock all your doors from here on in, okay? Not everyone is quite as honest as Manny."

"Thanks for telling me," she said icily. "And you might mention to your friend that when you go visiting it's customary to knock or ring a doorbell."

Jaime chuckled. "I'll see to it that Manny brushes up on his manners. Take care, *menina*."

Take care, *menina*. There had been that caressing note again in Jaime's voice as he spoke the Portuguese word. Evidently he'd forgotten—or was willing to overlook—the tenor of their recent parting.

Menina. As she turned away from the phone, Diana decided that her life would probably be a lot easier if he'd stayed angry at her.

DIANA SLEPT RESTLESSLY that night. She was plagued by bad dreams, but when she awakened to face the gray light of another December morning she couldn't remember what she'd been dreaming that had disturbed her so much.

As she breakfasted on coffee and toast she told herself that she had to get a work plan going. She needed to create a reasonably flexible schedule that would not be too confining—right now she couldn't face up to anything that would hem her in too much—but at the same time would ensure her getting a reasonable portion of her research done every day.

Regardless of her resolutions, though, she found it very difficult to concentrate on either the library books or any of the other reference material she'd brought with her. And as for her own findings about the Portuguese, about the only valid thing she could put into her large but virtually empty notebook was that Portuguese food was very good, and Portuguese men could be fascinating!

It was a raw day, snow threatened again, but as the hours passed, the house seemed to be closing in on Diana, and the feeling became so oppressive she knew she was on the verge of coming down with a bad case of cabin fever.

Much as she disliked the thought of driving with a weather forecast of snow, the idea of staying home was even worse. Finally she dressed warmly and started out.

It wasn't a day for sightseeing—there was an icy wind sweeping in from the water—and Diana was too restless to explore places like the Whaling Museum. She settled for making a return trip to the shopping plaza. She browsed in a large discount store, where she found a bulky white sweater that looked warm and comfortable. Then she stopped in the pharmacy and bought a bottle of bubble bath. Next she investigated a small book-and-card shop, where she purchased a paperback novel and a couple of birthday cards for future use.

The card shop had reminded her that she still had to write her Christmas cards, and time was dwindling. As it was, with the impossibly slow mail service, people probably wouldn't be getting the cards till after New Year's anyway, but the least she could do was get them on their way. She'd bought the cards in New York and had brought them with her.

When she arrived back home the house seemed so empty, and Diana had to fight off a real sense of oppression. She decided that the warmest and most comfortable place in which to do her cards would be right at the big, round kitchen table. She had quite a few to send, so writing messages on them whiled away the balance of the afternoon.

Darkness came early, and when she went to pull down the kitchen shade she found that the weather forecast had been right. It was starting to snow again, and the drifting flakes gave her a sense of isolation, heightening her growing loneliness.

She'd gone to pull the shade down because she wanted to blot out the sight of the house next door. She didn't want to know whether there was going to be a light in Jaime's window tonight or not. Didn't want to know? She laughed. She didn't dare know. The thought of having him so near to her in one sense and so far away in another was too provocative. Despite the snow, it would be so easy to bridge the distance.

Before drawing the shade, she couldn't fail to notice that the house was in darkness. Was he out? Or maybe taking a late nap? Or....

Diana turned away, trying to blot him out of her mind, which was as difficult a task as ever. She told herself it would help if she could get out and do more. As it was, she'd made a poor choice of seasons in which to come to New England to do her research. But then this house wouldn't have been available at any other time of the year, and Fairhaven did make a perfect base for her.

Well, winter wouldn't last forever. She'd been told that spring was slow in coming to New England and apt to be cold and rainy. But she didn't care about rain. Only about snow and sleet, and treacherous, glazed highways. . . .

Earlier, when she'd picked up a newspaper in the book-and-card store, the date had leaped out at her. She'd stood for a long moment clutching the paper, wrinkling it so much in the process that she'd bought it. It was exactly three years today since the accident, or it would be in a couple more hours.

She shuddered. Would the time ever come when she wouldn't blame herself for Gary's death?

TIME HUNG HEAVILY on Diana's hands that afternoon. Too many thoughts, too many memories were pressing in on her. If the weather hadn't been so miserable she would have gone for a long brisk walk, maybe over at Fort Phoenix, in the effort to rid her mind of some of the phantoms that haunted her. As it was, though, she was housebound.

The house needed a cleaning, and good physical work was supposed to be the best panacea of all, she knew that. But she wasn't in a mood for dusting and polishing and sweeping, no matter how therapeutic these activities might prove to be. She settled for dealing with trivia for a time—thumbing through magazines, rereading some of her mail, glancing at her mounting pile of reference books, and making a few desultory notes. But all of this soon paled, and finally she ran a hot bath and soaked for a while, using some of the bubbles she'd bought that afternoon.

There was no joy at all in fixing a supper of canned soup and toast, and even less in eating it. Nor could she escape in any of the programs on television. Finally she settled for making an early night of it—more from necessity than choice, she told herself grimly. But once in bed sleep eluded her and she began to think of a lot of things—including Christmas. Her parents, retired now and living in South Carolina, wanted her to come south and spend the holidays with them, but she'd sidestepped their invitation. Her mother had always been overly protective, and since the accident she'd become doubly so. Her parents had still been living in New York then, in a big old-fashioned apartment on Riverside Drive, and it had been natural to move in with them while she was convalescing. But before too long Diana had come to realize that she'd never be able to pull herself together as long as she let her mother smother her with well-intentioned kindness.

Fortunately her parents had already made their plans to move south and they'd followed through on them. There'd been some bad moments when Diana had flatly refused to go with them. "Just till you're feeling stronger, dear,'' her mother had said. But the resulting separation had worked well for all of them. Now she visited her parents two or three times a year, and the only bad part of the visits was the emotional wrench that always came when her mother tried to prevail upon her to settle in the Carolinas and she had to tear herself away.

This year, much as she loved her mother and her father, she didn't think she could face up to another one of those emotional scenes. On the other hand, Christmas had always been a very special time to her—except for that terrible Christmas three years ago.

Well, she told herself resolutely, she'd make her own Christmas. She'd get a tree and some ornaments and maybe she'd invite the Howlands and the Burroughses in for eggnog. Maybe Gail and her husband could drive over from Hyannis for the occasion.

And, of course, there was also Jaime. It would be the neighborly thing to do to ask him to drop by for an eggnog. The question was whether or not he'd come if she invited him.

IT WAS THURSDAY before Diana saw Jaime again. She nearly ran into his car as she was turning into her driveway.

She'd gone to the post office then stopped at the library to take out several more books and was trying not to panic as she started to drive back to Fort Street. It had begun to snow again, and the flakes were coming down thicker and thicker.

She couldn't wait to get home and put her car in the garage—where she'd leave it until spring, if necessary, she vowed. She wasn't about to try to go out again in icy winter weather.

Diana was going a shade too fast considering the conditions as she made the turn into the driveway. But it never occurred to her that she might meet someone else. Jaime was just backing out of his own driveway and was about to turn into the street.

When she saw his car looming in front of her a horrible memory swamped Diana. She became gripped by a terror so intense that her only thought was to avoid hitting him. She swerved sharply, careening across the lawn, and as she slammed on her brakes the car swerved crazily, then came to a lurching, skidding stop.

Fortunately she'd had her seat belt fastened. She knew if she hadn't, her head would probably have gone into the windshield, just as it had three years ago. She straightened, shaking uncontrollably, as Jaime loomed up at her side and began tapping insistently on the front window.

Instead of rolling the window down, Diana opened the car door and stared up at him dully.

"What in hell were you trying to do?" he demanded furiously.

Diana closed her eyes. She didn't want to get into an argument right now, she wasn't up to explanations. "Go away," she urged him, her voice low.

"Go away? What are you talking about?" he snapped. "Get out, damn it!"

"Please," she pleaded. "Leave me alone, Jaime. I need to be alone for a little while."

"Like hell I'll leave you alone!" he thundered. "What, for God's sake, were you trying to do? You came roaring in here...."

"I wasn't roaring," she protested mildly. "I wanted to get home, that's all. I...I don't like to drive in the snow."

He was surveying her narrowly, and suddenly he said, "Okay. Okay. Come on, now. Let's get you into the house."

He was leaning over her as he spoke, unfastening her seat belt with those wonderful hands of his. Then an arm slid around her, and very gently he eased her up, holding her until she was out of the car.

At that point, Diana's knees went weak and she sagged against him. He was wearing his heavy wool parka and the material was rough and scratchy on her cheeks, but it didn't matter. All she wanted was to feel the sanctuary of his arms around her.

He led her into the house, half carrying her. Then, carefully, he helped her off with her coat, and before she could protest he was gently tugging at her mohair beret, pulling it off with a backward motion so that it swept her puff of a bang with it, exposing her forehead.

For a tense moment he stared at the scar, and then he touched it, running his finger lightly along the length of it.

"Where did you get this?" he asked her softly.

Her gray eyes enormous, she shook her head numbly, unable to speak.

He frowned, but he only said, "Come on, Diana. That Victorian furniture in your living room wasn't exactly designed for comfort, but it's better than nothing."

He was guiding her toward the living room and she let herself be led by him. But her mouth had gone dry.

Would he recognize his own work? Did doctors recognize their own work?

He couldn't possibly! Common sense told her that. Jaime Medeiros must have attended to hundreds of facial cuts in the course of his career, and there was nothing distinguishing about hers, except that she'd obviously been attended by a very competent surgeon. But there were a lot of competent plastic surgeons.

He settled her onto a velvet-covered sofa, and she had to curl her legs up slightly in order to fit into the space. He propped a couple of satin pillows under her head, then took a crocheted afghan that was folded across the back of a nearby chair and carefully draped it over her.

"Wait here," he told her then, as if there was a chance of her going anywhere.

Jaime was carrying two glasses partially filled with an amber liquid when he came back. "Brandy," he said, handing one of them to her. "Sip it slowly."

She obeyed, letting the fiery liquid seep down her parched throat.

He crouched on the floor next to the couch, cupping her chin with one of his hands and staring intently at her face. He was looking into her eyes, but there was nothing emotional about his survey. He was assessing her clinically. Even if she hadn't already known he was a doctor she would have suspected it by the way he examined her now, carefully feeling her head and pressing certain points in her neck.

After a time he said, "I'd say you're okay. Frightened to death, that's all. But you're damned lucky. What were you thinking of, Diana?"

"I told you," she said. "I wanted to get home. It didn't occur to me that I'd meet another car... right in the driveway. When I saw you coming I...I guess I went out of control. I overreacted."

"It was a good thing that you were where you were, and not going any faster," he said grimly. "Otherwise, it could have been quite a different story." Again his finger reached out to touch the scar on her forehead. "Does this have something to do with your fear of driving in the snow?" he asked her.

"Yes," she whispered.

"When did it happen, Diana?"

"Three years ago," she said, her voice very low.

"That's when you lost your husband?"

His memory was much too good. "Yes," she admitted.

"Where were you when this happened?"

The questions were coming too close. "It was near here," she admitted. "On the Interstate...

near the bridge. It was very slippery and...and three cars and a bus piled up together. Mine was one of the cars.''

"You were driving?''

"Yes.''

"You must have been taken to St. Luke's,'' he mused.

"What?''

"St. Luke's Hospital, in New Bedford. Were you taken there?''

"Yes,'' she said reluctantly. "Yes, I was.''

"You're white as a sheet,'' Jaime observed dispassionately. "Drink some more brandy.''

She obeyed, but this time the fiery liquid nearly choked her. She sputtered, then coughed.

"Diana,'' Jaime said, watching her intently, "I'm presuming that you were taken into the emergency room at St. Luke's.''

She nodded, staring at the brandy glass, not wanting to meet his eyes.

"Who took care of you?'' he asked.

"What?'' It was an automatic query, a protective device. She didn't want to hear his question, she didn't want to answer it!

"I asked you who attended you in the emergency room,'' he repeated. "You must have had a very competent surgeon. The scar is minimal for the injury. Barely noticeable, as a matter of fact, and it'll fade even more with time.''

Diana's mouth twisted, and she turned her head away from him. He misunderstood the gesture. "Hey,'' he said, "you're overly sensitive about the scar. It doesn't detract in the least from your beauty.''

The moment of truth was at hand. Diana drew a long breath, and then, her voice wavering, she said, ''That's what the surgeon told me at the time. He told me I'd be as beautiful as ever.''

She knew he was staring at her, but she still couldn't bring herself to meet his eyes. His voice was husky as he demanded, ''What surgeon, Diana?''

''You,'' she said, her voice trembling. ''It was you, Jaime.''

CHAPTER SIX

DIANA HAD BEEN ONLY TOO AWARE that Jaime would resent the fact that she hadn't told him about their initial encounter in the hospital emergency room three years ago. But she was in no way prepared for the magnitude of his reaction.

He reared back as if she'd struck him. "So," he said, his words coming from between clenched teeth, "you've known all along who I was!"

"Please!" she implored.

"Are you denying that you recognized me?" The midnight eyes, usually so full of life, had dulled to opaque black coals. His laugh was harsh. "You're a poor liar, Diana."

His censure stung, and in the wake of the sting came her own rising anger. "No one's ever called me a liar!" she protested sharply.

Derision was plain upon his face as he looked at her. "Maybe no one's ever found you out before," he suggested.

"Damn it, Jaime, I'm not going to listen to this!" Diana protested. "You have no right to say these things to me!"

"On the contrary, I have every right," he contradicted. "Just what the hell are you *really* doing here? Did Cynthia send you down to spy on me?''

''Cynthia?'' she echoed sickly.

''My wife,'' he said dully, and Diana flinched.

Those black, unfathomable eyes were raking her face. ''Are you saying you don't know Cynthia?'' he demanded.

''No!'' she retorted, the word wrung out of her. ''But...if I *did* know Cynthia, just why do you think I'd be here spying for her?''

''I don't know,'' he said, after a moment. ''I don't know. Maybe when it comes to Cynthia I tend to become paranoid. She's caused me nothing but trouble, even since the divorce....''

The divorce? Diana sat up straighter. ''Are you saying you're divorced?''

''Of course I'm divorced!'' He stood up as he spoke, moving restlessly. Then he turned to peer down at her, and as she watched him, holding her breath, a small smile came to curve the corner of his mouth. ''So,'' he observed, ''that's been part of your problem, has it?''

''I don't know what you're saying, Jaime,'' she evaded, but her emotions were beginning to swirl, like slender ribbons caught in a breeze.

''Who told you I was married, Diana?'' he asked her.

''Jaime....''

''Don't hedge, it doesn't become you. Who told you I was married?''

''Amy Howland,'' she admitted.

He'd pulled up a straight-backed chair and now

he turned it around, straddling it, and propped his elbows on the laddered back. The look he shot her was triumphant, and she prepared herself to feel the full brunt of his anger. But instead, some of the bleakness seemed to go out of his eyes, and he said, "So, you and Amy have been discussing me. I suppose I should have expected it."

"No one's been *discussing* you, Jaime," Diana retorted. "I had coffee with Amy the other morning and she mentioned that we had a new neighbor in residence."

"A *new* neighbor?"

"Well, she said you'd come back," Diana qualified. "She said she understood you were going to sell the house."

"What else did she say?"

"Mostly that, well, that you'd never really lived here. She mentioned that your wife didn't care much for Fairhaven."

"That's an understatement if I've ever heard one," Jaime said, almost cheerfully. "I don't know why Amy would have told you I was married, though. She must know that Cynthia and I have been divorced for over five years."

"Five years?" Diana gaped at him.

"Yes," he said. "Why are you so surprised about that?"

"Oh, I don't know, I don't know," Diana muttered, wishing she could find some secret little closet to crawl into and pull the door closed behind her.

"Come on, Diana...."

"All right. I guess I thought that you hadn't been divorced very long because...because I assumed your giving up medicine had something to do with...with your wife."

"My giving up medicine?" Was it only her imagination, Diana asked herself, or had his hands really tightened on the chair back as he said this, so that the knuckles stood out whitely against his olive skin.

"Jaime, please," Diana said. "None of this is any of my business and I don't want to pry. I honestly *don't* want to pry! I don't like to be questioned, and that's taught me to respect other people's privacy."

"Even so," Jaime said, "there are things that I fully intend to ask you about yourself, and things that I want you to know about me. Okay?"

"I don't know," Diana muttered. "I just don't know."

"I *do* know." He surveyed her dispassionately. "You look like hell, *menina*," he said then. "And you're going to get cramps in your legs, twisting them up like that. Why didn't you tell me you knew who I was when you came over to my house that first night?"

He flung the question at her so swiftly that she was taken aback. Her answer came involuntarily. "I didn't want you to know who I was," she said honestly. "I...I didn't want to get into how I'd come to know you in the first place. I...I guess I've never gotten over the accident, despite everything I've tried...."

"Everything?"

"Counseling," she said. "Two different psychiatrists and one psychologist. I thought finally I'd made peace with myself and that's why I didn't hesitate to come to Fairhaven and rent Agatha DuBois's house. But I suppose I should have known. The same time of year, the same weather conditions, and then...and then seeing you."

"So," he said wryly, "all I brought back to you was a very bad memory?"

"No," she said honestly. "You...you were my Rock of Gibraltar in the midst of chaos, Jaime. You spoke to me, and I'll never forget your kindness, your strength, the caring in your eyes...and the tenderness in your voice. All of that for me, a stranger. That's what I clung to, and it got me through some very bad moments. I hoped to see you again, while I was in the hospital.... I wanted to thank you. But you didn't come back, and all I knew was that you came from Boston, and that you were famous. I never saw the emergency-room intern again who told me about you, who told me how I'd lucked out...."

"Lucked out?" he asked curiously.

"Well, he said that despite the fact there were excellent plastic surgeons in the area, I'd been very fortunate because I'd drawn the absolute best. You just happened to be there at that particular time."

He nodded. "I was visiting my great-aunt," he said. "She'd had a mild coronary. My car was parked not far from the emergency-room entrance. When I heard the ambulances coming in, I knew something big had happened. I went back into the hospital to see if I could be of any help. I had staff privileges there, and as it happens they were glad to see me. As I remember it, you had some rather severe head lacerations, so they took me to you. I remember being thankful because I knew most of your scars would be covered, once your hair grew back in again. There was just that single one on your forehead and, yes, I did do my best with it. I went back to Boston later that same night. I had to go back, otherwise I would have stopped by to see how you were doing. . . ."

"It was exactly three years ago yesterday," Diana said. "Exactly three years ago yesterday."

"I see." His eyes were steady. "Diana," he asked, "am I right in assuming that you feel responsible for the accident?"

"No," she said. "Not. . . not the accident itself. It was a multiple thing, as you probably know. There were several vehicles in a chain reaction. I. . . I blanked out. . . ."

"That's pretty normal," he assured her.

"So I've been told. But. . . I wish I could remember the. . . the details better than I do," she told him, the words emerging slowly, painfully. "I was driving and. . . and Gary and I were arguing. We'd gone down to the Cape for the weekend with Gail and Howard Landers in Hyannis. Gary hadn't really wanted to go. . . he never especially cared for Gail, probably because she was my best friend." The bitterness seeped out, though Diana tried to suppress it. "Gail's daughter, Melinda, was being christened, and I was to be her godmother, so Gary agreed to go along. But once we'd started back for New York things got worse and worse. He. . . he told me he wanted a divorce. But I didn't want a divorce, even though I knew Gary had become interested in someone else. I had this terrible sense of obligation to marriage, as marriage. I felt that we should try to put our marriage together.

"Gary got very angry when I told him I wasn't willing to give him a divorce. And I was so upset I had no right to be driving. The only reason I was driving was that he'd had a few drinks, so I thought I was in better shape to handle it than he was. There was this pickup truck ahead of us on the highway, and a bus in front of it. The pickup truck was trying to pass the bus—that's what the police told me—and there was a car trying to pass me. It was snowing, the road was getting very slippery. I skidded, and at that moment the car trying to pass me clipped my front left fender and my car went into a spin. Then the car behind me crashed into the rear of my car and I felt as if we were flying toward the bus and there was nothing I could do to stop the. . . the momentum. . . ."

"It seems to me your memory for the details is good," Jaime said grimly. "Maybe too good."

The tears were streaming down Diana's face. "I should have been able to stop," she murmured brokenly. "I should have been able to avoid going into the bus. I should have been able to do *something*. . . ."

"Oh, *menina, menina,*" Jaime said, his voice full of tenderness and sorrow for her. Despite the sofa's limited size he sat down beside her, drawing her close to him, pressing her head against his shoulder.

"Dearest," he said, "cry it out. Let it out. It's past time. It wasn't your fault. Without knowing any more than you've just told me I'd swear it wasn't your fault. It was one of those horrible things that happen. Maybe it wasn't anyone's fault, but that doesn't really matter. What matters is that you've suffered enough, Diana. Maybe if it had been Gary driving you would have been killed...God forbid! But that wouldn't have made him guilty, either. Some things just *happen*, Diana." He was nuzzling her hair with his chin as he spoke, and now he brushed her forehead with his lips. Then slowly, tenderly, he kissed her tears away.

Gradually Diana's vision cleared, and as she looked up at him she felt as if she were drowning in the velvet depths of his eyes. A surge of wanting, of longing, swept over her, and she raised trembling hands to touch the satin darkness of his hair, running her fingers over its smoothness. Then she clasped his neck, drawing his head down until their lips met in a kiss. It was she who commanded this time, he who responded. His tongue probed her mouth until she parted her lips to receive it, and then it teased and tantalized, setting off a series of cresting waves, each rising higher than the other across Diana's heightened emotions. Jaime's hands began to rove over her body, slipping up under her sweater to trail across her bare back.

"If I start," he whispered in her ear, "there's going to be no stopping, Diana. This time I won't go back. Be sure, *menina*!"

For answer her fingers found the buttons on the deep-red chamois shirt he was wearing. She fumbled as she unfastened first one button and then another. She buried her face in the curly, dark hair that grew at the base of his throat, breathing in the rich, male scent of him, his warmth, the feel of his skin, playing upon her own sensuality until she was vibrating with her need for him.

"This damned sofa!" he cursed. "There isn't room...."

She laughed softly and rose, holding out her hand. He grasped it, slowly coming to his feet. As if they were fellow conspirators she said, "Let's take the brandy upstairs with us," and he grinned.

"I won't need brandy to keep me warm," he told her.

"Neither will I," she admitted. "But even so...."

"Even so." He shrugged and picked up both their glasses, letting her lead the way out of the living room, along the hall and up the stairs.

There were four bedrooms on the second floor. Diana had chosen the large one at the back of the house because of its water view. The room had a big four-poster bed, covered with a thick white candlewick spread. A woodburning fireplace which, she had yet to use, was built into one wall. There was a supply of wood stacked next to it, and she said, "Let's make a fire."

He groaned. "I don't need a fire," he began, and then smiled down at her. "For atmosphere?" he suggested.

"For atmosphere."

"I can undress you in front of it?"

"Jaime...."

"If I can't undress you in front of it, *menina*..." he teased.

She moistened her lips. "All right. Yes...you can undress me in front of it."

She sat on the edge of the bed, watching him strike a match to the crushed newspapers under the log. The fire caught and the flames, spiraling up the brick chimney, echoed Diana's inner feelings.

Jaime turned toward her, his tall, powerful figure outlined by the firelight, and something very primitive and all consuming clutched at her throat. If this was desire, she told herself, then she'd never known the meaning of the word before.

Still, she was shy as he urged her to her feet. She didn't want to make comparisons; the past was the past, and she wanted to forget it. Yet she couldn't help but think that she'd never made love like this before. Gary had been almost businesslike about his lovemaking. There had been very few preliminaries. But now Jaime was taking his time, as if he wanted to slowly anticipate the moments they were going to share together, as if this was a natural part of the progression of events, the anticipation a part of the pleasure. And it *was* part of the pleasure. She knew this as he slowly eased her sweater over her head, and then let his hands trail across her shoulders and down her arms, his fingers massaging her flesh ever so slightly as he did so.

She shivered beneath his touch, but it was an ecstatic shivering, and he grinned knowingly. "Don't tell me you're cold!" he teased her.

"No," she said, wanting him to keep on touching her, to touch her until his fingers had explored every part of her. "No!"

He laughed, his hands moving to unfasten the buckle on her jeans. He slipped them down over her hips, his fingers lingering to caress her every inch of the way, and by the time she'd stepped out of the jeans she was quivering, vibrant, her own vitality at a peak.

She stood before him, wearing only a narrow beige satin bra and the skimpiest of matching bikini briefs. Jaime shook his head. "What a choice of clothes for the middle of December in New England!" he commented. "It's a wonder you haven't frozen to death. . . . But I'm very glad you didn't go for ankle-length thermals," he added, with that cajoling note she was coming to love underlining his deep, mellow voice. "Get closer to the fire, *menina*."

She edged closer to the fireplace and the warmth from the flames was an added caress. Then he said, gently, "Undress me, *menina*."

She stared up at him. "Jaime. . . ."

"Haven't you ever undressed a man before?"

She shook her head slowly, and something untranslatable flickered in his eyes. "I'm amazed," he said, "and delighted to think I'm going to be the first. Ah, *menina*, I want you to know me. All of me. Just as I want to know you."

He grasped her hands as he spoke, pressing her fingers against the buttons still to be opened on his shirt, and slowly, shakily, she began to help him out of his clothes until he was wearing only a pair of cotton briefs. There she faltered.

Jaime chuckled. "You've got another step to go, beautiful Diana," he told her. "You can tell, already, what you're doing to me, can't you?"

She nodded, desire merging with shyness as she stood back from him. Then, gently, he took her fingers again, and made her touch him, made her slip off the briefs until he was standing naked before her.

He was beautiful. Beautiful and powerful, and she swayed toward him, drawn by instinct. He eased the remaining bits of satin from her slender body and then for a long moment they clung together, bathed in the warmth and the light from the fire, which only seemed to ignite further the fire that had taken possession of Diana. She could feel her pulse thudding and her cheeks were flaming.

They moved toward the bed, and Jaime drew back the candlewick spread. Beneath it was a deep-blue quilt, and Diana sank into its softness, then felt him beside her. He clasped her to him, his hands roving over her skin as he held her, and she began to stroke his back, her ardor and impatience mounting. But Jaime was not about to be rushed.

Tenderly he took her by the shoulders and turned her until she was lying on her back, and then he leaned above her, his kisses beginning at her forehead then trailing across her neck and down to the hollow between her breasts. Gently his fingers caressed her tautened nipples, then moved lower, and lower, until they'd found the most intimate part of her, and she became suffused with a sharp delight that made her cry aloud.

Jaime stilled the cry with another kiss, taking her hands and moving them to his own hips, urging as he did so, "Touch me, Diana. Touch me."

Tentatively, at first, she fluttered her fingers across his smooth, muscular body, until they finally reached the core of his masculinity. Lightly she explored and caressed him. It was the first time she'd ever touched a man this way.

She kept touching him until he groaned, "You'd better stop, my darling, or I won't be responsible for my actions!" He rolled onto his back, looking across at her with eyes that were as black as night but had an inner glow to them now. "My God," he said, awed, "do you know what you do to me, Diana?"

Without waiting for an answer he moved until he was on top of her, and Diana's response to him was as natural as it was involuntary. She was possessed with her need for him, and when he entered her she was ready to move with him through the rhythms of mounting passion as they traveled together along the path to their final glorious culmination.

When the last of their ecstasy had abated, Diana lay very still within the circle of Jaime's arms, listening to his breathing, still ragged but slowly returning to its normal tempo. Impulsively she reached over to kiss the damp hair that ringed his forehead, and when she saw that his eyes were closed, her lips moved down to touch the dark lashes that fringed those eyes she loved so much.

The fire had died down, and gazing at the glowing embers, Diana wished that she and Jaime could stay in this room for a long, long time. Warm and alone, with the world and all its troubles shut out beyond closed doors.

After a time Jaime nibbled lazily at her ear, then complained, "I'm hungry. You'd be delicious, but I think I'll save you for dessert."

He raised himself on one elbow, then looked down at her, his full, beautifully shaped mouth curved in a smile that was at once tender and humorous. "Come to think of it," he said, "man does not live by bread alone. There are other appetites that should be satisfied first."

He rolled over on top of her as he spoke, pinning down her shoulders as he began to assault her with his kisses, his mouth leaving its trail across her forehead, his tongue probing the pearly inner circle of her ear until he had her gasping with the sheer, hot pleasure he brought her. And then, again, his hands were making magic with her body until slowly he moved closer to her, pressing his thighs against hers as he began to circle over her in an easy but pulsating rhythm that matched the tempo of her pulse. She was caught up in his cadence, arching her body in response to him, the need, the wanting, the desire cascading through her again as she matched her passion with his. It was a different sort of voyage this time. They were two rafts, plunging together into waves so great that they were drenched in their own emotions, riding the waves until they crested on the most magnificent one of all, then drifted slowly back to shore.

The embers were no longer glowing. It was dark in the room, and Jaime reached down to pull the quilt over them. Diana snuggled under it, pressing close to him, savoring his warmth and his nearness, and finally, with his arms around her, she drifted off into a wonderfully peaceful sleep.

She awakened to find that Jaime had put new logs in the fireplace. The flames cast gold and amber lights out into the darkness of the room. She saw, too, that he had dressed.

Hearing her move, he came over to her and sat down on the edge of the bed, reaching out to draw her to him, cradling her as he kissed her in a way so deep, so tender, it brought tears to her eyes.

Smiling down at her, he said, "Now I really am hungry. What do you have in your fridge?"

She stared at him in dismay. "Lots of things," she moaned, "but they're all frozen!"

"Modern women," he complained, shaking his head. "Okay, I froze some of the Portuguese soup I made the other day, and that thaws quickly. Suppose I go across and get it, with that other bottle of Beaujolais you gave me. Do you have some bread and butter."

"Better than that," she said triumphantly. "I have a whole bagful of Portuguese rolls!"

"Do tell!" he teased. "Does that mean that my ethnic lessons are taking effect, *menina*? No, don't answer that! Put your clothes back on before I lose all sense of reason again, and I'll go get the soup."

He left her, and she heard his footsteps going down the stairs, then the soft sound of the back door thudding closed behind him. She stretched languidly and stood naked in front of the fire for a moment, savoring its warmth on her bare skin.

She dressed slowly, then washed her face and decided to put on a little lip gloss, nothing more. Out of habit, she brushed her bang over the scar when she fixed her hair, then smiled. The scar obviously didn't matter to Jaime.

Thinking of the scar made her remember his anger when he'd realized that she'd been less than honest with him. It had been anger quickly dissipated. Yet there were still gaps, great gaps, to be filled in before she'd really know him. He'd told her there were things he wanted to know about her and things he wanted her to know about him. He'd already found out quite a bit about her today. *All my phobias,* Diana thought wryly. But she still had a lot to learn about him. Why he'd given up medicine, for one thing. If it hadn't been because of his ex-wife, then why had it been?

This was not the night to get into it, though. As she went downstairs, Diana told herself that it was not the right time to be inquisitive. And anyway, a newfound confidence in Jaime made her certain that when the time *was* right he would tell her all she wanted to know about him. Whatever his reasons for giving up medicine, they must be good ones. Very good ones. He'd been a dedicated doctor. She knew that from the single experience she'd had with him as a patient.

She put the oven on low so that she could warm up the rolls, and then set the table, put out wineglasses and butter. She was rummaging through the vegetable bin in the fridge to see if she had enough green things to put together a tossed salad when the telephone rang.

Reluctantly Diana picked up the receiver. Although a few hours ago she would have welcomed a phone call, just now she wasn't in the mood to let anyone other than Jaime into her private world.

But it was Jaime at the other end of the phone. A Jaime who sounded surprisingly—disconcertingly—crisp and businesslike.

"I'm sorry, Diana," he said without preamble, "but I can't get back over. Something's come up. Do you have enough food on hand to do you for supper?"

"Yes," she said. "Yes. But...."

"I'm sorry," he said again. "I'll call you in the morning." Before she could respond he hung up.

She stared down at the phone incredulously, as if willing him to come back on the line and speak to her again, and even when she'd returned the receiver to its hook she half expected the phone to ring again. She couldn't believe that Jaime would rebuff her like this, not after the afternoon they had shared.

She was in no mood to think about fixing anything to eat, as he'd suggested. She'd never been less hungry. She turned out the kitchen light and went to the side window that faced his house. As she watched from her vantage point in the darkness she saw him come out, stamp his way down the back steps and walk out to his car, which was still parked at the end of the driveway. As she saw his headlights sweep the garage then go past the house, she leaned her head against the window frame, puzzled beyond all measure.

CHAPTER SEVEN

DIANA TELEPHONED GAIL LANDERS at eight o'clock
the next morning. She didn't bother to apologize by
asking if she'd awakened her. She knew that Gail
was usually up early. Howard liked to get to his office before his secretarial staff arrived so that he'd
have some private time in which to think, as he
described it. And though Melinda was an exceptionally good child she seldom, according to her
mother, slept past seven.

"Can you get a sitter on the spur of the moment?" Diana asked without preamble. "I wondered if we could meet somewhere between there
and here and have lunch."

She sensed Gail's hesitation. "Melinda has a
cold," Gail said. "Nothing serious, but I hate to
leave her. Look, it's time you saw your godchild
again anyway, don't you think? Could you spare a
couple of days away from your research?"

Diana could imagine Gail's astonishment if she
told her she hadn't even gotten into her research
yet. Well, that revelation could come later. She
made a spur-of-the-moment decision. "Yes."

"Fantastic," Gail said enthusiastically. "Throw
some things into a tote bag and come on over. It

shouldn't take you much more than an hour to get here, and I'll have a fresh pot of coffee on the stove.''

Diana did exactly what Gail had suggested. She tossed a few clothes into a bag then streaked out of the house without permitting herself so much as a glance next door. If Jaime Medeiros was taking note of her departure she didn't want to know it. She couldn't help but be aware, though, that at some point he'd managed to back up her car, which had edged into a hedge, and return it to her garage.

She'd called Gail for two reasons. She needed to be with someone she knew, and she didn't want to be home if and when Jaime phoned her, as he'd said he would. She still couldn't believe his actions the night before. What could possibly have come up that would have caused him to tear off as he had? Had he suffered a quick change of heart, once he'd gone back to his own house? Had he regretted making love to her?

Disillusioned as she felt at the moment, Diana couldn't make herself believe this. No, deep in her heart she was certain that Jaime didn't regret their time together any more than she did.

Gail and Melinda were waiting for her at the door of the Landerses' house, and there was an exuberance to their respective greetings that was very warming. Melinda was slightly congested but her cold was on the mend, her mother said. The main thing now was to keep her indoors, and to keep her warm.

She was a charming miniature version of Gail. Copper haired, like her mother, with the same incredible blue eyes and a heart-tugging grin. Diana had stopped at a toy store and bought a game suitable for three-year-olds, and Melinda immediately became engrossed in its many brightly colored plastic pieces.

"You shouldn't have," Gail said, leading the way out of the kitchen. "You should have saved it for Christmas."

"Don't be ridiculous," Diana protested, as she settled in at Gail's kitchen table and accepted the steaming mug of freshly made coffee her friend handed her.

Gail sat down opposite her and surveyed her with a very discerning gaze. Mentally Diana found herself wriggling. She never had been able to keep secrets from Gail.

As usual, her friend got directly to the point. "How's the history project coming?" she asked.

Diana hesitated only briefly before confessing. "It isn't."

"Why?"

"I don't seem to be able to get off the ground with it," Diana said slowly. "I need to get a basic grasp on the subject, and then decide how I want to go about handling it for my thesis, and so far...."

Gail frowned. "Maybe it wasn't such a great idea, your renting Agatha's house," she suggested. "It's a barn of a place. You must be lonely rattling around in it all by yourself."

The quick flush of color that came to sting Diana's cheeks gave her away, and Gail said triumphantly, "Aha! The truth begins to come out. You've met someone and he's so devastating you can't get your mind on your work."

Diana shook her head, torn between chagrin and laughter. "You should be a crystal-ball gazer," she accused.

Gail's eyes widened. "I was only teasing. You mean you really *have* met someone? Di, that's wonderful!"

"No, it isn't," Diana contradicted quickly. "It isn't wonderful at all."

"Who is he?" Gail persisted.

Diana sighed. No use trying to evade, not now. And anyway, a secret was safer with Gail than gold was in Fort Knox. "He's your Aunt Agatha's next-door neighbor," she said.

Gail started visibly and set down her coffee mug with a thud. After a moment spent trying to regain her composure she asked incredulously, "Are you telling me you've fallen in love with Philip Howland?"

"Good heavens, no!" Diana exclaimed, appalled. "He's a nice enough man but. . . ."

"Whew! You startled me for a minute," Gail admitted frankly. She pursed her lips, and Diana knew she must be ticking off remembered names and faces in Fairhaven, people who lived near the DuBois house. Finally she said, "I give up. I wouldn't say Agatha has any other male neighbors who are of an age to interest you."

"Jaime Medeiros has come back, temporarily," Diana said. "I guess he's going to sell his house."

"Dr. Medeiros?"

"Yes. Do you know him? It seems to me I asked him if you'd met, and he said he didn't think so."

"We met once, ages ago, when he stopped by Aunt Agatha's one afternoon while Howard and I were visiting," Gail told her. "It was shortly before Melinda was born. I was very pregnant. He only stayed a few minutes. I'm not surprised he wouldn't remember me. But I have to admit I remember him."

"Oh?"

"I thought he was the best-looking man I'd ever seen in my life," Gail confessed. "I was so openly admiring about him that even Howard, who usually doesn't have a jealous bone in his entire body, was annoyed." Gail edged her chair closer to the table. "Di, tell me, tell me," she urged. "How did you meet him and...."

"Whoa!" Diana held up an admonishing hand. "Don't race it, Gail. There isn't that much to tell. I met him because I dropped the front-door key in a snow storm and it fell into the bushes...."

Slowly, very carefully, she went on to tell Gail how Jaime had come to her rescue, getting into the house via the cellar bulkhead. She went on to say that they'd had breakfast together the next day, and then he'd invited her to share his homemade soup with him, and finally she confessed that she'd nearly crashed into his car in the driveway the previous afternoon. She cautiously skirted the aftermath of that last encounter.

Gail listened with rapt attention. "Agatha's going to be absolutely enthralled by all of this!"

"Gail!" Diana was horrified. "You're not to tell her a thing, do you hear me? Everything I've said was in absolute confidence."

"I know, I know," Gail said placatingly. "And I won't say anything, unless a real romance develops between you and Dr. Medeiros. Then, of course, Agatha will be bound to know. And," Gail finished, more slowly, "I can't help but hope that a real romance does spring up between the two of you. Agatha adores him, I know that, and she detested his ex-wife."

"She knew his ex-wife?"

"Yes. But only in passing. I gather she was a regal, Boston beauty, related to more than one of the leading New England families. Aloof...a snow princess. There's enough warm French blood in Agatha's background so she didn't like Jaime Medeiros's wife at all.

"Then, when he gave up medicine, Agatha was devastated. She came out here for a visit about that time, and she was terribly upset."

Diana's mouth went dry as she heard this. She moistened her lips with the tip of her tongue and asked huskily, "Did Agatha say why he gave up medicine?"

Gail frowned. "I'm trying to remember. It had something to do with a patient. A death, I think. Someone died, and Dr. Medeiros felt he'd been responsible. Evidently he put down his scalpel and said he'd never operate again, and he walked out of the hospital and never went back. He left Boston. I guess for a while no one knew where he was, and Agatha was beside herself. I don't know whether you know it or not, but years ago Agatha taught English at Fairhaven High. Jaime Medeiros was a pupil of hers. She always took a special interest in him, he used to do lawn work for her after school, things like that. Agatha became very fond of him and she followed his career, of course, and was very proud of him.

"You have to remember," Gail went on, "I've never lived in Fairhaven myself. I was brought up in Providence. I used to visit Aunt Agatha occasionally, especially during summer vacations, but I don't remember Dr. Medeiros at all during those years. Probably he'd left the local scene by then. There'd be a fair difference in our ages."

"About nine years," Diana said. "He's thirty-eight."

"So you've gotten your statistics down," Gail observed with a grin. Her smile faded and she became thoughtful again. "You say he's going to sell the old Bennett place?"

"The old Bennett place?"

"The house he bought belonged to the Bennett family. They were very prominent locally at one time, so Agatha has told me. Jaime Medeiros's mother used to work for the Bennetts as a maid."

As a maid. The words clicked, and it was easy to imagine the rest of the story. Jaime's mother had worked for the Bennetts, and at one point he must have vowed that one day she'd have a house of her own as grand as theirs. And then, in a strange quirk of fate the Bennett house had been put on the market, and by then Jaime had been able to buy it. But it had been too late, as far as his mother was concerned. She'd never had the chance to live in her mansion.

"I wonder if Aunt Agatha knows he's planning to sell the Bennett place," mused Gail. "She'll be upset about it...."

Gail's conjecturing was interrupted by Melinda, who had exhausted her three-year-old attention span on the game Diana had brought her and was looking for both diversion and a glass of orange juice. After that, a neighbor stopped by for a visit, which called for the production of a new pot of coffee, and the rest of the day passed pleasantly. Gail was an easygoing young woman with her feet set firmly on the ground. Practical, she nevertheless had an impish sense of humor and was fun to be with. She and Diana still kept in contact with many of the friends they'd made during their college years, so whenever they managed to get together they always had a lot to talk about. To Diana's relief, they didn't return to the subject of Jaime.

Howard Landers came home at six o'clock, and his welcome was genuine. Howard wasn't an exciting man. He was tall and thin, and balding prematurely. In a crowd he would pass unnoticed. But his charming smile gave a clue to a personality he kept hidden from most people. When she'd first met him, Diana had thought he was a rather cold sort of person, and she'd wondered at Gail falling in love with him. Now that she'd come to know him better, she'd revised her first opinion. Howard was a loyal and caring person, completely devoted to Gail and their daughter. He was a man who could be depended upon, and Gail obviously was very happy with him.

As she got ready for bed that night, Diana felt a faint pang of envy for her friend. She'd never experienced that sort of relationship herself. She'd learned early in her marriage that Gary was not a person to be depended upon, and only her own stubbornness, her insistence that somehow she must make her marriage work, had kept her tied to him for nearly four years.

Would Jaime be a man a woman could depend upon? Sliding under the bedclothes in Gail's pretty, Colonial-style guest room, Diana instinctively knew the answer to that question. If Jaime really loved a woman, he'd never let her down. She was as sure of this as she was of the fact that somewhere up there in the sky, on this cloudy December night, there was a silver moon shining. Obscured, maybe, but there.

IT WAS BRIGHT AND SUNNY the next morning, and Melinda's cold was so much better that Gail decided she could go to the play school she usually attended on Saturdays.

"And you and I," Gail said conspiratorially, "will go off on a shopping spree."

They went to the Cape Cod Mall, which housed branches of the leading Boston department stores and specialty shops. Gail bought a dress to wear to a Christmas party she would be attending with Howard, then she insisted that Diana get herself a party dress, too.

"But I'm not going anywhere," Diana protested.

"Nonsense," Gail said brusquely. "You said you were invited to a party at the Burroughses' last week, didn't you?"

"Yes. But that was only because of your Aunt Agatha. Before she left for Florida she asked Emily Burroughs to look in on me."

"Well, I'm sure you'll be hearing from some others, too, over the next few days. Anyway, a new dress will perk up your morale. And if you have that little eggnog party you mentioned—believe me, Howard and I will come unless there's a blizzard—it would be nice for you to have something special to wear."

When Gail made up her mind about something she was a hard person to sway. Laughing, Diana went along with her and succumbed to a stunning ivory creation that was a blend of silk and angora with a cowl neck and a gold, wraparound belt. The gold sandals that had provoked such ridicule from Jaime would go very well with her new dress, she thought whimsically.

She and Gail stopped for lunch at a German restaurant in the mall, indulging in open-faced sauerbraten sandwiches accompanied by potato dumplings and red cabbage. It was delicious but hearty fare, and when she'd finished everything on her plate Diana groaned. "I could curl up and take a nap."

"Nonsense," Gail said briskly. "We'll have to work it off! Come on. I still haven't bought Howard's Christmas present, and I want to pick up a couple of extra little things for Melinda's stocking, too."

The mall was decorated for Christmas, and carols were playing softly in the background. Outside Filene's, Santa Claus had set up residence, and a wide-eyed little boy about Melinda's age was perched on his knee, volubly detailing all the things he wanted for Christmas.

Diana hadn't felt any Christmas spirit for years. Not since long before the accident. Knowing that Gary was seeing other women always put a damper on things. But now the warm and wonderful spirit of the season began to take hold of her, and as she watched Gail scanning all sorts of possible presents and then deciding on a soft-gray cashmere sweater for Howard, she wished she had someone to buy something for. She'd mailed her presents to her parents before leaving New York, knowing how slow the mails could be especially as the holidays approached. She'd brought along a gift for Gail, which she'd given her last night with the admonition that she was not to open it till Christmas morning. Other than that, there really weren't any people she regularly exchanged Christmas presents with; cards with handwritten messages had suffced for quite a while now.

She waited while Gail bought a doll for Melinda, and finally she faced up to the fact that it wasn't *people* she wanted to go Christmas shopping for. It was one specific person. Jaime Medeiros.

She repressed the impulse so sternly that she was tight-lipped as she and Gail left the mall, and Gail looked across at her curiously.

"What's the matter?" she asked. "I haven't worn you out, have I? Howard always swears I get an energy injection every time I go shopping."

"No," Diana said hastily. "No. I'm fine. I...I just ate too much lunch, that's all."

Gail spied a booth in the center of the mall where a woman was selling handmade Christmas corsages for the benefit of a local charity. Impulsively she paused to buy one for Diana and one for herself.

"Here," she said, handing Diana hers. "This'll get your Christmas spirit bubbling!"

The corsage was fashioned with fresh greens, intertwined with red and green velvet ribbons and small, glistening Christmas balls. Diana pinned it to her coat collar and smiled at her friend. "Thanks, Gail," she said. "I guess I need a few visions of sugar plums, though being here with you today has given me a shot in the arm in that department."

"I'm glad," Gail said sincerely. "More than almost anything I can think of, Di, I want you to have a really Merry Christmas."

DIANA HAD INTENDED to get a reasonably early start back to Fairhaven, but it was nearly four by the time she and Gail returned to the Landerses' house and she loaded up her car. At the last minute Gail presented her with two loaves of homemade cranberry bread and some of her beach-plum jelly.

"Remember," Gail told her as they hugged each other, "you're invited here for Christmas. Unless, of course, you get a better offer!" she added mischievously.

Diana protested, but as she drove away she knew that Gail, a romantic for all of her practicality, was already fantasizing about Jaime Medeiros and her. Gail would probably be phoning her Aunt Agatha in Florida between now and Christmas to tell her that Jaime had come home and he and Diana had already gotten to know each other.

Darkness came early these days, and by the time she reached the bridge over the Cape Cod Canal, the world had closed in on Diana. Although she didn't relish driving in the dark, she took the situation in stride. She'd be all right, she told herself firmly, and even if it did start to snow, she could handle it.

The skies were still cloudy, and the moon that was up there somewhere remained an unseen, silvery promise, but Diana's luck held. At Wareham she decided against going off onto the interstate highway and followed Route 6 along to Fairhaven instead. After all, she was in no hurry. At least that was the way she tried to rationalize her choice of routes to herself. But she knew she was avoiding following the same road where disaster had overtaken her three years before.

Traffic was light, and Diana felt considerably more relaxed than she'd thought she would. She switched on the radio. Christmas carols filled the car, and she was caught up in their sweet sound. This was such a special time of the year. A season of peace on earth, goodwill toward men...if it could only really be like that.

She was almost at Fairhaven when she remembered that she was out of milk and was getting close to the bottom of her can of coffee, as well. When she saw the lights of a convenience store she turned in. She quickly tossed a few things into a shopping cart, then, as she was passing the bread section, she saw a package of Portuguese *bolos*. She stared down at them, a melange of feelings welling up within her as she remembered that breakfast with Jaime. He'd filled the whole kitchen with his presence, his masculinity as refreshing as the salt breezes that swept in from the bay.

Without stopping to think, Diana reached out for the *bolos* and added them to the contents of her shopping cart. A few minutes later, back on the road again, she asked herself impatiently why she'd done such a silly thing. They'd go stale before she could eat them all. In fact, she didn't want to eat any of them. Just the taste of that sweet, delicious Portuguese dough would remind her of Jaime, and she didn't want to be reminded of him.

In spite of herself she found it impossible to

keep her eyes averted from the house next door as she swung into her driveway. The light was burning in his kitchen window, and as she looked at it Diana realized that she'd never seen a light in any other part of the house. Did Jaime spend all of his time in the kitchen when he was home? It was a spacious enough kitchen, though it was painted in a rather dull shade of yellow that would do little to lift a person's spirits. Even so, she couldn't imagine spending all of her time in even the best of kitchens.

Amy Howland had mentioned that Jaime had never really furnished the house when it became apparent that his mother would never be living in it. But it must be partially furnished. He had to be sleeping on something other than the kitchen floor.

Was he going to sell the house? And if he did, would he leave Fairhaven with the same kind of finality with which he'd evidently left Boston? Would he go off somewhere, simply vanish?

Why?

Diana remembered the brief but indelible impression Jaime had made on her that night in the emergency room. Maybe Gail was right, maybe he had lost a patient. But most doctors lost patients during the course of their careers. And heartbreaking though it must be, it didn't cause them to give up.

Jaime would have given up medicine only if he'd believed the patient's death to be the result of his own negligence, something she simply couldn't credit. No matter what anyone might say about Jaime, no matter how she might feel herself about his most recent actions toward her, as a doctor Jaime would never do anything that was less than his best.

Once inside her own kitchen Diana glanced through the side window toward Jaime's house, but she saw no silhouette tonight. She smiled wryly. She'd been flattering herself if she'd thought that Jaime might be standing there watching her come in.

She trudged up the stairs with the purchases she'd made in Hyannis, then slipped out of her clothes and into a deep, orange-colored velvet lounger. Back downstairs, she paused to turn up the thermostat. She'd put it down before she'd gone away and it was cold in the house.

To her surprise she found that she was hungry, despite her hearty German lunch. There was a pizza in the freezer compartment of the fridge, and she took it out, then turned on the oven to preheat it. She put on a kettle of water to boil for tea, and then switched on the light over the kitchen table. She would read the magazine she'd bought in the mall, while she waited for the pizza to bake and the water to boil.

But at that moment all the lights went out.

CHAPTER EIGHT

DIANA HAD NEVER BEEN AFRAID of the dark, but this sudden onslaught of blackness brought her close to panic.

She rallied quickly, her liberal endowment of common sense surfacing to tell her that probably nothing more catastrophic had happened than a power failure. She'd left her recently purchased flashlight on the kitchen counter. She groped around until she found it, and switched it on. The glaring beam was intensely reassuring in the dark room.

Maybe the kitchen light had burned out, she decided, but a glance at the stove told her that the oven was off, and the fridge, which had been humming a moment ago, was disconcertingly silent.

She made her way to the living room and checked the light fixtures there in the hope that whatever had happened had happened in the kitchen area alone. But she soon found that the power was off all through the house.

Glancing out the front window, she saw that the corner streetlight was on. She returned to the kitchen and pulled up the shade, which she'd drawn, and saw that the single, yellowish light next door was burning steadily. Obviously the power failure had occurred in her house alone.

She glanced at her watch. It was just past seven o'clock. There must be electricians in the area listed in the phone directory, but even if she was lucky enough to find one at home she wondered if he could be persuaded to come out this time of night. And when he asked what was wrong, what could she tell him? Only that her power was off, and she didn't know why.

So this was what came of growing up in an apartment on Manhattan Island, where so many of the modern amenities of daily living were taken for granted, Diana thought ruefully. Then, with a reluctant shrug, she put her pride in her pocket.

She thumbed through the telephone book with the help of her flashlight, stopping when she came to the listing under Medeiros. She was staggered at the number of people named Medeiros living in the Fairhaven-New Bedford area. There were literally dozens.

There was also the chance that Jaime wasn't even listed, but then she saw the simple "J. Medeiros, Fort Street," and felt an overwhelming sense of relief.

She wasted no time in dialing his number. She knew that if she thought too much about calling him for help she'd back down. His phone rang once, twice, three times, and her heart sank. He must have gone out again. But on the fourth ring he answered, and she sat down, weak-kneed at the sound of his voice. Until now she hadn't let herself admit how much she'd missed him.

"Hello?" he said again. She recognized the impatience in his tone and knew he'd probably hang up if she didn't respond quickly.

"Jaime," she said. "Jaime. . . it's Diana."

There was an intensity to the moment of silence that followed that permeated the telephone wires. Then, his tone heavy with irony, he asked, "Diana *Ashley*?"

"Yes," she said, "Diana Ashley. Jaime. . . ."

His voice became crisp with anger. "Where the hell have you been?"

"Away," she said. "In Hyannis. Visiting a friend."

"A friend?"

She resented his tone. She tried to tell herself that he had no right to take this kind of tack with her, but nevertheless she found herself explaining. "Gail Landers," she said. "I told you about her, remember? She's Agatha DuBois's niece. We went to college together. Jaime. . . ."

"Yes," he said, overly patient all of a sudden. "What is it, Diana? You must have a very good reason for calling me up."

Diana hadn't been aware of the tension mounting within her, but Jaime's mocking, indulgent tone of voice brought her to the breaking point. She'd cope without him, she decided. "Damn it!" she shouted into the receiver. "Forget it."

She'd called two electricians listed in the directory and had received an answering-machine message at each number when she heard the pounding at her back door. She knew it was Jaime. She hesitated, tempted not to answer. But she knew him well enough to know he'd go on pounding all night until she let him in.

She was holding the flashlight in one hand as she opened the door for him. She shone the beam on the floor, but even so, the little back hall was illuminated clearly enough that he was all too visible to her.

He needed a shave, his eyes were red rimmed—from lack of sleep, she surmised—and his usually well-combed hair was rumpled. But he was still the most overwhelmingly handsome man she'd ever seen. It was incredible how familiar his face had become to her in such a short space of time.

He glanced toward the dark kitchen then asked, "Aren't you taking energy conservation rather seriously?"

"The power went off all of a sudden," she replied defensively.

"Oh?" He was moving into the kitchen as he spoke, shrugging off his parka. He tossed it onto one of the straight-backed chairs. "Did you check the fuses?" he asked.

She stared at him dumbly. "What fuses?"

"You must have a fuse box in the cellar. Chances are one of the main fuses has blown, but there are probably some replacements around. If not, I have some extra fuses over at my house. Did you turn the furnace off?"

Diana stiffened and resisted the temptation to

start tapping her foot. "May I ask," she demanded icily, "just how in hell one turns a furnace off?"

"There's usually an emergency switch," Jaime told her, mockingly polite. "Here, give me that flashlight of yours." He beamed the light around the room, letting it come to rest on a small, square, red panel next to the fridge. Without commenting he walked across the room and pressed the switch, then turned back to her. "If you don't turn the furnace off, and the power comes on as suddenly, there's an electrical surge that can do some heavy damage to the furnace system," he explained. "Understand?"

"I don't know what I understand."

"Okay. We won't press the point. Why don't you get out a couple of glasses—here, I'll shine the light for you—and maybe some of that brandy. It's colder than hell in this place and it isn't going to get any warmer until we can safely get the furnace going again. Which I hope will be soon. While you fix the drinks, I'll dart down to the cellar and take a look at the fuse box."

She glared at his departing back, thoroughly annoyed despite her deep sense of relief. The man was so competent, damn him! And he had the easy ability to make her feel like an uncoordinated idiot. And besides, just seeing him again had had an effect on her that was out of all proportion to the circumstances.

She muttered a few words under her breath that were not regulars in her vocabulary. Jaime had left her in total darkness but he expected her to pour out a glass of brandy for him. It would serve him right if she dropped the whole damned bottle of brandy and it shattered to pieces, she thought, trying to whip up a healthy anger toward him as a first line of defense.

And as she was contemplating an "accident" with the bottle, the lights came on again.

The effect was dazzling. Diana had always thought the kitchen underilluminated if anything, but now she blinked. In the wake of the transition from darkness to light came Jaime. He grinned at her as he flicked the furnace switch back on again. She could hear the machinery begin to purr in the cellar, beneath her feet.

"So," she said. "So, it was a fuse."

"It certainly was," Jaime said succinctly. He took the brandy bottle out of her hand and poured them each a measure, then clicked his glass with hers. "Fortunately," he said, "I had my suit of armor polished to a high shine, and I was ready to leap into it. Otherwise I might not have been able to rush to your rescue quite so quickly."

She tried to be annoyed with him and failed completely. "Oh, Jaime!" she moaned helplessly.

"That's better, *menina*," he said approvingly. He pulled out one of the kitchen chairs and sat down at the table, stretching his long legs in front of him. "Tomorrow we'll venture into your cellar and I'll give you a lesson on how to tell whether or not a fuse has blown, and how to replace it if it has. You'll be surprised at how simple the whole operation is. I think a two-year-old child, properly instructed, could change a fuse.''

"Thanks a lot," she said testily.

"Well," he conceded, "that may be stretching it a bit. A two-year-old genius, perhaps. Diana, come on. Bring your brandy over and sit down and stop glaring at me like that. I'm the one who should be glaring at you!"

"How do you figure that?" The brandy glass in hand, she sat down next to him.

His eyes seemed darker than ever as he looked at her, and there was no levity in his tone as he said simply, "You worried the hell out of me!"

"*I* worried the hell out of you?" She couldn't have been more surprised.

"I told you I was going to call you yesterday morning and I did, and there was no answer. I kept calling you off and on all day, and I came over here a dozen different times, pounding on your back door and then going around and pounding on your front door. I even went over to Amy Howland's and asked her if she knew where you were. And she didn't."

"You went to Amy's?"

"Yes," he snapped. "Hermit that I am, *menina*, recluse, antisocial SOB, misanthrope—choose your own description—I came out of my damned shell and went over to Amy's because I was worried sick about you!"

"Jaime!"

"Don't sound so pleased, damn it!"

"It isn't that I'm pleased," she said, but a very

warm, wonderful feeling had invaded her. He'd cared enough about her to make inquiries of Amy Howland. She realized for Jaime to have embarked on such a safari meant a lot.

"Amy didn't know where you were," he pointed out. "Didn't you tell anyone where you were going?"

"No," she said. "No, I didn't."

"Not used to accounting for your actions, is that it?" he suggested.

She didn't especially like the way he was putting it, but she had to admit he was right. "For quite a while now," she hedged, "I've been something of a loner."

"For quite a while I've been something of a loner myself," he told her. "I appreciate your desire for independence, Diana, because I'm that way too. But don't you think it's somewhat irresponsible to—well, to simply run off and abandon a house in the middle of winter?"

"I didn't abandon the house," she protested. "I turned down the thermostat...."

"So low that the pipes might have frozen," he interrupted direly.

"That's ridiculous. Pipes don't freeze at a temperature of fifty-five," Diana said, and hoped she was right about this, "and that's what I set the thermostat for. I locked all the doors securely, and there was really nothing else to do."

"Except perhaps to have told me that you were taking off for a couple of days."

"It...it just didn't occur to me," Diana said.

And it really hadn't. She'd left to get away from him, and the memory of her reason for doing so was vivid. She nearly went on to say, "I didn't think you'd care where I went," but that sounded a bit too maudlin, a bid for sympathy, and she wasn't asking Jaime for sympathy.

He narrowed his eyes speculatively as he looked at her, and again she had the uncomfortable sense that he was reading her mind. "Of course," he said, as if there was no doubt at all about the veracity of what he was about to say, "you were angry with me. Is that why you took off?"

"You flatter yourself!" She spouted the cliché as an instant form of self-defense, and then wished she'd been more selective.

"Do I, Diana? No, I think you were angry. Maybe a little more than angry, maybe a little bit hurt. Am I presuming too much to think you were hurt?"

He didn't wait for her answer, but went on. "I had to do what I did the other night, and there was no time to make any explanations to you. For God's sake—" an anger of his own edged his voice now "—don't you think that what I wanted to do was to come over here and have supper with you, and then to make love to you all over again?"

Diana sat up straighter, her mouth tightening. "I'd rather not talk about it, Jaime," she said.

"You'd rather not talk about it?" he echoed. "That's the most ridiculous thing I've ever heard. It's between us, my leaving you like that—it's a sore spot. It can be cured easily enough. . . at least

I think it will be, once you've heard what I have to say. Left unattended the wound would only be aggravated...."

"If you say so, doctor," she said, her emphasis elaborate. When she saw the grimace of pain that crossed his face, she wished she hadn't spoken at all. It was a brief spasm, but to Diana it was very telling. That flash of anguish had been all too real, and Diana could hardly keep her distance from him. She wanted to encircle him in her arms and cradle his dark head against her. She wanted to console him, to kiss away his unhappiness. She wanted *him*.

He was staring straight ahead, his handsome face carefully composed. There was no reading his emotions at the moment, and his voice was carefully controlled as he said, "All right. The reason I took off so abruptly the other night was that I had a phone call from my brother as soon as I got into the house. His daughter Constance—my niece—had tried to commit suicide."

The statement, made without emphasis, was staggering in its starkness, and Diana was shocked. She stared at him, her gray eyes wide with the horror of what he'd just said.

"Oh, Jaime," she whispered, "I'm sorry. I'm *sorry*! I had no idea."

He turned toward her, still expressionless. "It might teach you not to leap to conclusions but to give a person a decent chance, Diana. I know when you've been burned once it's hard to trust again. I've been that route, too. But in our case...."

"Oh, Jaime," she said, her mind still on the terrible thing he'd told her. "What happened to your brother's daughter?"

"Connie? She's okay. I gave her an emetic. She took it willingly enough after I told her that if she didn't take it I'd cart her over to the emergency room at the hospital and they'd pump her stomach out, which would be considerably more unpleasant. She hadn't ingested that much. Some sleeping pills Flor, her mother, had. Flor knew there were only five or six pills left in the bottle. Not enough of a dose to be lethal, so there was no great risk. I suspect Connie knew that when she swallowed the pills. I suspect she was making a grandstand play. But it's the motivation behind it that worries me. When people talk or try suicide it's a cry for help. Sometimes they only utter that cry once. Next time it's too late. That's what I'm trying to get across to Bill and Flor. They've got to come to grips with Connie *now*."

"How old is she, Jaime?"

"Twenty," he said. "She's a pretty girl. A very bright girl, too. After high school she went to business school in Boston for a year. She's a secretary in a realtor's office in New Bedford, and I think she's contented enough with her work. Though Flor, of course, wanted her to go on to college and probably law school next, have an outstanding career and marry a dashing millionaire with a Boston Brahmin background in the bargain."

There was a suppressed bitterness in his tone,

but his next words were almost vehement. "Too bad certain people won't leave others alone."

Diana ignored this remark. "So what's Constance doing now?" she asked him.

"She stayed home yesterday, but I talked to Bill a while ago and he said she insisted on going back to work this morning. He thought maybe that would be the best thing for her to do, and I agree. The thing is, well, under ordinary circumstances I'd say the next step should be psychiatric counseling, but I'm not so sure that's what Connie really needs. I think this action on her part was pure protest...directed against her mother, particularly. The basic problem, as I see it, is that Flor is trying to break up the relationship between Connie and the boy she's very much in love with."

"Why?"

There was a weariness, a sadness, to Jaime's smile. "Well," he said, "I suppose it's partly because Flor and Bill are following the pattern most people do, in regard to their children. And Connie is an only child...they've centered a great deal of their lives around her. They've both worked very hard, and they want Connie to have a much easier life than they did when they were younger. In fact I'd say a major reason why Bill has been driven to work as hard as he has is so that he could give Connie all the things he and Flor never had themselves when they were young.

"They want to see her marry someone who will also provide her with the good things, someone who'll be able to take care of her and assure her a certain place in society. Manny, the boy she loves, doesn't fall into that category. But,'' Jaime added slowly, ''I have to admit that I'm certain a large part of their objection to him is because he's Portuguese. He's a fisherman. You've met him, matter of fact. Manuel Ribeiro. He's the young man who burst in on you unceremoniously the other night. He really did get the wrong house.''

Diana bit her lip. ''I've been sorry that I reacted so strongly about that.''

''It's understandable,'' Jaime said tolerantly. ''He scared the hell out of you. He was sorry about *that*.''

She frowned. ''I don't understand,'' she said. ''Why would your sister-in-law object to her daughter marrying someone who's Portuguese. After all....''

''You're going to say that Flor's Portuguese herself and married to a Portuguese, is that it?'' Jaime asked, when her words trailed off. ''Well, actually Flor is half Irish. Her mother was an O'Brien. Kathleen O'Brien. She married Ronnie Silva and her family disowned her.''

Diana stared at him. ''Are you serious?''

''Perfectly serious. The O'Briens were rich, they had a big house up on County Street in New Bedford, but they cut off their daughter without a cent, and Flor has never forgotten that.'' Jaime chuckled. ''Not that this has any relevance,'' he said, ''but there's a funeral home in the old O'Brien house today. Times change, neighborhoods change, but the old prejudices linger. Actually, this whole area is a melting pot today. The original Yankee-Quaker residents have long since become a minority, and the Portuguese predominate as far as ethnic background is concerned. But there is also a very large French population and plenty of Polish, Armenians, Germans, Italians, blacks and Hispanics, as well. But prejudice dies hard, Diana. That's something you've got to remember in doing this thesis you're planning, because it's people who make history, after all. There's good reason why minority people get chips on their shoulders...and my own sister-in-law's attitude, despite the fact that she's half-Portuguese herself, is enough to give me a fairly hefty chip of my own.''

''I see,'' Diana said slowly.

''Do you?'' he teased. ''I don't imagine you've ever encountered any slurs because of your national background, Diana. You look as if your ancestors must have come over on the *Mayflower*.''

She flushed, because he'd struck on the truth, and he laughed. ''Ah,'' he said. ''So they did, eh?''

''One of them,'' Diana admitted grudgingly. ''And I can't see that it matters. None of us choose our own ancestors, after all.''

''No, but we do inherit our genes from them,'' Jaime pointed out. ''We're a composition of the people who've gone before us.''

She shook her head. ''I don't like that concept.''

''Well, I like the result in you,'' he said disarmingly. ''*Menina*....''

"Yes?"

"Don't run off like that again without telling me," he said, and she was surprised at his intensity.

"All right," she agreed. "All right, I won't."

"I have no right to ask any favors of you," he went on. "But I know that you've still got a few problems kicking around that you haven't solved. No...don't look at me like that. You're not the only one with problems, *menina*, there's no reason to start retreating into your shell."

"I'm not going to retreat into my shell, Jaime," she told him, and knew—to her own surprise— that she really wasn't. What he'd just said was true. She did still have her problems. She couldn't deny this, especially to him. And she suspected that the doctor in him would make him keep at her "case" until he'd solved it to his satisfaction.

Could he solve it? Could he get her over the guilt, the fear that were still like dark specters riding herd in the night? How wonderful to be free of them!

But at the moment she was far more interested in the man at her side than she was in herself. She yearned to get on with her own investigations about *him*. But she was beginning to wonder if the right moment would ever come for her to try to draw him out of his own shell. Instinct told her it wasn't now.

She changed the subject. "Your niece is past the age of consent if she's twenty," she pointed out. "If she's so bitterly unhappy over Manuel Ribeiro that she'd think of taking her own life because of him, why doesn't she just run off and marry him?''

"It's not that simple,'' Jaime said gravely. "Manny works for my brother. He's a crew member on one of Bill's trawlers. Bill has a finger in a lot of commercial pies here in Fairhaven. A finger? Hell, he's in the fishing business up to his neck. He owns a large interest in the Pilgrim fish-packing plant down toward Fort Phoenix, and he's also a major owner of four trawlers, I believe, at last count. Although there are unions that cover the fishermen these days, if Bill were to fire Manny Ribeiro I'd venture that Manny would find it hard getting a job anyplace else along this waterfront, or across the river in New Bedford, either.''

"And you think your brother would actually fire Manny Ribeiro if he and Constance were to elope?''

"I'm damned sure of it,'' Jaime said grimly. "Not for the same motivation that Flor would have...there's none of the snob about Bill. But I think he would do almost anything he could to prevent Connie from marrying a fisherman. It's a hell of a life, Diana. At least it can be a hell of a life for many. But when the sea is in a man's blood, in his genes, and when it's the only way of life he's ever known, the lure is very strong. And after a time there's the practical consideration that there's not much else he can do and make a living at it.

"Bill knows what it is to be a fisherman. He

went to sea just as our father did and our grand-father before him. But fifteen years ago, when he was twenty-eight years old, he lost his leg in an accident aboard a trawler.''

"Oh, no!'' Diana protested.

"I was in my first year of med school,'' Jaime remembered. "Bill was over at St. Luke's, in New Bedford, and as soon as I could get out of class I went down to see him. I'll never forget it.

"It was a long way back for Bill. The amputation was above the knee, which always makes it more difficult to use a prosthesis, but he conquered his handicap so that today he gets around very well; he doesn't even use a cane. His days of going to sea were over, though. He was married, Connie was five years old, things looked pretty bleak for Bill. But he collected some insurance as a result of the accident, and he went to college with it. He took a number of business courses and he was an *A* student all the way through. After that he started working in the office of the fish-packing plant, and when the chance came to invest in the business Bill was ready to take it. Over these past fifteen years he's worked his way up to a point where he's not rich, maybe, but certainly comfortably fixed. He owns a nice home a few blocks from here, he's well respected. Connie is the only child, and he adores her. He'd like to see only the best for her, and I can't say I blame him. Though, renegade that I am,'' Jaime finished with a slight smile, "my sympathies tend to be with Manny.''

He shrugged. "But you asked me what I'm going to do about Connie. I'd like you to meet her, for one thing."

"Me?"

"Yes. I think the two of you would take to each other, and I'll be frank with you, right now Connie needs an escape—a place where she can go and be herself, feel free. I'd persuade Bill to let her come stay with me for a while, but I have no furniture in the house," he concluded wryly.

So Amy Howland had been right about that.

"*No* furniture?" Diana questioned, not quite believing him.

"The bare minimum. I keep the upstairs closed off, I have a folding cot in the living room, and my possessions are neatly stashed in the hall closet or stored in a couple of suitcases that make surprisingly adequate dressers. Don't look so shocked, *menina*. A solitary male can get by with very little in the way of creature comforts, I've found out. Living in an unfurnished house," he concluded, standing up and stretching, "is the least of my worries."

Diana was listening to what he was saying, but she was also watching him as he spoke, acutely aware of everything about him. He needed a shave, true, and his dark hair was uncombed, and there were deep shadows of fatigue beneath those midnight eyes, but the virile, masculine aura he emitted was what she was seeing, and her instinctive response to his sensuality was so powerful it jolted her.

She wanted him to take her upstairs again, she

wanted him to make love to her. She wanted to feel his warmth, his strength and to know his nearness. . . .

Their eyes met for just a second, but it was a naked second, enough to make Diana know that he wanted her every bit as much as she wanted him. Yet for reasons she couldn't even begin to understand, she knew that he was going to deny both of them their desires. She had the strong feeling that even if she were to take the initiative, Jaime had already decided that he was not going to make love with her that night.

CHAPTER NINE

"HAVE YOU NOTICED?" Jaime asked. "The sun is shining."

"Yes," Diana replied. "The sight's so dazzling it's blinding me, even though it's only a pale-lemon sun."

"Pale-lemon?"

"Yes. A winter sun."

He chuckled. "You're right. I like your description. What are your plans for today?"

"I don't have any," Diana admitted honestly. "For that matter, I haven't had the chance to make any. I just got up half an hour or so ago."

She didn't add that she'd been stepping out of the shower when she'd heard the phone ring, and she'd crossed her fingers and her toes hoping it would be Jaime. He'd kissed her the night before when he left, but it had been a gentle kiss, programmed, she decided, not to elicit too much of a response. She'd wondered, briefly, what he might have done if she'd responded anyway, if she'd telegraphed the message that she wanted him to stay. How she'd wanted him to stay! But again, that funny little seventh sense that seemed to be taking over when it came to dealing with Jaime had warned that this was not the time to try to hold him—in any way.

Now he said, "I think this would be a good day for me to prove to you that the Portuguese came to New England way ahead of the Pilgrims."

"Are you talking about the Dighton Rock?" she asked him curiously.

"Yes. It's only about an hour's drive away, and I thought we might take a picnic."

"A picnic? Jaime, it's freezing outside."

"Who said anything about eating outside?"

"I'm out of bread," Diana remembered.

"You're going to have to learn to get a better grip on your food supplies," he admonished. "But anyway, we don't need bread. This is going to be a Portuguese picnic, and I'll handle the whole thing."

Diana was smiling as she hung up the receiver. What a great persuader Jaime could be. It would not have even occurred to her to say no to him.

Since she'd been in Fairhaven, Diana had learned the value of layering clothing in cold weather. Now she donned snug flannel-lined jeans and a pale-green turtleneck. Over the turtleneck, she slipped on a darker-green shell, and then a cable-knit forest-green sweater.

She watched through the kitchen window until she saw Jaime come out his back door, then she put on her heavy hooded coat and went out to meet him. There was a salty tang to the morning air, and she licked her lips appreciatively, liking the taste of it. The day was crisp and cold, but not

freezingly cold, and the winter sun was like a bene-
diction. Diana's eyes were shining as she came up
to Jaime, and the cold was bringing a rosy tinge to
her cheeks. She felt vibrant and alive and healthy,
better than she'd felt since she could remember,
and she liked the appreciative gleam in Jaime's
eyes as he looked at her.

He looked glowingly healthy himself. Evidently
he'd managed a good night's sleep, because those
dark shadows had vanished. He was clear-eyed
and freshly shaven, and the knitted red cap pulled
down over his raven-black hair was absurdly becoming.

As they started out Diana said, "I haven't felt
like this since I was a teenager and played hooky."

"One of those, eh?" Jaime teased. "I never
played hooky myself. I was the serious type."

"I can imagine!" she scoffed.

"It's true. I was," he said rather ruefully. "My
grandfather'd had very little formal education,"
he elaborated, "and my father made it through
high school and then spent a good part of the rest
of his life on a fishing trawler between here and
the Georges Bank. He came a step up from my
grandfather. My grandfather always worked for
others. My father managed to buy a part interest
in the trawler; he was her captain when he retired."

"Did you always want to be a doctor?" He'd
led into the past, and she could see no reason why
she shouldn't ask him this question.

"Always? Well, when I was eight or so, my sister Rose got very sick. My mother thought she was going to die, and she took me to church with her to say prayers. I can remember praying for Rose. Praying and praying and praying. Then, when Rose was a little better, they let me go to the hospital to see her. Rose's doctor was in the room when we got there. I still remember him vividly. He had gray hair, and he wore glasses with silver rims on them." Jaime smiled faintly. "Rose told me that he was the man who'd made her well. In my book that meant he'd saved Rose's life, and he became a somewhat heroic figure to me. I decided that I wanted to save lives, and that the way to do it was to become a doctor."

He flashed a grin in Diana's direction. "I had very lofty motives in my early days," he said lightly, but she didn't let his tone fool her. She could imagine that he'd been a serious child. As a student he'd probably stuck to his books and never played hooky. Maybe he'd been alienated from a lot of the other kids because of this...a relative loner from an early age.

"So you went to med school," she said, when he grew silent.

"Not quite that easily," he told her. "My mother went to work cleaning people's houses and putting aside every cent she earned to help me get an education. My father was doing well enough by then, but there were always debts. He owed on the trawler, he owed on the house, he was always buying a car on credit. I don't think he ever got together enough cash in his whole life to buy anything he wanted outright. He didn't have the same feeling about my being a doctor that my mother did. I think he wanted all of us to follow in the family footsteps and go to sea, and of course Miguel did—and lost his life in the bargain—and so did Bill, and he lost a leg.''

He was staring straight ahead as he spoke, concentrating on the road, but there was a narrow, bitter line to his lips. Diana said carefully, ''You sound as if you hate the sea, Jaime.''

''Hate it?'' He flicked a glance toward her. ''No,'' he said. ''I love the sea. It's in my blood as much as it was in any of my forefathers. But I don't want the sea as my mistress, I never have. I don't want to beg her for my living. I want to be my own master, as much as a man can ever be his own master. That's something my father was never able to understand. I don't think Bill even understands it fully, though he was extremely proud when I graduated from med school.''

''Was your mother still alive?''

''Yes, thank God, she was. That was her day, far more than it was mine. Her moment of triumph. I cried when I looked at her. You should have seen the expression on her face. She'd had her vision of glory, she'd put all her hopes and all her dreams in me, and to her I'd succeeded. It was a terrible responsibility to handle, Diana. I would have died before I would have ever let her down.''

A small, inner voice nudged Diana. The time had come, but her voice was trembling as she posed the question. "What would your mother think now, Jaime?"

She could feel his dark eyes searching her face. "What do you mean?" he asked.

"How would your mother feel about your having given up medicine?"

Jaime drew a long breath, a ragged breath. Then he said, his voice husky with suppressed emotion, "I didn't give up medicine, Diana. Medicine gave up on me."

They'd driven across the river into New Bedford and were traveling along one of the main streets as he said this, and as if it had been prearranged, Jaime pulled over to the curb and came to a stop.

"I'll only be a minute," he promised, getting out of the car, and Diana watched him go through the door of the small neighborhood bakery he'd parked in front of. She wondered what sort of memories her questions had forced him to confront.

He'd suffered. Jaime had suffered. There was a certain veneer to his manner, an insouciance at times, that usually served as quite an adequate mask. But she'd seen the mask slip more than once now. The other night it had disappeared entirely when they'd made love, and she was intensely aware of this strong man's vulnerability. He was a person of great depth, great feeling, yet a camouflage expert when it came to himself. Diana was amazed that he'd let her get as close to him as she had. He wasn't a man who would share his true self easily.

She wished now that they hadn't gotten into the subject of medicine, not today. Much as she wanted her curiosity about him satisfied, she would have been willing to wait a little while longer rather than spoil the euphoric mood they'd both started out with that morning. When Jaime got back into the car, flashing her a smile that was enough to turn anyone's heart over, she saw that he, too, was determined to return to their earlier footing, and she easily followed his lead.

"We were in luck," he said cheerfully. "The Portuguese pops had just come out of the oven."

"Portuguese pops?"

"Linguiça, done up inside a roll," he enlightened her, turning to place a square cardboard box on the back seat. "And I've got some other goodies, as well. Plus fresh fruit and a chilled thermos of Portuguese rosé wine. Ambrosial fare, *menina*. We are about to have the picnic of the century."

She let herself be caught up in his enthusiasm, and it wasn't hard to yield to the moment and the pure pleasure of simply being with him. As they started off again he said, "I'll give you a history lesson as we go along, so that you'll be better prepared for the rock when you see it. It's a very old rock and quite large. It's about eleven feet long and nine feet wide, and maybe five feet high, and it weighs more than forty tons."

She shook her head. "How in the world do you know how much the Dighton Rock weighs?" she asked skeptically.

"Because its weight and measurements became public knowledge when it was lifted out of the river, back in 1963, and considerably later when I started investigating the rock myself, I gathered up all the facts there were about it."

"What do you mean, it was 'lifted' out of the river?" she asked curiously.

"Well," Jaime said, evidently enjoying his role as a teacher, "let me start by explaining that the town of Dighton is situated on the east side of the Taunton River, at a point where the river begins to widen as it flows toward Narragansett Bay. Then...."

"Please, Jaime," Diana protested teasingly. "I like geography but right now it's your rock that fascinates me. Why—and how—was it lifted out of the river?"

"It was necessary in this instance in order to preserve the rock and its inscriptions, or a combination of vandalism and the effects of natural forces would have ruined it before very long. As I started to say, the rock lay along the east bank of the Taunton, and for centuries it was nearly covered by water with each high tide. But as the tide ebbed, the rock's flat face made a perfect slate for voyagers to make their marks on. This route up the Taunton River has long been a water path for explorers from many different parts of the world. Over the centuries, hundreds of marks were made on the rock, and eventually the markings attracted the attention of a great many scholars and historians. So finally the Commonwealth of Massachusetts decided that it should be protected and preserved for posterity. An embankment was built out from the shore, and then, by using a huge derrick, the rock was lifted out of the river and placed on top of the embankment. It was quite an engineering feat. That's when it was discovered exactly how big the rock was, and how much it weighed.

"Ten years later the state decided to enclose the rock in a building that could also house a museum where details of the mysterious inscriptions could be put on display. Frankly, the building looks like a mausoleum to me. It's like a rather small, octagonal Greek temple. The rock is in a separate room on the river side. The museum occupies the rest of the space, and there are photo blowups of the inscriptions and a variety of opinions about their origin. Naturally I favor the Portuguese theory," he added with a grin. "I like to picture Miguel Corte-Real and his men carving the Portuguese Cross into that rock over a century before the English set foot on Plymouth Rock."

"But you're not really sure he did it? Carved the Portuguese Cross on the rock, that is?"

"I don't see why not," Jaime told her. "But you can soon judge for yourself."

A fifty-acre state park surrounded the building in which the rock was housed, Diana discovered, and as they parked near the building itself Jaime said, "This is a great place to picnic in the summer. They have camping facilities, too. You can even come here by boat. Right now, though, it's a little too cold for that sort of thing. Bundle up, *menina.* There's a stiff breeze blowing in off the water.''

Diana threw her hood up over her head and fastened the top button on her coat, but even so she shivered from the blast of cold air that met her as she got out of the car, and she wasted no time in scurrying up the walk to the museum entrance with Jaime.

It was cool enough even inside the building. But she was at once fascinated by the panels along the walls, large photographic blowups depicting the inscriptions that had been discovered on the rock.

Jaime wouldn't let her linger here, though. ''First, the rock,'' he said. ''Then you can look over the inscriptions and come to some of your own conclusions.''

He led her to the rear of the museum building, then opened the wide, heavy doors at the end and motioned to her to precede him. Diana stepped into an area that was much too tomblike for comfort. It was dank and chilly, and there was an aroma to the dampness that suffused her senses and made her shiver.

The huge rock was in its own enclosure, protected from prying fingers and bathed in ribbons of garish light streaming down from different-colored floodlights. The lights had been placed so that their rays would converge on the ''writing side.''

Despite the striated rainbow lighting, the markings were clearly visible, although there were so many it was difficult to separate them individually.

"See?" Jaime said. "That's the Portuguese Cross, and there's the name, Corte-Real."

She followed his pointing finger, and the marks he was speaking about were clearly legible to her. But despite her fascination, she couldn't wait to get out of the cryptlike room and back into the museum proper. Once the rear door had clanged closed behind them, she heaved a sigh of relief.

Jaime looked down at her anxiously. "Something wrong?"

"Not really," she said. "Just a feeling. Oppressive. I think it's partly the colors. I don't like them. But anyway it...it's so cloying in there." Thinking about it, she shivered again. "I've never thought I was claustrophobic, but I'd hate to be locked up overnight all by myself with that rock."

He laughed. "I wouldn't think of letting you be locked up all by yourself anywhere, *menina*," he assured her. "Now take a look at the inscriptions, and see which of the historians you agree with. There are a number of theories depicted here. Some scholars think that the marks, a few of them anyway, were made by the Wampanoag Indians, who lived in these parts for about nine thousand years. Others subscribe to the theory that the ancient Phoenicians traveled to North America, and that the markings were made by Phoenicians who came to live among the friendly Indians for a time before returning to their own land.

"Then," Jaime continued, urging her on to yet another pictorial display, "we usually get to the Vikings. There are those who are sure that at least some of the inscriptions on the rock were made by early Scandinavian explorers.''

He moved her along a little farther. "Now, as you'll note," he said, "the leading theory about the rock, the one widely advanced by scholars and historians, is that the most significant inscriptions were made by Miguel Corte-Real sometime between 1502 and 1511. I can't claim kinship to Corte-Real," he teased, "but I can say that my people got here way before that ancestor of yours sailed over on the *Mayflower*, if the historians are correct!''

"Such pride of origin!" she teased back.

"And why not?" The touch of his hand, guiding her elbow, was tantalizing as he moved her on to the next exhibit. "I'd be less than honest if I didn't point out to you that some of the marks may also have been made by the Taunton hayrakers, back around 1640. At that time haying was quite a business hereabouts, and hay for the area livestock was cut at various points along the river and then transported by rafts. The hayrakers may have used the rock for a record tablet." He stopped and smiled down at her. "Had enough?''

"I'd like to look at the blowup of the Portuguese Cross one more time," Diana told him.

"I think you're just trying to get in my good graces, *menina*, but look all you want.''

She was intrigued by the alleged Portuguese inscriptions and had to agree with Jaime. It really did seem as if Miguel Corte-Real, long ago, had put his own personal signature on the face of this enormous rock. He'd left a record that neither time nor weather had been able to erase.

As they left the building and went back to the car, Diana said, "It's fascinating, really fascinating. I'm going to look into this further in my research. You say that most historians think Corte-Real was the first one to write on the rock?"

"A large percentage, yes," Jaime said. "Actually, there's a possibility that all the theories have some validity. But what's important to me is the evidence that Corte-Real did sail up this river and touched land at this very point." He grinned. "Sometimes it makes me feel that we should be eating codfish instead of turkey on Thanksgiving," he teased. "Cod is such a staple of the Portuguese food economy that it's called *'o fiel amigo,* which means 'faithful friend.'"

Jaime opened the car door and Diana slid inside, amused by him and fascinated by what he'd been telling her. He started up the engine and said, "We'll get the heat going so we'll warm up, and then we can choose our picnic site."

"We're going to eat in your beautiful Mercedes?" Diana asked.

"Why not? What are cars for, if not to picnic in?"

They found an ideal spot at an overlook along the river. As Jaime had promised, the Portuguese pops were delicious, and the slightly dry, slightly sweet wine was perfect with them. He'd sliced oranges and wrapped them in foil. "The fruit of

Portugal," he told her as he presented one to her elaborately. The other "goodies" he'd mentioned included an assortment of Portuguese cakes and cookies, each one better than the last, in Diana's opinion.

"You've sold me on your native food," she announced when she'd finished the last crumb. "Eating like this all the time could do terrible things to a person's waistline, though."

"You don't have to worry about your waistline," he told her firmly. "I find you close to perfect, but to be honest you're a bit on the thin side. I suspect that's because, judging from the usual state of your larder, you never eat when you're alone."

"I do too!" she protested.

"What?"

"Canned soup, TV dinners, all sorts of ambrosial fare," she said, laughing.

"Can't you cook?"

"Yes, I can cook," she said, mockingly indignant. "It's just that I don't like to bother...for just one person."

"Well," Jaime said, "that can always be remedied. You can always take pity on your hungry next-door neighbor."

"And compete with your culinary skills? No way!"

He held the thermos of wine up to his ear and shook it slightly. "Sounds like enough for one more inch apiece," he said. "Hold out your glass."

"I'm going to get tipsy." Diana giggled. "I'm not used to drinking in the middle of the day."

"You'll be on the way to getting relaxed, which is the way I want you," Jaime told her. He'd moved close to her to pour the wine, and now he lingered. He was so near she could see the little lines that radiated out from the corners of his eyes. And his eyelashes... his eyelashes were incredibly long and dark.

He smiled. "Do I pass inspection, *menina*?"

Diana flushed, aware that she'd been staring at him.

"Hey," he said, when she averted her eyes, momentarily embarrassed. "Hey!" And then, more seriously, he asked, "*Do* I pass inspection, *menina*?"

"Yes," she whispered, her voice catching in her throat. "Oh, yes! Jaime...."

"What is it?"

"This has been such a glorious day. Such a wonderful day."

"Yes," he said. "Yes, it has been. Let's treasure it, *menina*."

The sky began to cloud over as they started back to Fairhaven, the winter sun fading as if it had lingered just long enough for them to enjoy their picnic.

Glancing skyward, Jaime said, "Looks like we may have some more snow." Then he added, "Tomorrow's Monday."

"So it is," Diana agreed.

"Well, I thought it might be about time to introduce you to Connie."

Diana was surprised. "Are you sure your niece

would want to meet me, Jaime? I mean, she must still be quite upset, emotionally, and...."

"Are you trying to tell me you're not comfortable at the thought of meeting her?" he asked quietly.

"No. I'd be happy to meet her."

"Then, if you mean that, I can assure you Connie would be very happy to meet you. There's a pleasant old inn in Mattapoisett, Fairhaven's neighboring town to the east," he said. "I think you might enjoy it. I thought we could have dinner there."

"I'd like that," she told him.

"Now, it's about time you started on your homework, don't you think?"

"What do you mean?"

"That thesis," he prompted, then added, "I know, you still have over five months left in which to find out all about the Portuguese, *menina*." He was baiting her, she knew, but he was doing it with a tenderness she loved. "You'd better start taking notes. And I can't think of a better place to begin than to delve into Miguel Corte-Real and the Dighton Rock inscriptions."

"Are you telling me that you took me out there today with my career solely in mind?" she taunted.

He laughed. "I could never take you any place with your career solely in mind, *cara*," he told her.

"Well, you're right about one thing. I'm primarily going into the historical aspects of the Portuguese in America, Jaime. That's what I have to build my thesis around. And Miguel Corte-Real is a fascinating figure.''

"What's past is prologue," Jaime stated.

"That has a familiar ring."

"It should have—to you, at least, student that you are. It's the inscription outside the National Archives building in Washington. I went to Washington on my high-school-senior trip, and it's funny, but that phrase stuck with me even after the memory of a lot of other things had faded. It's true, you know. What's past *is* prologue. We can't escape our past, *menina*. It's what comes to haunt us, what we have to deal with, when we try to start in all over again."

CHAPTER TEN

JAIME DREW THE CAR UP to the point nearest Diana's back steps and said, "This is where I'll leave you. I have a couple of phone calls to make and then I may have to go out again."

Diana's sense of letdown was considerable. After that last, enigmatic statement he had made about the past, they'd been silent most of the way back. Jaime had retreated into himself. As she'd glanced at his inscrutable profile, Diana had felt as if he'd gone miles away from her, and she didn't know how to begin to bridge the gap.

Now she said, "Thank you again, Jaime, for such a marvelous day."

She let herself out of the car, then walked around to his side, ready to tap on his window if she had to. He was acting so remote. But at least he did roll the window down voluntarily.

"I'm not doing what I want to do, Diana," he told her. "Try to understand that."

Try to understand? His statement only baffled her all the more. Why wasn't he doing what he wanted to do? If he wanted what she wanted... well, why didn't he put the damn car in the garage and come in the house with her?

Didn't he want to make love to her again? She had the uneasy feeling that maybe he didn't, and the thought was disconcerting, to say the least. It was a strange position for her to be in. She'd become a past master at turning men off. Now... well, now she was being turned off. Diana smiled wryly. She didn't like the feeling.

"I plan to see Connie tonight," Jaime said, "and I'm hoping she'll be able to have dinner with us tomorrow. I have some ideas I want to put before the two of you that I think might be of mutual advantage."

Diana frowned. "What kind of ideas?"

"Something I'd intended to talk to you about earlier," Jaime said vaguely, "but the time slipped away on me. This isn't the moment to get into it, Diana. I'm not going to keep you standing out in the cold, and I have to get on my way." He hesitated. "Look, whether or not Connie can join us, let's plan to go to the Mattapoisett Inn for dinner tomorrow. If it's okay with you, I'll pick you up at six."

"That'll be fine with me," Diana muttered, and then made her way up the back steps into the house, aware that he was watching her every inch of the way.

His final remark was puzzling. She wished he hadn't even mentioned that he had an idea concerning his niece and herself if he wasn't going to elaborate on it. She was uneasy enough as it was at the idea of having dinner with Connie. Anyone who'd been through that much emotional trauma so recently must still be in a shaky mental state. Diana had agreed to the dinner only to please Jaime, but she had reservations about getting into a situation that also involved his niece.

Though it was not even five o'clock, it was already getting dark, so it seemed much later. Diana wished it was time to go to bed. She didn't look forward to the next few lonely hours by herself. She brewed a cup of tea, then remembered what Jaime had said about the time having come for her to get going on her homework. He was right. She'd chosen this temporary niche in Fairhaven because it would be an ideal place in which to work on her thesis, and she was letting herself be diverted by a tall dark stranger.

Stranger? It was no longer the right word, Diana thought, as she sipped her tea. Could a man still be a stranger to a woman when they'd shared the ultimate in physical closeness? Physical wasn't the right word, either. There had been more than the purely physical between Jaime and herself that magical night. There had been a tremendous emotional current, a deep meshing that had given their union a very special significance. And ever since their initial meeting, she and Jaime had shared something else. A concern for each other, a caring. Even a while ago, when he'd watched her walk up the back steps and let herself into the house, she'd felt warmed by his concern, disappointed though she'd been at his leaving her alone.

But they still had a long way to go, and she

wasn't sure that Jaime wanted to let anyone else make that journey with him.

He'd given her glimpses of his background, and he talked quite readily about some parts of his past—but not all. He'd said very little about his marriage, Diana brooded, as she took her empty teacup over to the sink and rinsed it out. And he'd completely shut off the topic of his terminated medical career after one brief puzzling statement.

How could medicine have given up on Jaime Medeiros when he'd been such a talented and dedicated doctor, already at the top of his career by the time he was in his mid thirties? What had happened that would have made medicine "give him up"? It must have been something personally and emotionally catastrophic, because Diana felt sure there was nothing physically wrong with him that would prevent him from carrying on with his work. Unless it was something so hidden, so deadly—God forbid—that it was not yet apparent to an untrained eye such as hers.

The cold hand of fear clutched Diana as she contemplated the possibility of Jaime being the victim of some terrible disease. She paced the kitchen floor trying to force herself to put such negative thoughts out of her mind, and it was a relief when her fears were brought to a halt by a knock on the back door.

Jaime. It had to be Jaime. A smile curved her lips as she flung the door open, ready to greet him. But it wasn't Jaime standing on the threshold, it was Amy Howland, wrapped in a huge fake-fur coat. "I hate to intrude, Diana," she said quickly. "It's the blasted telephone. It's out of order, and Phil's off at a meeting tonight. Wouldn't you know!"

"You're not intruding, Amy," Diana assured her, and she meant it. After her initial disappointment at not finding Jaime on her doorstep, Diana had been grateful to see Amy. Right now, the last thing she needed was to be alone.

Amy came into the kitchen, tossed her coat on a chair, and then went to the telephone. She hung up after a few minutes, shaking her head. "They say they can't do a thing about it till tomorrow morning. It's not an emergency. Blast it! I wanted to make some long-distance holiday calls tonight."

"Make them here," Diana invited.

"Thanks, but you don't know me when I start talking on the phone," Amy informed her with a smile. "The calls can wait till tomorrow."

"Then how about sharing a cup of tea right now?" Diana suggested. "I was about to brew myself a second one."

"I'd love it," Amy replied promptly. "I seem to be all at odds and ends with myself tonight. Pre-holiday nerves, maybe. I'm always afraid I'm going to forget someone on my Christmas list."

Diana laughed. And to her relief, as she and Amy settled down at the kitchen table with their tea, the conversation revolved around the upcoming holidays, their memories of Christmases past, and other fond reminiscences. The subject of Jaime did not arise.

Amy left, and without her the house seemed emptier than ever. Diana tried to turn her attention to some Christmas cards that had arrived with the daily mail. They were from friends who lived all over the country, and they'd been forwarded to her from New York. Few people had caught up yet with her Fairhaven address.

The messages were cheery for the most part, but they did very little to lift her spirits. It was impossible to neatly fold away her concern for Jaime in the same, precise way that she put each card back into its envelope and then piled the entire stack on the hall table.

On the other hand, she told herself practically, she'd only drive herself crazy if she kept on thinking in negatives. Now was the time to begin doing something productive. Resolutely Diana attacked the stack of books she'd taken out of the Millicent Library and almost at once came across an account about the Dighton Rock and the presumption that Miguel Corte-Real had carved the Portuguese Cross and his name on the face of it centuries ago.

Diana plunged on in her reading and soon was immersed in it. The story of the Portuguese and the way they'd come to America fired her imagination. In the 1800s, whaling ships out from New England had put in at the Portuguese islands— especially the Cape Verde Islands, just off the coast of Africa—to replenish their supplies and give their crews shore leave. After months at sea, the men had usually set about celebrating being ashore with such exuberance that when the time came to sail they were far from ready to go to sea again. Often those who had been "crimped"—taken aboard ship against their will—deserted the ships entirely. The captains were forced to seek new crews, and they'd pressed local Portuguese men into service. More often than not, when these Portuguese crews reached the United States they jumped ship and sought work, usually in or around the seaports where they'd landed, which accounted for the present, clustered Portuguese population in New England.

Diana took a break from her reading to make a fire in the living-room fireplace, then, with the blaze roaring satisfactorily, pulled the most comfortable chair in the room up to it, propped her feet up on a needlepoint-covered stool, and went back to her books.

Thoughts of Jaime inevitably kept infiltrating as she read, because these were his people she was reading about. She wondered just when his grandfather had set sail for America, and whether he was one of those who'd signed on aboard a whaler or whether he'd put forth in a small boat, determined to escape conscription into the King's military service. Later in the nineteenth century, many of the young Portuguese had done exactly that.

She wondered if Jaime had ever heard the stories about Emanuel Caton, who was reputed to have been the first Portuguese ever to settle in Provincetown, at the tip of Cape Cod. According to the legends that had lingered about him,

Emanuel had run away from his home in Lisbon as a boy to sail on a ship that was captured by pirates. While the rest of the crew was made to walk the notorious plank, he was kept aboard to serve as a slave to the captain. When the ship finally put in at Provincetown, the captain had become very ill and was near death. As a dying gesture, he freed Emanuel, who later married a local girl, became a respected citizen of the town and lived to a healthy old age.

Jaime had spoken of the Portuguese affinity for the sea. Now Diana learned that the Portuguese were renowned as seamen and navigators. " 'When the seas ran high and storms came up,' " she read, " 'it was said that the Portuguese crews were the last into harbor and usually brought the largest catches. It was they, too, who sailed the trim, seaworthy schooners designed for use on the Georges Bank, those treacherous shoals that lie some eighty miles east of Chatham, on Cape Cod.' "

Jaime's grandfather and his father and two of his brothers had put to sea in trawlers to fish off the Georges Bank, Diana mused. Two had lost their lives, one had lost a leg.

She put aside her book and stared into the firelight, wishing that Jaime was there to talk to her about men who put to the sea to eke out a living from an invincible mistress they alternately feared, and loved, and hated.

What was it he had said? "I don't hate the sea, I love the sea." But he'd never wanted the sea to be his mistress, and he'd never wanted to owe his living to her.

Rising, Diana went upstairs in search of the large notebook she'd bought. Thoughts about the direction she wanted her thesis to take were already forming in her head, and she wanted to put them down.

As she gathered up the notebook and a couple of felt-tipped pens, she heard the sound of a car's engine. Her side bedroom window faced the back of Jaime's house, and it was impossible for her not to look out and see if it was Jaime returning from his visit with Connie.

She watched the Mercedes swing into the driveway and disappear from her view. Her pulse began to throb, and she could feel it beating against the hollow in her throat.

Was there a chance that he was going to come over?

None at all, she concluded dismally, as the minutes ticked by. With an effort she went downstairs again and set up a card table to work on in front of the fireplace.

She stacked her reference books neatly, opened the notebook, even took the top off one of the pens and held it between her fingers. But she stared into space without putting down so much as a single line, her thoughts entirely on the man next door.

CONSTANCE MEDEIROS WAS DARK-HAIRED, slim and very pretty. But there was a sadness in her eloquent dark eyes—eyes so much like Jaime's that

Diana could hardly refrain from staring at them—
and her manner was subdued.

The old inn in Mattapoisett was charming. They
were served in a dining room decorated with blue-
patterned wallpaper, the color theme echoed in the
lovely old china objects displayed on shelves and
mantels. Many of the china pieces were "Flow
Blue" or Canton, which had been brought back to
Massachusetts years before by the clipper ships
and whalers on their return from two- and three-
year voyages to the Orient.

The menu was presented on a huge blackboard
propped up on an easel, and the array of dishes offered was so tempting that Diana had a hard time
making a decision.

Jaime tried to make conversation, but it wasn't
easy, and although she attempted to help him,
Diana found it difficult to come up with any subjects that might be of mutual interest. Constance
was not unfriendly, but she was shy and much too
remote for an attractive young woman of twenty.

Finally Jaime said, "Manny nearly scared
Diana to death the other night, Connie."

Connie snapped quickly to attention, her gaze
swiveling between Diana and her uncle. "Manny?" she echoed.

"He burst into the DuBois house, where
Diana's living, and she thought he was a burglar,"
Jaime enlightened her.

"Why was Manny in the DuBois house?" Connie asked, focusing on the subject obviously
closest to her heart.

"He made a mistake." Jaime laughed. "He thought it was my house. I think he'd only been to my house once before, quite some time ago, so it was an easy enough mistake to make in the dark."

"He just... burst in?" Connie was incredulous.

"Well, he came walking in," Diana said. "He was as startled to see me as I was to see him. He was terribly apologetic, once he'd realized his error. I... well, I definitely overreacted. I'll say one thing, though—" she smiled at Connie "—if a woman was going to have a real intruder, it would be nice to have one as good-looking as Manny is!"

Connie returned the smile. Then she said softly, "Manny is more than just outwardly handsome, Ms Ashley. He's as good inside as he's good-looking outside. The only other person in my life I've ever known who is at all like him is...."

She paused, and Jaime prompted, "Is who, Connie?"

"Well," his niece said, fingering the blue napkin she was holding, "you, if you must know, Jaime."

Jaime was so disconcerted by her reply that Diana had to laugh aloud. "You see," she told him. "If you ask leading questions...."

He managed a grin. "I didn't expect that particular answer," he confessed. "Connie, love, there's something you shouldn't forget. All idols have clay feet. If you don't remind yourself of that once in a while you're apt to be hurt pretty badly one of these days."

"Neither you nor Manny have clay feet," Connie said, with a firmness that led Diana to believe she was a stronger young woman than she'd seemed at first. "I have absolute faith in both of you, and no fear at all that my faith is going to be undermined!"

"So there, eh?" Jaime teased.

"Yes... so there!"

"Rebellious youth!" Jaime said laughingly, but then he sobered. "Look, I might as well get to it. I had a purpose in bringing the two of you together tonight."

"Oh?" the two women said simultaneously.

"I should have discussed this with you first, Diana," Jaime began. "I fully intended to. So I hope you'll both forgive me for... well, for springing it on you like this. You see, Connie wants to give up her job in the real-estate office, Diana. It's a good enough job, but she's gotten all she can out of it. She wants to branch out into something entirely new, and what I'd like... no, don't interrupt me, Connie, I'm going to have my say, and there's no need for you to be embarrassed about it. What I'd like is for Connie to go to work for you."

Diana could not have been more surprised. "Me?"

"Ms Ashley, don't even listen to him," Connie said quickly, and turned to her uncle, anger flashing in her dark eyes. "I hope you know you're absolutely mortifying me, Jaime."

"No," Diana responded immediately. "Please, Connie, don't feel that way. I'm sure Jaime has a reason for thinking you and I should be working together."

"Thanks, Diana." Jaime's relief at her reaction to what he'd been saying was so obvious it was almost amusing. Almost, but not quite. He should have discussed the matter with her before so she could have given it some thought.

"Diana," Jaime said, "the fact is that you need someone to help you get your history thesis off the ground. Connie has a Portuguese-American background. I think she'd have a feeling for the research you're doing, I think she could be a definite help to you there. She could also open up some contacts in the area, put you in touch with people in organizations like the Portuguese-American Civic League, whose membership is composed of people from all the New England communities with sizable Portuguese populations. One of their reasons for being is to try to perpetuate Portuguese history, customs and traditions.

"Also," Jaime continued, "Connie is a very good secretary. She's an excellent typist, she could transcribe your notes for you. You know," he concluded, with a mischievous grin, "she could get you organized."

"Jaime. . ." his niece protested.

"Diana knows very well that she has to get organized at some point along the line," Jaime replied affably. "Don't you, Diana?"

"*Really* . . ." she began, nettled, but he cut her off.

"There'd be another good thing about having

Connie go to work for you. She's willing to work for nothing."

Diana bristled. "That would be completely out of the question."

Connie reached out a hand and placed it lightly on her uncle's sleeve. "Jaime," she said, "I know you mean well...but you're really putting your foot in things!"

"I am?" he asked, surveying her with exaggerated amazement.

"Yes. Ms Ashley...."

"Call me Diana, won't you please, Connie?"

"All right. Diana, what he's really trying to say is that he's hoping to find something I can do that I'll be interested in. Something that will take my mind off myself and my...my problems. Right now I don't need to make money."

"She's right, Diana," said Jaime. "Connie needs to be around someone who is...well, someone who can relate to her."

"Thanks for the implied compliment," Diana replied tartly. "But I can't help but feel you're putting Connie in an awkward position."

Connie smiled. "I think he's putting *you* in an awkward position, Diana."

"I think the two of you are being stubborn," Jaime remarked, scowling at both of them. "Look, Christmas is right around the corner. There will be a lot of holiday things going on over the next few days, which, when you hear what I have in mind, won't prevent you from getting started in a sense. But as far as the routine is concerned, I suggest we get things lined up so you can both go to work the Monday after Christmas. I'll provide a typewriter and a desk for Connie. You're not really using the dining room in the house anyway, Diana. It could easily be converted into an office.''

"You're coming on like an efficiency expert, Jaime,'' Diana warned.

"You need an efficiency expert in your life, *menina*. You also need to have someone around you. You're alone in that house too much. All that solitude isn't good for you.''

And you're not about to fill those lonely hours of mine yourself, is that it? The question was a silent one. Diana only hoped that he couldn't read its message in her eyes because he was looking directly at her.

"In the meantime,'' Jaime went on, "I think we could give Diana a good insight into the old Portuguese Christmas customs via Aunt Profetina, don't you, Connie?''

Connie laughed. "Definitely.''

"And who is Aunt Profetina?'' Diana asked.

"My great-aunt, Connie's great-great aunt,'' Jaime told her. "She's ninety-eight years old. She was my grandmother's older sister, and she's quite a character. I was visiting her at the hospital that night. . . .''

He hesitated a moment before going on, and Diana prompted, "Yes?''

"She'd had a mild coronary, but she's been fine ever since,'' Jaime continued. "I keep an eye on her, but Profetina is a hard woman to keep down! She lives in an old house over in New Bedford's South End. There's such a large Portuguese population there you sometimes can't believe you're in the United States. You hear Portuguese spoken all around you. And Profetina is a zealot when it comes to trying to keep up the old traditions. The Portuguese are great for celebrating Saints Days with festivals, and there's no end to the number of Saints Days that can be put on the calendar. There are twenty-seven Saint Johns alone. Sometimes I think Profetina honors all of them.

"She gets into her real stride at Christmas, though," Jaime went on. "She deplores the fact that the younger generations have given up the old customs, to a large extent. There was a time when the men used to gather together on Christmas Eve and go from house to house, strumming their seven-stringed *guitarres* as they sang carols in Portuguese. Back before the days of strict immigration and customs law, there'd often be Portuguese ships in the harbor here, and in Provincetown, and other places along the coast, and the crews would come ashore and stroll through the streets, serenading the townspeople.

"That was Profetina's era, and she recalls it with a great deal of nostalgia and considerably more annoyance for the succeeding generations. When she was a young woman, every Portuguese household had its *Menino Jesus*, no matter how small. As Christmas approached, the front windows of the house would be filled with lighted candles, unless the *Menino Jesus* itself was placed in the window. In either case, this was considered an invitation to friends and strangers to drop in and share in the spirit of the season. There was a continual open house from Christmas Eve right to New Year's Day. When guests came they'd be served either homemade beach-plum or elderberry wine, or maybe Portuguese port or madeira. Then there would be trays of special holiday sweets, like *trutas* and *suspiros*. Profetina says that in those old days anyone at all was welcome. In fact, she says that strangers were considered the most welcome and honored guests of all.''

Jaime's lips twisted in a wry smile. ''It's another age we're living in,'' he said quietly. ''But Profetina doesn't like to admit it. Anyway, she does her best to keep the past alive, and so every Christmas she clears out the front parlor in her house and sets up her *Menino*, and she holds her own open house.''

''What is a *Menino Jesus*?'' Diana asked curiously.

''I think we'll let Diana find that out for herself. All right, Connie?'' Jaime asked his niece. ''Profetina can certainly give her a more authentic introduction than anyone else I can think of. Do you have anything planned for Christmas Eve, Diana?''

She shook her head. ''No.''

''Okay, then you and I and Connie. . . and Manny Ribeiro,'' Jaime added significantly, ''will visit Profetina.''

CHAPTER ELEVEN

DIANA HAD PROMISED HERSELF she would get a Christmas tree, some ornaments, and instill some holiday spirit into the old DuBois house, but she hadn't done anything about it.

Tuesday morning she drove up Route 6 until she came to a place where Christmas trees were being sold, and after long and careful scrutiny she bought an eight-foot-tall balsam. The man who sold her the tree bound it up for her and loaded it into the trunk of her car, carefully tying the trunk lid open just enough so she could still see out of her rear-vision mirror.

Diana stopped at her house just long enough to lean the tree against the back steps. Then she set out for New Bedford. She'd made up her mind she was going to give Jaime a Christmas present, no matter what he might think of such a gesture.... She wanted him to have a tangible reminder of her for the time when she'd leave this area and would be gone out of his life.

She shopped carefully, scanning the contents of a number of stores before she finally settled upon a scrimshaw tie tack that she discovered in a small antique shop. It had been carved onto a segment of a whale's tooth, and the carving was exquisite, depicting a tall-masted sailing ship. The price was considerably more than Diana had expected it to be, but after only a moment's hesitation she decided it was worth it. The workmanship was far superior to that of the modern scrimshaw items she'd been looking at.

Her purchase snugly tucked into her purse, Diana turned her attention to shopping for Christmas ornaments. She went to three different stores before she found everything she wanted, then wound up in a variety store, where she bought tinsel icicles and candy canes. By the time she went back to her car, which she'd parked on a public lot, she was feeling well satisfied with her purchases. She secured them in the trunk, then set forth on her final errand, to take out a card at the New Bedford Public Library.

The library was an impressive building in the Greek Revival style, and after an exploratory tour Diana felt certain she'd be able to get a lot of the information she needed right there. She acquired the card and was on her way out when she almost collided with Jaime.

Their surprise was mutual. Instinctively Jaime reached out a hand, as if to restrain her, and Diana knew she was staring at him. He was wearing a heavy, black wool jacket over a thick, creamy-white turtleneck, and the combination made a perfect foil for his dramatic coloring. He was bareheaded, and his ebony satin hair glinted with blue lights in the pale winter sun, which had momentarily poked out from behind the clouds.

"Now I really begin to believe in *sorte*," he said.

"What's *sorte*?" Diana asked him.

"Luck." He smiled. "*Sorte bom*, I should say, and I don't need to translate that, do I?"

"No, I don't think so."

He took her arm, obviously prepared to start walking along the sidewalk with her, but Diana drew back. "Weren't you going into the library?"

"It's an errand that can wait," he assured her. He raised his eyebrows in a mock frown. "You don't really think I'm going to let you go now that I've found you, do you? Have you had lunch?"

"No."

"Neither have I. Come on, I'll take you to a seafood place down on the waterfront where they have the most fantastic fish and chips you've ever tasted."

She shook her head. "Jaime, is food all you ever think of? I mean...it seems to me that when we're together all we do is eat."

She wished she could have bitten off the words as soon as she'd spoken them, and she could feel the rush of color flooding her cheeks.

Jaime made no attempt to hide his amusement at her discomfiture. "I wouldn't say it's the *only* thing we've done, would you, Diana?" he remarked. But then an odd expression flitted across his handsome face as if he, too, wished he hadn't said what he had.

"Come on," he urged. "My car's parked down on the next block."

"My car's parked on the lot in the block beyond that," she said.

"Okay. Leave it there, why don't you? You can pick it up later."

"Well. . .I suppose so."

They had begun to walk along, but now it was Jaime who stopped, and he stood looking down at her, his expression unexpectedly serious.

"Menina," he said gently, "stop worrying."

"I. . .I'm not worrying, Jaime."

"Ah, but I think you are," he corrected. "I can't say I blame you. There is so much. . .unfinished business between us. That's something I want to talk to you about, but not now. Now, let's simply enjoy the day, as we did the other day at Dighton Rock. Okay?"

Jaime could be the most charming man Diana had ever met, and when he looked at her as he was looking at her now, it was very hard to refuse to do what he wanted.

"All right," she said, hoping that her voice didn't sound as weak as she felt. She'd never liked weak-willed women. But then she'd never believed a man could be so irresistible.

The seafood restaurant to which Jaime took her was on a point of land overlooking the Acushnet River, and every window in it commanded a water view. The harbor was a busy one, and it was fascinating to watch as boats of every size and shape went about their nautical business, from a sleek

Coast Guard cutter putting out on patrol to trawlers and draggers coming back from trips to Georges Bank. The restaurant was a popular place, so crowded they had to wait awhile for a table. But once they'd been seated and their plates of fish and chips placed before them, Diana agreed that the wait had been worthwhile.

"It's the best fish I've ever tasted," she said between bites.

"That's because it's really fresh," Jaime told her. "This place buys most of its finfish from Bill's trawlers, right at the dock."

"Finfish?"

"As opposed to shellfish, like scallops," he said. "The New Bedford and Fairhaven ports bring in the largest supply of scallops, commercially, on the entire coast. Bill's never gotten into scalloping, although he's entertained the thought. I've tried to dissuade him and I've been successful so far. He has his hands full enough with his interests in the trawlers and the packing plant. By the way. . . ."

"Yes?"

"Bill and Flor would like it very much if you'd share Christmas dinner with them."

"*Me?*"

"You, *menina*. Flor called me this morning. Connie'd told her about our dinner yesterday and said she was going to go to work for you right after Christmas. Flor seemed pleased about it, which surprised me. She hasn't always been known to go along with other people's ideas. Naturally she's very anxious to meet you."

"But Christmas is such a...private time," Diana protested.

"I know. But it's not a time to be alone, either. You weren't planning to go back to New York for it, were you? Or to your friends in Hyannis?"

"I wasn't planning to go to New York, no," Diana said slowly. "Gail and Howard did ask me to come to them for Christmas, but they said I could wait till the last minute to give them an answer. But about going to your brother's house.... Well, I don't know."

"I think you'll like Bill, Diana."

"I don't doubt it. But...."

"I think you'll like Flor, too," Jaime persisted, "once you get past the phony front she tends to put up when she meets people. Flor's all right underneath it all. Like a lot of us, life hasn't entirely gone the way she wanted it to go. Flor's never going to be the social butterfly she wants to be, and I think she's beginning to realize that Connie is not going to become the world's greatest female lawyer one day, either. But in the long run, Flor will handle all that. She coped very well when Bill lost his leg. She stayed by him, she was intensely loyal to him through some very bad times. There are moments," Jaime confessed, "when I have to remind myself of that, because Flor can, on occasion, be hard to take. I've never been much for pretense, and at times she irritates me." He smiled apologetically. "Probably I shouldn't be telling you this. I should let you judge Flor for yourself. You might relate to her quite differently from the way I often do."

Diana hesitated. It was very important that she use the right choice of words in what she was about to say. Above all, she didn't want to offend Jaime by making him think she didn't *want* to have dinner with his family.

"Jaime," she said carefully, "I really am going to have to decline the invitation, much as I appreciate it. And it isn't anything you've said about your sister-in-law or your brother that makes me hesitate at the idea of going to your family's for Christmas dinner. It's just that I feel, well, I feel I wouldn't belong."

"On the contrary," Jaime told her, "you'd be very welcome." He flashed a smile at her. "If I make a personal appeal to you, will you consider sharing Christmas with me?"

Put that way, the offer was extremely difficult to refuse. Still, Diana hesitated. "I don't know," she said doubtfully. "Christmas is a very special, private time. I can't help but think I'd be an intruder, though I think it's very kind of them to ask me."

Jaime grinned. "Maybe Flor feels that if you agree to come, there'll be no danger of me backing out at the last minute, as I've been known to do."

Diana scowled at him. "Thanks a lot!" she retorted.

"Do you know, your eyes actually flash when you get angry?" he told her. "Like streaks of silver lightning against a cloudy sky. *Menina*, I was only teasing you...."

"I'll go," Diana said suddenly.

"What?"

"Tell your brother and his wife that I accept their invitation with pleasure."

He stared at her. "Just what caused that turn-about?"

"I think I have a few things to prove to you, Jaime Medeiros," she told him. "And I agree with you. We do have a lot of...issues between us that we're going to have to talk about one of these days. But right now," she added, glancing at her watch, "I have to get home. I have a Christmas tree to put up."

"I know. I saw it. Did you get the tallest tree on the lot?"

"No. The ceilings in the house are high, you know that. I didn't want something that would be dwarfed before I even began to decorate it."

"Speaking of decorations—do you have some stuff to trim the tree with?"

"My trunk's full of ornaments," Diana told him happily. "I bought all sorts of different decorations, some of them the imported ones from Germany that look so delightfully old-fashioned." She laughed. "I was ridiculously extravagant. But it was fun."

"What about lights?" Jaime asked her.

"Lights?"

"Lights for the tree," he said patiently.

Dismayed, she moaned, "Oh good heavens! I forgot all about lights, and I don't think I have enough money with me...." She pressed her lips together and shook her head. "I'll have to go home and get my checkbook and go to the bank."

"Not at all," Jaime told her firmly. "I'll buy the lights on my way back. I might as well get the kind I like since I'm going to have to string them on anyway."

"You?"

"Yes, me. In my wildest imagination I can't imagine you getting the lights strung up on a Christmas tree without all sorts of dreadful things happening," he teased. "You'd probably fall off the ladder. And for an eight-foot tree you'd definitely need to do some ladder climbing, to say nothing of doing something with the basic electrical system so you'd blow out all the fuses. Then—"

"I think that's quite enough," Diana told him primly.

"Lightning's threatening again," Jaime said, smiling into her eyes. "You're beautiful when you're angry, *menina*. But then you're also beautiful when you're not angry. Come on, let me pay the bill and we'll get out of here. We have our work cut out for us."

IT WAS JAIME who carried the Christmas tree into the house, and he was the one who decided that it should be placed in the corner by the front window so its lights would be visible to passersby.

It was also Jaime who went across to borrow a ladder from Amy Howland, since there wasn't one to be found in either his place or on the DuBois property. He came back to cheerfully inform her that Amy had asked them to stop by for a drink later in the afternoon.

"I told her we couldn't make it this afternoon but we'd be glad to take a rain check," he said, to Diana's astonishment. "She asked if tomorrow would be okay, and I told her we'd see her around five, unless you had some plans I didn't know about. Do you have any plans for tomorrow, Diana?"

"No," she replied, amazed that Jaime, who'd been reputed to be such a recluse, was willing to go to the Howlands' with her.

"Then it's a date," he said cheerfully.

Jaime had bought several strings of multi-colored lights for the tree, and he positioned them with the care of an artist creating a mural for posterity, stepping back to survey his spacing and making small changes until, finally, he was satisfied.

He had even thought to buy a shimmering silver star for the top of the tree, and he was the one to hang all the ornaments on the highest branches, telling Diana that she could get into the act when they got down to a level she could reach without too much peril.

As she watched him, Diana marveled that he could enter so wholeheartedly into something like trimming a Christmas tree. But there was no doubt he was enjoying himself immensely. Jaime was not at all a simple person, yet there was a simplicity to his nature. He was so genuine. Not for the first time Diana told herself that she'd never met anyone like him.

He turned to her and held out a shimmering

green bauble. "Okay," he said. "Your turn. You can start decorating some of the lower branches."

"Thanks a lot, master," she said, feigning subservience. That was another thing about Jaime, she thought, as she hung the ornament near the end of a branch. He was accustomed to giving orders, although there was nothing at all autocratic about the way he did so. It was simply that he was used to being in command. She could imagine him standing at an operating-room table, dressed in surgical greens. She could imagine him in complete charge of the operation, everyone around him doing exactly what he told them to do....

"Move it back."

"What?" asked Diana, startled.

"That green ball. You have it too close to the end, Diana. It weights the branch down when you do that, and the tree droops prematurely."

She was amused by his seriousness. "Well," she said, picking up another green glass sphere, "it wouldn't do to have the tree droop prematurely."

She was placing the ornament as she spoke, and he protested, "Hey, wait! Don't put one green ball so close to another. You want to vary the colors, just as I did with the lights."

"What a perfectionist!" she complained.

"Yes, I've been accused of that," he admitted wryly. "I'm also of the school where instead of throwing a whole heap of tinsel toward the tree and letting it land anywhere, I believe in making it really look like icicles, hanging a strand at a time."

"Ouch!" Diana said, backing off. "At this rate we're going to be here until midnight."

He was standing behind her, and she caught the spicy scent of his after-shave. He said, almost under his breath, "I wouldn't mind being here until long after midnight, *menina*."

Diana felt her treacherous pulse race again, and she was afraid to turn around to face him. She'd had such a distinct impression that Jaime, for reasons she couldn't hope to understand at this point in their relationship, had decided against any further lovemaking. But now....

She felt his hands on her shoulders, and he slowly turned her around toward him. To her surprise, he looked bitterly unhappy, his eyes, darker than ever, were tormented. "I'm breaking all my own promises," he said huskily. "I swore I wouldn't make love to you again until we'd cleared the obstacles in our path, and we're still a long way from doing that. But I can't be so near to you without my need for you...overflowing. I want you so damned much." He swallowed hard. "I used to think I was a pretty strong character," he muttered, "but where you're concerned...."

He held out his arms, and Diana needed no second invitation. She went into them, tilting her head, her mouth ready to receive his kiss. She touched her tongue to his lips, urging him to let her know this small but intimate part of him. He matched her action with his own, his tongue probing, teasing, setting off the spark of desire deep inside her that was only too ready to be ignited whenever he was near.

A moment later he was nibbling at her chin, and then his kisses trailed up her cheek, his tongue lingering to trace small, fiery patterns along the rim of her ear. "Shall we settle for your sofa, *menina*?" he whispered huskily. Without waiting for her answer his encircling arm guided her across the room. He laughed. "Remind me to buy a comfortable couch for your living room one day, will you?"

Spellbound, Diana was not up to a reply. Nor was she even conscious that the sofa was narrow and uncomfortable. She was immersed only in Jaime, and this time there was a wonderful familiarity to their lovemaking. They'd already known each other in the total sense of the word, but that only enhanced the pleasure they found in each other now. Diana felt freer with Jaime than she ever had before with a man. With him, she tossed off inhibitions that had always plagued her, setting them aside as lightly as if they were wisps of clothing.

She loved the touch of Jaime's body beneath her fingers. She loved to feel the swell of his muscles, the smoothness of his skin, the softness of the hair that made a curly vee down the front of his chest. She loved the tautness of his thighs, and when she touched the masculine core of him and felt his response, an unexpected thrill coursed through her, her own needs mounting to match his.

He groaned as she touched him, and, his hands clasping her head, he pulled her toward him.

"Oh my God, *menina*," he said. "What you do to me!"

Diana couldn't answer. She felt the breath being drawn out of her and she arched toward him, every atom in her body vibrant with her desire for him.

Jaime was a master musician playing upon an exquisite instrument as he made love to her, his hands roving over her body, followed by his lips. First he touched her breasts, encircling her tautened nipples with those magic fingers of his, and then his mouth followed to claim each nipple in its turn, rocking her with darts of ecstatic pleasure. He came finally to the most intimate part of her, and Diana cried out in sharp delight as he sent her off on a voyage entirely her own. But when this first ecstasy had passed she wanted him with her even more than she had before. She was ready for him when he entered her, ready to travel with him all the way to their own shared paradise.

IT WAS WELL AFTER MIDNIGHT when they finished trimming the Christmas tree. They had stopped for a supper of soup and hot rolls and a chocolate cake Diana had bought in a neighborhood bakery, then they'd made love again. Afterward, they'd put on the radio, tuning to a program of Christmas carols, which set a background mood while they continued trimming the tree. The project was abandoned once again when Diana inadvertently stepped backward right into Jaime's arms, and his initial caresses soon led to a trip to the upstairs bedroom. There, in the darkness, they found a way entirely their own to light their lives.

Diana had bought a quart of eggnog in the supermarket, and once they'd hung the last of the ornaments she mixed it with some bourbon and rum and took it into the living room to him.

The tree was beautiful. The lights were like twinkling stars, and the ornaments glowed in soft, shimmering colors. Jaime had opened the box of icicles and he was meticulously hanging a strand at a time over the branches.

He paused to accept the eggnog and clicked his mug to Diana's in an unspoken toast. Later, looking back, Diana decided it was exactly at this moment that she'd first realized she was falling in love with Jaime Medeiros. A wave of feeling swept over her that was a thing apart from passion. She felt a tenderness toward this man such as she'd never felt toward anyone before, and with it came the sweet-sad, plainly hopeless wish that she could prolong this moment with him forever.

CHRISTMAS, which had promised to be a bleak and lonely affair for Diana, suddenly began to take on new overtones. When Gail Landers called to repeat her invitation to come to Hyannis, Diana had to report that she was going to have dinner with Jaime Medeiros and his family. Gail laughed delightedly.

"Wait till I tell Aunt Agatha that!" she crowed.

"Do you suppose you and Howard really could come for eggnog the afternoon after Christmas?"

Diana asked quickly, not wanting to get any further into the subject of Jaime.

"Unless we have a blizzard, we'd love to," Gail assured her.

After that, Diana called the Burroughses and extended the same invitation to them, and it was quickly accepted. In return, Emily Burroughs asked her to come for Christmas dinner at her house.

Three Christmas dinner invitations when she'd expected to eat a TV dinner all by herself, Diana thought whimsically. She knew that Jaime was somehow responsible for all of this. He was responsible for a change in her that she, herself, still couldn't analyze.

Eventually, on what Diana now considered a miracle night, they had gone back to putting last touches on the tree. Finally, when the icicles had all been hung and the candy canes put into proper place, they had trailed upstairs together in a wordless accord. Their lovemaking this time had begun on a languorous note, the tempo increasing with a certain laziness until once again they became caught up in passion's whirl. Afterward Diana had fallen asleep in the circle of his arms, knowing that she had never felt so thoroughly content, so secure.

She'd awakened in the early hours of the morning to find Jaime slipping out of bed, and she'd muttered an instinctive protest, which came out so sleepily it was virtually unintelligible. He'd laughed and said, "Shh, go back to sleep! I want to get next door before the neighborhood starts stirring for the day. Can't ruin your reputation, *menina*," he teased.

He bent down to kiss her, and automatically her arms reached out to entwine his neck. He gently removed them, kissing her once more as he said, "I'm meeting with Bill early this morning for a coffee and a much-needed discussion. Later, my love." And she had to be content with that.

Diana drifted back to sleep, but it was not a deep sleep, and when she awakened she felt an acute sense of desolation on seeing the empty space beside her. As she worked around the house during the day, doing some cleaning and polishing silver in preparation for her party, she found herself wandering over at almost regular intervals to the wide windows that faced Jaime's house. But the house presented a blank facade; there was no sign of life about at all.

After lunch she made a stab at working on an outline for her thesis. She wanted to be ready for Connie before they started working together. But her heart wasn't in history today, and she wondered if it ever would be at the rate she was going. At the moment her heart was fully occupied by her handsome next-door neighbor—and where was he?

By midafternoon she was beginning to wonder if Jaime had forgotten about their engagement for drinks at the Howlands. There was still no sign of life next door. After a time she stacked up her books and papers and went upstairs to dress. She selected a deep-green wool dress that had a becoming blouson top and flared skirt, and with it she decided to wear her grandmother's pearls. As she slipped on her high-heeled, black-patent shoes, she thought of Jaime. But this time she wouldn't have far to go, she told herself with a smile, and she'd have his arm to lean on...unless he forgot all about his promise to Amy Howland.

He hadn't forgotten. He knocked at the kitchen door at exactly five minutes to five, and Diana was so staggered when she opened the door and saw him that she actually gaped.

She'd never seen him in anything but casual clothes. Now he was wearing a three-piece gray suit. His shirt was a pale gold, and his figured tie picked up the gold and the gray and was accented with black. She'd thought he was handsome before, but he was devastating dressed like this. She felt an urge to pinch him, to prove that he was real.

There was nothing ephemeral about his grin, however. "From the look on your face," he observed, "I don't know whether to be flattered or horrified."

"Be flattered," she said rather shortly, fighting to keep her composure in check. She felt an overpowering urge to throw herself into his arms. "Shall we go out the front door or the back?"

"Why don't we try the front, this time?" he suggested amiably. "I think the only other time I've explored the front entrance with you was the night you lost your key."

"Let's not even go into that," Diana said, slipping on her coat. "I don't think you'll ever let me live it down."

"No," he agreed, "I don't think I ever will. It was a high point of my life. I don't know when I've ever enjoyed myself so much."

"You didn't look as if you were enjoying yourself," she pointed out. "Unless you scowl when you're happy."

"Not necessarily. But appearances can be deceiving," he warned her, opening the front door for her. Then, straight-faced, he asked, "Have you got your key?"

"I have my key and I also have another one hidden behind the fifth shingle up from the ground three shingles in to the right of the steps," she informed him. "And...."

"Yes?"

"Well, I have another spare key that I meant to give to you."

"A key to your house?" he asked, eyebrows upraised.

"Just as a safeguard," she said quickly.

He laughed. "I'm not sure I'd consider it a safeguard. But anyhow...."

"Anyhow," Diana said firmly, clamping a lid on the subject.

She was looking straight ahead of her as she spoke and she had completely forgotten there was snow on the steps. Her foot slipped out from under her, and she would have fallen if Jaime hadn't reached out and gripped her arm so firmly that she was able to right herself.

"Damn!" Diana exploded. "I should have shoveled off the steps!"

"I should have thought to do it for you," he told her. "Come on, *menina*, don't look so stricken. Nothing happened, and if you'll just be a little careful about where you put your feet you'll be fine. Matter of fact, you can hold on to my arm. I'll take care of you."

He was smiling as he looked down at her, but it was a smile that didn't reach all the way to his eyes.

"If it were possible, *menina*," he said softly, "I would like to take care of you forever!"

CHAPTER TWELVE

IT BEGAN TO SNOW late in the afternoon on Christmas Eve, and as she glanced out the window toward the drifting white flakes, Diana wondered what to wear for her meeting with Jaime's great-aunt.

She settled for a simple, winter-white wool dress, and she wore her Victorian crystal jewelry with it. The effect was dressy enough, but not overly so.

She'd seen very little of Jaime since they'd gone to the Howlands' for cocktails together, an afternoon that had proved to be very pleasant. Diana was aware that Jaime valued his privacy and had wanted to keep a very low profile on his return to Fairhaven, and she had wondered if he'd be hopelessly stiff and formal with the Howlands. But he couldn't have been more at ease. He and Phil picked up their friendship as easily as if it had never been interrupted, and there was no doubt at all that Amy was thoroughly mesmerized by his charm.

Amy had proved to be an adept and very enthusiastic hostess, proffering tray after tray of succulent hot hors d'oeuvres until Diana had protested that she'd never be able to eat again if she didn't start refusing them. The conversation had been kept on a light note, and there had been soft Christmas music playing in the background all the while.

At the door when they were leaving, Diana had said, "Amy, this has really put me in the holiday spirit." And she meant it.

Amy, looking like one of Santa's elves herself in a vivid green dress, had beamed with pleasure. She and her husband had stood in their bewreathed doorway, waving after Jaime and Diana as they made their way back over to the DuBois house, and there'd been a lovely warm feeling to the day.

Back at the house, though, Jaime's mood had seemed to change. He'd become preoccupied, and he hadn't lingered. He'd paused to admire the Christmas tree he had had such a hand in decorating, and then had said that he'd promised his brother he'd stop by to go over some things with him. He didn't enlighten her about whether the "things" in question involved Connie or not.

He'd phoned the following morning, though, to tell her that he'd pick her up at a quarter to eight. "I'll stop by for Connie first," he'd said, and Diana felt a throb of disappointment. She'd wanted to be alone with him for just a little while, especially before this meeting with his great-aunt. For one thing, she'd wanted to get a few cues from him on how she should behave. She was curious now as to whether or not they'd also be picking up Manuel Ribeiro on their way to Profetina's house.

And she wondered at Jaime having said in the first place that Manny would be going with him. It seemed to Diana that this was directly going against his brother and sister-in-law's wishes, and she wondered how he could handle such a situation with them.

Secrecy? No, she doubted very much that Jaime would hide the fact he was taking both Connie and Manuel to his Aunt Profetina's. Dissembling wasn't his style.

She was ready when he pulled the car up in front of the house. To her surprise, when she opened the front door she discovered that the steps had been shoveled off to the bare concrete. Jaime must have done it at some point when she was out.

She saw at once that Connie was sitting in the front seat beside her uncle. Diana wished the arrangement had been otherwise, but she swiftly made her way down the steps and across the sidewalk, opening the rear door of the car herself before Jaime had time to get out and do it for her.

She slipped in with a bright greeting for both of them. Then, as they started up, she said, "I hate going to your aunt's empty-handed, Jaime, but I didn't know what I should get her. Do you think we could stop for a bottle of rosé, or something like that?"

"Profetina will have her own homemade wine," Jaime assured her. "And there's no need for you to take anything. I bought her a box of chocolates because I know her favorite kind, and Connie has a loaf of sweet bread Flor made. But you're the guest tonight, Diana. The most honored one of all," he added, under his breath.

It was less than a ten-minute drive to Profetina's house, one of a number of nondescript, two-story frame houses that lined the street. As they approached it, Jaime said ruefully, "I can see that I'm going to have to hunt for a parking space. Profetina's evidently gathered her full coterie in honor of the *Menino*."

"Don't you think that at this point you should tell me what the *Menino Jesus* is?" Diana asked, faintly irritated. Whatever the occasion in Profetina Rodrigues's house, she didn't welcome walking in on it without being forewarned.

It was Connie who answered her. "Translated, *Menino Jesus* means 'the little boy Jesus,'" Connie said. "The Portuguese often use the figure of the standing Christ Child, rather than that of the Holy Infant. When we speak of the *Menino Jesus*, though, we really mean the whole display people used to put out at Christmas. In the old days, every home had its own *Menino Jesus*—"

"I've already mentioned that, Connie," Jaime interrupted.

"Well, traditionally the effect of the entire scene is supposed to be triangular. Usually a series of shelves are set up, covered with a white cloth, and arranged so the center top is the focal point of the display. Jaime, you really should be telling Diana all this. You know more about it than I do."

"Each generation knows less about it. Is that

what you're saying? Well, I suppose you're right," Jaime conceded, "and certainly Profetina would be the first to agree with you. But right now I'm concentrating on finding a place to park. I'll take one more swing around the block, and if nothing turns up I'll let you two girls out."

Going into the Rodrigues house without Jaime beside her was the last thing in the world Diana wanted to do. She stared at the back of his head in dismay, then found herself concentrating on the way his hair contoured to his perfectly shaped head.

She found herself clutching her hands tightly together. She longed to reach out and touch his hair, to finger its smoothness, and the impulse was so strong it shocked her.

Control yourself, menina, she warned herself, the silent words tinged with irony.

She sought emotional refuge in asking questions. "So, most people don't have this display any longer at Christmas, is that it?" she asked. "But your Aunt Profetina still keeps the custom going?"

Jaime was heading around a corner back toward the street Profetina's house was on, and he flung a reply over his shoulder. "Profetina has an especially elaborate display, because she makes it a kind of neighborhood enterprise," he told her. "Ah, we're in luck. There's a car pulling out just a couple of doors down from Profetina's. If you ladies don't mind a short walk, I'll park there."

He brought the car to a standstill at the curb.

"As I was saying, what makes Profetina's *Menino* different is that she makes something of a community event out of it. She clears all the furniture out of her front parlor, then she rents a bunch of straight-backed chairs from a local funeral parlor. She sets them up in rows, so that her guests will have time to sit and meditate for a while if they want to...and most of them do. She invites anyone who's interested to bring some of their own favorite figures and objects to help her decorate the display. If you have time to really look at the different things, I think you'll be impressed by them. But I'm afraid Profetina may not leave you alone long enough for you to be able to do that!"

He laughed as he unlatched the front door of the car. "I should tell you about the shoes in the display," he said. "There are a number of shoes placed at its base, filled with coal, oranges and nuts. Traditionally the oranges represent happiness, the coal humility, and the nuts fertility. Portuguese children put out their shoes on Christmas Eve instead of stockings. If they're bad during the year they'll find their shoes filled with coals. If they've been good, they'll get oranges and other goodies."

"Did you ever put out your shoes, Jaime?" Connie asked him.

"Once," he said. "One year Profetina persuaded my mother to adhere to the old customs. And before you ask, no, I didn't find my shoes filled with coals. The next year we went back to good old American stockings, though, which my brothers and sister and I preferred. They held a lot more," he said, laughing.

Diana smiled softly when she heard this. She was picturing Jaime as a little boy, and it was a very endearing vision. She could imagine him at Christmas with his two brothers and his sister Rose. Had his been a happy family? She hoped so.

He was getting out of the car, and this time he held her door open for her and, as she alighted, grasped her elbow. He led her across the sidewalk and said in a voice so low only she could hear him, "You look especially lovely tonight, Diana. Stop worrying. Profetina is going to be crazy about you!"

PROFETINA RODRIGUES was small and wiry. Though her face was crisscrossed heavily with wrinkles, her deep-set dark eyes were bright and plainly inquisitive as they rested on Diana, and she was so lively it was impossible to believe that she was ninety-eight years old.

"So, Jaime," she teased her nephew, "you have brought your *noiva* to meet me!"

Jaime said something to his great-aunt in Portuguese, and Diana was surprised that he spoke the language so swiftly and fluently. Jaime was so thoroughly American in most ways that she hadn't expected him to be so fluent in another tongue.

Profetina laughed when he'd finished speaking and answered him with a brief Portuguese comment of her own. Then she took Diana by the arm and said, "Come! You must have a glass of elder-berry wine, and then Jaime tells me you want to see the *Menino*."

Before Diana could answer, Profetina was propelling her into a small dining room. The center table had been covered with a lace cloth. On it were two large crystal decanters filled with a deep-red wine, and platters laden with assorted small cakes and cookies.

Profetina poured a glass of wine for Diana, her hand as steady as if she were years younger. Handing it to her guest, she said, "Here. This is elder-berry wine. Homemade. There is also Madeira, which may be more Portuguese, but this is more traditional here."

Diana took a tentative sip of the wine and found it delicious. She turned, expecting to see Jaime right behind her, but to her consternation he wasn't in sight. Had he deliberately done this disappearing act in order to leave her alone with his aunt?

"Jaime tells me that you are his neighbor," Profetina said, fixing her lively, dark eyes directly on Diana's face. "I tell him he is lucky to have such a lovely *vizinha*."

Profetina's English was fluent, but more than a hint of an accent still lingered, and Diana realized that she must have come to New Bedford directly from Portugal, or more probably the Azores. Perhaps as a bride? Her curiosity was heightened.

"You know," Profetina confided, with a wink that was so conspiratorial it was all Diana could do not to laugh out loud, "I think you are good for Jaime. And I am glad of that. I will tell you something, Diana. You do not mind that I call you Diana?"

"Of course not," Diana said quickly.

"This is the first time that Jaime has ever brought a woman to my house, except his own mother," Profetina stated. "The first time," she repeated, giving the phrase a highly significant emphasis.

What Profetina was saying was that during the time Jaime had been married, he'd never brought his wife there.

"I feel very flattered by that, Mrs. Rodrigues," Diana fumbled.

"Profetina," the elderly lady insisted. "If you are to be Diana to me, I am to be Profetina to you. Both Jaime and Connie call me Profetina, and so do most of the other young people. Sometimes they remember to add *tia* if they are feeling formal, but most of the time they do not feel formal with me. That makes me happy." Profetina reached over to select a sugar-covered cookie from one of the plates and took an appreciative bite out of it before she continued. "It is good to have a meeting of the young and the old, Diana. Today, the ages are kept apart too much. Youth Centers. Senior Citizens Centers. People have—how shall I say it?—they have labels put on them, depending on how old they are, and then they are put in their own little zoos." She shook her head. "I do not like that, I like to see everyone mixed up. At least some of the time. It is not good to always be with either the old or the young.''

"Yes, I agree with that," Diana said.

"Then perhaps you will come back to visit me by yourself," Profetina suggested. "You do not have to wait for anyone to bring you. My door is at all times open to you. And you and I can talk.''

"I would love to talk to you, Profetina," Diana said, and she was sincere. Someone like Profetina could be of inestimable value to her from a professional point of view. And from a personal point of view Profetina had known Jaime all his life!

"Now we will go see the *Menino*," Profetina said, having noticed that Diana had finished her wine. "I do this, I admit, because I hate so much to see the old customs dying away. The young people, they all want to be American, Diana. They don't want to remember their Portuguese background, they don't want to even learn to speak our language. As for the customs, like the *Menino Jesus*, like the serenading at Christmas and so many other things, they are dying out, and when people like me are gone there will be no one left to observe them.

"I can understand that," Profetina said reflectively, "even though I do not like it. To me, the old customs and traditions make life interesting, but that is because I am an old woman." She shook her head. "No, there is no doubt that the old traditions are gradually dying out, and one day they will be gone. The passing of time, deaths in the family, lack of interest on the part of the young—all of these things take their toll.

"There was a time," she added, "when everyone had a *Menino Jesus* in their house at Christmas. And they held open house all through the Christmas season. Now most people do put out a crèche, but they don't take the time and the care to arrange the *Menino*. People have open house, but by invitation. There is nothing very open about it. Sometimes there is carol singing in a neighborhood, but there is nothing like the old serenading. And the carols are more often sung in English, not Portuguese."

"You said that the younger people don't learn the language," Diana ventured, "but I noticed that Jaime speaks Portuguese."

"Yes, Jaime speaks Portuguese as if he had been born in São Miguel," Profetina agreed. "That is because of his grandfather, in whose house Jaime and his family lived when Jaime was a small boy. Jaime's grandfather never learned to speak English."

"Your brother, Profetina?"

"No. Jaime's grandmother was my sister," Profetina said. "Like me, she was born in São Miguel—in the Azores. When I came to this country—my husband had come first, he sent for me—she came with me. She went out to work, as I did myself, and we both learned English. But it was different with the fishermen. Most of them were Portuguese anyway, there was no need for them to learn English. At least, they didn't think so. For that matter, you will find many people of all ages around here today who speak very little English. Some of them speak no English at all, only Portuguese. Jaime's own father grew up speaking Portuguese. Though he was born here, English was his second language not his first. With Jaime and his brothers and his sister, of course, it was different. They consider themselves Americans."

"And you don't?" Diana asked softly.

"I love your country," Profetina said simply, "but no, I have never truly considered myself an American, Diana. If I had had children, it would have been different. They would have been Americans, and their children, of course, would have been like Jaime...."

Profetina's eyes misted. "Jaime is like a son to me, more than a nephew," she confided. "A grandson, I guess I should say, but when I think of him to myself I call him my son. You can understand that? Now...I will show you the *Menino*."

Jaime had been right when he'd said Profetina had taken everything out of her front parlor in order to accommodate the display. The room was devoid of any furniture except the rows of straight-backed chairs and the elaborate triangle of shelves that stretched across the far wall between the two front windows.

It was very quiet in the room, although there were a number of people sitting there, most of them elderly women dressed either in black or in dark, drab colors. Some of them were talking quietly among themselves, others seemed lost in contemplation, others were praying.

The light was dim in the room, so that the glow cast by the flickering white candles seemed especially bright. Profetina took Diana by the hand and led her directly up to the display.

"People bring here what they have," she whispered, indicating one of the many crèches placed on a shelf. "It is all of significance to them. As you see, the holy figures are scattered throughout the display, with other objects that are considered symbolic. See, the figure of the Christ Child—the Boy Jesus—is always in the front. Many of these figures are real works of art, Diana. They were brought from Portugal and the Azores and have been in the family for a long, long time. They mean a great deal to their owners. You will see that most of the favorite saints are included. The top shelf is the most important. See, that's where the most important figures are placed."

Diana nodded. Then, pointing, she whispered, surprised, "Is that wheat?"

Profetina nodded. "You will always find wheat and many candles in a *Menino* display," she said. "You see, wheat has been sprouted in those small dishes to represent the Resurrection. The sheaves of wheat you first noticed represent the staff of life, and the white candles represent the Light. The Holy Light, you would say.

"Then," Profetina continued, "there are always many roses strewn along the shelves. Maybe that looks strange to you at Christmas here, but the rose is the flower of Portugal. Roses bloom at Christmas in Portugal, and they are plentiful. Most of these roses we use are artificial, as you can see. The real flowers are too expensive for most pocketbooks in this part of the world.''

"The carved doves are exquisite,'' Diana said softly.

Profetina nodded approval. "They symbolize the Holy Spirit, and they are my favorites. Some of them have been done so very beautifully. And—you see those with the red ribbons around their necks?''

"Yes.''

"That means that their owners are giving thanks for wishes that have been granted.''

Diana smiled. "I'd say quite a few dreams have come true, then.''

"Let us hope so,'' Profetina said with a nod. She drew Diana's attention to a circular object, which seemed to be made of interwoven dried leaves. "That is the curative crown,'' she explained. "Many believe that it has rare healing powers. And at the base of the display you see the shoes?''

"Yes,'' Diana whispered. "Jaime told me about the shoes.''

"That Jaime!'' Profetina said dryly. But she was smiling.

"Now there are new friends arriving,'' Profetina murmured. "I must leave you, but you can look for yourself all you want, Diana.''

"Thank you,'' Diana whispered, and for a few

minutes she did move along the length of the display, studying the many different objects in detail. But she could not avoid the feeling that she was an intruder here, and that some of these quiet women watching her must think her decidedly out of place. She wished she'd worn something less conspicuous than the winter-white dress and the crystal jewelry.

A voice at her elbow queried, "Does it live up to your expectations, *menina*?"

Diana started visibly, and Jaime asked swiftly, "What's wrong?"

"Nothing," she whispered. She couldn't possibly tell him that just hearing his voice had sent a tremor through her body, a small emotional earthquake.

"I didn't mean to make you jump," he said softly.

"You startled me, that's all."

"Have you seen enough of the *Menino*?"

She nodded and let him guide her away, painfully aware of the fact that nearly every eye in the room was upon them.

"Where were you?" Diana whispered, once they'd cleared the front parlor and were in the narrow hallway that led to the back of the house.

"In the kitchen, with Connie and Manny," Jaime said. "And, yes, I left you alone with Profetina deliberately. I wanted the two of you to get acquainted, and I felt the best way for you to do it was without my inhibiting presence."

"Your inhibiting presence?"

He grinned. "Are you saying that I'm not inhibiting? Does that mean I actually make you lose your inhibitions?"

"Don't leap to conclusions so rapidly," Diana warned him, then asked, "What's a *noiva*?"

It was Jaime who looked startled this time. "What a good memory for words you have! A *noiva* is a sweetheart. Sometimes the word is also used to mean a bride."

"I see!" Diana's cheeks became so hot she was sure they must be scarlet, and she told herself fiercely that she should have known better than to ask Jaime such a question. When Profetina had asked him if she, Diana, was his *noiva*, his quick reply had obviously been negative. Well...what had she expected?

"You're right," he said quietly. "I told Profetina that you were not my *noiva*, but rather my neighbor and my friend. I thought it would be presumptuous of me to...."

"Please!" she interrupted wildly. "You don't have to explain, Jaime."

"No, I know I don't have to explain, Diana, but...."

"Please!" she said again, and he shrugged.

"All right," he conceded. "Would you like some more elderberry wine, or perhaps a glass of Madeira?"

"No. No, thank you."

"Let's go out to the kitchen and find Connie and Manny before Profetina drags us over to introduce us to those people she's talking to. I don't think a single one of them speaks a word of English, if I'm remembering them correctly."

"Well," she said, an edge to her voice, "that wouldn't make any difference to you, would it?"

His mouth tightened slightly but he said only, "No. But it would to you."

He was leading her toward the kitchen as he spoke, and Diana asked, "Don't you think we'll be intruding?"

"No," Jaime said shortly. "People pop in and out of the kitchen constantly. There's no privacy guaranteed around here. Anyway, Connie and Manny are happy just to be together."

This was true enough, Diana saw, once they'd joined the younger couple. Connie and Manny were so obviously in love and so glad to be with each other that it almost hurt to watch them.

Manny looked very young, very handsome and very vulnerable tonight. He was wearing a dark-blue suit that was a far cry from the beautifully tailored clothes Jaime was wearing, but Diana felt sure he'd donned his elaborate best. His white shirt and blue tie were ultraconservative. The thought came to Diana that these must be his Sunday, church-going clothes.

He seemed somewhat abashed when he saw her, and after a moment Connie said, "Manny's still embarrassed about breaking into your house like that the other night, Diana."

"I didn't break into Miss Ashley's house, Connie," Manny protested. "I. . . ."

Diana laughed. "It's all right," she assured

him. "Forget it, please! I panicked much too easily."

"I don't know about that," Connie intervened, a teasing note in her voice that reminded Diana very much of her uncle. "If I were alone and someone like Manny suddenly broke in on the scene...."

"That's enough," Manny warned her, but there was a fond gleam in his dark eyes as he spoke.

Jaime chuckled. "I think Diana and I are going to leave you two to quibble by yourself. You'll remember that midnight's the curfew, Manny?"

"I'll remember," Manny said seriously.

"Let's say good night to Profetina," Jaime suggested, and Diana looked at him in surprise. She hadn't thought that he'd want to leave quite so soon.

Profetina was the center of a group of people who were holding a conversation in rapid Portuguese, but she quickly excused herself when she saw Jaime and Diana.

When Jaime said they were leaving she protested, "But you have not eaten anything, and you should also have another glass of wine."

"I've sampled every one of your delicious cakes," Diana said, which was true. "And I think I've had three glasses of Madeira."

"We've been out in the kitchen," Jaime explained, "so we snitched things right off the stove top! If you don't have enough to put out for the other guests, blame us," he teased.

Profetina laughed, her eyes fond as she gazed

up at them. "There is no danger of that," she assured him.

"I didn't think there was." He turned to Diana. "When my Aunt Profetina cooks she makes enough good things for all of New Bedford."

Jaime bent and kissed the old lady on both cheeks, and she reached out her arms to Diana, inviting the same gesture. Diana responded, giving Jaime's aunt an added hug.

"You will be back to see me?" Profetina asked her.

"You can depend on it," Diana assured her. "And...*Bom Natal*, Profetina."

Quick tears glistened in Profetina's eyes. *"Bom Natal, menina minha,"* she answered softly.

Once they closed the front door of the house behind them, Jaime turned to Diana to ask suspiciously, "Where did you learn how to say Merry Christmas in Portuguese?"

She lifted her head high, her lips curving in a satisfied smile. "I think I'll keep that my secret."

"And I think I'll kiss that smirk right off your face!" he threatened. "Come on, Diana! Have you been holding out on me?"

"Not really," she said, waiting for him to open the car door for her. "My knowledge of Portuguese is extremely limited, but I'm trying to learn a few phrases. That one came directly from pages of a Portuguese phrase book I picked up in a bookstore yesterday."

"You're putting me on!"

"No...it's true. I can also say, 'Where can we

go swimming?' and 'How much does it cost to send a postcard to England?' if you'd really like to hear me, though I'm a bit shaky on the pronunciation.''

He shouted with laughter. "I don't believe it."

He settled in next to her, looking across at her speculatively before he started up the car. "I think you will never cease to surprise me, *menina*," he told her. "And don't look so damned smug about it. I just might have a few surprises of my own!"

CHAPTER THIRTEEN

FLOR AND BILL MEDEIROS went out of their way to be hospitable on Christmas Day, and Diana fully appreciated their efforts. But it was still impossible for her not to feel constrained around them.

She was more comfortable with Bill than she was with Flor. He was an older, shorter, not quite so handsome version of Jaime and very likable. He managed his handicap remarkably well. If Jaime had not told her about it, Diana wouldn't have suspected he had an artificial leg. He looked tired, though, almost harried despite a surface geniality, and when his eyes lingered on Connie and he didn't think anyone was watching, there was a deeply worried expression in them.

The problem with Flor Medeiros, Diana soon saw, was that she tried too hard. She was a fairly tall, thin, nervous woman, stylishly dressed, with carefully coiffed, sleek black hair. She, too, had those gorgeous dark, Portuguese eyes, but she was not especially pretty. Connie, Diana thought, had inherited her looks from the Medeiros side of the family.

Connie seemed like a wraith, very subdued and into herself. It was difficult to believe this was the same radiant girl who'd been at Profetina's the night before, and the change worried Diana. She could well understand why Bill was so concerned about his daughter.

She could also understand what Jaime had meant when he said that his sister-in-law could sometimes be hard to take. There was nothing natural or relaxed about Flor; she was the complete antithesis of Profetina.

Diana could imagine Profetina having dinner in her own home today, surrounded by friends, and she wished, guiltily, that she could be there with her. Even Jaime seemed different here...constrained. Diana caught his eye upon her every now and then and she was sure that he suspected she was every bit as uncomfortable as she had hinted to him she might be.

She'd asked him what she could bring Bill and Flor in the way of a gift for their hospitality, and Jaime had said, somewhat abruptly, that it wasn't necessary to bring them anything. So after having dismissed the traditional bottle of wine or box of chocolates, Diana had ordered a Christmas table centerpiece from a local florist.

It graced the center of Flor's dining-room table, which was covered with a lavish lace spread, and Flor had thanked her for it so profusely that it had been embarrassing. But Diana was glad she'd sent it. The bright arrangement of poinsettias and white carnations gave a touch of holiday decor to the stark dining room, with its white walls and heavy, dark wood furniture.

There was a Christmas tree in the corner of the living room, but it was the kind of tree Diana had personally never liked—a bright silver aluminum "tree" decorated with huge blue balls, blue lights and blue tinsel trim. Diana decided that Flor, Bill and Connie must have opened their presents on Christmas Eve after Connie had returned from Profetina's, or very early that morning. The gifts were tucked away neatly under the tree. Diana glimpsed a peach satin nightgown and a vivid red sweater and a plaid shirt, which evidently had been a gift to Bill.

Mimosas were served in the living room, Connie passing around the tall-stemmed glasses, and Bill proposed a toast. "To peace and a good year for everyone," he said.

"To all of us," Flor added.

Connie took one sip of her drink and set it aside. She went out to the kitchen and returned with a platter of assorted appetizers. Flor offered caviar on thin crackers, a liver pâté and a variety of fancy little hors d'oeuvres, which she'd evidently made herself and which must have required a good deal of time and effort.

The conversation lagged, and Jaime, usually so quick when it came to words, obviously was not interested in filling in any of the gaps.

Flor tried, by turning her attention upon Diana.

"Are you enjoying Fairhaven?" she asked.

It was a trite question, and Diana could think of nothing but a trite response. "Yes, very much," she replied.

"Jaime says you're from New York," Flor persisted. "I should think it would seem pretty dead to you around here when you're used to living in a city."

"Diana's here because of her work, Flor," Jaime interjected rather impatiently.

"Yes, I know," Flor replied quickly, but she didn't seem inclined to get into the subject of Diana's interest in the Portuguese, historical or otherwise. She quickly switched to questions about Diana's family, learning that, like Connie, Diana was an only child and that her parents were now retired and living in the Carolinas.

Since Diana had exchanged telephone greetings with her mother and father that morning she was able to give an update, even a weather report, on life in the South, and Flor said rather wistfully that it must be nice to get away from the cold of New England winters.

With this she rose to go take a look at the turkey. Although Diana promptly offered to help with the final dinner preparations, Flor insisted that she stay in the living room with the men while she and Connie put the food on the table. This did nothing at all to appease Diana's discomfort. She chatted idly with Bill and Jaime, all too aware of Connie and her mother at work just a few steps away.

Flor's dinner was delicious, but it had no Portuguese overtones. She served turkey with the usual trimmings, and mince pie for dessert. Afterward they had coffee in the living room and Flor proffered chocolate mints. She'd strived so hard to please, all the way around, that Diana couldn't help but feel sorry for her.

It was a last-minute decision to ask Flor and Bill to stop by for an eggnog the following afternoon. Diana hoped she conveyed the invitation graciously enough that Flor would not be offended by such spur of the moment timing, and evidently she wasn't. To Diana's relief, she said quickly that they'd love to come.

Jaime was silent on the short ride back to Fort Street, and it wasn't until he'd parked his car and was walking toward her house with her that he said simply, "I'm sorry for getting you into that. You didn't belong."

The statement stung. Diana could only think that she'd let him down in front of his family. Her voice quavered despite herself, as she asked, "Why do you say that, Jaime?"

"Ever seen a fish out of water?" he asked. "It's more than a cliché. It's a sad fact. Don't misunderstand me. You did your best."

"But it wasn't good enough, is that it?" she asked, hurt by what he was saying.

"Oh my God," Jaime said abjectly, "it wasn't you! It was the whole scene. Flor, trying to come on like the social arbiter she isn't. Bill, trying not to make any gaffes that Flor would upbraid him for later. Connie, about as miserable as a kid could be...."

Diana reached up to press a slender finger against his lips. "Jaime, dear Jaime, don't say things like that," she chastised him gently.

"Neither Flor nor Bill nor Connie deserve those kind of comments. I'll admit I wasn't as comfortable as I'd like to have been, but you're drawing the wrong conclusions."

"Am I?"

"Yes, you are. I've already become very fond of Connie. My heart went out to her today. That's something I want to ask you about, incidentally." She paused, then managed a faint smile. "It's cold out here," she said. "Won't you come in?"

"Diana...."

She summoned up her courage. "I think I know all about your resolutions, Jaime," she told him. "But it *is* Christmas."

For a moment he simply stared down at her, and then he smiled. "So it is," he said softly.

Once inside the kitchen, Diana shrugged off her coat. "I have some eggnog. Or brandy, if you prefer. Or...."

"I'll settle for brandy. What about you?"

"I think I'll settle for eggnog," she said. "Brandy tends to take a direct route to my head."

"Why don't you get the drinks and I'll turn on the tree lights and start a fire," he suggested.

Diana was more than willing to agree. She needed a little time away from him to pull herself together. Jaime could cause her no end of emotional turmoil by just a few words. This time he'd thoroughly upset her by saying that she hadn't belonged at his brother's house, but her fear that she'd disappointed him had diminished when he'd added fervently, "It wasn't you!"

That wasn't quite enough, though. Somehow

she had to convince Jaime that she wanted to relate to his family, to get to know them better.

She took her time about preparing their drinks and putting their glasses on a tray. When she reached the living room, the Christmas tree sparkled with rainbow-colored lights, and Jaime was standing in front of the fireplace, watching the flames lick their way up the chimney bricks. Pausing in the doorway a moment, Diana decided this was a scene she wanted to photograph mentally so that it would stay in her memory forever.

She pulled a chair up near the fire and sat down in it. After picking up his brandy, Jaime sprawled on the rug in front of the fireplace.

He stared into the flames, the wood sparking out occasional flares of orange-red, and he said moodily, "What a strange Christmas for you!"

"Please don't say that!" she protested. "It's been a wonderful Christmas, it *is* a wonderful Christmas. Which reminds me. I have a present for you."

She got up quickly and moved over to the old secretary desk. She'd hidden the little box with the scrimshaw tie tack there after first wrapping it in red gilt paper. She handed the box to him smiling. "Here."

Jaime looked up at her as if she'd struck him. Then he said, "You're embarrassing me. I didn't get a gift for you."

"That doesn't matter," she assured him. She fibbed slightly. "I just happened to see this, and it reminded me of you."

"Look, Diana," he persisted, "it wasn't that I didn't think about getting something for you...."

"It doesn't *matter*, Jaime," she said again. "Go ahead. Open it."

He gave her a strange look, and she guessed that he hadn't been the recipient of too many unexpected gifts in his lifetime, which seemed odd. What kind of marriage had he had, she wondered. Hadn't Cynthia ever surprised him with a gift, just for the fun of it?

Thinking this, she realized that Gary had never exactly "surprised" her with a gift, for that matter. But despite the other failings in their marriage—and there had been all too many of them— he had always given her a valentine, he'd been good about remembering their anniversary, and he'd never forgotten her birthday, to say nothing of such an obvious gift-giving occasion as Christmas. True, she was sure that Gary had kept a record of all these dates in a neat little notebook, so that he wouldn't overlook anything. Whatever else, Gary had been both efficient and methodical. She smiled, and then was almost shocked at herself. She was smiling about something that concerned Gary.

She felt awkward simply standing there, watching Jaime turn the small, colorfully wrapped box around his slender, strong fingers. Finally she went and sat down again, putting a little distance between them.

He unwrapped the package carefully, then folded the piece of paper and put it aside as if it were something to be saved before he opened the box itself. He lifted out the tie tack, then moved to a lamp with it, holding it under the light as he scrutinized it.

"It's a beautiful piece of work," he said finally, and there was a thickness to his voice that surprised Diana. "You must have done a lot of looking before you found this. This is the really genuine, old scrimshaw."

"I know that, Jaime," she teased. "And, no, I didn't do all that much looking. I was lucky. But the workmanship was so much finer than it is in the new scrimshaw...and I wanted you to have something special to remember me by."

She hadn't intended to add that last phrase. It struck her ears as sounding downright maudlin.

He raised his head, his dark eyes meeting her gray ones directly across the intervening space. "I will treasure this always," he told her. "But...I don't need anything to remember you by, Diana." He hesitated, then the words were wrung out of him. "Can you honestly believe I could ever forget you?"

"Jaime...I didn't mean that seriously."

"Are you sure?" he asked skeptically. "I couldn't blame you if you did. I know the things I do must puzzle you. Sometimes they puzzle *me*." He drew a deep breath. "The last thing in God's world I intended to do at this point in my life was to get involved with a woman," he said bleakly.

Diana stiffened. This wasn't what she'd expected to hear. Yet when she thought about it, she supposed there'd been signposts all along the way that should have warned her.

But it had never been her intention—nor was it now—to lay any sort of claim on this man, even though she found him overpoweringly attractive physically, and even though, for reasons far beyond the physical, she was in real danger of falling in love with him.

Falling in love with him? *Be honest with yourself, Diana!* Her inner voice was sharp. *You've fallen in love with him . . . it's already too late to backtrack.*

"What are you thinking?" he asked suddenly.

She shook her head. "I don't think you'd want to know."

"That bad, huh?" he asked, a bittersweet smile curving his lips. "Diana, Diana, why the hell is it that I find it so difficult to say the right things to you? I keep on saying the wrong things, or at least phrasing what I want to say in the wrong way. Like telling you that you didn't belong at Bill and Flor's." He put the tie tack back in its box and put the box on the table under the lamp. Then, while she watched, he ran an agitated hand through his smooth dark hair, an unconscious gesture that gave her a real clue to his inner turmoil. Jaime didn't usually make gestures like that. As a doctor, she surmised, he'd become far too accustomed to facing the world with perfect composure.

He crossed the room to sit in a chair opposite her, close enough to the fire that the flickering flames highlighted his near-perfect features. As she watched him, Diana thought that for a man so singularly good-looking he was surprisingly unconceited.

He said, without preamble, "I wasn't going to come in tonight, even though it's Christmas. I was going to kiss you good-night at the door, and then leave quickly before I could change my mind."

She tried to accept his statement without reacting visibly to the impact it was having on her. But she felt a heavy thud deep inside her as she read his meaning—or thought she did. It took considerable effort for her to say calmly, "Am I right in assuming that what you're saying, Jaime, is that our relationship has progressed too far too fast, as far as you're concerned?"

He winced at her bluntness, but he said uncomfortably, "You do have a way, sometimes, of hitting the nail directly on the head, Diana. I wouldn't have put it that way myself, but I suppose you're right. Not for the reasons I suspect you think, though."

"Oh?"

"I had no intention of making love to you the first night we made love," he said honestly. "It just...happened. Hell, you and I both know that this physical tug between us is very strong. I'd need to have lost all five senses not to know that you find it very difficult to resist me, and I find it almost impossible to resist you!"

Diana bit back the words she longed to speak. She wanted to tell him that, on her part at least, this tide that had risen between them was far more than a physical urge. She no longer negated the sweeping intensity of physical urges. Jaime had taught her fully what desire, passion and sexual need really meant. But even so, those sublime moments she'd spent with him had transcended merely satisfying her body. Jaime had penetrated her soul, as well.

He ran his hand through his hair again, and his expression was pained. "I'm saying this very badly," he confessed. "Actually, it's a continuation of what I've said to you before. But I've never spelled it out." He hesitated. "Try to understand what I mean, will you, Diana? Try to read between the lines if I don't find the words to express myself the way I want to. The fact is that although I didn't intend to make love to you, I could no more have resisted our coming together than I could have turned back the rhythm of the sea. I wanted you more desperately than you can possibly realize. You filled a hunger so deep that it was like a chasm. I was insatiable in my need for you, and when you...when you made love with me...."

He broke off and stared across at her helplessly. "It's hard as hell for me to talk about things like this," he said quietly.

The ache inside her had begun to dull a little, but though she wanted to smile at him she found it impossible to do so. Her voice was very small as she said, "Yes, I suppose it is."

"You suppose? Ah, come on, *menina*. Could you put it into words for me? No, I can see by

your face that you couldn't do any better than I
am. But in fairness to both of us I have to say
what I...must say. That first time made me realize how—how much you could matter to me.''

This was not what Diana had expected to hear,
either.

"I knew, you see, that this could be no casual
affair between us," he went on, staring into the
fire. "I also knew that neither of us was entirely
free. And my feeling was—my feeling *is*—that
what we have between us is far too valuable to trifle with.''

"Trifle?" Diana's voice was higher than she
wanted it to be, an indication that she wasn't far
from tears. She forced herself to speak steadily. "I
don't think either of us has trifled with the other,
Jaime.''

"All right," he conceded. "I guess what I'm
saying is that I don't think there can be much of a
real future for us unless we first clear up our pasts.
I told you that there are still obstacles in our way.
That's how I feel. And when I hold you in my
arms, when I make love to you, I don't like to
think that there is anything at all to come between
our feelings for each other.''

Diana sighed. Then she said carefully, "Don't
you think you're being awfully idealistic?"

"Is that a fault?"

"No, of course not. But I'd say that sometimes
it creates impossible problems...when you're
dealing with people like us.''

"What's that supposed to mean?"

"Well, we've both been married, we've both been through tragedies in our lives. There's been a lot written on our slates, and I think you'd have to agree that some of it is so indelible it can never be erased."

"No," he said shortly. "No, I don't agree with that."

"Then you're being illogical," she said. "I... I'm not a sixteen-year-old virgin, Jaime."

"I know that," he exclaimed impatiently. "For God's sake, Diana, what place would a sixteen-year-old virgin have in my life? What I'm saying is that scars can be dealt with. Not erased entirely, perhaps—maybe no one can ever do that—but handled so that they no longer matter."

This was the closest he'd come to talking about his own work, and Diana held her breath. But he went on. "I'm not such a fool that I think we can both start to live tomorrow as if we've never lived before. The past has made us what we are; we're its products, both the good and the bad of us. What I'm saying, though, is that old ghosts should be exorcised before two people try to achieve a significant relationship. You have your ghosts and I have my ghosts. We need time to deal with them, that's all."

"Are you sure you *can* deal with yours?" The question terrified her, but she had to ask it.

He stared across at her bleakly. "I honestly don't know."

"When you discovered that we'd met before, you asked me if your ex-wife had had anything to do with my coming to Fairhaven. Why did you ask me such a question, Jaime?"

This was something that had been haunting Diana.

"Because even though Cynthia and I have been divorced for a long time she has a way of intruding into my life periodically, sometimes in rather nasty ways," he explained. "It was ridiculous of me to think that you could have had anything to do with her, of course. I realized that the moment I spoke, and I would have given a lot to take back those words. But seeing your scar, having you tell me that I was the doctor who'd handled your case, completely rocked me. It struck me then that you'd known this from the moment you saw me again...."

"I did know it from the moment I saw you again."

His eyes were black as coals, and there was a coldness to them that made her shiver. "Yes, and why the hell didn't you say so?"

"I had the strong feeling that you didn't want to be recognized," she replied. "I respected your desire for privacy. Maybe I shouldn't have."

"I don't know," he said unhappily. "I really don't know. And as far as my desire for privacy is concerned...yes, I wanted to hide away for a while to get my thoughts together and make some sort of intelligent decision about what to do with the rest of my life. But I was insane, of course, to pick Fairhaven as a retreat. I did so only because the house was here, and I also knew that I should come to some decision about it. It's been five years since my mother died, and she was in a nursing home for a year before that. So the house has been sitting empty for a long time."

The fire was dying down, but Jaime made no move to put another log on it. He stared into the glowing embers. "I suppose if I hadn't been such a sentimental fool I would have put the house up for sale years ago. But for some crazy reason I couldn't bring myself to do that. Maybe the house is symbolic to me. Maybe it's come to represent the Portuguese kid who made good and was able to afford a mansion on one of the best streets in town. Though, as it turned out, this Portuguese kid didn't do such a great job of making good after all."

"Why do you say that?"

By way of answer he stood up, prodding the embers with a poker, then adding a log to the fire. It was a diversionary tactic that made it clear to Diana he still wasn't ready to speak about his reasons for giving up medicine.

"This is turning out to be a pretty sorry Christmas," he said. "You give me a present and I have nothing to give you. . . ."

"Jaime, will you please forget that? Sometimes giving a gift can be more satisfying than receiving one."

He looked at her over his shoulder, his grin sheepish. "You're the only woman I've ever known who could say something like that and mean it— except maybe my mother, and Profetina."

"I'm not going to comment on that."

"Thank you. No, I mean it. If you were to comment it would only involve a conclusion about the kind of women I've known, and I think that's something we can skip."

"There's something I can't skip," Diana said steadily. "Do you still love Cynthia?"

He turned away from the fireplace, staring at her in shocked surprise. "Do I still love Cynthia?" he echoed. He stood with his arms akimbo, looking across at her, and it was impossible for her not to react to the masculine vitality that radiated from him. "Do you seriously think I could still love another woman and make love to you as I have?"

"I wouldn't like to think so," she admitted. "But. . . you still haven't answered my question."

He glared at her. "Of course I don't still love Cynthia!" he snapped. "I haven't loved Cynthia for years, if I ever really loved her in the first place. When I look back, when I'm honest with myself, I have to admit that marrying her may have been just another case of trying to prove that the Portuguese kid could make good." Abruptly, he changed the subject. "Would you like another eggnog? I'm going to get another brandy."

"No," she said. "No, thank you."

She sat very still while he went out to the kitchen to get his drink, every muscle in her body so tensed she felt like a wound-up watch spring.

Jaime came back and sat down opposite her again, twirling the glass of brandy between his fingers and staring down into the amber liquid. After a time, he said, ''Well, why don't we exorcise one ghost? Not that Cynthia really is a ghost, but she might as well be if you think she's coming between us. No—'' he held up a restraining hand ''—don't protest. Let me tell you about her, which I can do quickly and easily.

''I got through college and med school by means of scholarships, and my mother toiling like hell and giving me every cent she made, and me working every spare minute during holiday periods and on vacations. There wasn't much time for fun and games. But on one break, during my senior year of med school, a classmate invited me to go skiing up in New Hampshire with him. His family had a small chalet up in the mountains, so it cost me next to nothing. I'd never skied before, but I was more than willing to try it. As it happened, I did pretty well for a rank beginner.

''After we'd spent our afternoon on the slopes,'' Jaime continued, ''we stopped in at the lodge. That's where I met Cynthia. Without meaning any disrespect to your national origins, I have to say she was the ultimate WASP. She was blond, she was blue-eyed, she was gorgeous, and she was willing, which astonished me. She was also a Boston Brahmin on both sides of her family. In short, totally out of my league, but it took me very little time to decide it was a league I wanted to work my way into.

''I was doing a general surgery rotation at the time,'' Jaime went on. ''A week or so later, on my day off, I called Cynthia, who was back in Boston by then, and suggested we have a drink together. She invited me to her house, which turned out to be one of those mansions on Louisburg Square. I don't know how well you know Boston. . . ."

"Not very well at all," Diana said.

"Well, let's say you couldn't have a much better in-city address. Louisburg Square is in the posh part of Beacon Hill. Anyway, I put on my best clothes and polished up my best manners and went over. Cynthia's parents were there and they detested me on sight."

"You probably imagined that," Diana protested.

"The hell I imagined it! Even if they could have brought themselves to like me personally, it was like waving a red flag in front of them when they thought about me in connection with their daughter. But Cynthia had a mind of her own and I have a very strong will when I want something. I decided I wanted *her*, and I went all out to get her. We were engaged by Easter, I graduated from med school in May, and we were married in June.

"I had a fairly long vacation before starting my internship. Her family had a place in Chatham, down on the Cape, and so we went down there. I had next to no money, certainly not enough to take Cynthia on a honeymoon in the style to which she was accustomed.

"From the very beginning of that time on the Cape," Jaime said, still gazing down into the brandy glass, "I knew what a terrible mistake I'd made. But by fall she was pregnant, and I decided there was no way out of it.''

''You have a child?'' Diana whispered, shocked.

He shook his head. ''No. Cynthia had a miscarriage when she was four months along, and I made damn sure she wouldn't get pregnant again. Which brings me to a question I've been meaning to ask you. Have you been... protected, Diana?''

She shook her head. ''No, but it's been a safe time of the month.''

''Famous last words,'' Jaime said grimly. ''Let's hope you're right!''

Diana went cold when she heard this. Would he really think it so terrible if she did find she was pregnant? As far as she was concerned, she couldn't imagine anything in the world more wonderful than having his child.

CHAPTER FOURTEEN

BY THE TIME Diana began to prepare for her Christmas party she wished she'd never thought of having it.

Her conversation with Jaime Christmas night had left her emotionally exhausted. When they'd finished talking, she'd been too tired to possibly think of making love, even if Jaime had not already made his position clear on that score.

The morning of the party she washed out the lovely old cut-glass punch bowl she'd found in the dining-room closet and the cups that went with it. She made her favorite recipe for small mushroom turnovers, which would be served hot, and as the hour for the party approached she set out an array of cheese and crackers, salted nuts, slices of fruit-cake, mints and other sweets. Then, before filling the punch bowl with eggnog, she rushed upstairs to dress. She'd allowed herself only a minimum of time to do so.

She had decided to wear her favorite dress. It was black crepe, its low vee neck decorated with rhinestones. The dropped waist and shirred skirt made it fashionable as well as flattering. Diana just had time to zip it up, slip on her high-heeled black patent-leather shoes and to clip on some dangling rhinestone earrings when the doorbell rang.

She flew down the stairs, hoping that it was Jaime who had arrived first, but she found Connie standing on the threshold.

"My parents will be along soon," Connie promised as she slipped off her coat. She peered into the living room. "Oh! Your tree is beautiful, Diana," she complimented.

"Tell Jaime," Diana said. "He did most of it."

"Jaime decorated the tree?" Connie laughed. "That doesn't sound much like my uncle! Look, I came early because I thought maybe I could help."

"You can," Diana assured her. "I have to fill up the punch bowl with the eggnog."

They accomplished this by carrying containers of eggnog back and forth from the kitchen. At the last instant, Diana remembered to place a shaker of nutmeg near the punch bowl for those who wanted it.

As she did this, she turned to Connie, wanting to get something off her mind that had been bothering her.

"Connie," she said frankly, "I wanted to invite Manny, but I didn't know what to do. I suppose I should have asked Jaime...."

"He would have told you not to," Connie said. "My parents know that Manny was at Aunt Profetina's Christmas Eve and that he brought me home. They went to Profetina's early themselves so they wouldn't run into Manny. They didn't like the idea of my meeting him, you can be sure of that, but I guess they went along with it because of Jaime. He came right out and told them, and I guess he must have said a few other things, too, because they didn't make any fuss. That's one thing about Jaime: whatever he does is out in the open. He hates people doing things behind other people's backs."

Connie was rearranging the small poinsettia-decorated cocktail napkins Diana had placed on the table, fanning them out into a pretty pattern. "As far as having Manny come here today, my parents would have been miserable and so would he," Connie admitted. "I don't know." She looked up at Diana with a shy smile. "Maybe another time?"

"Definitely another time," Diana said.

The doorbell rang again. This time it was the Howlands who were standing on the threshold, and then Gail and Howard Landers arrived, and after that Bill and Flor Medeiros, followed shortly by the Burroughses.

There was a pleasant hum of conversation, everyone was being very affable, Diana noted as she circulated among her guests, but she was intensely aware that the most important person of all, as far as she was concerned, was missing.

Had Jaime decided not to come to her party? They'd parted on a tired note last night but not a bad one.

As the time passed, Diana found it increasingly

difficult to play the hostess role. Again and again she caught herself glancing toward the door, hoping to see Jaime's tall, familiar figure standing on the threshold. She was increasingly aware of Gail's observation. Gail was becoming curious, and the last thing in the world Diana wanted to do right now was to have to fend off any questions, even from her best friend.

She noticed Bill Medeiros sitting in a corner, and he looked very much alone. Glancing around, she saw that Flor had joined the Howlands and the Burroughses. Flor was dramatic tonight in a stunning white dress, her only jewelry some beautiful ruby earrings that looked antique. Family pieces, Diana supposed. Jaime had indicated that Flor had come from a well-to-do family. But for all of her striking appearance Flor seemed as nervous as ever. Her brittle laughter floated across the room.

Diana made her way to Bill's side, glad of a chance to be alone with him, if only briefly. She wanted to get to know Jaime's brother better.

"I think you need a refill on that eggnog," she said. "May I get you one?"

"Thanks." Bill smiled. "But I think I'll pass for a little while. This is a very nice party, Diana, and you were kind to invite us."

"You were kind to come," Diana replied. "This is a busy season." She hesitated. "Bill...?"

"Yes?"

"I'm glad I have this chance to tell you how glad I am that Connie and I are going to be working together. I think we'll get along very well."

"I hope so," Bill said, and for a moment his guard slipped, and Diana saw that he was still very troubled about his daughter. "We all make mistakes," he said then. "I guess maybe Flor and I have made a few where Connie is concerned. But I don't think anything could be better for her right now than this opportunity to work with you."

Diana's throat tightened. She liked this man, she would have liked him even if he wasn't Jaime's brother, and if anything could inspire her to make a success of her upcoming working relationship with Connie, Bill's vote of confidence would do it.

As she was about to think of something to say in return, a small kitchen timer she'd been holding in her hand suddenly rang, and she quickly said, "Excuse me, will you please?" Bill nodded.

Diana's mushroom turnovers had been a terrific success, and she'd already been out to the kitchen twice to replenish trays from the oven. The bell that had just rung was a signal that the latest batch must be done, and she hurried toward the kitchen.

She stopped short on the threshold when she saw Jaime standing at the stove, carefully loosening the turnovers with a spatula.

He glanced at her over his shoulder. "If I hadn't happened by, these would have burned up," he commented.

"I suppose I should consider myself grateful that you decided to put in an appearance," Diana snapped.

"Here," he said. "Give me that dish you're carrying." He deftly transferred the turnovers from the baking sheet to the serving dish, and then faced her, the dish in hand.

"I don't blame you for being upset..." he began.

Diana could feel tears sting her eyes, which made her even more furious. "I'm not upset, damn it!" she sputtered.

"Diana...."

"Jaime, you don't have to make any excuses to me."

He put the dish down on the kitchen table and reached out to clasp her chin with one firm hand. Her eyes were glistening with the unshed tears, she knew, and she hated to have him see how damnably weak she was where he was concerned.

He said gently, "Okay, I won't make any excuses, *menina*, not now. Maybe later I'll tell you why I was late. Now, shall we go in and join your guests?"

Jaime merged into the scene so easily that it seemed as if he'd been there all along. Watching him as he chatted easily with her guests, Diana was once again painfully aware that he was the most attractive man she'd ever known...and without a doubt, she loved him.

He was not only handsome and virile, his sexuality a magnet to her, but warm, generous and wonderful. He was everything a woman could ever hope to find in a man. Few were so lucky in the course of their lives. But because she'd "found" Jaime didn't mean that they were going to have a future together, Diana reminded herself bleakly.

He was too aware of what he called the obstacles in their paths. It was his conviction, she knew, that there could be no total togetherness for them until these were removed. Yet some obstacles in life were insurmountable, she thought, helping herself to a cup of eggnog. Were theirs?

Giving up the practice of medicine had left a dark chasm in Jaime's life. Diana knew that, though others might not think it looking at him now, urbane, charming and smiling as he stood talking with Gail and Howard Landers. He had terrific self-control and he'd become a camouflage artist. To a point, she'd become one herself, though she was not as good at it as Jaime was. And, she admitted sadly, Jaime was right. She still did have obstacles of her own to deal with.

Could she ever rid herself of the conviction that she was responsible for Gary's death?

At her side Flor said, "This is a very nice party, Diana. It was thoughtful of you to include us."

"It was thoughtful of you to include me in your Christmas," Diana said sincerely.

"We enjoyed having you." Flor hesitated. "There is something I've been wanting to say to you. . ." she began.

"Yes?" Diana encouraged.

"Jaime's told us that you know about Constance's problem," Flor said. "I want you to know that Bill and I appreciate your giving her a job. She needs something different to take her out of herself. But there's one thing I'm going to ask of you, Diana."

Diana felt a stab of apprehension, but she managed to merely smile politely as she asked, "Yes?"

"Don't let Manuel Ribeiro come here when she's here," Flor said, her face so drawn as she spoke that her tension was communicable. "Oh, I know that Jaime arranged that meeting with Constance and Manuel at Profetina Rodrigues's Christmas Eve. He told us that he felt it was essential to let Constance see Manuel after what... what she'd tried to do. Something to do with basic psychology in cases like this, that's the way Jaime put it. He sold Bill—Jaime's a doctor, Bill's always looked up to him, so what could I say—but it can't continue." Flor spoke with a vehemence she couldn't suppress. "I'm not saying that's what Jaime has in mind, fixing it so Constance can work here with you. And I certainly don't mean to suggest that you have anything to do with this at all. There's no reason why you should. But...."

Flor looked so unhappy it was impossible not to feel sorry for her. But this was a family matter in which Diana didn't want to get involved. She said carefully, "I think this is something you should discuss with Jaime, Flor."

"What should my sister-in-law discuss with me?" Jaime asked lightly. He'd come up behind the two women, evidently bent on refilling his empty punch cup. He smiled down at Flor and Diana in a way that could have been called benevolent, except that Diana caught the glint in his dark eyes and knew he was not nearly as pleased as he appeared to be.

It was Flor who said, "This isn't the place to go into it, Jaime. I'll get in touch with you tomorrow. Diana, I would love to have the recipe for those turnovers—if you'd be willing to give it, of course. They're delicious."

"I'd love to give it to you, Flor," Diana assured her. "I'll write it out for you tomorrow."

Diana moved away, circulating among the others, but at the back of her mind was the uneasy suspicion that maybe Jaime really had arranged this job for Connie so that she would be free to see Manny. This would indicate, of course, that Jaime endorsed the romance, which Diana found puzzling. Jaime had spoken with considerable bitterness of the toll the sea took from the men who worked her for their living. He'd lost both a grandfather and a brother to the sea. It was difficult to think that he'd welcome Connie marrying a man committed to that kind of life. But then maybe Jaime wasn't even thinking about anything as binding as marriage. Maybe it was his educated guess that if Connie and Manny were permitted to see each other freely their romance would wear out of its own accord.

This might be true, Diana conceded. Keeping them apart could prove true the old cliché that forbidden fruit always tends to seem the sweetest.

Gail came up to say she and Howard would have to be heading back to the Cape, and the little gathering gradually began to break up. Connie left with her parents, the Howlands went in one direction and the Burroughses in another, and finally

Diana closed the car door to turn and find herself alone with Jaime.

He wasted no time in taking her into his arms, plundering her mouth with his lips, his kiss so long, so insistent and so torturingly sweet that it threatened to shred the last vestiges of her composure.

He stepped back from her, still holding her arms, and he said, his eyes devouring her, "I don't think you've ever been so beautiful as you are tonight. Maybe it's that thing you're wearing. . . ."

"That thing?" Diana laughed shakily. "I'll have you know I ate beans for a week in order to be able to afford this particular 'thing.' "

"It was worth the sacrifice," Jaime said. "It's been all I could do to keep my hands off you, and with every man in the room sneaking lecherous glances at you. . . ."

"What an imagination!" Diana managed to release herself from his grip gently but firmly and headed back toward the dining room. "Another eggnog?" she offered.

"I don't think I could go another eggnog," Jaime said frankly. "But I'd love an honest drink of bourbon."

Diana was spreading a cracker with some cheese. "By all means," she invited. "Go on out to the kitchen and make yourself a drink."

"Can I fix one for you?"

"No thanks," she said. "Not this time around."

By the time he came back to the dining room

she'd gathered up the empty punch cups and stacked them on a tray, and she was scooping the crumpled paper napkins in a heap, planning to burn them in the living-room fireplace.

Watching her, Jaime said, "Okay, I know you're displeased with me, so we might as well get the explanations over with."

She shook her head. "I told you. There are no explanations necessary."

"Don't be stiff with me, Diana. Come on. Leave the damned cleanup, will you? I'll help you with it later."

She hesitated. There had been a certain buildup toward having this little party. It was the first time she'd entertained, even on such a small scale, in a very long while. As a result she was tired, and it was true that Jaime had upset her. But it wasn't that she was displeased with him. That was the wrong word, she decided. She'd been dismayed when he hadn't shown up in time, then fearful that he might not come at all, and then hurt to think that he'd let her down.

He was standing in the living-room doorway. Impatiently he asked, "Will you come in here and sit down and let me talk to you?"

"All right," she said reluctantly. She took the crumpled napkins with her and tossed them into the burning fire before sitting down on one of the stiff old Victorian chairs. She tried very hard not to look at Jaime because she felt as if his eyes were boring a hole through her.

After a time he said abruptly, "I admit it wasn't

easy for me to come over here tonight. It wasn't easy for me to go to the Howlands' with you the other afternoon. But in both cases I made up my mind it was something I had to do. No, don't look at me like that, Diana. The matter of my going to the Howlands' or coming here tonight really has very little to do with you, can you understand that? But it has a lot to do with me. Of course, if it hadn't been for you, the need to mingle like this probably wouldn't have arisen. At least I wouldn't have let it arise. I. . . ."

He paused. "I'm saying this badly."

"Yes, you are," she agreed, so tired, so dispirited, that right now it didn't matter if he didn't like her agreement.

He smiled faintly, then continued. "You know that when I came back to Fairhaven I did so because I wanted to be alone, I wanted time and space in which to think. I've told you that. I expected my family to have the courtesy to leave me alone, and I made that point clear to them. But then you came on the scene. . . ."

"It's too bad I ever rented the house," she said bitterly.

"Do you really believe that, Diana?"

"I don't want to get into it, Jaime."

"Do you really believe that?" he repeated.

"Does it make any difference whether I do or not?"

"You know damned well that it makes one hell of a lot of difference whether you do or not!" he exploded. "Look, Diana, what I'm trying to say is that after you got me involved with your blasted key I came to realize that John Donne was right when he wrote that no man is an island. No man can ever be an island. I don't mean to fill you full of platitudes, but it's a fact that a person can't live completely alone and be happy. You, well, you made me realize the emptiness in my life, you made me realize that I'd been living in a vacuum. You also brought me to new grips with a truth I'd known all along, but I was trying not to admit it. You made me face up to the knowledge that it's impossible to run away, because in the end our self always catches up with us."

Diana didn't reply. She stared down at her black patent shoes and tried to focus on the fact that her feet were tired.

"Why don't you take them off?" Jaime suggested.

"What?"

"Your shoes. Why don't you take them off?"

She had to smile, despite herself. "You're impossible. Where do you keep your crystal ball?"

"Where you are concerned I have two crystal balls," he said blithely. "One in my head, and one in my heart."

Diana made a small face at him. But she reached down and slipped off the shoes and wriggled her toes. It felt wonderful.

"To get back to this...strange confession of mine," Jaime said. "It wasn't easy for me to go to the Howlands' the other day or to face up to coming here tonight. I know that everyone's curious as hell about me. I can't blame them. I knew they'd probably be too polite to ask any leading questions—and they were—but even so I shrank from the thought of all the conjecturing that would be going on.... I would never have let you down by not showing up tonight, and what bothers me is that I think *you* think that's what I was on the verge of doing. Am I right?''

She nodded slowly.

Jaime's smile was pained. "Do you have so little faith in me, Diana?''

"It isn't a question of faith, Jaime.''

"No? I think it is. But if I haven't built up that kind of faith in you yet, that's my fault. And when we get right down to it, there hasn't been very much time. To establish a basis of real faith takes a long while.''

He stretched his legs out toward the fire as he spoke, and Diana felt her throat tighten as her eyes traced the long line of his semireclining figure. She'd come to know every inch of him, and memories filled her, both provocative and disturbing.

"Actually,'' Jaime said, "I was on my way out the door when the phone rang. And please don't say, 'How convenient!' It wasn't convenient at all.'' His voice lowered. "The call was from Cynthia.''

"Cynthia!''

"That's right,'' he said. "We talked a long time, she had a lot to say. I felt I should listen.'' He sighed. "At the conclusion of our conversation, I agreed to meet her in Boston for lunch to-morrow.''

"I see," Diana said dully.

"No, you don't." Jaime contradicted her. "Don't start making mirages where there shouldn't be any, *menina*."

Menina merely meant girl, or girl child, Diana knew that. But the way he'd always used the word had come to have a very special significance. When Jaime spoke it, it was a term of endearment. It hurt to hear him say it in the same breath with the announcement that he was going to have lunch the next day with his ex-wife.

"I had a number of different reasons for telling Cynthia I'd have lunch with her," he explained. "I've been wanting to talk to her anyway, and as it happened it would have been cruel to refuse her. Her marriage has broken up. . . ."

Diana's gray eyes were puzzled. "Her marriage?"

"I'm talking about her second marriage. She married a Boston lawyer about a year after we were divorced. Now it seems that he's fallen in love with someone else. Cynthia's saying she never loved him in the first place, but I gather she'd like to take him to the cleaner's if she can, just for spite. It's been a terrific blow to her ego."

"I can imagine," Diana said dryly.

"Sarcasm doesn't become you," Jaime commented quietly. "Would I be presuming too much if I say that you sound. . . a bit jealous?"

"Yes, you would be," she replied testily.

"My loss," he said, but he was smiling slightly. Then, sobering, he continued, "Anyway, I'll be going up to Boston tomorrow. While I'm there I'm going to try to pick up a used electric typewriter for Connie."

"I can rent one locally," Diana said quickly.

"There's no reason why you should. I've been intending to get a typewriter for myself, anyway. My handwriting is terrible...."

"A typical doctor?" she suggested. "All doctors have terrible handwriting."

"The reputation for it, at least," he said indifferently. "Anyway, I do better on a typewriter when I have to write a letter, at least if I want anyone to be able to read it."

"Fine, then." She nodded. "If you really want a typewriter anyway, go ahead and get one. About Connie, though...."

"Yes." Jaime's gaze narrowed. "Just what was Flor saying to you?"

"She seems to think that the job offer may be camouflaging a potential point of rendezvous for Connie and Manny. She asked me not to let Manny come here." Diana saw no point in being less than truthful.

"And what did you tell her?"

"You heard the major part of my reply, I'm sure. I told her I thought she should talk to you about it."

"You were right," he agreed. "She said she wanted to talk to me tomorrow and I should have told her I wouldn't be around, but it slipped my mind. No matter. I'll call her up when I get back from Boston. I shouldn't be late.''

He rose, stretching. "As far as Connie and Manny are concerned, I don't want you to think I'm trying to put you in the middle. I've already told Manny I think it would be a good idea if he stays away when Connie is working here, and Connie knows this. My feeling is that it would only stir up dissension between Flor and you, and there's no point in doing that. Connie and Manny can meet at my place occasionally, while I'm there, of course."

Diana thought about this for a moment and then said, "Am I to assume that you wouldn't object if Connie and Manny decided to get married one of these months?"

Jaime shrugged. "It would be futile if I did. If they're as much in love with each other as they seem to think they are, this is going to turn into a tragic Romeo and Juliet situation, which is where Connie appeared to be heading, or else there'll be an elopement one of these days. I doubt very much if they'd tell anyone until the deed had been accomplished!

"On the other hand," he added, "if it's merely a case of puppy love, then they'll outgrow it. And the worst thing anyone could do right now is try to keep them apart, as I've tried to explain to Flor and Bill. That will only force them to get together. I think Bill understands that, but I'm still having a problem with Flor."

"I like your brother," Diana said.

"Bill likes you," Jaime told her. "He tends to be rather introverted when he first meets people. It's a kind of shyness...part of it due to his leg, I think. He covers it up well, but he's never gotten over losing his leg. He's overly conscious of the fact that he's a cripple."

"I'd never think of Bill as a cripple," Diana said quickly.

"Someday I'm going to tell him you said that," Jaime told her. "When the time is right. Just now, Bill's got his hands so full that I don't think he's really hearing anything. He's worried to death about Connie, for one thing, and then there's constant trouble with his business interests."

"In what way?"

"Well, a few years back things hit bottom when the fishermen got so fed up with low prices they tied their boats up in protest for three weeks, right in the beginning of the summer. What had happened was that even though the fishermen in the area had set a record the previous year—their catches had totalled up to nearly seventy and a half million dollars—the competition, the escalating operating costs and lower dockside prices were leaving a good many of them with holes instead of money in their pockets.

"It was a bad time," Jaime said, "and Bill was in the thick of it. He's part owner of several trawlers, as I've told you, but he's also involved in the processing end of the business. So he was torn two ways. He had to go along with the fishermen and the other boat owners where the tie-up was concerned, but he also had to stand fast with the processors when it came to the fishermen's demands for guaranteed minimum fish prices. You see, what happened was there was so much fish that the market became glutted and the prices dropped next to nothing. But the area processors couldn't remain competitive with other New England ports serving similar markets if they made a minimum guarantee.

"As one of the local newspaper accounts put it at the time, the tie-up vented a lot of anger and frustration...but it didn't accomplish much more than that. After a while the fishermen put back out to sea after a temporary plan had been agreed upon whereby they'd force prices up by deliberately limiting the catches.

"Every time something like that happens, though, it leaves a lot of bad feeling in its wake. About a year after the tie-up, the workers in the processing houses went on strike, and that crippled the whole industry. The processors include workers who trim, weigh and fillet the fish, and those who pack it. You're dealing with both skilled and unskilled labor, which was one of the problems. There was a wage differential, as you might expect, and what the plant owners proposed was a pay cut for most of the trimmers, weighers and packers, and a slight increase for the cutters. The idea didn't go over very well." Jaime paused. "Am I boring you?"

"No," Diana said quickly. "No. It's very interesting."

"Just about everyone involved with fishing, as with almost everything else these days, belongs to a union," Jaime went on. "And of course things came to a grinding halt when the fish lumpers—they're the men who unload the boats—decided to honor the seafood workers' picket lines.

"Fish is a highly perishable commodity. Despite everything, the plant owners managed to keep fish moving out of the area—without the workers who had gone on strike.

"It was a long strike, finally it was settled, but not to everyone's satisfaction, and it left a great deal of bitterness," Jaime concluded. "The whole thing took a lot out of Bill, and I was so busy myself during the time when he was dealing with a lot of his problems, that I wasn't able to be of much help to him. He still has constantly nagging problems, for that matter, in connection with his work.

"If he had a son," Jaime said reflectively, "it would be different. He'd have someone else to take over some of the burden, just as he did from my father. As it is. . . . Yes, I wish in a way that it would work out so that Connie does marry Manny Ribeiro, because it would be a big break for Bill. Manny's a smart boy, and God knows fishing is in his blood. Bill could take him in as a partner, one day he could take over for Bill. What I'd like to see is for Bill to get a long, long rest away from the whole picture.

"But," Jaime said, a rather strange smile curving his lips, "we seldom can have things exactly as we want them, can we?"

CHAPTER FIFTEEN

CONNIE APPEARED at nine o'clock the Monday morning after Christmas, ready to go to work. Jaime had brought back a typewriter from Boston and had helped convert the dining room into a temporary office. He'd brought Connie with him when he'd done so, and the three of them worked together. Diana had suggested that Connie make most of the decisions about what was to go where, since it was to be her working space.

The atmosphere was friendly and relaxed, and it was a real letdown for Diana when Jaime and Connie left...especially since she'd had no chance at all to talk to him alone.

Actually, there'd been no opportunity for Diana to be alone with him since that evening after her party, and she began to be convinced that the situation was by his own design.

She didn't know how to interpret any of this. It was impossible to evaluate much where Jaime was concerned without knowing what had transpired between him and his ex-wife the day they'd had lunch together. And Jaime didn't seem to be about to satisfy her curiosity.

With Connie on hand, Diana forced herself to

get down to work, and it proved to be good therapy. Connie was an excellent typist and well organized, and she was very quick to grasp new concepts.

Diana discovered the convenience of having someone who could transcribe her notes into beautifully typed segments that made perfect sense. Connie was such a quick typist it was often easier to have her copy selected paragraphs from reference books than it was to xerox entire pages.

"Just don't forget to list the author, the publisher and the date of publication with everything you copy," Diana warned, "so that we can get copyright permission later, wherever we need it."

She knew that having told Connie this once, she'd never have to tell her again.

As the week passed, they made steady progress. Connie had a real talent for research and was fascinated by history. Diana could not have asked for a better assistant, and she began to relax, knowing that finally she had a real grip on her project, a sense of direction. She was reaching the point where she'd be going out and talking to people next. She'd made notes of organizations like the Portuguese-American Civic League, which she wanted to contact, and she was sure that once she'd begun to do so one thing would lead to another.

And there was, of course, Profetina. Profetina had asked her to come back by herself for a visit, and Diana had every intention of doing so. She'd decided, though, that she would wait till after New Year's. Once the *Menino Jesus* display had been taken down in her front parlor, Profetina would doubtless have more time to herself.

The day before New Year's Eve Jaime appeared unexpectedly to announce that he had an invitation. "For both of you," he said, smiling at Diana and Connie.

"There's a small Portuguese café over in Fall River that I've gone to occasionally. Tonight they're going to have a *fadista* right from Lisbon and I thought you might like to go hear her."

"A *fadista*?" Diana repeated.

"The *fado* is the song of Portugal," Jaime told her. "To some it's the soul of Portugal. *Fado* means fate, and the music is haunting, tremendously sad. Usually lost loves are wept for, lost illusions are deplored and," Jaime added, with a soberness that surprised Diana, "the inevitability of death is lamented. The music is bittersweet and melancholic...it's almost always in a minor key. There are male *fado* singers, but the *fadistas* are the most famous and the best, in my opinion. They usually dress in black and wear black shawls over their shoulders. Are you intrigued?"

"Tremendously."

"And you, Connie? I spoke to Manny and he's free to come, if you're interested."

The expression on Connie's face made it clear that she'd be interested, at this point, no matter what form of entertainment the evening was offering.

THE CAFÉ WAS VERY SMALL, and crowded. Diana marveled that there was space enough in which to seat four more people. Their table was close to the tiny dance floor and bandstand and she suspected that Jaime knew the owner or else he must have done some elaborate tipping in order to secure it for them.

They'd stopped at a fast-food place for something to eat on the way over and it was nine or so when they walked into the little Portuguese night club. Jaime ordered an imported Portuguese beer for himself and Manny, and glasses of port for the two women.

Manny was wearing the same suit he'd worn to Profetina's on Christmas Eve, but tonight he wore a vivid gold turtleneck with it that highlighted his dark coloring. He was pensive, and Connie kept darting anxious glances at him.

Jaime carried the conversation, commenting on the beer, which, he said, was especially full flavored. He offered Diana a taste of it, but she declined. "Another time, but not with port," she told him.

"You're probably right. Do you like the *fado*, Manny?"

Manny shrugged. "I've never heard much *fado*," he admitted.

"I guess you know more about rock and new wave," Jaime suggested.

"I guess I do," Manny admitted sheepishly.

"I don't imagine you've heard too much *fado* either, have you, Connie?"

"No," she replied. "My father has a *fado* record but my mother doesn't like him to play it. She says it gives her gooseflesh."

Jaime laughed. "I suppose it could," he admitted. "Particularly if you understand the lyrics."

The music in the little café had been strictly jukebox variety so far, but now the lights dimmed, the jukebox was shut off, and the room became so quiet it was hard to believe that everyone in it had been chattering noisily only a moment before.

In the hush, three people came through a door that opened to the back of the café. A short, rather dumpy woman and two men, each carrying a guitar.

"The one on the left has a Portuguese guitar," Jaime whispered to Diana. "If you look closely, you'll see it has seven strings. The man on the right will play the better-known six-string Spanish guitar."

Diana nodded, but her eyes were fixed on the *fadista*. Although she was a woman you would pass on the street a hundred times without noticing, when you looked directly into her face the effect was dramatic and compelling.

She wore a black dress as shapeless as her figure, and a black shawl, heavily fringed, was draped around her shoulders. Her hair, as black as Jaime's, was parted in the center then drawn back into a bun at the nape of her neck. Her eyes, too, were as dark as Jaime's, eloquent and full of a deep sadness as they roamed around the room. Her skin, in contrast to the dark hair and eyes, was gardenia white, and her full, sensual mouth was a deep carmine.

There was no particular style to her manner as

she stepped up to the microphone, but then the guitarists, behind her, began to strum their instruments, and the atmosphere became electric. The *fadista* started to sing, and for the first time Diana fully realized that the human voice was truly an instrument. The woman's range was astonishing. She seemed to take high notes and low with equal ease, but it was the tone and quality of her singing that made it so unique. She ran the gamut of emotions in her song, happy to the point of laughter at one moment, then plunged into a bottomless abyss of sorrow the next.

When she'd finished the first song the applause was thunderous, and the *fadista* bowed, as if she was slightly tired of all this and wanted to get back to her singing. Over and over she muttered in low tones, *"Muita obrigada. Muita obrigada."* Then she said, *"Coimbra,"* and someone in the back of the room cheered before that breathless silence came to reign again.

Jaime whispered in Diana's ear, "This melody will be familiar to you. It is the original version of 'April in Portugal.' Coimbra is a very old university town in Portugal, and in this song the *fadista* tells us that the real teachers in Coimbra are the singers who teach the language of dreams. She says that the faculty is on the moon, and the books are beautiful women. And she also sings of a very sad and famous love affair that took place in Coimbra a long time ago...."

Jaime stopped speaking as the guitarists began to strum, doing magical things with their flying fingers. Then the *fadista* began to sing again, and Diana was transfixed. The melody was familiar as Jaime had pointed out, but if he hadn't told her she doubted she would have recognized the song, so unusual was the *fadista*'s treatment of it.

This time, after acknowledging the applause, the *fadista* said, *"Barco Negro,"* and Diana, who had studied a little Spanish in school, asked Jaime, "Would that mean 'Black Boat'?"

Reluctantly he nodded. "It is a very sad song," he said quietly. "It tells the story of a woman whose lover, a fisherman, has been lost at sea, but she doesn't want to believe he is dead. Then she sees a black cross on a rock and she is filled with fear. She goes down to the beach to search for her lover, and she meets some old women who tell her he is dead, that he will never come back, but she thinks they are crazy. She refuses to believe them. Then she sees a black boat out on the waves and she sees an arm upthrust from the water, and she knows it is her lover. She knows that he is saying goodbye to her. But after that she sees him everywhere: when the wind is blowing, when the waves are high, in her empty house, in the very deepest part of her soul. And she tells herself that he will never leave her, that he will always be there. She tells herself that the old women were insane."

Jaime's voice trailed off as the *fadista* began to sing, and for a moment Diana didn't think she could bear to listen to the song. There had been something in Jaime's tone—a note of doom—that made her shudder. She tried to tell herself she was being overly imaginative. The *fadista* was reaching new emotional heights, and it was impossible not to fall under the magic of her incredible spell. But then Diana glanced at Connie. She was staring ahead, her face a mask of agony.

So Connie understood Portuguese and knew what the lyrics meant. Diana glanced at Manny and realized that even though he'd said he didn't know anything about the *fado*, he, too, understood what the singer was saying. His lips were compressed, and he was staring down at the table in front of him as intently as Connie was looking out into space.

No wonder Jaime had said that the *fado* was the heart of Portugal, the spirit of the Portuguese people. So many of the people in this little café were themselves close to the sea, and it was a long moment after the *fadista* had finished the song before the applause broke out.

DIANA SAT IN THE FRONT SEAT of the Mercedes with Jaime on the way back to Fairhaven. The evening had had a powerful effect on her. The *fadista* had moved her tremendously, the memory of the song about the black boat was both sobering and ominous.

"Did you enjoy it?" Jaime asked quietly.

"Enjoy it? That's too moderate a word, Jaime. It was an experience I'll never forget."

"I was watching you," he said. "I hope you won't take offense at this, but I didn't expect someone as quintessentially Anglo-Saxon as you are to react the way you did."

"Do you think a person has to be Portuguese to feel things?" she asked, miffed.

He laughed. "No. No, of course not. You don't really think I'm as narrow as that, do you?"

Diana didn't answer him. She was aware of Connie and Manny in the back seat. They were talking in low tones, and they sounded very intense.

"Hey," Jaime persisted, "you *don't* think I'm such a narrow-minded idiot as that, do you?"

"No," she said shortly.

"*Menina*, I told you I didn't mean to offend you."

"Well, I don't like to think I'm considered incapable of any real depth of feeling because my ancestry dates back to the *Mayflower*," she said defiantly.

His laugh was open and completely genuine. "That's the last thing I would ever accuse you of," he assured her. "You've done more to relieve me of some of my previous misconceptions than anyone I've ever known."

"Including your ex-wife?" Diana could have bitten her tongue off for having let this question explode from her.

"Especially my ex-wife! And what brought out that kind of remark?"

Diana didn't want Manny and Connie to hear them bickering. "Don't speak so loud, do you mind?" she said irritably. "What brought it out? I've been wondering if you've decided to go back to her, that's all."

Jaime diverted his attention from the road ahead just long enough to bestow a knowing smile on her. "I was under the impression that you weren't jealous of Cynthia."

"I'm not," Diana told him hastily.

"You're fibbing, *menina*," Jaime told her, his low, mellow voice very tender. "And I'm delighted!"

There was nothing she could say to this, and Jaime, for his part, seemed to be perfectly content with the ensuing silence.

To her surprise, he dropped her off first before taking Connie and Manny home. He got out of the car and insisted on unlocking the front door for Diana then waited until she'd switched on some lights. "I'll see you tomorrow, *menina*," he said, and with that he left her.

By the time she went to bed that night Diana had come to the conclusion that Jaime Medeiros was the most unpredictable man she'd ever met.

Gail and Howard had suggested that she come to the Cape for New Year's Eve and go to a party with them in Hyannis, but she'd declined. Now she wished she'd accepted, but it was too late to call and say she'd changed her mind.

With morning's arrival, Diana decided that if she was going to see the New Year in by herself she'd do it in style. Once Connie had left she drove to a supermarket and bought some fancy hors d'oeuvres, and then she stopped at a package store and bought a bottle of chilled champagne. Home again, she took a fragrant bubble bath, then curled up for a long nap, just as if she was getting ready for a very special date.

Well, in a sense she was, she told herself, as she put on an emerald-green lounger and some slim silver slippers. She had a date with herself tonight, and she was determined that she was going to enjoy her own company!

She turned on the TV, willing to accept any fare it had to offer, and was trying to decide when she should open the champagne when Jaime walked into her living room as casually as if he owned the house.

He stopped short when he saw her. "I didn't think you were here."

"What gave you that idea?" Diana asked coldly.

"I saw you go out a while ago. Then I guess I must have dozed off. I didn't hear you come back. When I looked across, your car wasn't in the driveway. Then I saw lights on over here and decided I'd better use the key you gave me to investigate."

"I put my car in the garage," Diana said stiffly. "But I appreciate your concern."

"I brought along a bottle of champagne in case you came back. But I was getting worried that you might not come back. I'm afraid I didn't make myself very clear last night."

"Oh?"

"When I told you I'd see you tonight I meant that I wanted to see the New Year in with you, *menina*," Jaime said rather lamely.

"Oh?" she repeated again.

He frowned. "Okay, I hedged," he admitted. "But I also knew I couldn't possibly stay over there—" he pointed in the direction of his house "—with you over here. So. . ."

"Yes?"

"Monosyllabic tonight, aren't you? So I bought some champagne and. . .will you join me in a glass?"

"I bought some champagne myself," Diana said ungraciously.

Jaime was a shade too casual as he asked the next question. "Are you expecting someone?"

"Tonight?" Diana hesitated, knowing that it would be fun to tell him that she was, and he had it coming, damn it! But her innate sense of honesty triumphed. "No," she replied.

Jaime grinned. "Good," he told her, "because I think if I'd come in here and found you drinking champagne with someone else I'd have tossed him out on his ear. What you do at the beginning of a new year is very important, you know."

Diana smiled. "I didn't know you were superstitious."

"Everyone's superstitious to some extent," Jaime informed her. "Anyway, there's an old saying that whatever you do as the new year starts—and all through New Year's Day—will set the pattern for what you'll be doing the rest of the year. That, *menina*, is why I want to be with you at midnight. Now, shall we open my bottle of champagne first, before it gets warm?"

He was on his way out to the kitchen before she could answer, and she slowly trailed along behind him. He was already busy with the cork on the champagne bottle. "Before I actually pop this you'd better have a couple of glasses ready. I don't always do a perfect job and I don't want to lose all the bubbles down the sink."

Diana found a couple of long-stemmed glasses and took them over to him. They weren't exactly champagne glasses but they'd do. She watched him thumb out the cork, heard the resounding pop, and then quickly held out a glass while Jaime poured some champagne into it. He filled his own glass and clicked it with hers. His voice was low and mellow as he said, "May this be the best year of your life—so far—*menina*!"

She felt a sudden lump in her throat and said shakily, "And the best year of yours!"

"I'll drink to that," Jaime agreed.

The champagne bubbles tickled Diana's nose. She'd never been particularly fond of the taste of champagne, but there was no doubt that it was the most festive of all beverages.

"Shall we go back to the living room or sit here at the kitchen table for a while?" Jaime asked.

His proximity was already becoming too disturbing, and in the interest of her emotional safety she said, "Let's stay here."

As he sat down, Jaime said, "That robe thing you're wearing is very becoming. I should have changed my clothes before I came over here."

In Diana's opinion, he couldn't have looked

better. He was wearing a handknit fisherman's sweater in an ivory shade and black corduroy slacks.

"That's a really beautiful sweater," she said.

"Profetina made it. She's terrific with knitting needles and she loves to do things like this. Would you like one?"

"Jaime, for heaven's sake, that's a labor of love!"

"I think Profetina would be happy to perform a labor of love for you. Incidentally, are you going to go see her one of these days?"

"Yes. Yes, I am," Diana told him. "I was thinking about it only this afternoon."

"Menina . . . ."

"Yes?"

"I don't know how to put this. It sounds pretty crazy, I know, to make this particular analogy, but on the Chinese New Year's Eve—they go by a different calendar than we do—the Chinese people aim to settle up all their debts, to clear the past and make room for the future."

"I didn't know that, but I like the concept," Diana said.

"I'd like to expand upon it. I've done a lot of talking about the obstacles that stand in our way, and I'd like to clear them up."

"How?" Diana asked directly.

"Well, I'd say we have two obstacles where you're concerned—about me, that is—and one obstacle where I'm concerned, about you. One of mine is major, one is minor. Shall I start with the minor one first?"

"Y-yes," Diana replied doubtfully, wondering just what they were about to get into.

"I'd say Cynthia has been an obstacle in my path, from your point of view," Jaime told her. "But I told you the truth when I said it's a long while since I've felt any love for Cynthia. More than that—and I've gone into this with you, too—I doubt that I ever really *loved* her in the first place."

"So you've said," Diana admitted.

"*Querida minha,* don't look so unhappy. That's not the point of this discussion. Look, I admit I've deliberately held off telling you what transpired with Cynthia at lunch the other day because you tried to make it so plain to me that you didn't give a damn!"

"Jaime!"

"Then you do give a damn?" There was a devilish glint in his eyes.

"Stop it!"

"Okay, so you don't have to answer that question. I think I once mentioned to you that Cynthia has had a habit of popping into my life at various odd and inconvenient times since our divorce. That's why I made that ill-chosen remark to you when we first met. I asked you if she'd sent you here to spy on me, which was ridiculous, as I've since admitted. Well...when I agreed to go to lunch with her the other day, it was because I wanted to tell her it was the last time I intended to have an arranged meeting with her. If we bump into each other somewhere, I'll be civilized, but I want her out of my life, that's all. There's no room for her in it.''

"You told her *that*?"

"Precisely."

"My God, Jaime. How did she react?"

"Not very well. It turned out she'd called me because she decided that she'd made a terrible mistake in agreeing to our divorce in the first place. She said she wanted to come back to me. I can assure you that her wanting to come back had absolutely nothing at all to do with love. It was a matter of her salvaging some of her wounded pride after the failure of her second marriage. Anyway," Jaime said quietly, "we were not the best of friends when we parted. Cynthia quickly became her old, vituperative self when she realized I wasn't interested, and she said a lot of things that would have been better left unsaid. But she no longer has the power to hurt me. If anything, I feel sorry for her. End of chapter." Jaime smiled. "I want you to know there's no obstacle at all, where my past marriage is concerned."

Diana didn't know how to answer him. She finished off her champagne to give herself a momentary diversion, and to her consternation Jaime immediately refilled her glass.

"Now," he said, "we've got to talk about you, Diana."

She wasn't ready for this. An onrush of tension made her voice tight as she spoke. "I'm not sure I want to talk about me."

"We have to talk about you," Jaime said firmly. "As a starter, am I right in assuming from some of the things you've said that love had died out of your marriage long before Gary was killed?"

He spoke so matter of factly that it had a calming effect. Still, Diana's voice was tense as she said, "Yes. Yes, that's true."

"Do you want to tell me about Gary—and your marriage?"

"There isn't all that much to tell," she answered sadly. "I met him at a party some mutual friends gave. That was while I was in graduate school."

"Was he in history, too?"

"No," she said. "He was an environment-systems analyst. He was involved in designing, developing and executing air-pollution control systems at the time he...died. All very technical work. Gary was definitely hi-tech, in every sense of the word."

She gazed at Jaime imploringly. "There really is so little to tell. Our marriage didn't work from the very beginning. Gary was not a one-woman man, I don't know any other way to put it. I wanted to keep trying, not because I imagined that there was any love left in our relationship but because I, well, I guess I believed in marriage as an institution," she finished, smiling faintly.

"So," he said, "it isn't because you're mourning Gary as a husband and lover that you can't come to grips with your life but because you think you're responsible for his death. Am I right?"

She moistened her lips. "Yes," she admitted. "Yes, you're right."

"You're not responsible, Diana," Jaime said. "And I can prove it!"

Diana closed her eyes tightly. Already the memories of that terrible night were surfacing, and she didn't want to deal with them. "Jaime, you don't know what you're saying!" she said shakily.

"But I do," he assured her. "Remember the day you met me at the New Bedford Library, when you were coming out and I was going in?"

"Yes, of course I remember."

"Well, I postponed what I'd intended to do so that I could take you to lunch and then trim the Christmas tree with you. But I went back the next day, and I found what I wanted. There was a detailed account of your accident in the local papers."

Her eyes were huge. "What are you saying?" she demanded.

"I'm saying that I wanted to get at the facts, for the sake of my own peace of mind as well as yours. As it happens, Paul St. Pierre, who went to high school with me here just as Phil Howland did, is now on the Fairhaven police force. I found out from the newspaper account he was the one who responded to the accident call that night, and he was immediately followed by the state police. They got further assistance from the New Bedford police. So, I went and saw Paul—"

"I can't believe this," Diana whispered. "Why are you doing this? Why are you bringing all of this up?"

"Because you've got to exorcise your ghost,

that's why,'' Jaime said abruptly. ''And you can't do it by deciding you were guilty and then retreating while you try to thrust the whole thing deep into your subconscious. Believe me, I know what I'm saying, Diana. I've pushed a lot of things deep into my own subconscious, and they've stayed there and become very heavy weights. That's why I talked to Paul, and why he got out the official accident reports and let me see them. Then I went and talked to the medical examiner who pronounced your husband dead at the scene. And. . . .''

Diana pushed back her chair and got to her feet, shaking. ''Will you stop?'' she pleaded, her voice edging toward a scream. ''I've already been through this once. The police made their investigation while I was still in the hospital and they told me there would be no charges laid against me. . . .''

''But you couldn't believe that what they were saying meant you were innocent, could you?'' Jaime accused. And then he said firmly, ''No. I'm not going to stop. You're going to hear this, Diana, and you're going to get it into your mind once and for all that you were in no way responsible for the accident. I've got xeroxes of the reports, thanks to Paul. You can read them. I've also jotted down notes from things the medical examiner told me, and I've talked to the state police. It all adds up to the same conclusion. The road conditions were hazardous that night. There was a pickup truck passing the bus in front of you, and he cut in sharply. The bus driver automatically slammed on his brakes, a foolish thing to do on an icy road but he didn't have much choice. He started to skid. At the same time there was a car passing you. You were trapped. Obviously you slowed immediately, but there was an icy patch on the road and you also skidded. The car that was behind you plowed into you and there was a chain reaction. The pickup truck, whose driver caused the whole thing to happen, got away free. They put out an All Points Bulletin for him but nothing ever came of it. The weather was against any police search, and probably the truck was just going to some point in New Bedford and easily dropped out of sight."

Diana had stopped shaking and she was standing still as a statue by the time he'd finished.

"As I've said," Jaime told her, "I have all the reports, all the notes. You can read them for yourself."

She shook her head. "I don't want to read them," she said. And she added, very softly, "I believe you, Jaime. I don't know what to say, that's all. I believe you, but I still can't simply... absolve myself. I believe what you're saying, but it doesn't sink in!"

He came over to her and put his arms around her, and she rested her head against his shoulder. "It'll take a little time, *menina*. Ghosts may be ephemeral creatures, but they don't tend to float away easily and leave you in peace. You have to throw them out. You're going to have to put this out of yourself, my dear one, and it'll take a little time. But the worst is over. You'll know, one of these days, deep down inside you, all the way through you, what happened that night was an accident. A terrible, tragic accident. But still an accident, and not your fault at all.''

Jaime stroked her hair as she clung to him. Then he said softly, ''And now we have one more ghost to exorcise, don't we, *menina*? My ghost.''

CHAPTER SIXTEEN

JAIME RELEASED DIANA. "I'm going to open the other bottle of champagne."

She was astonished to think that they'd finished the first one. She'd consumed her share, she knew. Jaime had refilled her glass more than once, but she wasn't even feeling it. Or could it be that the effect had been negated by her emotionally intense response to his discussion of the accident?

And now. She was almost afraid to hear what he was going to say next.

"Let's go into the living room," he suggested abruptly.

Jaime, Diana noted, was bringing the bottle of champagne with him. But it was the sole festive note in the staid, Victorian living room. The darkened Christmas tree standing in the corner seemed more of a reminder of a time gone by than a symbol of the holiday spirit. She turned on the lights and their multicolored radiance was as lovely as ever, but her mood didn't brighten.

Jaime was silent for a long moment, and it was a silence Diana didn't know how to go about breaking. Finally he looked at her, his smile wistful. "It was one thing to talk about Cynthia," he admitted, "but this is something else again. I...."

His words trailed off, and she saw the pain in his eyes and wished she could help him. She cared enough about him to be able to say, "You don't have to talk about it if you don't want to."

"No, I *do* have to talk about it. I've put off talking about it long enough—even to myself. I've been just as guilty as you've been about sweeping things under the rug, Diana. Now...."

"This still may not be the time, Jaime."

He managed a short laugh. "The time will never be right for this particular confession." He drew a long breath. "All right," he said, "all right. Once, when you asked me why I'd given up medicine, I told you that I hadn't.... That medicine had given me up."

She nodded. "Yes."

"That was an oversimplification," Jaime said slowly. "The facts are that a series of events transpired that made it clear I had no rightful place in medicine."

Diana shook her head slowly. "I can't believe that. Just from my own experience, I can't believe that."

"Your experience, as you put it, came only a month or so before what was to be the beginning of the end for me," he told her wryly. "Only, of course, I didn't recognize the signposts when they were put up for me.

"It was the middle of January, and I'd had a rough week. One thing after the other. Things go in cycles like that, I know, but this had been an especially difficult time. You seldom have fatalities among your patients in reconstructive surgery, but sometimes despite your best efforts the results are not what you'd wish for. There are scars that sometimes can't be minimized, no matter how good the plastic surgeon is. Burn scars can be especially difficult, and that week I'd had two cases involving people who'd been burned. One was a young woman who must once have been very pretty. It's impossible not to think of the effect such a drastic change in appearance is going to have on the life of someone like that.

"The other patient was a child, and those cases are always tough. It's very hard to tell parents, who've come to you thinking that you can repair the damage, that you can't entirely. You can do something to minimize it, but you can't erase it.

"Those had been just two of the cases I'd had to deal with that week, and on this particular day I was putting in overtime in the operating room. My patient was a child, and the operation was to correct a congenital cleft palate.

"I'd just finished when I had a call from my assistant, who was handling our patients at my office across town that afternoon. He said he wanted to ask my opinion about a young woman who'd come in for consultation about a mole on her cheek she wanted removed.

"He'd examined the mole and he told me he was convinced it was a benign lesion, and in his opinion if it was removed, the scar would definitely be more unsightly than the mole itself. He'd told the young woman that and she wasn't too happy with his decision, so he thought he'd ask me about it. In fact, he wondered if I'd like to take a look at the girl myself.''

Jaime sighed deeply. "Frankly, I was exhausted, so I told my assistant that unless he felt it really necessary I'd pass, and go with his opinion. I suggested that if the girl wanted to come in the next day, I'd be glad to take a look at her. But I felt he was right. It would have been unwise to excise the lesion, if it was benign, for purely cosmetic reasons because it would have been impossible to do so without leaving a scar.

"Well...that was that. The girl didn't come back the next day, and for the next year or so both my assistant and I forgot all about her. It was just about a year later that the roof fell in,'' Jaime said. "That was another one of those periods when things go wrong in bunches. This time I'd also operated on a child with a congenital cleft palate, but—something that happens in one out of God knows how many times—infection set in and the child died. And on the heels of that, my assistant and I were slapped with a malpractice suit. That mole the girl'd had on her cheek hadn't been benign after all. We were informed that she'd died—malignant melanoma was the final diagnosis. Her parents were suing us because of the misdiagnosis made when she'd come to my office wishing to have the mole removed.''

"A suit was brought against you after a whole year?'' Diana asked.

"Yes. Actually, the suit was instituted about a month after the girl's death. And we lost it," Jaime added bitterly. "The court found negligence. A considerable sum was awarded to the bereaved parents. Fortunately my malpractice insurance covered it. Every doctor in practice today pays an arm and a leg for his malpractice insurance, because suing doctors has become such a popular sport.

"I don't mean to say," he added hastily, "that I feel the parents in this case were completely unjustified. On the contrary, they had a very good case."

"But not against you," Diana protested.

"Very definitely against me! It was my practice, Diana."

"But it was your assistant who made the diagnosis."

He shook his head. "That doesn't count. It was my responsibility. When he consulted me about his decision, I should have responded. I should have insisted upon seeing the young woman for myself. I should have recognized an element of his own uncertainty in what he was telling me. I wish she had come back the next day, as I'd asked, but that's neither here nor there."

"Well," Diana said reasonably, "you'd had an especially difficult time, you were tired. Aren't doctors allowed to get tired?"

"Not at the expense of someone's life," he said tersely.

"And what about the child who died?" Diana persisted. "You consider that your fault, too?"

"I was the one who operated. The incision *did*

become infected. The child *did* die,'' Jaime said tonelessly. "How could I possibly absolve myself of responsibility?"

"Because it seems to me that there must have been many other factors," Diana said. "Many other ways in which the incision could have become infected. I don't know that much about hospital routine, but it doesn't seem to me that a surgeon is responsible for absolutely everything...."

There was a cynical twist to Jaime's smile. "You're very much in the minority, when it comes to the general opinion of the lay public," he informed her.

"Perhaps I am. But if that's so, then the lay public is being exceedingly unfair," Diana said hotly. "Jaime, I can't believe that you gave up operating because of what you've just told me!"

His laugh was grim. "Do you think it should have taken more than that, Diana?"

"Yes, I think it should have taken more than that. A hell of a lot more than that!"

He surveyed her sadly. "You don't know what you're saying."

"I think I do know what I'm saying. Two unfortunate incidents—very unfortunate incidents, I admit—happened within a short space of time. And for some perverse reason you decided to let them wreck your career—and the rest of your life."

"I appreciate your trying to defend me," Jaime said slowly. "But believe me, my reasons were not perverse. I had to tell that child's parents their son was dead. Dead as the result of an operation that normally held a minimal risk. I had to testify in court with that dead girl's father and mother staring me in the face as if I was some kind of monster...."

"How many people have you given new life to, because of your skill?" Diana asked him, a tight edge to her voice. She was too close to tears, she warned herself, and the very last thing she should do, she knew, was to go to pieces in front of him right now. Still, her voice broke slightly as she said, "How many people have you made...as beautiful as ever?"

"That's what I said to you that night in the emergency room, isn't it?" he mused.

"Yes. And it's true, Jaime. My scar is minimal. I'm not saying that I considered myself beautiful before the accident or that I do now, but...."

"Your mirror must tell you that you're beautiful, *menina*," he said softly.

"I'm not interested in what my mirror tells me. What I'm interested in, Jaime, is your thinking about the many, many people who've been able to look into their mirrors without flinching, because of your talent."

"I appreciate what you're trying to say, what you're trying to do, but I went through everything there was to go through a long time ago." He held out his hands. "They're steady enough now," he said, "but would they be steady if I were to pick up a scalpel again? Do you think I could ever risk operating on anybody again, knowing that my confidence has been shot to hell? A surgeon without confidence shouldn't be let inside an operating room. A doctor who's afraid that he'll fall apart before he even starts in to work has no place in surgery. In that sense, medicine kicked me out the door. Medicine robbed me of that particular kind of ego without which a man can't possibly function as a surgeon.... It's an irreversible theft, Diana. Once it's taken away from you, nothing can bring it back.''

Jaime glanced at his wristwatch and said abruptly, "It's almost midnight. This is a hell of a way to see in the new year!"

He got up and refilled their glasses with champagne. Forcing a smile, he said, "The least we can do is drink a toast to the twelve months ahead of us.''

Diana hesitated. "So we're not to be like the Chinese after all?"

"What?"

"You said the Chinese set their records straight on New Year's Eve. They pay their debts. I presume that if they have ghosts to exorcise, they exorcise them. Well, we've exorcised two of our ghosts, Jaime. But the third...."

Jaime shook his head and his expression was so sad it tore at her, because she knew that there was no formula she could hope to find that would bring him instant happiness. "The third ghost is my nemesis," he said. "I wish I could live up to the Chinese tradition I've told you about, but I can't. It isn't that I haven't wanted to, that I don't want to...."

"Jaime," she moaned, sharing his suffering.

"Please, darling," he told her softly, "don't look at me like that. It isn't the end of the world, sweetheart! Come on! It's time to drink a toast to a new year, and a new future. The devil with our ghosts!"

IT WAS BITTERLY COLD the first few days of the new year. Connie came to the house to work one morning and she looked very worried. Her mind obviously was elsewhere, and finally Diana asked her if something was wrong.

"The *Miguel M* is going out today." When Diana looked puzzled she explained, "That's one of my father's trawlers. The...the one Manny works on."

"The *Miguel M*." Diana frowned, and then realized what the name must signify. "The trawler was named after your uncle who died at sea?"

"That's right." Connie nodded. "Macabre, isn't it? But it wasn't my father's idea. His father named the trawler before he died. I suppose maybe my dad could have changed it, but he didn't. Out of respect, I guess."

She shuddered. "I've always hated Manny being on that boat, maybe because of the name, maybe because my Uncle Miguel was lost at sea when he was even younger than Manny is now." Connie shivered. "I'm sorry, Diana. Look, let me get back to work and I promise I'll do better. I need something to occupy my mind."

Diana could understand. She, too, needed something to occupy her mind. She left Connie with a stack of notes to transcribe and then drove into New Bedford, parking her car in a lot as close to the public library as possible.

Entering the library building made her think of Jaime. It touched her deeply to think that he'd gone to so much trouble to try to "exorcise her ghost," as he'd put it. Amazingly, since New Year's Eve she'd thought so much about him and his own staggering problem that there'd been no time left in which to think about herself.

Now, in a sudden burst of clarity, she realized the magnitude of what Jaime had done for her. The very fact that she hadn't dwelled on the details he'd gone into proved more than anything else that he'd made it possible for her to erase her major "obstacle."

That terrible sense of guilt, that dreadful burden, had dissipated. Diana drew a long breath, still not quite able to believe it. Not quite able to believe that after three years, in which she'd lived a nightmare over and over again, she finally was free!

If only she could do the same thing for Jaime.

As she went upstairs to the genealogy room, where both back newspapers and books on area history and related subjects were kept, Diana realized how very helpless she felt where Jaime was concerned. They'd drunk their toast at midnight on New Year's Eve, and then she'd suggested that she make them something to eat. She had the fancy hors d'oeuvres she'd bought, and she was prepared to fix scrambled eggs and hot biscuits to go with them.

But Jaime, for once, had said that he wasn't hungry. He'd looked so tired it alarmed her. She'd wanted to make love to him, but she hadn't wanted to be spurned. Spurned? That was a word with echoes as Victorian as the furniture in Agatha DuBois's living room, yet it expressed her feelings. She didn't want Jaime to turn away from her. She couldn't bear the thought, and when he'd said it was time to say good night she'd let him go.

He'd kissed her with a tenderness that brought tears to her eyes, and she'd stood at the kitchen window, watching him trudge across to his house, her love for him overflowing. There had been a dejectedness to his figure that had torn at her heart.

These thoughts about Jaime kept overwhelming her as she scanned through old books and made meticulous notes and finally Diana gave up. It was impossible to concentrate, and if she persisted in trying to work she'd only make a hash of things.

Back in her car she contemplated doing some sightseeing, but it was too cold to wander around the New Bedford historic district, as she would like to have done.

New Bedford fascinated her as much as Fairhaven did. In both towns, the sea was always a presence. There was a perpetual salt tang to the air that became less noticeable after a time, yet it was there. Diana had only to sniff to remind herself she was close to the ocean.

Fairhaven had its fabulous architecture as a signature, but it also had its waterfront, usually choked with fishing boats of all description. Diana had learned, to her surprise, that Fairhaven boasted the largest fishing fleet in all of New England.

In New Bedford, too, life revolved around the waterfront, and ever since she'd been in the area Diana had been wanting to read *Moby Dick* again. She'd read a quote recently from Melville's famous book and had learned for the first time that he'd lived in New Bedford in between voyages as a whaling-ship seaman. In *Moby Dick*, he'd written that it seemed as if "the brave houses and flowery gardens of New Bedford were one and all harpooned and dragged up from the bottom of the sea."

That might not hold true today, for at the time Melville was writing, whaling had been New Bedford's life. Jaime had spoken to her about this one night, Diana remembered, when they were sitting in front of the fireplace in her living room together. He'd told her that in those days of whaling, the men from Fairhaven and New Bedford had set out from the harbor, which the two towns shared, on voyages that would take them away for two and three years at a time. Their search had been for the giant whales that yielded the oil to light the world's lamps. But this era had come to an end when petroleum was discovered in Pennsylvania in the mid-nineteenth century, and in a very short time the famous Whaling City had become a ghost town.

Then, later, Jaime had explained, New Bedford

had risen again to become one of the glass centers of the world. Some of the most beautiful glass ever made had been fashioned in New Bedford, and prized specimens of the Mount Washington and Pairpoint glass that had been made locally were museum pieces today.

Later the town had become a textile center, which accounted for the long, multistoried red brick mills that still lined the banks of the Acushnet River. Some of them were now abandoned, and some had been put to other uses. Eventually depressions had taken their toll until New Bedford had become a shabby town.

But over the past twenty years there had been a renaissance largely due to the effort of a group known as the Waterfront Historic Area League, or WHALE. A rescue mission had been mounted to save old structures, and an unbelievable amount of research had gone into restoring the historic area in the center of town. Driving around, Diana had already seen some of the results, and the effect was charming. The efforts to make embellishments such as the gaslit street lamps, the fences and storefronts absolutely authentic had more than paid off. The entire historic area had been repaved with cobblestones right up over Johnny Cake Hill, which, Diana had learned, was the historic heart of New Bedford.

"You can follow Melville's footsteps along those streets," Jaime had said. "You could spend hours in the Whaling Museum, which extends all the way to the top of the hill. It wasn't here in

Melville's day, of course, but the Seaman's Bethel, which stands directly across the street from the museum, was. It was built in 1832, and Melville immortalized it in *Moby Dick*. The Mariner's Home, right next door to it, was here long before Melville ever came to New Bedford. It dates back to 1790, and it has been providing a home to sailors for over a century. At twilight, the red and green port and starboard lanterns that light the doorway come on, and sometimes I've wondered if the men living inside imagine that they're back aboard ship again. . . ."

Jaime had told her he was going to show her all these things, but winter wasn't an ideal season in which to go sightseeing. As it was, Diana was shivering as she sat behind the wheel of her car, and she made a spur-of-the-moment decision.

It was no time to go sightseeing, but it would be a perfect time to visit Profetina.

She thought of calling Profetina first to see if such a visit would be convenient for her, and then decided to take a chance and just drop in. She'd paid careful attention to the streets they'd driven along on the way home Christmas Eve, knowing that she wanted to accept Profetina's invitation for a return call. She had no trouble reversing the direction now.

Along the way she spied a florist's shop, where she stopped and bought a dozen red roses. The price made her wince, but Profetina was more than worth it.

She couldn't have chosen a gift that would be

appreciated more. Profetina, Diana was sure, would have been glad to see her anyway, but the roses gave her visit a special meaning. Profetina put them in her best cut-crystal vase and proudly displayed them on an antique round table in her front parlor.

The parlor had been totally transformed from the setting for the *Menino Jesus* into a room much too cluttered for Diana's taste. There was a lot of furniture and all sorts of pictures, bric-a-brac and several religious statues, but it perfectly suited Profetina.

She insisted on making coffee and with it served plump molasses cookies that were "very Portuguese."

"In the old times," Profetina said, stirring sugar into her coffee, "as you may have heard, a lot of the men set sail for America from Portugal to escape the draft. And by the time they got here, all they had left to eat was molasses."

She looked across at Diana, her black eyes twinkling. "Jaime tells me you would like me to make you a sweater like his."

"Profetina!" Diana was embarrassed. "He never should have said such a thing!"

"You don't want a sweater?" The older woman seemed almost offended.

"I think his sweater is absolutely beautiful. But there's so much work involved in anything like that."

"I like to keep my hands busy," Profetina said. "I will make you a sweater, Diana. Perhaps you would like it in a color, rather than ivory, like Jaime's."

"I'd like anything you did," Diana said sincerely, and the old lady beamed.

"Jaime tells me that he took you to Fall River to hear a *fadista* from Portugal," Profetina commented.

"Yes, he did."

"He said you were very moved by the *fado*."

"Yes, I was. But I can't imagine anyone not being moved by the *fado*."

Profetina nodded. "It is like the cry of the soul," she said. "So different from our dances. Portuguese dance music is usually very lively... and the dances are such fun to do. There was a time, when I was young, that those of us who had come to this country kept up the old customs. There would be dances every Saturday night, usually in a place like a public hall. The girls would get all dressed up in bright-colored costumes. Then, first there would be a procession, with the girls in one line and the men in the other. After that, we would begin the dance.

"The favorite dance of all was *La Charmarita*. The name means to charm, so it was a very—how shall I say it—a very flirtatious sort of dance. Anyway, we thought we were flirting. To young people today it would seem very tame. But we had such good times.

"Later, when Jaime's father was young, they still had dances, but already the *Charmarita* was giving way to American dances, the young people all wanted to be 'modern' by then," Profetina said, sniffing slightly at the idea. "That is what makes me sad, that all of our old ways and our customs will fade away, as I think I told you when you were here at Christmas. That is why I have the *Menino Jesus* every year...."

"I'm so glad you do," Diana said. "I will never forget seeing it."

"Jaime has told me of your work," Profetina said. "I find it very interesting that you want to write so seriously about the Portuguese. I think there are many, many things I can tell you, Diana. I've lived for nearly a century."

"I know there are many things you can tell me," Diana said with a smile.

"Some of the old superstitions have lasted," Profetina reflected. "Not the way they used to be, of course, but especially around All Hallow's Eve— you call it Halloween—there are still old stories that the children like to hear. Sometimes some of the neighborhood children come in and I tell them these things, and one little girl told me this past Halloween that she loved the way I scared her."

Profetina smiled at the memory. "You see, in Portugal and in the islands—the Azores, I am speaking of—there were all kinds of witches and spirits, and of course those of us who came here were sure they'd followed us. There were *imaginarios* and *magicos, agoureiros, bruxas,* and *feiticeiras*. All very important, all very frightening. You could avoid their evil influences, though, by opening a pair of scissors in the form of a cross.

"Then," Profetina continued, "there were those things that everyone knew. If your hair started to fall out you had only to cut off a lock of it on Saint John's Night and bury it under a quick-growing plant, such as a pumpkin vine, and very soon you would have beautiful hair again."

"Which Saint John's Night?" Diana asked, knowing the question would delight the old lady. "As I understand it, there are at least twenty-seven Saint Johns!"

Profetina chortled. "So, just like Jaime tells me, you have been doing your homework! Well, the major feast of Saint John is on December twenty-seventh, but there is also a summertime feast, which was always my favorite. The men made large wooden crosses and decorated them with greens. To these they would attach fresh fruit and loaves of Portuguese bread wrapped in cellophane. We used to auction off the bread to raise money for the church. It was the tourist season, so the bread would bring some very high prices.

"In Portugal," Profetina said, "June thirteenth, which is St. Anthony's Day, is a favorite day for weddings. In fact it is considered such a fortunate day on which to get married that nuptial Masses are held all over the country. My husband—he was my fiancé then—didn't want to go in the military, he was never cut out for such a life. So when he knew he was going to be conscripted he decided to take his chance and go to America. It *was* a chance in those days. Sometimes the boats they sailed in were not very seaworthy.

"After he arrived here, he sent for me. We were married on June thirteenth," Profetina said, the light of memory shining in her eloquent eyes. "It was a very fortunate day. Perhaps you, one day, will choose that day for your wedding, Diana."

"I've been married, Profetina," Diana said honestly.

"I know." Profetina nodded. "Jaime told me. Like myself, you are a *viúva*."

"A widow? Yes, I am."

"But you are young, *cara*. Young and very pretty and, if you ask me, ready for true love. I think you will find true love, Diana. I think you already have found it, perhaps?"

It was more question than statement, and Diana was touched by the hopefulness in Profetina's voice.

"I think I have, Profetina," she said huskily. "I think I have. Oh, you can't know how much I hope I have!"

She was rewarded by the old woman's nod, and a beautifully knowing smile.

CHAPTER SEVENTEEN

THE DAY AFTER HER VISIT to Profetina Diana woke up with a sore throat, chills and a temperature of one hundred and two. She staggered downstairs, appalled by her own weakness, and was brewing herself a cup of tea when Connie arrived.

Connie took one look at her, assessed the situation, and ordered her back to bed. Diana was more than willing to comply. She felt as if her legs were going to go out from under her at any second.

Connie brought her tea up to her, plus a large glass of fruit juice, and insisted on adding an extra quilt to the bedclothes. She said she had plenty of transcribing to catch up on and added firmly that Diana was to get some rest and not worry about a thing.

Diana dozed off into the kind of deep, almost euphoric sleep that fever often brings. She had no idea how long she slept, but when she awakened she wondered if she could be hallucinating. Jaime was standing at her bedside, staring down at her with concerned eyes.

She managed a feeble, ''What are you doing here?'' Her throat hurt so much that it was painful to talk.

"Connie called me," he said briefly.

"She shouldn't have," Diana began, but he waved a dismissing hand at her.

"Don't try to talk," he told her, then a moment later he made sure she couldn't, by thrusting a thermometer into her mouth.

He sat down on the edge of the bed, his fingers encircling her wrist while he felt for her pulse with unmistakable expertise. When he read the thermometer he frowned slightly, then he drew back the bedclothes and held out his arms. "Here," he said, "I'll help you. I want you to try to sit up so I can listen to your chest."

From somewhere he produced a stethoscope, which he first moved across her back, then to various other strategic places on her chest all the way down to the hollow between her breasts.

Diana stole a glance at him and saw that he was deeply intent upon what he was doing. Right now she was not his *menina*. She was a patient.

He eased her back onto the pillows and said with a smile, "You'll live. I diagnose a case of plain, miserable, old-fashioned flu. About all we can do is see that you drink plenty of fluids and take some aspirin to reduce the fever. And, needless to say, stay in bed."

"I can't stay in bed," Diana protested feebly.

"Would you care to explain why?"

"I—I have to do things for myself," she told him.

"I won't even bother with an answer to that," he replied. "Connie and I will spell each other today, and I'll sleep on that bed in your guest room tonight so I can hear you if you want anything.'' He grinned. ''You're in excellent hands, *menina*. Connie's gone to the store to get some chicken. She's going to make homemade chicken soup for you. Maybe we've got some Jewish heritage somewhere in our background. And wait till Profetina hears you're sick. I'm sure she'll be sending over some potent Portuguese brew for you.''

He drew the covers back up over her, tucking them gently and securely around her shoulders. Then he bent and kissed her lightly on the forehead. ''Get some sleep. I'll look in on you from time to time, but whatever you do, don't try to come downstairs.''

Diana watched him leave the room and then closed her eyes. She had a headache, she had a sore throat, she felt sick, but she also felt as if she'd been wrapped in a cocoon of tenderness, and it was a warm and wonderful feeling. She succumbed to it and drifted off to sleep again, and when she awakened, someone had pulled down the window blinds to shut out the light, so she had no idea what time it was.

Not that it mattered. She wasn't going anyplace today; even *she* knew she wasn't in shape to navigate very far. She was content just to lie there, which surprised her considering she felt so miserable physically.

Connie appeared with another tall glass of fruit juice, moving stealthily until she saw that Diana was awake. Then she smiled, a smile that reminded Diana very much of Jaime.

"You've been asleep three hours, and Jaime's delighted with that," she reported. "Ready for a little chicken soup?"

"I'll try it," Diana said. "But I don't want you running up and down stairs...."

"Don't worry. I can use the exercise!"

"What time is it, Connie?"

"One o'clock. Jaime's gone to get you a prescription for something or other, but he'll be back shortly."

The only light showing around the window shades was a deep gray. "Is it snowing again?" Diana asked.

"No. It's foggy. A thick fog. The temperature's warmed up. The fog will melt away the snow."

"Really?"

"Yes. Maybe it's because there's so much salt in the fog here, I don't know exactly. But when we get a fog and there's snow on the ground, the snow begins to disappear as if by magic. Don't be surprised if there's nothing but bare ground when you're up and about again. Look, I'll go get your soup."

The soup was delicious, but Diana couldn't finish the entire bowl that Connie had brought her.

"That's all right," Connie assured her when she apologized for this. She smiled. "There's plenty more where this came from. You'll probably get tired of it. But I can remember my grandmother saying that chicken soup is the best thing for you when you're sick."

Connie's grandmother. That would be Jaime's mother. The beloved mother, for whom he'd bought the house next door...and then she'd never been able to live in it.

"What was she like, Connie?" Diana asked.

"What was who like?" Connie was busy setting out a box of tissues, the thermometer and a large, fresh glass of fruit juice on the table next to Diana's bed.

"Your grandmother."

"She was the dearest person I've ever known," Connie said. "She was small, not much taller than Profetina, and really beautiful. At the time I remember her she was old, of course—relatively old, anyway—but to me her face was beautiful even though life had left a lot of lines in it. She had eyes like Jaime's. You know?"

"Yes," Diana nodded. She didn't have to be told that Jaime had the most beautiful eyes in the world.

"My grandfather was a very stern man, except where she was concerned. He loved her so much. When he died, I remember my father saying that it was as well he'd died first because he never would have survived her death anyway." Connie paused. "Sometimes love is so great that one person doesn't want to live without the other," she finished soberly.

Diana knew that Connie was thinking of herself and Manny. Was it possible that Connie's love for this slender, dark-haired boy was really that intense?

And what about her own love for Jaime? Yes, her love for Jaime was that strong.

The medicine had put a temporary halt to her coughing. She nodded. "Yes."

"These things have to run their course. It takes patience, I know, and I suspect that patience isn't your greatest virtue."

"Oh?"

"It's not mine, either," Jaime admitted. "Do you think you can drift back to sleep?"

"Not just now," she croaked. "I've slept and slept and slept."

"All right. Then I'll stay here and talk to you for a little while. Don't try to talk back too much, though. That voice of yours has limitations at the moment."

"Tell me about it," she whispered grimly. But despite her difficulty talking, there was something she had to know.

"Did you—did you write the prescription for the cough medicine?" she asked him.

He looked surprised. "Yes. Why?"

"I. . . I guess I didn't know you could do things like that when you. . . when you're not practicing."

"I wasn't thrown out of the profession, *menina*," he told her. "I didn't lose my license, if that's what you've been thinking. I'm still legally entitled to practice, and I keep up with everything that's going on in my field." He forced a smile. "For the first time in my professional life I read the *New England Journal of Medicine* from cover to cover. I never had enough hours for that before. Like most physicians I used to skim the contents and concentrate on those articles of especial interest to me.''

A faint glimmer of hope coursed through Diana. If Jaime was still that intent on keeping abreast of what was going on in medicine, might that not mean his decision to abandon his profession was not as final as he'd indicated?

He seemed to read her mind, and he shook his head slowly. ''If there has to be a reason why,'' he said, ''let's call it habit. Like a person renewing his driver's license even though he knows he's in no shape to drive. He knows he'll never drive again, yet he perversely keeps the piece of paper that gives him the right to do so.'' He stood. ''Don't jump to false conclusions.... Now, I think if I leave you alone maybe you'll go back to sleep again after all.''

Diana didn't go back to sleep, though, for quite some time. Maybe Jaime was still convinced that he'd never return to surgery... but *she* wasn't, she decided stubbornly. He *had* to go back. Somehow, some way, she was going to have to make him see that. It was the one real contribution she could make to him, even if she aroused his antagonism in the process to the point where she... lost him.

Jaime was a dedicated doctor and a master at what he did. It was wrong of him to deprive people of his talents, and she had to convince him so. She felt strongly that the two terrible experiences that had caused him so much suffering would only, in the final analysis, make him an even better doctor. People were sometimes strengthened by tragedy, if they could manage to live through its trauma.

With this thought Diana drifted back into fever-induced slumber, and she dreamed of Jaime, dark and handsome in his operating gown.

DIANA FELT WORSE before she felt better, which Jaime told her was par for the course. But despite her own physical misery she noticed that Connie was going through another kind of misery. There were dark circles under her eyes, and she was jittery. Even the slightest unexpected sound made her jump.

When Connie had gone home one evening, and Diana was alone with Jaime, she asked him about his niece.

He frowned. "She's worried about Manny. The *Miguel M* set out to fish off Georges Bank, but Bill said they were going to go farther, depending on the way the fish are running. Henry Andrade's the captain of the boat, and I know Henry. He's not one to put back until he's got all the fish the boat will hold. The problem is, there's a storm brewing out at sea, to the southwest of here. . . ."

"The southwest?"

Jaime nodded. "Think of a map of the United States, and then picture how the coastline curves. New York, for example, is more west than south of us. This storm is off the Carolinas and it's moving slowly. There's a chance it may veer out to the open sea, but if it follows the coast we're apt to be right in its path. If it intensifies and turns into a full-fledged winter storm, there could be trouble."

"But the trawlers get the marine advisories, don't they?" Diana asked.

She was sitting in an armchair in her bedroom, the most comfortable chair in the house, Jaime had discovered. He'd even offered to move it downstairs so she could have a change of scene in a day or so. Diana fully intended to be up and around and on her own before much more time passed, though. Between Connie and Jaime she'd had superlative care, and she was feeling much stronger.

"The marine advisories?" Jaime repeated. "Yes, of course the trawlers get all the weather bulletins. I tell Connie there's nothing to worry about. Even Henry should have the sense to start back if the situation gets any worse than it is now."

Diana glanced out the window. It was late afternoon, and twilight was just beginning to cast a mauve haze over the winter landscape outside her window. But now it was a winter landscape devoid of snow. Connie had been right. The fog she'd spoken of had melted away all traces of snow and ice.

"Can't your brother get in touch with the trawler captains and tell them to start back?" she asked.

"Yes, he could. But decisions like that are left to the men doing the job, Diana. They're supposed to know what they're doing, and it's their hide too, after all. Like most things, the cost of operating a trawler has risen tremendously over the past few years. Fuel prices are the biggest culprits. The trawlers use diesel, and I don't know what the latest price is, but last time I heard it was well over a dollar a gallon. A typical trawler will use around 4,000 gallons of diesel fuel on the average week-long fishing trip, so no captain wants to bring a boat in before he's gotten his full load of fish. He gets a share of the profits, so he wants to make the potential net profit as high as possible."

"If you had a greedy captain, that could be awfully dangerous," Diana observed.

"Yes, I suppose some men will take more risk than others," Jaime admitted. "But as I said, the captain also has his own hide to think of. He can drown just as easily as a crewman can. The men captaining the trawlers are veterans, remember. I think few if any of them would take needless chances. And anyway, there's a good chance the storm I'm talking about will go out to sea, well beyond the fishing grounds."

Diana thought back to Jaime's words, during the night when the wind began to howl. Windows rattled in the old DuBois house, boards creaked. She shivered. There was an unearthly, doleful sound to the wind's cry that made her go cold all over.

She got up, slipped on a warm robe and went to the window. The corner streetlight lit up the scene, and she could see the bare tree branches dancing a grotesque ballet as they were whipped by the wind. It was impossible not to think of the *Miguel M* out there somewhere in the vastness of the North Atlantic.

A voice behind her said, "Just what do you think you're doing out of bed?"

She turned to face Jaime, who was wearing the same clothes she'd seen him in earlier in the evening.

"Do you sleep in those?" she asked him.

"Yes."

"You've been sleeping in your clothes ever since you've been staying over here?"

"Yes. Don't look so horrified, Diana. I learned how to sleep comfortably with my clothes on way back when I was a med student doing my clinical rotations. Matter of fact, I learned how to go to sleep anywhere, anytime the opportunity presented itself. Friends of mine swore I could even sleep standing up, and I think maybe they were right. But," he added gently, "you haven't answered my question. It's two o'clock in the morning. Why are you up?"

"The wind woke me," Diana confessed. "Jaime, I can't get the thought of Manny's boat out of my mind."

"That makes two of us," Jaime said grimly. "Look, get back into bed, *menina*, and I'll go make us both some hot chocolate."

"I'll go downstairs with you."

"You will not go downstairs with me," he said firmly. "Here...." He crossed to turn on her bedside lamp. "Pull up the covers, keep yourself warm. I'll be back in a few minutes."

When he returned he was carrying a tray with two cups of hot chocolate on it and a plateful of cookies. But he couldn't suppress the anxiety in his eyes, and Diana asked quickly, "What is it?"

"That radio Agatha left in the kitchen has a weather band on it," he told her. "I got the marine forecast that's issued on a round-the-clock basis by the National Oceanic and Atmospheric Administration. It's not good. There's a winter-storm watch out for this area and one hundred miles out to sea. The storm's picked up speed, and it's intensifying."

He handed her the cup of hot chocolate and sat down on the side of her bed. "I don't like the sound of it. I hope the wind doesn't waken Connie. I don't want her going off the deep end again. I wish I could talk to Bill."

"Why don't you call him?" Diana suggested.

"I would, but I'm afraid Connie would hear the phone, and it would wake Flor up for sure. I may anyway, after a while. I'll listen to another forecast in half an hour or so. They update them regularly."

"Surely the captain.... What did you say his name is?"

"Henry Andrade."

"Well, surely Captain Andrade has had the weather forecast and he'll be heading back. Don't you think so, Jaime?"

"Very possibly. But it depends on when he decided to return and how far out they are. They may head directly into the full force of the storm on the way back. Right now there's no way of telling. A winter storm can be very unpredictable." He tried to smile at her, but it was a sketchy smile.

"There must be other trawlers out there too, don't you think?" she asked.

"Quite a few of them came back into port this afternoon," Jaime said. "Both here and in New Bedford. I stopped by to see Bill at the packing plant when I went out to get a few supplies while Connie was here. Two of his boats were coming in, he said, but he still didn't know about the *Miguel M.*"

"Wasn't he worried?"

"Yes. But in his business you get used to being worried. There's something for Bill to worry about most of the time. He has a lot of confidence in Andrade, though." Jaime shrugged. "We'll just have to wait and see."

"I don't know," Diana brooded. "I think that if I were your brother...."

Jaime looked amused, but he only said, "Yes?"

"Well, I think no matter how much confidence I had in a trawler captain, I'd tell him to head back if there was a storm warning out," Diana said firmly. "Especially if my...."

"Go on."

"Well, I was going to say especially if my son-in-law was on board as a crewmember," Diana told him. "But then, Manny isn't Bill's son-in-law, is he?"

"No," Jaime said soberly. "No, he isn't."

After a time Jaime left her, and Diana tried to go back to sleep. The moaning wind orchestrated her dreams. They were wild and turbulent, and when she awakened again she imagined that she could hear crashing waves in the distance and she knew she'd been dreaming about something terrible that involved the sea.

Still groggy, she heard a new sound, and opening her eyes she saw rain slashing against the bedroom window. It was a steady, pelting rain, and in another moment it changed to hail, icy round white globes that hit the glass like frozen mothballs.

She got up and went into the bathroom, and when she'd washed her face and brushed her hair she slipped on her warm robe and thrust her feet into her furry blue slippers, determined that she was going to go downstairs and do something constructive like making a pot of coffee for Jaime and herself.

Jaime was ahead of her, though. He was sitting at the kitchen table drinking a mug of coffee, his hair tousled, his face unshaven. A look at his red-rimmed eyes told Diana that he hadn't even slept as well as she had.

"Look," he began warningly, "I thought I told you...."

"Please, Jaime," she said quickly. "I'm all right, and I couldn't stay up there any longer. I...I had nightmares," she confessed, "and you...well, you look as if you didn't sleep at all."

"I didn't, not too much," he admitted. "I came down a while ago because I wanted to get the latest forecast...."

"Yes?"

"What's going on outside gives you some clue," Jaime said, glancing toward the window. "But we're only getting the edge of the storm. Out there—" he gestured toward the water "—it must be like being in hell." He sighed. "It's only six o'clock. You should still be asleep. No, don't say anything. For purely selfish reasons, I'm glad you're here. I...."

He broke off as the telephone rang, and in an instant he was across the kitchen, taking the receiver off the wall.

Diana watched his face and saw his mouth tighten. Then he said simply, the single phrase so full of misery that she flinched at the sound of it. "Oh, God!"

Jaime listened, then he said, "Okay. I'll be here. Keep in touch."

He hung up, then turned to face her. When he spoke his voice was rough with emotion. "It was Bill. He's been trying to reach Andrade, but he can't make radio contact with the *Miguel M.*" Jaime turned bleakly toward the window. The hail had reverted to a freezing rain that slashed viciously against the glass panes.

"With all that going on out there," Jaime said, gesturing in the direction of the sea, "Bill says there's not much doubt the *Miguel M* has run into trouble."

CHAPTER EIGHTEEN

"We shouldn't stay here, Jaime," Diana insisted. "We should go to Bill's house!"

"Don't be ridiculous!" Jaime snapped. "You're not going anywhere. If necessary, I'll go over there later. But right now...."

"Right now I think it would be a good idea for Connie to have you or me with her...or both of us," Diana said firmly. "Look, I'm all right, Jaime. I can take a thermos of fruit juice along with me."

"It's not your juice consumption I'm worried about. It's having you get chilled with the result that this whole thing could boomerang back on you...only with added complications the next time."

"Stop sounding like a doctor!" she demanded.

"I *am* a doctor!" he shot back, and then his lips twisted in a self-mocking smile. "I walked into that, didn't I," he observed quietly. "All right, *menina*, I guess you win. Go upstairs and get dressed. Slowly, do you hear? I'll go across and shave and put some other clothes on. You wear something warm. And don't step foot out of this house until I come and get you. I'm going to warm the car up first."

Diana obeyed instructions, knowing very well that Jaime would refuse to take her with him unless she did so. She dressed warmly and waited for him in the kitchen. Her heart was thumping madly all the time, and she felt as if she had something pressing on her chest. Her condition had nothing to do with the aftermath of the flu. She diagnosed what she was feeling as fear, pure, stark fear. In her dreams something terrible had happened out at sea. It was fuzzy now, as dreams are in the light of consciousness, but the effect it had left was enough to make her shudder. And the memory of the night when she and Jaime and Connie and Manny had gone to hear the *fadista* swept over her. She remembered Connie's face as she listened to the lyrics of the *fado* about the black boat, knowing what they meant.

Diana shivered. The song about the black boat, last night's dream...they seemed like premonitions of disaster.

And I'm the one who's always scoffed at superstition, Diana thought, waiting for Jaime. But no matter how she tried to deride her inner feelings, they clung. It was a great relief when Jaime finally appeared at the back door. Right now, weak though she was, Diana needed action.

They were silent during the course of the short drive. Jaime said only, "I called Flor and told her we were coming, and I asked her to put a couple of pillows and a blanket for you on her living-room couch."

"That wasn't necessary," Diana protested.

"Let her fuss over you," Jaime said roughly. "She'll need something to keep her occupied over these next hours.... We all will."

Bill was waiting for them at the front door of his house when they pulled up, and Flor was right behind him. Bill welcomed them warmly, but as he led the way into the living room Diana noticed that his limp was more discernible than usual.

"I suppose I should be down on the docks, or at the plant, but I stayed home because of Connie," he told them.

"Where is Connie?" Jaime asked quickly.

"She's locked herself up in her room," Flor replied. A glance at Flor had already told Diana that she had been crying. She seemed at the edge of tears once again.

This was a different Flor. She was wearing a pair of slacks that had seen better days and a sweater, and she'd put on very little makeup. Her hair was combed back smoothly and there was nothing chic about it, in contrast to her usual style. But it was surprisingly becoming. Without the strain that usually etched her face, Flor would be an attractive woman.

"I'll go up and talk to Connie," Jaime said. "Flor, get Diana settled in, will you? She's just gotten out of bed and this is the first day she hasn't run a fever. I didn't want her to come over here, but she insisted."

Diana started to protest that she didn't need any help, then she thought better of it. Remembering Jaime's admonition, she let Flor prop pillows behind her head and draw a hand-crocheted afghan up over her.

"It was wonderful of you to come, Diana," Flor said. "I know you must feel terrible still. The flu really takes it out of you. But if Connie will come down for anyone it will be you. She's taken a real liking to you."

"And I have to her, Flor," Diana replied warmly. "I've become very fond of Connie. She's a super assistant, but it's a lot more than that. She's a wonderful person."

Tears welled in Flor's eloquent black eyes, and Bill said, "Hey come on, you two. Look, Diana...."

"Yes?"

He hesitated. Unlike Jaime, Bill didn't have an easy way with words. Diana could sense this. But then Jaime had learned his own brand of eloquence the hard way. He'd had to be fluid verbally, once he'd become a successful surgeon. She remembered him speaking about the personal trauma involved in giving parents news about their children that they didn't want to hear. Yes, Jaime had become well-spoken out of necessity.

But it was a struggle for his brother. "Look...." Bill began again. "Flor and I really do appreciate you coming over here like this, Diana. And...what you've done for Connie. And I want to tell you right now, I only pray to God that Manny Ribeiro...."

He broke off, choked by his own emotion, and Flor said brokenly, "Bill!"

"Hey," Bill said, pulling himself together. "Hey, look, how about a drink. What do you say? I think we could all do with a drink, Flor."

"What would you like?" she asked, brushing back a stray tear with the back of her hand.

"What would you like, Diana?" Bill said, turning the question to his guest.

"I don't know," she confessed. "Anything that's fairly tall and cold."

"Vodka and tonic, maybe?" Bill suggested. "Unless you're taking medication. Are you on any medication?"

"No," Diana said. With the fever gone, she hadn't even had any aspirin today.

"Okay," Bill said, settling himself down in an armchair near the couch Diana was occupying. "Flor, you make the drinks, okay? You do it better than I do anyway."

Flor only nodded, but then she disappeared in the direction of the kitchen.

When Bill was sure his wife was out of earshot, he said, "Look, Diana, there's something I have to say to you. Flor and I have made a mistake with Connie and Manny. Don't think we don't know it. I admit it, I didn't want my daughter to marry a fisherman. I...I've seen what the sea can do." His voice was bitter.

"Yes," Diana said. "Yes, I know you have, Bill."

"I didn't want to see her let in for the kind of grief Flor has had," he went on, keeping his voice low. "Flor's been through a hell of a lot because of me. But now...well, you can't pick the person you want your kid to fall in love with, Diana.''

Diana smiled sadly. "You can't usually pick the person you want to fall in love with yourself, Bill. Sometimes...it just happens.''

Their eyes met, and she had the uncanny feeling that Bill Medeiros could also read her mind. Maybe it ran in the family, she thought wryly. But she was sure he knew she loved Jaime, as sure as if she'd just told him so.

"Don't give up on my brother, Diana," he said softly. "He's got a way to go to get back to himself. But you might be surprised at the long way he's already come...in a very short time. Since he met you.''

"Bill...'' she began.

He raised his hand, cutting her off. "No," he said, and he smiled, a smile that was so like Jaime's Diana could see why Flor had fallen in love with him. "You don't have to say anything, Diana. It's enough for me that I see something in Jaime these days that I haven't seen for a long time. It's like you've pushed the clouds away and brought out the sun. Jaime's living again. But....''

"Yes?"

"To get back to Connie and Manny," Bill said slowly, "well, if Manny gets back from this trip I'm going to give them my blessing, and so will Flor.''

Diana felt as if she'd swallowed a cold stone. She gulped. "*If*, Bill?"

"Yes," Bill said moodily. He sat forward, clasping his hands together, and she flinched from the torment she saw in his face. "I've been out on a trawler in a winter storm," he told her simply. "She ices all over, you could break your neck on the decks, and the rigging looks like it was made out of frozen crystal." He sighed deeply. "I should have had the guts to tell Henry Andrade to turn back two days ago, when I first heard there was a depression forming far, far south of here. But I didn't. I wanted the catch, Diana. We all want the catch. That's what means money. Hell, how I hate money!"

Diana had been lounging back against her pillows, but now she sat up straight. "Bill," she said, her tone more authoritative than she'd intended. "Don't start blaming yourself for this!"

He looked across at her quizzically. "Look," she continued. "I've been on a guilt trip for three years. Your brother just got me off my own emotional merry-go-round and I don't want to see anyone else getting on. Especially someone like you."

He raised his eyebrows, reminding her so much of Jaime that she felt a catch in her throat. "Especially someone like me?" he repeated.

"Yes... yes," Diana said softly. "In more ways than you may think, you're so very much like Jaime."

Jaime came downstairs just then. "Connie's going to join us after a while," he said. "Bill, what's the latest word?"

"There isn't any word," Bill answered glumly. "The minute anyone hears anything, that phone out in the hall will ring."

"Okay, then, let me change the question. What did you hear last?"

"I talked to Andrade at two o'clock this morning," Bill told him. "The radio was still okay then. He said they were getting a real blow. I told him I hoped he'd have the sense to start back. He said he'd already started back, they'd been on their way in for several hours. He told me he'd check with me again at 6:00 A.M. He didn't. That's when we started to try to raise the *Miguel M.*"

"Look," Jaime said, "because their radio is out doesn't mean they're necessarily in any great danger. That's what I've been trying to tell Connie."

"Would you like to take odds on that?" Bill asked ironically.

"With you? No. You're a pessimist, as I damned well know."

"I have a reason to be a pessimist, thanks," Bill said heavily.

"So do a lot of us. That doesn't mean it's commendable," Jaime retorted shortly.

Bill looked up at his brother, his lips tightening. "What are you saying?"

"That when Connie comes down I wish both you and Flor—and you too, Diana—would put up a little better front," Jaime snapped. "When I walked into this room I felt as if I was at a Portuguese wake! There's no reason for the gloom yet, and if anyone around here's got any religion they might start praying that there never will be!'' Jaime blurted out. Then he drew a long breath and smiled. "Okay, now that's out of my system! Flor, how about making me one of those drinks you've been passing out?''

Flor went to the kitchen, and the door had just closed behind her when the phone rang. Bill started to struggle to his feet, but Jaime said swiftly, "Want me to catch it?''

Bill nodded and sank back into his chair.

Jaime's telephone conversation was a brief one, but the tension of wondering what message he was going to bring back into the living room mounted.

Returning, he said at once, "That was Profetina.''

"Profetina?'' his brother echoed.

"Yes. She was listening to the news on the local radio station and they said something about the *Miguel M* being in trouble. There are times,'' Jaime added vehemently, "when I think the media should be strangled.''

"Look, you can't keep things like this a secret,'' Bill said. "A ship gets in trouble, it's news.''

"Sure, I know,'' Jaime observed bitterly. "Real life-and-death drama. I'd like some of the jerks who get such a charge hearing about it to get out there and live a little of it!''

They heard footsteps on the stairs and Connie came into the room. Like her mother, she'd combed her hair back without bothering to style it, and she wore no makeup at all to relieve her pallor.

But she was surprisingly composed as she asked, "Who called?"

"Profetina," Jaime answered. "She heard something on the radio about the *Miguel M* being in trouble and she wanted to know what we knew about it. That's all."

Connie turned to her father. "Dad," she asked him, "is anyone still trying to raise the boat?"

Bill nodded. "Joe Tavares is down at the dock office. He's got a couple of other men spelling him. They try to contact Andrade every ten minutes, and of course there's someone right there in case Andrade can make contact with them. Look, Connie, because the radio breaks down aboard a boat doesn't mean the boat's in danger. It could be just the radio, is what I'm saying...."

"Dad, please," Connie said. "I don't need to be coddled."

"Your father isn't trying to coddle you, Connie," Jaime said quietly. "It's the truth. Sometimes the radio goes out on a boat when there's nothing else wrong. Especially in a storm."

"And lots of other things happen in a storm too, don't they?" Connie asked. On the surface she was still calm, but her inner tension was obvious. Watching her, Diana wondered how much strain the vulnerable young woman was going to be able to take.

"Look, dad," Connie said, "I want to go down to the dock."

Bill sighed. "There's no point, Connie. Believe me, you're better off waiting here. The minute there's any word about anything Joe will call me. I guarantee it.''

"I want to be there when Manny comes in," she explained, and for the first time her voice faltered slightly.

"You'll be there when Manny comes in," her father promised her. "Look, Connie, it's going to be all right."

"All right?" There was an edge to her voice, and it was higher than it usually was. "Was there a storm at sea the day you lost your leg?"

Bill stared at her. "Oh God, Connie!" he groaned.

"Connie," Jaime said, "accidents happen... on calm days as well as stormy ones. It happens that the sea was as smooth as a mirror the day your father lost his leg. So don't start trying to make comparisons." He flashed an appealing grin at his niece. "How about helping me make some sandwiches?" he suggested. "It's time for lunch."

Connie nodded and followed Jaime out to the kitchen. Once the door had closed behind them, Flor collapsed into the nearest chair. "I don't know how much of this I'm going to be able to take, Bill."

"If the damned wind would ease up, the Coast Guard could send a chopper out," Bill said tersely. He turned to Diana. "Search and rescue. That's part of the Coast Guard's job. But even they can't carry it out in this kind of weather."

Bill was clenching and unclenching his fists as he spoke, and Diana could imagine the extent of his frustration. She, herself, felt gripped by a terrible sense of helplessness. She listened to the wind, still howling through the trees outside. The rain seemed to have slackened, but the wind sounded strong as ever. She could only dimly imagine what it must be like to be out at sea in a relatively small boat, bearing the full force of nature's fury. But Bill knew what it was like. He must have ridden out many winter storms aboard a fishing trawler.

Knowing makes it all the worse for him, she thought, and wished there were something she could say to him. Something that would make his vigil easier.

Flor straightened. "Diana, would you like another drink?"

"Thank you, no," Diana said with a faint smile. "I'd fall flat on my face if I had another one. I haven't eaten much these past few days."

Bill held out his glass. "I wouldn't mind another one. Flor, look, you're doing fine."

Flor bent and kissed the top of his head, and there was a poignancy to the gesture that touched Diana deeply. These two people had been through a lot, and their marriage seemed stronger because of it. She admired them for that.

After Flor left, Bill turned to Diana. "This is rough on her. She has this crazy feeling that if she hadn't been so much against Manny Ribeiro he wouldn't be out there now, maybe fighting for his life." He shrugged. "There's no point in telling her she's wrong. Manny would be out there anyway. It's his job...."

The phone rang, and Bill heaved himself out of his chair and limped across the room to answer it. He spoke tersely, in monosyllables, and his face was strained as he hung up. Diana became conscious of the fact that she was staring at him, her heart beating faster. Then she saw that Jaime, Flor and Connie had all come in from the kitchen and were grouped in the doorway staring at Bill, too.

"It was Joe," Bill said, not looking at any of them. "He just talked to the captain of the scalloper *Eduardo T*. They say they picked up a Mayday signal...very weak. The position the boat gave was about thirty miles northeast of Nantucket. That's about ten miles west of where the *Miguel M* was, the last time I talked to Andrade."

"Oh, God!" Flor moaned. Connie stood still and silent as a statue.

Bill limped back to his chair and sat down heavily. "The Coast Guard's got a cutter in the general area. They're on their way. The *Eduardo T* has changed course, and they're heading for the location, too." He shook his head. "They got gale-force winds out there, and the waves are like mountains."

"Are they sure it was the *Miguel M* they heard?" Jaime asked.

Bill shook his head. "No. And they're probably not the only boat out there, it could be someone else."

"If the radio on the boat's not working, dad, how could the scalloper have gotten their Mayday signal?'' Connie asked. She seemed far too controlled, Diana decided.

"The radio could be working to a point," Bill said. "That is, it could be giving off a faint signal...not strong enough to reach beyond a few miles. The scalloper said what they got was pretty broken up, that's why they couldn't make out the name of the boat. Fortunately they got its position.''

Connie walked over to the front window, her back ramrod straight. Then she turned to face her father, her eyes blazing.

"I want to go out there," she said.

"Connie, come on..." Bill began.

"Dad, I want to go out there!" Her voice was vibrant with passion. "There must be some kind of a boat you could get out there in. I want to go. I want to go to Manny!"

"Honey, look," her father said. "You don't know what you're saying. Come on and sit down, will you?"

"No!" Connie blurted, her face contorted. "No, no, no!"

Jaime went to her, enfolding her in his arms, and she leaned against him, the sobs beginning, shaking her body as she cried uncontrollably.

"Get it out, Connie," Jaime murmured softly. "Let it go, baby, get it out."

Flor turned away, but Diana had a glimpse of her face before she did so, and what she saw was pure, distilled anguish. She got to her feet, determined to overcome her lingering shakiness, and quickly went to Flor, touching her tentatively on the shoulder.

"Flor," she said, "come on. Let's you and I go finish making the sandwiches."

Once inside the kitchen, Flor sagged. There was desperation in her eyes as she turned to Diana. "If anything has happened to Manuel Ribeiro, I don't know what will become of Connie."

Diana gripped the other woman's shoulders. "I pray to God that nothing's happened to Manny," she said, her voice husky with her own emotion. "But Connie's stronger than you think. I'm sure of it. She's your daughter, Flor. Yours and Bill's. She comes from strong stock."

Flor managed a weak smile. "Thank you, Diana. Now it looks as if Jaime and Connie have started to make some sandwich fillings."

"Yes," Diana said. "Tuna salad, I think."

"We also have cheese, cold cuts...and I have cookies, fruitcake...."

"Why don't we settle for tuna-fish sandwiches and some cookies," Diana suggested. "And maybe some coffee. Shall I make a pot of coffee?"

"Why don't you make the sandwiches and I'll make the coffee," Flor said.

Both women worked busily for a few minutes, and then Flor remarked, "You've done enough, Diana. You shouldn't be on your feet at all. Go on back into the living room. I'll bring these things in."

"I can take the sandwiches," Diana insisted.

"No, no, I'll do it," Flor argued. "Go ahead,

now. Jaime will be out here in another minute asking what I'm trying to do to you.''

Actually, though, Jaime flashed a grateful glance in her direction as Diana went back into the living room. But he came over to her to say, ''Back onto that couch with you. You're still an invalid, remember?''

''I'm feeling stronger with every passing second,'' she told him.

He gripped her arm and led her toward the couch. ''Don't push it,'' he warned, but his fingers were giving a different sort of message to her. She'd never known before that fingers had their own way of saying thank-you.

Coming in with a tray of sandwiches and cookies, Flor looked around the room and asked, ''Where's Connie?''

''She went upstairs for a minute, Flor,'' Jaime said quickly. ''She cried a little, she wanted to wash her face off. But she's all right. She'll be right back down.''

Flor nodded, put down the tray and went back to the kitchen for the coffee, but she cast an apprehensive glance toward the staircase. Diana could appreciate her concern. She was wishing, too, that Connie would finish washing her face, or whatever she was doing, and come back to join the rest of them. Finally she heard footsteps on the stairs and saw Connie coming down slowly.

Connie's foot was on the bottom step when the phone rang, and she headed for it so quickly there was no way Bill or anyone else could have intercepted her.

"Yes?" she said. "No, this is Connie Medeiros, Mr. Tavares. You can tell me, I'll get your message to my father."

Bill was already on his feet and had begun to limp across the room, and Diana saw that his face was creased with lines of deep anxiety. Then her gaze switched to Connie, who was crying, "Oh, no! Oh my God! No!"

She dropped the phone receiver the second before Bill reached out to take it from her. He recovered the receiver and began talking into the phone in low, urgent tones. But Connie, her hands over her face, was rocking back and forth, moaning, and Jaime strode to her side.

"What is it, Connie?" he demanded, gripping her and shaking her slightly as he spoke. "What is it?"

"They've heard from the *Eduardo T*," Connie whispered. "The *Miguel M*...they've got her crew off, but one of the men is dead, and two are badly injured. Oh my God," Connie said, staring up at her uncle, her eyes twin pools of horror. "Oh my God, Manny!"

CHAPTER NINETEEN

BILL, HIS TONE GENTLE BUT FIRM, said, "Connie, it will be hours before the *Eduardo T* can hope to put into port. They've been coping with gale-force winds, remember, to say nothing of a sea with twelve-foot waves. In the meantime there is nothing we can do. Nothing!"

Connie turned away from him. "The winds have begun to die down," she said. "The Coast Guard could send out a helicopter."

"The Coast Guard couldn't send out a helicopter," her father corrected her. "No chopper could make it in this kind of weather. It would only mean...a further loss of life."

Bill got up and limped to the window, staring out at the rain-drenched street. "Don't you think I'd give anything in this world to be able to do something?" he asked, his usual calm overcome by a kind of savagery. "Waiting like this is the worst thing anyone's ever called upon to handle, Connie. But when you deal with the sea, it's part of the game."

"Connie, look," said Jaime. "I'll help you wash up the lunch dishes."

Connie turned on her uncle. "Stop trying to

provide therapy for me, will you, Jaime? Dad, can't you get Mr. Tavares to radio out to the *Eduardo T* and see who it is that's been hurt? And who... who died?" Her voice faltered.

"The captain of the *Eduardo T* has his hands full right now, Connie," Jaime reasoned with her. "Extra men on board, and a storm of this magnitude to handle—"

"Oh, stop!" Connie told him, her dark eyes flashing angrily. "You don't want to find out who's been hurt, who's dead, that's it, isn't it? You know it's Manny, just like I know it!"

"Look," Jaime said, "there were six men aboard the *Miguel M*. There have been three casualties, but from everything we can learn the other three men are all right. Manny is young, he's strong, my bet is that he's one of those three."

"You're playing games with me, Jaime," Connie accused. "You're playing games with me! How can you just stand around like this and do nothing? You, more than anyone else, should be able to do something! You're a doctor!"

Jaime flinched as if she'd hit him, and Diana saw his mouth compress so tightly that it became edged with a chalklike line. He said tightly, "Doctors aren't gods, Connie. I think maybe I know that a little better than most people."

He turned and walked out of the room. They heard the kitchen door thud closed behind him. Flor, who had been sitting in a chair sipping at a cold cup of coffee, straightened and said, "Connie, you shouldn't have spoken to Jaime like that."

"She didn't mean it, Flor," Bill interjected. "Look, we're all on edge."

Diana stood up, wishing that her legs weren't still so wobbly. "I...I want to speak to Jaime by myself, if you don't mind."

Bill nodded. "Go ahead, Diana."

Jaime was standing at the kitchen window, looking out at the rain-spattered backyard. He was standing straight, his hands thrust into the pockets of his corduroy slacks. There was no dejection in his attitude...but Diana knew only too well that Jaime was a past master when it came to the art of camouflage.

"Jaime," she said softly, and he turned to face her. His eyes were dull black coals, the fire gone out of them, and she shrank from the bleakness of his expression. But her voice was steady as she said, "Connie didn't mean anything. You know that."

"Yes, of course I know that. She's beside herself with worry, she doesn't even know what she's saying. And she didn't say all that much. It's me, that's all. I take any statement to do with medicine as if it's an arrow being aimed right at me. Diana...."

She moved toward him, her arms went out to him, and he let her draw him to her. She clasped his neck and heard him sigh, a sigh so deep it went all the way through him and found an echoing shudder in her.

"Oh my God!" Jaime said. And then, in little more than a whisper, "I love you so much!"

There was an extension phone in the kitchen and now it rang, a jangling, discordant sound. Jaime straightened. "I suppose I'd better let Bill answer it."

"It chills me right to the bone every time that phone rings," Diana said.

Jaime's voice was sober. "This isn't the time to bring it up, I suppose, but maybe now you can understand why Bill and Flor didn't want Connie to fall in love with a fisherman. All their lives they've been close to the sea. They know what a toll it can take."

Diana stared at him. "You think it's Manny, don't you?"

"No," Jaime said. "No. Oh, hell! I don't know!"

Bill came into the kitchen, carefully closing the door behind him. He didn't speak until he'd crossed the room to where they stood, and then he kept his voice so low that it couldn't be heard beyond a few feet.

"It was Joe again," he said. "Joe Tavares. The worst of the storm has veered east, so the *Eduardo T* has made better time than we thought she could. They'll be coming in, in maybe two more hours, Jaime. Look...." He swallowed hard.

"What is it, Bill?" Jaime asked swiftly.

"Manny Ribeiro...no," he said hastily, as he heard Diana gasp, "he's not dead. Vincent Cabral's dead." His voice was heavy with pain. "He's about Manny's age, he's got a family too, people who love him. It...it's always hell on someone."

Jaime winced. "I remember Vince Cabral," he said. "Just a kid. I...." His words trailed off, and he forced himself back to the present. "Manny's been hurt?"

Bill nodded. "I knew it the first time I spoke to Joe... after I took the phone away from Connie. But I don't want her to know it until we see how bad it is."

"I'm not sure that's wise," Jaime said gravely.

"I don't want her to know," Bill insisted. "She'll face it when she has to, Jaime, whatever it is. Just like...well, like Flor did. But there's no point in her going through any more, these next couple of hours, than she's going to go through anyway. It may not be bad...."

Bill was grasping at a slim straw of hope, and Diana could empathize with him. Yet she wondered if Jaime might not be right...if it might not be better to warn Connie.

"What's Connie doing now?" Jaime asked.

"Flor's with her. They're just talking together. I think Flor's doing most of the talking, but Connie seems to be listening, anyway. Sometimes she stares out into space. It tears my heart out to see her like this. Flor's holding her own, though. When you get into the tight places, Flor has a lot of guts."

"I know she has, Bill," Jaime said, and he patted his brother on the shoulder. "Look, go on back to them. I'll do what you want, of course. Diana will too, I'm sure. If you don't want Connie to know that Manny's been injured we won't say anything."

"Another half hour or so, I'm going down to the dock," Bill said. "I want to be there when she comes in."

"I'll go with you," Jaime responded quickly.

"I was hoping you'd say that. Connie's going to want to come, but that's one thing I'm not going to allow," Bill said firmly. "I don't want her to be there when that boat comes in."

THERE WAS AN OLD SETH THOMAS CLOCK on the mantel in the Medeiros's living room, and Diana thought she'd never heard a clock that ticked quite so loudly. It seemed to be measuring out every second with a dolefulness that set her nerves on edge.

Finally Bill stood up, stretching elaborately, and said, "I think I'll take a run down to the dock. The wind's died down. I'd like to take a look at things. Care to come along, Jaime?"

"Yes. We can take my car."

"I'll come with you," Connie said quickly.

Her father shook his head. "No point, this trip, honey. We'll be back in half an hour or so. Meantime, I'll get Joe Tavares to radio the *Eduardo T*...."

Bill was not the best of prevaricators. Whether Connie suspected that her father was hedging or not, Diana didn't know. But there was an added insistence in her voice as she said, "I want to go with you, dad."

"Look," Bill said, "it's still raining out, there's no point in you going out in this kind of weather. Stay here with your mother and Diana, Connie. If there's anything to report, I'll call you right away. I promise you that.''

"No," Connie insisted.

"Connie, I'm not taking you," Bill said, and there was a steeliness to his tone. "That's all there is to it. Come along, Jaime.''

Connie watched the two men leave, and Diana saw the muscle at her jawline twitching. There were bright-red spots of color on her cheeks, and her eyes were flashing.

"How can my own father think he can pull the wool over my eyes like that?" she demanded.

Flor sighed. "What are you talking about, Connie?''

"Dad knows damned well when the *Eduardo T* is due in, and don't tell me he doesn't. And he knows Manny's...in bad trouble." Her voice broke as she spoke Manny's name. "What does he think I am? Some kind of idiot child? I have every bit as much right as he has to be down there on that damned dock! More right!''

"Connie," Diana said, trying to sound reasonable. "Your father wants to spare you a lot of needless worry, that's all. Have a little faith in him.''

"Faith in him? Diana, how would you feel if it was Jaime out on that boat?''

The question took Diana totally by surprise and her face gave the answer before she could reply. She couldn't imagine what she'd do if it were Jaime out on the *Eduardo T*. She'd be frantic with worry.

I love you so much! Had Jaime really said that to her? She closed her eyes tightly, wishing they'd had just a few minutes more together out there in the kitchen. Just a few minutes more.

"I love Manny just like you love Jaime," Connie said to her. "Yes, yes, I know you love Jaime. It's in your eyes every time you look at him, in your voice every time you speak to him. If it were Jaime coming in on that boat, wouldn't you want to be there? No matter... no matter what might have happened to him?"

There was only one honest answer to this. Diana's gray eyes met Connie's dark ones, and she drew a long breath. "Yes," she said simply. "And though Jaime will probably have my neck for it, I'll go with you, Connie."

"No," Flor interposed quickly. "You can't go out in this weather, Diana! Jaime will—"

"Flor," Diana said, "please. You have enough to worry about without worrying about me. I'll handle Jaime," she added, with a conviction she was far from feeling.

"I'll get dad's car out of the garage," Connie said. She hesitated, then turned to Flor. "Mother... why don't you come with us?"

There was an appeal in Connie's face, and Diana held her breath. Would Flor respond to it?

"All right. I'll come," Flor replied.

The Fairhaven docks bordered the Acushnet River. Across the water, New Bedford rose along a series of low hills, back from the waterfront.

So many fishing draggers and trawlers and scallopers were tied up at the docks that Diana wondered if there'd be space enough left for the *Eduardo T.*

Connie worked her way into a parking space between two trucks. "Dad's got an office in that building back of the dock over there," she told Diana, pointing. "Why don't you and mother wait and I'll go tell him we're here."

"No," Flor said, suddenly resolute. "You and Diana stay here, Connie. I'll go."

Flor got out of the car, slim, determined, an entirely new expression on her face. Watching her, Diana knew that she was seeing the real Flor, a Flor that might not have been around for a while. But the tense woman who'd been so overly anxious to please had vanished, and Diana liked the person who stood in her stead much better.

Time passed...and Diana couldn't have counted its passing rationally. Time had come to take on a different dimension. A minute could stretch out of all proportion. And finally, when it seemed as if Flor had been gone forever, she saw Jaime striding toward them. She was afraid to look at his face, but Connie said, "He looks furious, Diana."

Jaime opened the door on Diana's side of the car. "Get out of there, will you? What are the two of you trying to do, freeze yourselves to death? You should have had the sense to keep the engine running so you'd have some heat, Connie."

He was tight-lipped. "Get on over to the office. At least you'll be warm there. You'll also be in the

way, both of you, but I don't suppose you give a
damn about that!''

Neither Diana nor Connie replied. They followed Jaime silently across the parking lot and
through the door of a low, concrete building. Inside were several small offices, furnished with steel
filing cabinets, desks and chairs of the same dull,
metallic green. There was a calendar on the wall in
Bill's office but little else.

Bill was sitting at a desk, and Flor was sitting in
a chair beside the desk. A man with gray hair and
weathered, near-mahogany skin was sitting at
another desk, a telephone in his hand, and once
he'd hung up Bill made brief introductions. ''You
know my daughter Connie, Joe,'' he said. ''And
this is Diana Ashley. Joe Tavares.''

Joe Tavares nodded, but his attention was fixed
on Bill. ''She's cleared the breakwater,'' he said,
and Diana saw Connie put her hand to her throat.

Bill struggled to his feet. ''Okay. Let's get down
there. Jaime?''

''I'm coming with you,'' Jaime said tersely.

Bill turned to his wife and his daughter. ''The
two of you stay in here,'' he commanded. ''Look,
Connie, right now you'll only be in the way. If you
want to do something for Manny, give the rest of
us a chance, will you?''

When the men had left, Connie exploded.
''How could my own father say something like
that to me? Doesn't he know there's nothing I
wouldn't do to help Manny?''

''Connie, your father's got his hands full right

now," Flor said. "And you...you've got to get a grip on yourself."

Connie turned to her mother, her eyes brimming with tears. "Mother," she demanded, "do you think Manny's dead? Do you?"

It was Diana who spoke. The torture in Connie's voice was enough to convince her that the time had come to say something.

"Manny isn't dead, Connie," she said, "but he's been hurt. Joe Tavares told your father on the phone but he didn't want you to know until they found out what's happened to him. I shouldn't be telling you this now but I...I can't stand to see you punishing yourself."

"My father knew Manny was hurt?" Connie asked, her voice rising. "Jaime knew?"

"Don't start holding things against them, Connie," Diana advised. "Your mother's right. Just now your father has all he can handle. And he's only been thinking of you, Connie, no matter how you may feel about it. So has Jaime. They were only trying to protect you."

Connie shook her head vehemently. "I'm a woman," she said. "I don't need...protection." And before either Diana or Flor had any idea of what she was going to do, she'd fled through the outer door of the little office building and was running down the dock.

"Oh, no," Flor moaned.

"It'll be all right, Flor," Diana soothed. "It'll be all right. But...I'm sorry, but I had to tell her."

Flor reached out and grasped Diana's hand. "You did right," she said. "No matter what anyone tells you, I know.... You did right, Diana!"

OUTSIDE THE WIND HAD DIED DOWN, and the rain had abated to a drizzle that was little more than a mist. Flor went to the front window of the office building, which overlooked the dock and the water, and said, "Dear God! They're bringing off Vincent Cabral."

Diana felt her throat go tight and she said, "Flor, don't stand watching! Don't torture yourself."

"The men from Harry Gomes Funeral Home are here for him," Flor said. "The rescue-squad people are going down now with stretchers."

Diana moved over to take her place with Flor by the window. She saw the first stretcher bearing a still form covered by a gray blanket, and she swallowed hard. She saw the emergency medical technicians going in another direction with two more stretchers... to be used for the living. Please God, for the living, Diana prayed silently.

After a time, two of the men came back carrying the first of the stretchers, and as they passed by the office Diana saw the face of the man lying on it. It was not Manny. This man was older, with the stubble of a red beard. His eyes were open, and he seemed to be talking to the rescue-squad men.

And then nothing else happened. Nothing happened for an eternity. Years passed, in this new way in which Diana was measuring time, before she finally saw Bill limping toward the little office building. With him were several men whom Diana realized must be fishermen. They wore heavy wool jackets, knitted caps and knee-high black boots, and they looked utterly exhausted. Three of them, she knew, must be from the *Miguel M*. The three who hadn't been injured. The rest must be from the *Eduardo T*. And as far as she was concerned, every man deserved his own weight in gold medals.

Bill came into the office, weary and spent, yet he managed to smile at the two women as he looked across at them.

"Pete Higgins was hurt," he said, speaking to Flor. "He's got a busted arm. Maybe you saw them go by here with him."

"Yes," Flor nodded.

"They'll be coming along with Manny in a minute," Bill said. His eyes met Diana's. "Manny's hurt...critically. But he'd be dead if it wasn't for Jaime. Henry Andrade said that Manny's breathing had been getting worse and worse and Jaime took one look at him and told someone to get him a knife. A sharp knife." Bill swallowed. "Just an old...fishing knife!"

Diana felt as if her own breathing was about to stop. "Yes?" she urged.

"Jaime said there wasn't any time to waste," Bill reported. "He said it was a miracle Manny had lasted as long as he had. Almost as if he was waiting to...to make port. Anyway...."

"Bill, for God's sake, tell us!" his wife implored.

"Jaime said the only chance Manny had was if someone did an emergency tracheotomy. And Jaime was the only person around who...who knew how to do something like that. My God, he took the knife and...and he slit Manny's throat with it. And then...Manny began to breathe again. It was like a miracle!" Bill shook his head wearily, his voice hoarse with wonder. "Jaime saved Manny Ribeiro's life!"

He limped over to his desk, pulled out the chair behind it, and sat down. "Connie's going to the hospital to be with Manny. Jaime will drive her over in his car. He wants to be there, too. He said the three of us should go back to the house. He's worried about you, Diana."

"There's no need for him to worry about me," Diana said quickly.

Bill managed a grin. "You can talk to him about that later," he told her. "Come on, you two, come on," he urged. "As far as I'm concerned, I could use one helluva big drink!"

CHAPTER TWENTY

THE SUNLIGHT WAS DAZZLING, the sky was an incredible shade of blue, and a faint, salt-laden breeze swept in from the bay.

As she walked down the back steps of the DuBois house and across to the garage, Diana found it hard to believe that the entire world had been so transformed in a matter of a few hours. The external world, that is, she amended hastily. Her own internal world was still a very shaky, shadowy place.

She glanced at the house next door, but there was no sign of life. She supposed that Jaime must still be sleeping. She'd heard his car come in during the very early morning and had glanced at her bedside clock. The hands had stood at twenty minutes past three. She'd yearned to get up, to go to Jaime, but instead she'd stayed in bed, lying very still...hoping that perhaps he'd come to her.

But he hadn't.

Now, steering her car out of the driveway, all sorts of thoughts crowded in on Diana, so pressing that they were giving her a headache.

At the end of the driveway she turned left instead of right, as she'd intended to do. She'd planned to go up to the shopping center on Route 6 to take care of a few mundane details like buying bread and eggs and milk and toothpaste. But that could wait a little while longer. Right now she needed to get out and... and *breathe* a little.

She'd driven down to the end of the town twice before and come out at the Revolutionary War fort. The fort had invited exploration, but the weather had been too cold to even get out of the car. Now it was still cold, but she'd bundled up warmly.

There was a spacious parking lot at the end of the road, and beyond it a beach that curved along the Buzzard's Bay shoreline. This historic area was now a popular state park, and Diana could imagine that in a few more months the beach, the picnic tables and the adjacent tennis courts would be thronged with people. But right now she had the place all to herself.

The restored fortifications were atop a rocky rise to her right. Diana paused to read a plaque that had been set into the rocks. It told of the first naval battle of the Revolution, which had been fought here at Fort Phoenix in 1775, when two British sloops were captured "by a gallant force of Fairhaven men." Then, slowly, she climbed upward.

A sea gull shrieked overhead, interrupting her solitude, but it was the right sort of interruption. The gulls were a part of this landscape, they soared above the waters of the world. Following the gull's flight with her eyes, Diana envied the bird its freedom.

Atop the rocky knoll, she paused to look out at New Bedford across the way, and at the massive hurricane dike, which stretched as a breakwater between Fairhaven and New Bedford, protecting the inner harbor.

Last night the *Eduardo T* had come through that breakwater, bringing Manny Ribeiro back to shore. Now he lay in the intensive care unit at St. Luke's Hospital in New Bedford, but he was going to be all right. Jaime had said he was going to be all right.

Jaime had called Bill's house from the hospital late the previous night. By then Flor had made another pot of coffee, and Flor, Bill and Diana were sitting together around the kitchen table, not minding the fact that they were finding it impossible to keep up a conversation.

Then Jaime had called, and Diana, anxiously watching Bill's face, saw him relax, heard him say finally, "That's fine, Jaime. That's fine. Okay." Bill had turned to tell them that Jaime and Connie would be staying at the hospital awhile longer, but that Manny was out of surgery and he was going to be all right.

Diana was shaking inwardly as she posed the question. "Did Jaime operate?"

Bill looked puzzled. "No...no, Jaime didn't operate. Jaime wouldn't operate—"

He didn't finish the sentence, because Flor interrupted with a question of her own.

After he answered Flor, Bill said, "Jaime asked me to run you home, Diana. He says you should have been back in bed long ago."

Diana hated the thought of dragging Bill out of the house at such a late hour when she knew he must be exhausted. She even thought of suggesting that she walk home—it wasn't all that far and the rain had stopped—but she realized Bill would be offended at the mere idea of such a thing, so she waited while he brought his car around to the front of the house. As she left, she impulsively kissed Flor good night. They'd built up a rapport tonight that was going to endure, even if—after this was all over—Flor went back to being her old self outwardly.

Bill hadn't said much on the drive over to the DuBois house. But when he left her at the door he said and smiled at her and said, "Thanks a lot, Diana. A lot."

She mumbled something in return, and once inside she'd succumbed to the flood of tears she'd been holding back for hours. It had been an emotionally draining evening, peaking, for Diana, with that simple statement of Bill's: "Jaime saved Manny Ribeiro's life." Diana knew that if she lived to be a thousand she'd never forget hearing Bill say that.

Now, as she stood on the knoll at Fort Phoenix looking out across the water, the thought came to Diana that a tide had turned last night for Jaime. He had responded to Manny Ribeiro's life-and-death need. He had responded as a doctor, and his instant action had saved a life. But it had left a strange aftermath for Diana. She was in awe of someone who could do what Jaime had done, maybe because she knew she couldn't possibly do such a thing herself. Right now he seemed larger than life to her, and she was endowing him with near-heroic proportions. But even more than that...she had the deep sense that what he'd done last night had returned him to his own world, and he no longer needed her.

They'd come together because of a mutual need, she recognized that. They'd been at low ebbs, both of them. She'd been caught up in her own past, Jaime had been caught up in his. In each other they'd found compassion and under-standing and they had made wonderful love to-gether. Jaime had helped her exorcise her ghost. Both mentally and emotionally she would be more free right now than she had been in years, except for one thing. In a surprisingly short space of time she'd filled her heart, herself, her whole being with Jaime Medeiros.

She thought about this as she climbed back down the rocky knoll then slowly walked across the parking lot to her car. Jaime had given her so much. So much. And she couldn't help but be deeply thankful that his tide had turned for him, that he'd be going back where he belonged...even if it meant losing him. She loved him so much.

She was thoughtful as she drove up to the shop-ping center. There were decisions to be made, the first of which must be whether or not to stay in Fairhaven over these next few months and get on with her thesis. *Could* she get on with her thesis? Everything Portuguese would remind her of

Jaime, and she wasn't sure she could handle that much emotional association. And how bleak it would be to know that the house next door was empty once Jaime went back to Boston. After last night she had no doubt that he'd be going back to Boston. And...if the house were put up for sale, if it sold, it would only be worse. She couldn't imagine strangers taking possession of Jaime's house.

Her brooding was getting her nowhere, she told herself sharply. She had never especially enjoyed grocery shopping, but now even poking around in a supermarket came under the heading of a diversion. She explored shelves she usually bypassed and put a lot of things into her cart that she didn't really need. She had two full bags of food when she got back to the DuBois house instead of the couple of things she'd anticipated buying.

She was struggling up the steps with them when her back door suddenly opened, and Jaime said, "Here. Let me take those!"

If he hadn't lifted the grocery bags out of her arms at that precise moment, Diana might very well have dropped them. Surprise made her stammer as she asked, "W-what are you doing here?"

Jaime grinned at her. "You gave me a key to your house, remember? So instead of hanging around out in the cold I came in here to wait for you."

"To...to wait for me?" she echoed.

He was putting the grocery bags down on the kitchen sideboard, and he shot a quizzical glance at her. "Yes, to wait for you," he said patiently. "I saw you drive off, and I thought maybe you were just going to the store for a few things so I decided to come over. You took longer than I thought you would."

"I . . . I went down to Fort Phoenix first," Diana explained weakly.

"Fort Phoenix?" His eyebrows shot upward. "What on earth were you doing at Fort Phoenix?"

"I . . . I just wanted to see it," Diana mumbled.

"On a bitter cold January morning when you're just getting over the flu? Honestly, Diana, I would think you'd have better sense!" He came across to her and put his palm against her forehead. "You don't feel like you have any fever," he observed, scowling. "But I think I'll take your temperature anyway."

"No," she said, flinching at the touch of his hand, and Jaime drew back from her, his eyes narrowing.

"What's with you, Diana?" he asked simply.

"Nothing. Nothing," she said. "Have you had any late word about Manny?"

He nodded slowly. "Yes. They've moved him out of intensive care into a semiprivate room. . . . He's doing fine." He grinned briefly. "I suspect we'll be having a wedding in the family come June."

"St. Anthony's Day?" Diana suggested.

"How did you know about St. Anthony's Day?"

"Profetina told me."

"I might have suspected that. Incidentally, I called Profetina a while ago to tell her about Manny. She's knitting a sweater for you. A match to mine, she said."

Diana sighed. "I told her she shouldn't do that."

"And why not, may I ask?"

"Because a sweater like that's a . . . a real labor of love. I already told you that." Diana's voice began to falter.

Jaime frowned and reached out to cup her chin with his long fingers. Then, as she tried to evade his grasp, he said sternly, "Stop trying to wriggle away from me! What's with you this morning? You don't seem to want me to touch you."

"It . . . it isn't that . . ." she began.

"Then what is it?" he interrupted.

"Last night," Diana said feebly. "Last night . . . you saved Manny's life. . . ."

He stared at her, perplexed. "That may be a slight overdramatization," he said, "but even if it were true I can't see what it has to do with my touching you. . . ."

It was her turn to interrupt. "I . . . I can't imagine being able to do something like that."

He smiled slightly. "It's largely a matter of training, *menina*. And I still can't see. . . ."

"What happened to Manny, Jaime? No one's really said."

"The trawler was pitching, the cable let go, the boom swung out and it caught both Manny and

Vincent Cabral. It was a fatal blow for Vince. Manny was luckier.'' Jaime's eyes never left her face as he spoke. ''Manny suffered injuries to his neck and shoulder. The bleeding inside his neck was so severe that the expanding hematoma was compressing his trachea.''

At Diana's puzzled expression, Jaime explained gently, ''A hematoma is a localized swelling, filled with blood. The trachea's more commonly known as the windpipe. Manny couldn't get enough air past the hematoma—the obstruction—and he was nearly unconscious when we got to him.''

''And you saved his life,'' Diana said again. ''But. . . but why didn't you operate on him at St. Luke's?''

''Because the kind of surgery he required isn't within my specialty,'' Jaime said levelly. ''It's one thing to act in an emergency, but quite another thing when there are people more capable in their field than you are on hand, waiting to take over. Diana. . . just what is this, anyway? What's this fixation you seem to have developed about my saving Manny's life. I'm thankful to God that I was there when I was, and that I knew what to do. I was able to keep him alive until we got him into surgery, yes. But there were others also involved in saving his life, believe me. However. . . even if you insist on giving me the full credit, what do you think that makes me, Diana?''

''I. . . I don't know,'' she said, her voice very low. ''I suppose it makes you seem. . . different. . . that's all.''

"All?" There was a dangerous glint in his dark eyes. "Diana, you're not by any chance polishing a pedestal, are you?"

"What do you mean?"

Surprisingly, he laughed. "People have some weird ideas about doctors sometimes. They tend to view them as either saints or sinners. Personally I don't endorse either viewpoint. But if you have to hold to one of them, I'd much prefer you looked upon me as a sinner rather than a saint! Don't you think you know me too well to try putting a halo on my head? The damned thing would probably slip off. You know that. And anyway, this whole discussion is ridiculous."

He still was holding her chin with the tip of his fingers, but now he released it. "That stuff you bought...does any of it have to go into the fridge or the freezer?"

"Just the milk," she said. "I concentrated on canned things today."

"So I suspected from the weight of these grocery bags," Jaime said dryly. He was foraging in one of the bags as he spoke, and he drew out a carton of milk and put it into the fridge. "Okay," he said. "Now put your coat back on and come with me."

"My coat back on?" Diana asked shakily.

"You're repeating yourself this morning, *menina*," Jaime said. "Come on!"

He held her coat for her, and she shrugged into it. "Where are we going?" she asked.

"Not far," he said. "Not far at all. Just over to my house."

"Your house?"

"There you go, doing it again. Yes, to my house. You've never seen my house. You've only been in the kitchen...right?"

"Yes."

"Don't look so apprehensive," he said and smiled, ushering her out the back door and closing it behind them. "I just want to show you my house, that's all. I have a reason for wanting you to see it."

"What reason?"

"You'll find that out when the time comes." They were walking across the stretch of lawn that separated the two houses. The snow was gone, but the grass underfoot was spongy from the rain the day before.

"We'll go around to the front this time," Jaime told Diana. "I want you to use a little imagination as we go into the entrance and to visualize how the house could be if it were fixed up. Okay?"

She nodded, mystified by all of this. But once Jaime had opened the front door and motioned to her to precede him into the entrance foyer, she was transfixed.

She was standing in a large square foyer, and a staircase swept up from the center of it to the floors above. There was a landing part way up, and above the landing a tall window stretched toward the ceiling. There the staircase separated, a section of it continuing up on either side.

A large front room—a drawing room, really—opened to the left of the foyer. Beyond that, on the same side, was a second room, which had probably been used as a family living room, and behind that lay a small wood-panelled room with a fireplace flanked by bookshelves, all empty now.

"What a perfect room this would be on a snowy night," Diana found herself exclaiming. "Oh, Jaime, this place could be...spectacular. Everything's been made so beautifully, the woodwork, the moldings, the details on the fireplaces."

He nodded. "You go through the library to that big glassed-in porch you may have noticed when you've driven by," he said. "It's cold out there, though, so we'll skip it for the moment. Anyway, I want to show you the other side. Come on."

A spacious room opened to the right of the foyer, and in the center of the ceiling hung an elaborate crystal chandelier. "The dining room," Jaime said. "There's a smaller room just beyond that was called the breakfast room, if I remember rightly. I think the family ate there unless they were entertaining. Now we come to the pantry and beyond that the kitchen, with which you're already familiar. It needs modernization, of course, but I think a sort of old-fashioned quality could be kept to it. Maybe a big round maple table, something like that."

Diana smiled. "And a rocking chair in the corner," she suggested.

"Yes, of course. A rocking chair in the corner. Now, would you like to go upstairs?"

She nodded yes. When they'd passed through the breakfast room she'd noted the cot in the corner and had surmised that this was where he'd been sleeping since coming back to Fairhaven. It seemed so wrong to her, though she wasn't about to say anything. But this beautiful home didn't deserve to be empty and barren. It deserved people living in it who would restore it to all its former glory. It deserved love. . . and laughter.

Upstairs there were four large bedrooms and an equal number of baths. "The bathrooms need some modernizing," Jaime observed, "but with painting and some bright color touches they wouldn't be too bad for the time being. What do you think of this master bedroom?"

The master bedroom stretched across the rear of the house. Large windows across the back and side offered a magnificent view of the Acushnet River, sparkling in the sunlight today, and on the opposite wall was a wood-burning fireplace.

Diana sighed, her mind busy visualizing the way all this could be. "It's absolutely fabulous."

"What color would you like to do this room in, do you think?" he asked her.

"I don't know for sure. A pale yellow, a very clear shade of yellow, would be lovely, with white trim. . . ." She broke off with a wry smile. "Whoever decorates this for you may have entirely different ideas."

He shook his head. "You're the only person in this world who will ever decorate this house for me, *menina*."

Diana felt as if someone had hit her in the middle of her stomach. She stood very still, not daring to look at him, and Jaime made no move to come any closer to her.

He said, his voice incredibly soft, "I love you, *menina*. And though you haven't come out and told me so, in so many words, you've shown me that you love me, too. . . or can learn to love me.

"A long time ago," he went on, "I bought this house because I had a dream. A dream for someone else, not for myself. Now the dream I have is for me, *menina*. I want to make this house beautiful again, and I want you to live here in it with me. How long have I known you? Not much more than a month, but in that month I've come to know you better than I have anyone else in my entire life. I want you with me for the rest of my life, sharing in both the good things and the bad. . . and I'm sure there will be plenty of both. I never want to spend another night apart from you."

Diana shuddered. It was all she could do not to cover the short space between them and fling herself into his arms. She never wanted to spend another night apart from him, either. But it wasn't that simple.

It took all her strength to say, "You can't live here, Jaime."

He stared at her incredulously, then he scowled. "What are you saying?"

Diana got a firm grip on her courage and her voice was remarkably steady as she said, "Your world is in Boston, Jaime. In Boston and some other places, too, maybe, but mostly in Boston. You've got to go back there, back to your hospital, back to your work. I think you knew that last night, after you saved Manny's life... even though you still may not want to admit it to yourself.''

She walked over to the empty fireplace and could almost see her own dreams evaporating up its chimney. "This isn't the place for you. This house could be beautiful, yes, absolutely beautiful, a wonderful place to live in. But just... living here... wouldn't be enough for you, even though right now you may think it would be. You're young and vigorous and... and so very talented in your own field. You'll never be really happy with me or with anything or anyone else unless... unless you go back, Jaime.''

Silence filled the room, a silence so heavy Diana felt oppressed by its weight. Then Jaime said quietly, "I did tell you I love you, didn't I, Diana? Well, that's not even the half of it. I adore you, with every fiber of my being. You're my light and my breath and my life, *querida minha. Te quero, vida minha.*''

Jaime laughed, and Diana swung around sharply to see that he was smiling ruefully.

"You do bring out the Portuguese in me. Never before in my life have I gone around scattering Portuguese love words through my phrases. Maybe I'm doing it now because I'm trying to convince you that as a historian bent on doing a thesis about the Portuguese in America you could hardly do better than to marry someone from that background.''

An answering smile trembled on Diana's lips. "Oh, Jaime, Jaime," she said, "you are hopeless!"

"Hopeless? I don't know about that, but I do know that I'm completely helpless where you're concerned. Will you rescue me, Diana? Will you please put me out of my misery and tell me you'll marry me?"

He still had made no move toward her, and it took all of Diana's willpower to keep her distance. She asked shakily, "On St. Anthony's Day?"

"Hell, no!" Jaime protested. "Do you really think I could wait over five more months? Valentine's Day, maybe," he mused, then grinned at her. "But even that seems an awfully long time away!"

Now he did come to her and enfolded her in his arms, and their kiss was much more than a kiss. It sealed a bond between them. A bond that would never be broken.

Then his hands began to rove, and as he touched her an emotional fountain was set off deep inside Diana, the torrent of her desire spiraling upward to find its match in him. He was holding her so close that she had no doubts about his arousal, about his needs and his passion equaling hers.

After a time he said huskily, "There's a certain disadvantage to a house being without furniture that I never fully appreciated before." He laughed. "That cot downstairs is so rickety I've nearly broken it down all by myself. I don't think...."

Diana smiled. "Let's go next door."

"It will take all my self-control to make it that far," he teased. "And I'm not sure—"

"Jaime," she said, lovely laughter lighting her eyes. "Come on!"

They walked across the lawn hand in hand, and glancing at the house ahead of them, Jaime said, "I don't think Agatha DuBois would mind if I moved in with you, once we're married, till we get our place fixed up. We should be able to get enough done before she comes back from the South in June to make it habitable. Meantime. . . ."

Diana stopped, still holding onto his hand, and looked up at him. "Jaime," she said, "because you and I have gone off into a kind of fantasy world doesn't alter what I said to you a while ago."

"I know, I know," he said gently. "And I won't pretend that you may not be right, *menina*. Notice, I'm not saying that you *are* right, only that you may be."

He drew a long breath. "Last night when I saw Manny, when I knew what I had to do. . .it did something to me. I thanked God that I had the knowledge to act quickly. . .and correctly. And I had the very strange feeling, once we'd gotten Manny to the hospital, once he'd gone into surgery, that I'd just been given a test, and that I'd passed it. But. . . ."

Diana waited, and after a moment Jaime said, "I'm still not sure." He looked down into her eyes, and she saw his doubt, his uncertainty, and only wished that she could set his fears at rest. But she knew this was something he was going to have to do himself.

"I want to go back, Diana. It's not a question of my not wanting to go back. The question is whether or not I'm fit to go back. How I'll be, not in an emergency situation, where one tends to react instinctively, but standing in an operating room with a scalpel in my hand. This isn't something you can play with. It's a matter of constant life and death. There's a power involved that you have to be very sure about. I think my questions are ones that only time can answer, and I think I still have a way to go before I'll know what the answer's to be."

He hesitated, then asked, an oddly humble note in his voice, "Will you travel that way with me, *menina*?"

Diana's eyes were shining with unshed tears as she looked up at him, but these were tears of happiness, not of sorrow. Jaime, she told herself, might still wonder about his future, but she had no doubts at all.

And as she stood with the January sun shining down upon her, Diana threw her arms around Jaime, pulling his head down so that his lips could meet hers, and gave him no doubts at all about her answer.

EPILOGUE

DR. JAIME REMINGIO MEDEIROS strode out of the operating room with a single thought in mind. He found the nearest empty office with a phone in it, sat down at the desk, and dialed.

As he did so, he took off his green surgeon's cap and laid it aside, rubbing tired fingers across his forehead. It had been a long morning.

Diana was sitting at the window of their apartment overlooking Boston's Charles River, waiting for the phone to ring. She'd been trying to read a book so the time would pass more quickly, but her mind had been focused on Jaime to such an extent that she hadn't turned a single page.

This was one of the most important days in their lives. So much depended on the outcome of it. She sighed deeply, wishing she could help him, hoping that she was, perhaps, by somehow communicating the message of her love and never-ending support.

These first months of their marriage had been glorious. That special time in Jaime's life had come. They'd made the trip to Portugal, dividing their honeymoon time between Lisbon, the Algarve, and the Azores, lingering on São Miguel.

Diana had fallen in love with the island. She'd never forget the day they'd picnicked by a lake, its banks covered with pink azaleas and blue hydrangeas, and she'd said to Jaime, "We have to come back here."

Well, they would go back. They both loved to travel, and there would be time for it. But their beautiful house in Fairhaven would always be home. They'd come a long way toward getting it exactly as they wanted it, and Manny and Connie would be living in it this winter. A house in cold weather was better off if it was lived in, Jaime had said. But once Connie had her baby in the spring, she and Manny would be wanting to get a place of their own.

Diana had traveled along Jaime's "way," as he'd asked her, but she'd refrained from pressuring him. And finally one morning he told her he thought the time had come for them to go up to Boston and do some apartment hunting. He didn't need to say anything more.

They'd taken a number of their favorite things to the Boston apartment, and once it was furnished Jaime told her she could make any place a home. The Boston Public Library had excellent research facilities, and before long she'd be getting back to her thesis. But right now. . . .

Right now it was Jaime who occupied every second of her waking day, and she told herself that even though he slept right next to her every night, she dreamed of him, as well.

Today was a clear, early October day, and there were still sailboats out on the Charles. Diana watched one small boat, its white sails billowing in the wind, and wished she and Jaime were aboard it. He'd taken her sailing several times since they'd come to Boston.

Then the phone rang, interrupting her reverie. Diana froze. It was not until the third ring that she was able to pick up the receiver and utter a shaky, "Hello?"

"I hate to ask you to go out on a single errand," Jaime said without preamble.

"What?" she demanded. This wasn't what she had expected to hear.

"I'd like you to get a bottle of Dom Perignon," Jaime said, his voice remarkably steady. "A bottle of chilled Dom Perignon. I'm coming home as soon as I can possibly make it, so I think maybe you'd better chill two champagne glasses, too."

"Darling," Diana said, her voice breaking.

"The girl I operated on this morning was just about the same age you were when I first met you," Jaime said. "She even looked a little bit like you. Her scars were considerably more extensive. . . and visible. She was in an accident several months ago and the operation was strictly reconstructive work. But. . . ."

"Yes."

"With perhaps just a little bit of makeup as camouflage, she will be as beautiful as ever." Jaime could no longer keep the emotion out of his voice. "As beautiful as ever," he repeated, then added softly, "but she'll never be as beautiful as you."

His voice was a caress as he added, "To me, no one could ever be as beautiful as you are, *menina*."

COMING NEXT MONTH FROM
HARLEQUIN SUPERROMANCE

142 SILVER HORIZONS, Deborah Joyce
From the moment they met, Minta suspected Brad was involved in something dangerous. When she learned the devastating truth about him, she was forced to make a choice. Either turn in the man she loved or turn her back on justice. . . .

143 WHEN MORNING COMES, Judith Duncan
Christine Spencer had secretly arranged for the rescue of her estranged husband, David, from a prison camp in Central America. Now, in a rustic cabin on Vancouver Island, she had the chance to heal their wounded relationship—if only David would let her.

144 RICHES TO HOLD, Christine Hella Cott
Sharli Cook's relatives coveted what had been dropped in her lap—the ancestral cottage complete with hidden wealth. Sharli thought Rochan Richet wanted only her—until she discovered he too could be just another fortune hunter. . . .

145 DELTA NIGHTS, Jean DeCoto
Love should have given Alisa Fairlight the warm feeling of belonging she'd always craved, but Pace Lofton had vowed never to marry an outsider to his beloved Delta for reasons even Alisa couldn't challenge.

THE DREAM LASTS LONGER
WITH SUPERROMANCE....

The Fourth
Harlequin American Romance
Premier Edition

GENTLY INTO NIGHT

KATHERINE COFFARO

Emily Ruska and Joel Kline
are two New York City police detectives
caught between conflicting values
and an undeniable attraction
for each other.

BARBARA DELINSKY

Fingerprints

Carly Quinn is a
woman with a past.
Born Robyn Hart, she
was forced to don a new
identity when her intensive
investigation of an arson-ring
resulted in a photographer's death
and threats against her life.

Ryan Cornell's entrance into her life
was a gradual one. The handsome
lawyer's interest was piqued, and then
captivated, by the mysterious Carly—a
woman of soaring passions and a
secret past.

FP-2

Harlequin Intrigue

Because romance can be quite an adventure.

Enter a uniquely exciting new world with

Harlequin American Romance ™

Harlequin American Romances are the first romances to explore today's love relationships. These compelling novels reach into the hearts and minds of women across America... probing the most intimate moments of romance, love and desire.

You'll follow romantic heroines and irresistible men as they boldly face confusing choices. Career first, love later? Love without marriage? Long-distance relationships? All the experiences that make love real are captured in the tender, loving pages of **Harlequin American Romances.**

What makes American women so different when it comes to love? Find out with **Harlequin American Romance!**

Send for your introductory FREE book now!

Get this book FREE!

Mail to:
Harlequin Reader Service

In the U.S.	In Canada
2504 West Southern Ave.	P.O. Box 2800, Postal Station A
Tempe, AZ 85282	5170 Yonge St., Willowdale, Ont. M2N 5T5

YES! I want to be one of the first to discover **Harlequin American Romance.** Send me FREE and without obligation *Twice in a Lifetime.* If you do not hear from me after I have examined my FREE book, please send me the 4 new **Harlequin American Romances** each month as soon as they come off the presses. I understand that I will be billed only $2.25 for each book (total $9.00). There are no shipping or handling charges. There is no minimum number of books that I have to purchase. In fact, I may cancel this arrangement at any time. *Twice in a Lifetime* is mine to keep as a FREE gift, even if I do not buy any additional books.

Name _____ (please print)

Address _____ Apt. no. _____

City _____ State/Prov. _____ Zip/Postal Code _____

Signature (If under 18, parent or guardian must sign.)

154-BPA-NAXJ

52

When Iain Auld broke, he shattered into pieces. It was as if Karen had taken a crowbar to the shell he'd been hiding inside since the interview had begun. He threw off his glasses and buried his face in his hands, weeping like an inconsolable child. The dam had burst, yet Karen felt no satisfaction. It was grief and not guilt that possessed him; to her that was obvious. Grief for his brother, but also grief for the lives he would never recover.

Karen cast a quick look over her shoulder at Nugent. He gave her an approving nod. Auld continued to weep, great shuddering sobs that shook his whole body. It felt like an unconscionable time before the tears subsided but it was probably only a couple of minutes. He sat with his head bowed, panting as if he'd run a hard race. Daisy took some tissues from her bag and passed them across to him. He looked up then, his eyes swollen and red, his face strangely mottled.

'This wasn't where you expected it to end up when you fell in love with David,' Karen said gently, transforming herself into the caring face of interrogation.

He shook his head and blew his nose. 'Nobody was supposed to get hurt.' His mouth twisted up at one corner

you. He must have been raging after what you'd done to him and Mary. But still, he agreed to meet you, didn't he? Because deep in his heart, Jamie still loved you.'

'Can I get a drink of water?'

Clever move, Karen thought. Break up the rhythm of her relentless attack. 'Sergeant, get Mr Auld some water, would you?'

Daisy stood up as Nugent leaned in and said, 'DS Mortimer is leaving the room.'

'Jamie loved you. So it never crossed his mind that agreeing to meet you was a dangerous thing. He came over from France – did he tell you anything about his life in Paris, by the way? He played saxophone in a well-respected jazz quintet. If you're ever in a position to listen to Spotify again, you can check them out. Comme des Etrangers, they were called. They're gutted at losing him. Oh, and he had a girlfriend too. We met her. Pascale. Lovely woman. She owns a jazz club in Caen. She's devastated. She really loved him. She doesn't understand why he was murdered. To be honest, I don't understand either. The very fact that he'd agreed to meet you says to me he was a long way down the road of forgiveness. So what happened, Iain? How did it all go wrong? How did it end up with David whacking him round the head with a crowbar?'

Shock flashed across Auld's face. He tried to cover it with a cough, but Karen was no stranger to the bombshell moment. He'd had no idea. He hadn't been there and, whatever story David Greig had concocted, it hadn't involved a crowbar.

Daisy couldn't have picked a worse moment to return with a paper cup of water. 'DS Mortimer has entered the room,' Nugent sighed. She put the water on the table in front of Auld and sat down, her expression puzzled.

Auld seized the water and drained the cup. By the time he put it down, he had almost recovered his composure.

'I know what you're thinking, Iain. You're thinking I'm making it up. You're sitting there clinging to the hope that I'm making it up. You don't want to believe that the man you love, the man you tore up your life for, the man you committed all these crimes for – you can't bring yourself to believe he caved Jamie's head in. That David could ever do that to your lovely brother. But it's true. I'm not making it up. Sergeant, show Iain the DNA analyses.'

Daisy opened the folder she'd brought to the table and took out three sheets of paper. Karen took the first and showed it to Auld. 'Look at this. It's a lab report from the Police Scotland lab at Gartcosh. See what it says? "DNA pro-files extracted from Exhibit 73, Case 5/13022020." See the labels? The top one, that's your brother's DNA, the victim. That's the DNA we'll be comparing to yours. But see the other one? "Unknown" it says.'

She placed the page that showed David Greig's certified DNA next to the Police Scotland report. 'They match, don't they?' Her voice sharpened. 'Don't they, Iain?'

'If you say so.' His voice was so soft she could hardly hear him.

'Could you say that more loudly, for the tape?'

'If you say so.' This time it was almost a shout.

'You know what this piece of paper is, don't you, Iain? It's the piece of paper that confirms the identity of the unknown assailant who brutally beat your brother to death.' She dropped in front of him the final piece of the jigsaw. The legal confirmation of David Greig's DNA.

Auld stared bleakly at the papers in front of him. He rubbed his forehead with the tips of his fingers. He looked

up at Karen, a plea in his eyes. 'How do I know that piece of paper' – he flicked the legal document with a finger-nail – 'refers to this? It could be anybody's DNA. This is entrapment.'

'Why are you even trying this? I took the original from Francis Flaxner Geary yesterday. Right before he texted you to come to Dublin for an important meeting. I didn't bring the original into this interview in case you decided to rip it up. Geary's not on your side any longer, Iain. He's all about saving his own skin now. I bet he's closeted with his lawyer right now, concocting a version of events that covers his back. That'll be why he wasn't answering his phone when you tried to call him from the police car on the way here.' She took Geary's phone from her pocket and tossed it on the table. 'Three missed calls from Daniel Connolly.'

There was a long silence. Karen could hear Nugent breathing. She leaned forward, forearms on the table, hands clasped. 'All you've done over the years, you've done for David. All the hazards you've faced, all the laws you've broken, you did that for David. You were never the one in love with risk. That was David. Iain, the man you live with killed your brother. In cold blood. There's nowhere for you to hide from that. How safe do you feel now?'

in a bitter smile. 'I thought it was a moment of madness. Something that would be over in a matter of weeks, months at the most. I thought he'd get tired of somebody as dull as me.'

'I understand, Iain. Now you need to help us. You need to make sure your side of the story gets out there first. Because I have a sense that David will not hesitate to throw shade on you.' She reached out and put a hand over one of his. It was hot to the touch, as if he'd suddenly developed a fever.

'We met at a Tate Gallery party in 2007.' He gave her a piteous look. 'He's so charismatic. Charming, dangerous, funny, clever. I couldn't understand why he was talking to me for so long. I've never been exciting.'

'But there was some sort of chemistry between you?'

He frowned, baffled. 'I still don't get it. I'd never had a relationship with a man before. Hell, since I met Mary, I'd never slept with anybody else, man or woman. But I felt as if David had cast a spell on me. We were like magnetic poles, drawn irresistibly to each other.'

That had the feel of a well-worn line, Karen thought. 'So you started having an affair?'

'So we fell in love,' he corrected her. 'We saw as much of each other as we could. When I was working down in London, Mary was mostly back in Scotland. And although David travelled a lot – giving lectures, appearing at gallery events all over the world, going to other people's openings – we managed to spend a lot of time together. But we never went out in public.' He smiled. 'Oddly enough, it never felt like a restriction. We loved being at home together. Cooking, eating, talking, watching movies, making love.'

'Why were you so obsessed with keeping it private? In 2007, even in Scotland, even in the upper echelons of the

Civil Service, being gay wasn't going to destroy your career.'
There was nothing aggressive in Karen's tone; she gave the
impression of genuine curiosity and nothing more.

Auld sighed. He took his hand away from Karen's and
linked his fingers together, almost wringing his hands.
'Admitting to a relationship with David would have
stopped my career in its tracks. He's not just any old artist.
He was one of the bad boys of BritArt. Drugs, partying,
drinking, outraging the establishment with his pro-
nouncements about anything and everything that caught
his attention. It would have been like saying a giant "Fuck
you!" to my bosses.'

'And then there was Mary.' His shoulders slumped. 'I
didn't stop loving Mary when I fell in love with David. But
we'd been married a long time, it wasn't an overwhelming
passion. If I'm honest, it never was, I was probably in denial
about my sexuality for years. But I loved her, truly I did. I
knew that it would be devastating for her if I told her about
David. And as I say, I was convinced for a very long time
that it would fizzle out. That he'd get bored and move on.
It seemed crazy to destroy my life for what would almost
certainly be nothing more than a fling.'

He gave a wistful smile. 'And he was – he *is* so much fun.'

'Was that how the thing with the Dover House paintings
came about? A bit of fun? Thumbing your noses at the dull
old establishment.'

Auld studied the tabletop. 'Exactly that. It was a joke.
David is a brilliant copyist. You'll know that already if
you've done your homework. The first time I took him to see
my office, he spent half the time examining the art and telling me how easy it would be to copy. He took a few photos
and I thought nothing of it. Then the next time we met,

he presented me with a perfect replica of the Joan Eardley painting in my office. I was genuinely astonished. Then he proposed swapping it for the genuine article.'

'And you agreed?'

He shrugged. 'It felt like a game. And it was easy enough to get away with. I had keys and access to the building 24/7, so it was easy to do. It was like taking the self-important down a peg or two. Ministers always make a thing about choosing paintings, but they generally go for what makes a statement rather than ones they love. David thought it would be funny to see how long it took to dawn on them that what they were looking at were fakes.'

'Only it never did dawn on them, did it? So when did it dawn on you that the joke had gone too far?'

He darted a quick look at her and she saw a flash of the intelligence that had helped him rise so far so fast. 'You may remember that there was a lot of talk in late 2009 that Gordon Brown was about to call a General Election?'

She recalled it perfectly. Brown had had a following wind but he'd bottled it. Ultimately opening the door for David Cameron and Boris Johnson and ten years of austerity politics dealt out by people whose only experience of poverty lay in their lack of imagination and compassion. 'I remember,' was all she said.

'The very prospect was enough to worry me. Whatever the outcome, I knew a change of government would likely mean a change of personnel in the Scotland Office and that in its turn would mean a change-around in the artwork on the walls. I told David we needed to swap the originals back before the artworks were sent back to the National Galleries of Scotland. He gave me the strangest look. A mixture of amusement and shamefacedness. "That's not going to be possible," he said. I asked why and he said, "Because I've already sold the originals."'

'That was the first you'd heard of this?'

'It had never even crossed my mind.' He scoffed. 'Why would it? I told you I was dull. I didn't know anybody who would even contemplate a scheme like that. I didn't even know how such a thing was possible. How could you sell paintings when two minutes on the internet would tell you the work in question was part of a national collection?' A bitter laugh. 'God, I was naïve. I knew nothing about private collectors with zero scruples, I had no notion of the way art is used to launder organised crime proceeds. I was an innocent abroad.'

'But sadly not for long.'

'What could I do? I was in it up to my neck. And then David came up with a proposal. He'd used the money to buy a property in Donegal, so he hadn't lost it in the financial crash. He said he wanted to live there with me. He'd grown fed up of the life he'd been living. Since we'd been together, he'd tried to escape the constant attention, the parties, the travel. He wanted to be somewhere he could just paint. But people wouldn't leave him alone. They were always pestering him. Making demands. He'd obviously been thinking about how to escape from it all for a while. He had all the details worked out.'

'What about the passports? How did you come by those?'

'An artist David knew. He'd been using the concept of identity theft in his work. He put us on to a man who created a whole false ID for us both. I was scared shitless the first time I used my passport, but it's never been questioned.'

'So you made your plans. And you set up a very loud row with your brother and made sure the neighbours heard?'

For the first time, Auld looked ashamed. 'Yes. That was David's idea.'

'What was the row about?' Karen pushed back.

Auld bit his lip. 'I told Jamie I had fallen in love with someone else. A man. And that I was planning to leave Mary. He was outraged, exactly like I knew he would be. Not because it was a man. He'd have been equally angry if it had been a woman. No, he was furious that I could even contemplate leaving Mary and all we'd built together. He called it a shitty little fling, and that gave me an excuse to lose my temper in return. I hated it, but it had to be done if our plan was going to work.'

'That makes more sense. The only thing Mary could imagine the two of you almost coming to blows over was Scottish independence, but I never thought it was enough of a provocation for a murderous row. But were you not afraid that Jamie would tell Mary the truth? Especially when he came under suspicion?'

He met her eyes. 'Why would he do that, when the sole reason for his anger was how much pain my betrayal would cause Mary? I was never comfortable about taking advantage of the care he felt towards Mary. But I truly assumed Jamie would have an alibi for later in the evening, after our row. He was always very sociable, always hanging out with musicians in bars and clubs.'

'And was it also David's idea to stuff your bloodstained T-shirt into the bin in the basement of Jamie's flat?' She couldn't keep an edge out of her voice this time.

His head came up and she saw that moment of shock again. Had he not taken in what she'd said earlier? 'I don't know what you're talking about.'

'A crime scene officer found a bloodstained T-shirt in one

415

of the bins in the basement of Jamie's block of flats. It was your blood.'

He stared at her, shaking his head. 'How?'

'That's what I'm asking. Your blood, in your brother's bin. How?'

He gripped the sides of his face with his hands, so hard he left white fingermarks when he stopped. 'I can't ... No, wait. The week before. I was at David's, he's got these sharp Japanese knives, I took a chunk out of my thumb when I was cooking. It bled like crazy. David binned my T-shirt and gave me one of his. Are you seriously telling me he kept it to incriminate Jamie?'

'What do you think? If you've got another explanation, I'd love to hear it.'

He looked ready to burst into tears again. 'Jamie was only supposed to be a distraction, a diversion. Not a serious suspect.'

'And what about Mary in all of this? You say you loved her but you left her in limbo. Grieving your loss but never knowing whether you were alive or dead. How did you justify that to yourself?' Again, she fought to sound merely curious rather than judgemental. Sometimes it was almost a physical struggle to turn away from what often felt like her default state.

'I thought she'd be better off without me. I'd turned our marriage into second best and I thought she deserved the chance to find happiness with someone else.' He couldn't meet her eye now.

Self-serving, selfish, self-indulgent bawbag. 'That's a big ask when she didn't know if you were alive or dead. How could she embark on a new relationship when she had no idea whether you were going to walk back through the door like the first episode of a TV drama?'

416

'She had me declared dead,' he said, defensive. 'She decided there was no room for me in her life.'

'She had you declared dead because her life had been on hold for more than seven years. Have you any idea the hoops she had to jump through to conduct her financial affairs? How she couldn't even sell the car that was registered to you because you were still officially alive and unaccounted for?' Karen let one hand drop below the tabletop and pressed her fingernails into her palm to contain her anger.

'I'm sorry for all of that. But what use would I have been to her if I'd said no to David's plan? I'd have been languishing in jail, my career in ruins. Living with the disgrace and the humiliation would have been worse for her, surely?'

You think? Karen took a deep breath. 'What happened the night you disappeared?'

'Simple. It was a summer evening, lots of people around. I walked up to Soho and David picked me up in his car. We drove through the night to Holyhead and crossed to Ireland. Nobody gave my new passport a second glance. We took the long way round to Donegal so we wouldn't have to cross the border, and David left me at Hill House with a fridge full of food and a cupboard full of booze. Three weeks later, he faked his own death and joined me in Ramelton. It's a nice town, people are friendly without being too nosy.' He spread his hands in a gesture of completion. 'We've been there ever since.'

Karen turned to Daisy. 'Is that what we think, Sergeant?'

'More or less. Apart from a side trip to Brighton in 2017.'

Karen smiled. 'Oh yes, I'd almost forgotten about the arson. There's a lovely picture of you among the rubber-neckers at an art gallery fire. Sadly the Goldman Gallery lost three – or was it four? – of David Greig's paintings. What was the problem, Iain? Was your lovely lifestyle working out more expensive than you'd planned? Was the bottom dropping out of his market? Did you need to up the scarcity value of the work he was still churning out?'

'Got it in one,' he said, rueful. 'We were burning through our capital faster than we'd anticipated. David thought we needed to give his prices an artificial leg-up to boost our nest-egg.'

'It certainly did that. And it was your first mistake, Iain. You know what happened, don't you?'

'No. All I know is that I got an email from Francis Geary, passing on a message from Jamie. It was like a punch in the chest.'

'What did it say?'

'It's carved on my memory. "Dear Daniel Connolly, Apologies for contacting you out of the blue but I believe you may know something of the whereabouts of my brother, Iain Auld, who knew David Greig very well. I would like to meet to discuss this." I was so shocked, I threw up. I barely made it to the bathroom. I couldn't make sense of it.'

'So what did you do?'

'I told David.'

53

Auld's words hung in the air. He might as well have said, 'I signed my brother's death warrant,' Karen thought. Auld knew how ruthless his lover was; he must have understood the risk he was exposing his brother to. But she knew from long experience that people's capacity for self-delusion was pretty much unlimited.

'You told David. How did he react?'

'He could see how upset I was. He told me not to worry. He insisted that he'd handle it.'

Karen let the words settle between them. 'What did you take that to mean?'

'I was so relieved. I knew he'd find a better way to explain things to Jamie than I would. I'd have been too emotional, we both knew that. So David said he'd meet Jamie and see how the land lay.' He gave her a beseeching look. 'He's good with people, he knows how to persuade them to see things differently.' He gave a laugh that turned into a cough. His eyes were all over the place, everywhere except Karen's gaze. 'I mean, look how well he did with me, and I was as strait-laced as they come.'

Karen bit down again on her anger. 'What happened next?'

'David replied to the email and set up a meeting in Fife. Jamie was up there, visiting Mary. They arranged to meet in Elie and walked out along the coastal path together. They were talking for a long time. There was a lot to explain. Jamie was angry at first, David said. But he calmed down when he understood he could be back in my life again. They were out for so long it got dark.' Auld closed his eyes, his expression one of anguish. 'And Jamie lost his footing and fell down the cliff. David went after him but there was no sign.' He opened his eyes, meeting Karen's in a piteous stare. 'He must have hit his head on the way down. That's what David said.'

'David lied, Iain. I don't think there was ever a conversation. I think he went there with the express purpose of removing the threat to his lovely life.'

'You're wrong. You don't know him. He's not a cold-blooded killer. I've lived with him for ten years. He's warm and loving and generous.'

'He killed your brother.' She pushed her chair back. 'I think we all need a break now. Do you want a coffee, or a tea? Something to eat?'

Auld shook his head. 'A cup of black tea, that's all. No sugar.'

Nugent intoned the formula for the interview suspension and the three officers filed out. Karen leaned against the wall, exhaling slowly. She allowed herself to feel the tension in her body, the damp in her armpits, the dull ache at the base of her skull. 'I need something to eat,' she said. 'Daisy, away and find me chocolate. Please. And coffee.'

When they were alone, Nugent said, 'That was a helluva performance in there.'

'Mine or his?'

'Well, both, I suppose, but I meant yours. You pushed all the right buttons at the right time.'

'I thought I'd lost him at the end there, when he started on about it being an accident.'

Nugent gave a dark chuckle. 'Last desperate throw of the dice. You could see he didn't believe it himself. So what now?'

'I have to persuade him to trick David into coming on to your turf.'

'You have a plan?'

Karen managed a weak laugh. 'I wouldn't pay it the compliment of calling it a plan. I have an idea.'

Daisy reappeared. 'I got you a Snickers because peanuts are protein.' She handed over the bar. 'And a bag of Maltesers. Sergeant Tiernan's bringing coffee.'

Karen forced herself to eat the Snickers bar with something approaching restraint in spite of her desire to demolish it in three bites. 'Oh God, that's better,' she sighed as Tiernan arrived with the coffee.

'You were amazing in there,' Daisy said. 'I mean, wow. I'm learning so much, working with you.'

Karen nodded her thanks, drank the coffee and ate the Maltesers without another word. 'Bathroom break,' she said. 'Then it's showtime.'

Iain Auld was beginning to look dishevelled. His tie was loose, the top button of his shirt undone. He'd taken off his jacket and there were dark circles under his armpits. Even his hair had started to go limp, its curl loosening.

Karen, who had washed her face and pimped her hair, sat up straight and gave him a look of pity. 'You know you're looking at jail time, Iain? I won't pretend there's any way out of that. I'll tell you what else there's no way out of, and that's the end of your relationship with David. You've woken up next to him for the last time. No more cosy cups of tea in bed in the morning. Whatever happens now, you're on your own. Either you help us bring him to justice. And I'm guessing he won't be too happy about that. Or you take the rap for all you've done together, all his crimes as well as your own. And what will he do then? Well, based on his past history, he'll run as far and as fast as he can. So what's it to be? Decency or martyrdom? I'll be honest. I believe in justice, and there's nothing just about you carrying the can for the murder of your brother.'

He hung his head and spoke softly. 'I'm glad our parents are dead. I couldn't face them. The shame. The disappointment. That's what I was thinking about when you were outside. Everything you said, when I had to listen to it like that, I couldn't believe it was me you were talking about. That I'd lost my way so badly that I let myself be carried along without stopping to think. Deep down, I knew it was wrong.' He looked up. 'But I love him so much. I couldn't bear the thought of losing him.'

'But you do see now that he's lost to you, whatever happens?'

He gave a sigh that was more like a sob in the back of his throat. 'It sounds crazy, but I still want him to think well of me.'

Karen leaned in again. Her voice was soft, almost a caress. 'I've been doing this job a long time, Iain. I've seen people like David Greig before. People who think they're special, above the rules that confine the rest of us. And I swear there is no way he's going to think well of you after this. He'll either despise you for your weakness if you try to save

422

him, or he'll hate you for your treachery if you do the right thing. You're dead to him now. Your only chance to survive this is to work with me.'

He took off his glasses, polished them on his tie and replaced them. 'What do you want me to do?'

Karen felt something loosen inside her, something she hadn't even realised she was holding so tightly. The headache lifted miraculously and she smiled tenderly at him. 'It's really simple. I want you to send him a text. You've been in a car accident. You're absolutely fine but the car is too damaged to drive. Can he come and pick you up? He'll do that for you, won't he?'

Auld nodded. 'He'll come like a shot.' He took out his phone. 'There's no signal here.'

'Never mind, we'll compose it in here then I'll take it and find a signal and send it.'

'I should say something about Dublin, he'll be thinking I'm there and back by now.' He started tapping the phone then showed it to Karen.

Dublin a waste of time, definitely not your work! Need a favour now – bloody stupid woman drove into me coming out of petrol station in Omagh. Front wing smashed to fuck, undriveable. It's at the BMW garage bodyshop, they're saying the end of the week!!! Can you come and get me? Love you. Xxx

Karen took the phone from him and flicked back past some exchanges between them. The tone and the sign-off matched. He wasn't trying to alert Greig. 'Thank you. Sergeant Mortimer will wait with you while Chief Inspector Nugent and I sort this out.'

Nugent followed her from the room and they walked back to his office, where the phone signal was clear. Karen pressed send and they waited. 'You think he'll go for it?' Nugent asked, propping one buttock on the edge of desk.

Karen couldn't keep still. She needed to stretch her legs, her back, her neck. 'Why wouldn't he? I don't think I've done anything to rattle his cage. My only concern was whether Geary would talk – I called him at the gallery this morning and told him Daniel Connolly wouldn't be coming and he should keep his mouth shut unless he wanted the Gardai all over him like a very bad rash. Given that Greig hasn't been in touch with Auld, I'd say Geary has done what I told him.'

'How are we going to do this? I take it you want Auld staked out in full view to draw him in?'

'You'll know a good spot? I'm thinking a coffee shop. Somewhere without alternative exits and entrances?'

'There's a nice wee coffee shop opposite the Sacred Heart church on George's Street. About five minutes away from here. There's probably a back door but you'd have to jump the counter and fight your way through the kitchen to get to it and we can stick a couple of uniforms out there.'

Before he'd finished speaking, the phone vibrated with a text:

Shit, that's not good. You sure you're OK? I'll jump in the car now, I'll be there soon as. Where are you? Xx

Karen typed a reply:

I'm in a café on George's Street opposite the Sacred Heart. Thanks. Love you. Xxx.

The response was instant:

Don't eat too many scones! Xx

She let out a breath and felt her shoulders drop. 'Thank fuck,' she said.

Nugent grinned. 'Aye,' he said. 'We'll get that all set up and walk Auld over there. Now, tell me. That crystal ball of yours, I don't suppose it knows where Greig is right now?'

'Look away now, nothing to see here,' Karen said, taking her own phone out and opening the app. 'He's not hanging about. He's coming down the road into Ramelton.' She looked up. 'I am so looking forward to this.'

54

Karen had to admit that Nugent was a serious operator. He'd proved it twice in one day. With less than an hour to work with, he'd cleared the café of customers and replaced the owner behind the counter with the woman who ran the police station canteen.

He had chosen well. The café was small – three four-top booths along one wall, five small round tables in the rest of the space. Auld was in the booth nearest the counter, facing the door. Daisy had managed to get Auld spruced up a bit – hair tidied, shirt button fastened, tie straight. Karen hoped Greig would write off his partner's worried and weary expression as the result of his car crash.

There was an unmarked car stationed outside with a plain-clothes detective in the passenger seat, and Sergeant Tiernan apparently interviewing a suspect in a liveried Land Rover in the lane behind. Inside, a young officer sat with a glass of Coke, seemingly absorbed in his phone. Daisy and another plain-clothes cop sat facing each other across the table nearest the door, drinking tea and working their way through a plate of scones. Between mouthfuls, having a quiet conversation about their favourite bands. They almost looked convincing as a couple, Karen thought. Two women

426

from the clerical support team occupied a booth with strict instructions not to get involved.

She conducted a quick sound check with Nugent, parked a few streets away. He could hear her, she could hear him. She took a look at her app again. Greig's Mercedes was on the outskirts of Omagh now. He'd be with them within minutes. A final circuit of the room; it appeared entirely normal to her. 'Right, everybody. Get set.' She smiled at Auld. 'Keep the heid and it'll all be over soon.' She sat down at the table nearest the booth, ready to spring into action as soon as Greig reached his partner.

Karen sipped the coffee in front of her. It was cold now, but it was still better than nothing. She looked at the app again. Greig was closer, it was true. But his car was no longer moving. She expanded the map, looking for clues. Was it a petrol station? Had he stopped to pick something up in a convenience store? The phone map settled and told her his Merc was in the car park of the BMW dealership. What the fuck?

'Nugent?' Urgent now. 'He's stopped at the BMW dealership.' She got up and leaned on the table of Auld's booth. 'Why would he do that? Why would he go to the BMW dealership?'

Auld looked scared. 'He'll be convinced he can get them to fix the car faster than they told me. He thinks I'm too soft with tradesmen.' He swallowed hard. 'He's going to find out I've lied to him.'

'You hear that, Nugent?' Karen shouted. In her earpiece she could hear the sound of an engine, the crackle of a police radio, Nugent instructing the team in the Land Rover to head for the BMW dealership.

'I'm on it, Pirie,' Nugent said. 'We're less than two minutes away.'

427

Karen ran for the door. 'Stay with Auld, Daisy,' she cried as she ran into the street and hauled open the door of the unmarked car.

'Drive,' she yelled at the startled detective. He looked terrified but did as he was told, clambering across the central console and starting the engine. 'The BMW dealership,' she told him. 'Fast as you can. But no siren,' she added, seeing his hand creep towards the button.

'Best-laid fucking plans,' she muttered as they wove through the busy streets. 'Nugent, what's happening?' she said, checking her phone. 'He's still there. Or at least, his car is.'

'We're here but I can't see the bastard,' Nugent said. 'We're going in, but I don't know where.' His voice faded out.

Karen's driver turned into the showroom car park. 'Go straight round the back,' Karen said. 'Where it says "Service and MOT".'

Obediently, he raced through the car park and screeched round the corner to the rear of the showroom. The wide roller doors leading to the service bays and the body shop were open to reveal a dozen mechanics and technicians working on a variety of cars and SUVs. Karen was out and running almost before the car skidded to a halt, looking wildly around her, alert for anyone who didn't fit in.

There was an office area behind the bays. As she drew near, she could hear raised voices. 'Are you calling me a liar?' a man was shouting in an accent that definitely wasn't local.

'Look for yourself, there's no black X5 in the workshop. I'll take you round the bodyshop myself if you don't believe me. Maybe it's not been towed in yet.'

Through the window, she could see the man who had

walked out of Hill House with Iain Auld two days ago. David Greig, or whatever he was calling himself these days. His fists were on the desk, arms straight, head jutting forward, aggression personified. The man behind the desk in a uniform blouson was pink-cheeked but not giving an inch.

Karen glanced over her shoulder. The detective had left the car, ignoring the protest of a mechanic who wanted it out of the way, and he was trotting behind her as if he was out for a slow jog in the park. Impatient, Karen pushed the door open. Both men turned to face her, startled. She planted her feet in a wide stance and said. 'David Greig, I am arresting you on suspicion of the murder of James Auld. You do not have—'

He launched himself at her, smashing his forearm into her throat. Karen collapsed to her knees, choking for breath. Greig moved to get past her but spotted the other officer coming up behind. He didn't hesitate for a second. He picked up a chair and threw it through the window that looked on to the service bays and vaulted through the frame, miraculously managing not to open a vein. He took off at speed, pursued a moment later by the Irish detective. Greig was moving fast for a man of his age.

Karen struggled to her feet, still making noises like a damaged animal and saw he was opening up the gap with his pursuer. She wanted to howl with rage, but she could barely breathe. All this, and now Greig was getting away.

And then a mechanic stepped out from behind a great brute of an SUV and swung a long spanner at Greig's trailing leg. He hit the ground with a scream and a crunch. And then the detective was on top of him and Karen thought she might possibly breathe again.

55

Jason hirpled into the HCU office still leaning on his crutch but moving better than the last time they'd gathered there. Somehow they'd squeezed another desk into the room; Daisy's temporary attachment had become a permanent assignment. The Chief Constable's pleasure at the media response to their results on two high-profile cases had trumped the Dog Biscuit's hostility to all things Pirie and she'd been forced to paste a smile on.

Now the prosecutorial system was grinding its way through the long hard road to the courtroom. Ruth Wardlaw and her boss were still wrangling over how many different crimes they could lay at the door of a still-protesting David Greig, and how much leeway they were prepared to grant the wreckage of Iain Auld in exchange for his full cooperation. The McAndrew case was less complex, but the prosecution lawyers knew they would struggle to persuade a jury not to fall for the defence argument that Dani Gilmartin's death had been a tragic accident, followed by panic.

Amanda McAndrew's parents had flown back from Greece to support their daughter. But the spectre of being

430

trapped in Edinburgh by the fallout from Covid-19 had driven them back to their olive grove. 'She should have been a more devoted daughter,' Daisy had remarked. 'What goes around comes around.'

Karen would never forget Mary Auld's reaction to the revelations about her husband. Karen had insisted on being the person to tell her. 'It's my responsibility,' she said. 'I'm the person she'll want to lash out at.' But Mary hadn't lashed out. She hadn't even tried denial. She'd simply crumpled before Karen's words, her face seeming to collapse in on itself. Karen didn't know how you would even begin to recover from such a seismic upheaval of all you had believed to be true. 'Is she even still technically married to him?' she'd asked Hamish as they'd lain in bed together the night after she'd come back from Omagh. 'That poor woman. Everything she thought she knew, shattered into pieces.'

Hamish had sighed. 'I can't comprehend how he could do that. You said they were married for years, happily by all accounts. So how the actual fuck could he tear up all those years? It's magical thinking, isn't it? He set a time-bomb down in the middle of her life and kidded himself it would never go off.'

'That's a good way of putting it. He never intended her to find out. But that doesn't excuse it. He says he was mad with love. But that doesn't excuse it either.'

'He wanted the thrill. He wanted to be a bad boy and get away with it.' Hamish sighed. 'I've known guys like that. They were lucky enough to avoid hooking up with one of the genuine bad boys like David fucking Greig.'

It had taken weeks for Karen, Daisy and Jason to complete the detailed reports that the prosecution needed. Latterly, it had been a race against time. The virus that had been a whisper on the wind when they'd been running around assorted jurisdictions had taken firm root in Scotland and they'd been warned that in the morning, lockdown was scheduled to begin. They'd be working from home, whatever that meant in practice.

So today they were clearing their desks, making sure everything they needed was on their laptops or accessible on the cloud. Karen had earmarked for review half a dozen cases whose notes, photographs and reports had all been previously digitised. 'We'll take another detailed look at them,' she'd explained. 'And see whether we can tease out any new possibilities.'

'What about lab work, if we need it?' Daisy asked.

Jason laughed. 'I bet Tamsin will bring in her sleeping bag and go into lockdown in the lab.'

'I wouldn't put it past her,' Karen said. 'River's heading back to Cumbria, though. She's been planning to write a book for ages. A mash-up of the scientific stuff and her own case experiences. She's looking forward to hanging out with Ewan for a few weeks.'

Now they'd taken the giant step of becoming affianced, Jason and Eilidh had decided to do lockdown in his flat at the bottom of Leith Walk. 'Lucky you,' Karen had said. 'Lockdown with a hairdresser. At the end of all this, you'll be the only well-groomed polis in Edinburgh.'

Hamish had decided he needed to lockdown in his croft in Wester Ross. 'The coffee shops are shut, there's nothing I can do in Edinburgh, and there's always work needs doing on the land. Come with me. There's no reason for you to stay in Edinburgh.'

Karen had been tempted. But she knew she didn't have the right to escape to a community that wasn't her own, whose scarce resources would be stretched thin if this pandemic turned out anything like the worst-case scenario. 'I can't do it,' she said. 'I need to show solidarity with my neighbours. And my colleagues. If this gets really bad, HCU is going to be a luxury Police Scotland will have to put on the back burner. Like the Met's Art Squad after Grenfell. I might have to go back to front-line policing with a stab vest and a baton.' She'd made a joke of it, but she knew it was a very real possibility.

That left Daisy. The obvious solution was for her to go back to her flat in Fife and lockdown on her own. Karen knew her sergeant was dreading the isolation. Unlike Karen, who revelled in her own company, Daisy was a social creature. Karen had considered inviting her to hunker down with her, but while her waterfront flat was perfect for one, it would be intolerable with two, one of whom needed space. She'd voiced her concerns to Hamish, and he'd immediately proposed a solution.

'I'm going to be in Clashstronach, Karen. My place will be empty. It's way big enough for two. And I've got keys for the private gardens in the square.' He was right, of course. His flat at the top of the New Town had two bedrooms, a study, a big living room and a dining kitchen with a table that sat eight. And its private roof garden had views over the Georgian rooftops across the Forth to Fife, so she couldn't even complain about losing her sea view. It was seven minutes' walk from her office, should she be called back in. Karen loved Hamish's flat in the detached way one can afford to love a place that will never be within one's own budget.

It was a generous offer. But was it a devious way of trying to get her to move in with him? He'd shown a capacity for manipulation before. And the business with Merrick Shand was still fresh in her memory.

In the end, she'd accepted his offer, as much for Daisy as for herself. Hamish had left for Clashstronach two days previously, and Karen and Daisy had moved in the evening before. Karen had no idea how it was going to work. But she was slowly learning that change wasn't always something to chafe against. And she was one of the fortunate ones. A roof over her head. Access to healthcare if the worst came to her door. And a secure job – because people would always need the polis – and even in a pandemic, murder should never go unprosecuted.

She'd deal with the survivor guilt later. Right now, what mattered was survival.

Acknowledgements

Writers never fly solo. The more I do this, the more I understand all the contributions that make a book. Many of them go unnoticed, especially by the author, but there are others I am well aware of.

I owe grateful thanks to Patrice Hoffman of my French publisher, Flammarion, for his help with French policing arrangements. The bits I've got wrong are literary licence!

Closer to home, Dorothy Bain QC, Sheriff Norman McFadyen and Sheriff Tom Welsh clarified legal process and the administration of European Arrest Warrants for me.

Liz Nugent offered excellent location suggestions; in these constrained times, I wasn't able to go and scout them for myself!

As always, I lean on the generosity and patience of forensic scientists who happily share their expertise and their experience. In these days of lockdown, they don't even get cake in exchange ... Thanks to Professor Wolfram Meier-Augenstein for information on stable isotope analysis and to Dame Professor Sue Black for the Coco Pops, among other things.

Thanks too to James Auld and David Greig whose generous charitable donations to Breast Cancer Now, the

Homeless World Cup Foundation and Raith Rovers FC have been rewarded by their questionable appearances in these pages. Your kindness, forbearance and good nature are appreciated by all who know you!

Most of this book was written and all the editorial work was carried out in the strange half-world of lockdown. Like most of the writers I know, I found sustained concentration very difficult. Throughout the process, my support team at Little, Brown have been patient, dedicated and immensely competent in spite of their other responsibilities. Hats off to all of you, and thanks for always being cheery on the screen! Lucy Malagoni and Laura Sherlock at LB and the indomitable Jane Gregory at DHA kept me going through the difficult days.

What saved me in lockdown was sharing it with my partner Jo Sharp. She discovered new skills as a video producer (Check out *Cooking the Books – Val McDermid* on YouTube), a hairdresser, and a gardener. Through it all she's made me laugh, made me think and made me believe in myself. Jo, I couldn't have done it without you. You are my Wonder Woman.

Read on for an excerpt
from Val McDermid's first new series launch
in nearly twenty years, *1979*.

Available in hardcover and ebook.

Prologue

Fat flakes blew into his face, cold wet kisses on his cheeks and eyelids. Last time there had been a winter like this, he'd been a wee boy and all he remembered was the fun – sledging down the big hill, throwing snowballs in the playground, sliding across the frozen lake in the park. Now, it was a pain in the arse. Driving was a nightmare of slush and black ice. Walking was worse. He'd already wrecked his favourite pair of shoes and every time he took his socks off, his toes were wrinkled pink sultanas.

But there were advantages. No one would ever know he'd been here. His footprints would be erased within the hour. There was nobody else on the street. All the curtains were drawn tight to keep the night out and the heat in. The children were indoors now, their every outdoor garment drying on kitchen pulleys and steaming clothes horses after a day in the snow. Everybody else was huddled in front of the TV. There had been enough snow this January for the novelty to have worn off. Even the corporation bus he'd overtaken on the main drag had been empty, a ghost ship in the night. The only people he'd passed had been a couple of die-hards headed for the pub. There was an eerie stillness in this side street, though. The snow suffocated the engine noise from the few vehicles that had braved the blizzard. He felt like the last man standing.

Head bowed against the weather, he almost missed his destination. At the last moment, he realised his mistake and wheeled abruptly into the lobby of the tenement close. He took a deep breath, brushing the snow from his eyebrows.

He climbed the stairs, rehearsing what he'd been planning all day. He was standing on the edge of the road to nowhere. Maybe it was late in the day to start thinking about protecting his future, but better late than never. And he'd figured a way out. Maybe more than one.

It wouldn't be easy. It might not be straightforward. But he deserved better than this.

And tonight, there was going to be a reckoning.

1

I t started badly and only got worse. Blizzards, strikes, unburied bodies, power cuts, terrorist threats and Showaddywaddy's *Greatest Hits* topping the album charts; 1979 was a cascade of catastrophe. Unless, like Allie Burns, you were a journalist. For her tribe, someone else's bad news was the unmistakable sound of opportunity knocking.

Allie Burns stared out of the train carriage window at white, broken only by a line of telegraph poles. They were miraculously still dark on one side, sheltered from the blustery wind whipping the snow in sudden flurries. The train sat motionless, trapped in mid-journey by drifts blocking the tracks. She glanced across at Danny Sullivan. 'How come winter always brings Scotland to a standstill?'

He chuckled. 'It's just like *Murder on the Orient Express*. Stuck on a train in a snowdrift.'

'Only without the murder,' Allie pointed out.

'OK, only without the murder.'

'And the luxury. And the cocktails. And Albert Finney in a hairnet.'

Danny pulled a face. 'Picky, picky, picky. Anybody

would think you were on the subs' table, fiddling with my commas and misrelated participles.'

Allie laughed. 'I don't even know what a misrelated participle is. And I doubt you do.'

'I did once, if that counts?'

They subsided into silence again. They'd met unintentionally on the freezing platform of Haymarket station on the second day of the year, colleagues returning to work after spending Hogmanay with their families. There were plenty of her fellow hacks Allie would have hidden behind a platform pillar to avoid, but Danny was probably the least objectionable of them. If he was sexist, racist and sectarian to the core, he'd done a good job of hiding it. And there was no escaping the fact that after time spent with her parents, she was desperate for any conversation from her own world. The nearest she'd come was the first paper of the year, with its coverage of the International Year of the Child, an imminent lorry drivers' strike and cut-price blouses in Frasers' sale.

She'd met up with a couple of school friends for a drink in the village pub, but that had been no better. The chat started awkward and stilted, veered on to the comforting common ground of reminiscence, then backed into a cul-de-sac of gossip about people she didn't remember or had never met. The past few years seemed to have severed her from old acquaintance.

As the train had pulled out of Kirkcaldy on the first leg of the journey back to Glasgow, Allie had felt the lightness of reprieve. She'd waved dutifully to her parents, standing on the snowy platform. They'd driven her the eight miles to the station from the former mining village of East Wemyss where she'd grown up, and she wondered whether they shared her sense of relief.

They had nothing to say to each other. That was at the heart of the discomfort she felt whenever she returned home. She'd slowly come to the realisation that they never had. Only, when she was growing up, that lack of connection had been masked by the daily routines of work and school, Girl Guides and bowling club, Women's Guild and hockey team.

Then Allie had gone to university in another country and been parachuted into life on Mars. Everything in Cambridge had been strange. The accents, the food, the expectations, the preoccupations. She'd quickly assimilated. She believed she'd found her tribe at last. Three years flew by, but then she was unceremoniously cast adrift.

And now, after two years in the North East of England learning a trade, she was back in Scotland. It wasn't what she'd planned. She'd been aiming for Fleet Street and a national daily. But the news editor on her final training scheme post was an old drinking buddy of his opposite number on the *Daily Clarion* in Glasgow. And it was a national daily, if you counted Scotland as a nation. The strapline on the paper said, 'One adult in two in Scotland reads the *Clarion*'. The wags in the office added, 'The other one cannae read.' Strings had been pulled, an offer made. She couldn't refuse.

She'd had five years of a sufficient distance to keep her visits home to a minimum. But now it was impossible to avoid the significant dates. Birthdays. Family celebrations. And because it was Scotland, Hogmanay.

Which meant three evenings of endless Festive Specials and musicals – *Oliver!*, *My Fair Lady*, *Half a Sixpence*. She'd wanted to watch Jack Lemmon and Shirley MacLaine in *The Apartment*, but once her mother had read the brief

5

summary in the newspaper listings, that had been firmly off the agenda. Allie didn't want to revisit the torture so she simply said, 'How was your New Year?'

Danny scoffed. 'Like every New Year I can remember. We've got the biggest flat, so everybody piles in to ours. My dad's got five sisters – Auntie Mary, Auntie Cathy, Aunty Theresa, Auntie Bernie and Auntie Senga.'

Allie giggled. 'You've got an Auntie Senga? For real? I thought Senga was just a joke name?'

'No. It's "Agnes" backwards. She was baptised Agnes, but she goes by Senga. She says, anything to avoid being called Aggie.'

'I get that. So your five aunties come over?'

Danny nodded. 'Five aunties, four uncles and assorted cousins.'

'Only four uncles?'

'Yeah, Uncle Paul got killed at his work. He was crushed by a whisky barrel in the bonded warehouse down at Leith.' He pulled a face. 'My dad said it might have had something to do with a significant amount of the whisky being inside Uncle Paul at the time.'

'So you have a big family party?'

'Yep. Same every year. The aunties all do their specialities. Theresa borrows the big soup pot from the church and makes a vat of lentil soup. Mary does rolls on potted hough. Cathy bakes the best sausage rolls in Edinburgh, my mum makes meat loaf, Bernie brings black bun that nobody eats, plus shop-bought shortbread, and Senga produces three flavours of tablet.'

'Bloody hell, that's some feast.' He didn't look like someone who existed on that kind of traditional Scottish diet. Danny was slender as a greyhound, with the high cheekbones, narrow nose and sharp chin of a medieval ascetic. Only his tumble of collar-length curls made him look of his time.

He grinned. 'No kidding. There's enough in the house to feed half of Gorgie. And enough drink to open our own pub.'

'So what do you do? Eat and drink and blether?'

'Well, we eat and drink and then everybody does their party piece. That keeps us going till it's time to turn on the telly for the bells. And then Dad puts the Corries on the record player and it just gets more raucous. A few of the neighbours come in to first-foot.'

'Sounds like a form of self-defence!'

Danny shrugged. 'It's a friendly close. What about you?'

Allie was spared from answering when the door at the end of the carriage clattered open and the conductor staggered through, loaded with a pile of blankets. As he approached, he distributed them among the handful of other passengers. 'We're going to be stuck here a while yet,' he announced, a gloomy relish in his voice. 'We've got to wait for the snowplough to get here from Falkirk and it's making slow progress, I'm told. And the heating's went off. Sorry about that, but at least we've got some blankets.'

He handed each of them a coarse grey blanket that felt more suitable for a horse than a human. Allie wrapped it around her, nose wrinkling at the smell of mothballs. 'Are you feeling the cold?' Danny asked.

'Not really. But now the heating's off, we'll lose our body heat pretty quickly.'

He eyed her across the narrow gap between their seats. 'If you came and sat next to me, we could share the blankets. And the body heat.' He gave her a wide-eyed smile.

'I'm not trying anything on. Just being selfish. Look at me, there's nothing of me. I really suffer with the cold.'

There was no denying that he was well wrapped up. Walking boots, corduroy trousers tucked into thick woollen socks, chunky polo-neck sweater peeping out of his heavy overcoat. Woolly gloves, and a knitted hat sticking out of a pocket. Allie didn't think she'd ever seen anyone better equipped for the cold. Not even her grandfather, a man addicted to being out in the fresh air whatever the weather. A lifetime of the coal face would do that to you. 'OK,' she said, pretending a reluctance she didn't feel. He was probably the only man in the newsroom who didn't give off a predatory vibe. Arguably, you had to have the instincts of a predator to be a good reporter. But equally, you should know when to turn them off.

Allie swapped seats. They fussed with the blankets till they'd constructed a double-thickness shroud around themselves. 'What shift are you on next?' she asked him.

'Day shift tomorrow. You?'

She pulled a face. 'I'm supposed to be on the night shift tonight. Unless that bloody snowplough gets a move on, I'm going to be in big trouble.'

'You've got time. It's barely gone three. And even if you don't make it in on time, you'll not be the only one. You working on anything or just the day-to-day?' He spoke with a casualness that begged the return question.

'Waiting for the next news story to drop. You know what it's like on the night shift. What about you?'

He smiled. 'I've been chasing a big one. An investigation. I've been on it for a few weeks, in between chasing ambulances. I got a whisper from somebody who didn't even know what he was telling me and I've been trying to

8

bottom it ever since. Mostly in my own time. Grunts like you and me, we're not supposed to do stories like this. We're supposed to pass it on to the news desk and let one of the glory boys lead the charge. We get to do the dirty work round the edges, but we don't get the bylines.'

It was no less than the truth. There was a cohort of reporters who had titles – crime correspondent, chief reporter, education correspondent, court reporter and half a dozen others. When the lower orders uncovered a big story, it would immediately be snapped up by one of the guys who could claim it for his fiefdom. 'So how did you hang on to it?'

'I haven't told anybody about it yet,' Danny said simply. 'I'm holding on to it till it's too far down the line for anybody to take it off me. But it's dynamite.'

Allie felt a pang of jealousy. But it wasn't directed at Danny. It was more a longing for a major story of her own. 'What's it about? When's it going to be ready?'

'Soon. All I need is the last piece of the jigsaw. Next long weekend, I've got to make a wee trip down south and find the final bits of sky.'

So, not long then. The Clarion staff worked four long shifts per week, a pattern that was so arranged that it gave them five consecutive days off every three weeks. Allie still hadn't entirely worked out how best to use the time, though until the winter had set in she'd been developing a taste for hillwalking. But she was working up to buying a flat and she could see an endless vista of decorating and home improvement in her future. 'Good for you. If you need a grunt—'

Again the door clattered open. This time, the guard was red-faced and agitated. 'Are any of youse a doctor?' He looked around, desperate. 'Or a nurse?'

Before anyone could respond, from behind him, a woman's scream split the air. 'I'm going to fucking kill you, ya bastard.'

2

Allie sprang to her feet, open-mouthed. Her eyes met Danny's and without a word spoken, they both raced for the door. Danny pushed past the guard, shouting, 'I'm a first-aider.' Allie used his momentum to carry her through at his back. A woman lay sprawled along one of the three-seater bench seats, trackie bottoms round her ankles, blood smeared down her thighs and soaking into the coarse velour upholstery. A man stood over her, lips drawn back in a rictus. Allie stopped in her tracks.

Her first thought was that the woman was the victim of a violent attack. Then she registered the pale dome of her belly. 'She's having a baby.' As redundant comments go, she knew it was right up there even as she spoke.

Danny kept going though, not breaking stride till he was at the woman's side. 'I'm a first-aider, OK, pal?' he said to the man, who took a couple of stumbling steps backwards, nodding like one of those novelty dogs that old men had on the parcel shelves of their cars.

The woman hadn't stopped roaring and yelling since they'd entered the carriage and it didn't sound like she was about to quit any time soon. Danny shifted so he could see what was going on between her legs then looked

11

up at Allie. In spite of his air of confidence, she could see apprehension in his eyes, 'Hold her hand,' he said. 'Try and calm her down.'

Terrified at the responsibility, Allie edged forward and grabbed one of the woman's flailing hands. Somehow it was simultaneously clammy with sweat and sticky with blood. She turned to the man, whose expression had turned piteous. 'What's her name?'

'J-J-Jenny,' he stammered. Then, more firmly. 'Jenny. She's not due for another fortnight.' He fished a battered packet of No. 6 out of his jeans, jittered a cigarette out of the packet and sparked up, dragging the smoke deep into his lungs.

'Baby's got a whole different schedule,' Danny muttered, shrugging out of his overcoat and pushing up his sleeves.

Allie gripped Jenny's hand and stretched out to push her thick dark hair back from her sweating face. 'It's going to be all right, Jenny.'

'Fuck you, fuck do you know?' Jenny yelled.

'My pal knows what he's doing.' Allie gave Danny a pleading glance.

'That's right, Jenny.' He gave a nervous laugh. 'I was brought up on *Emergency Ward 10*. You need to take some deep breaths, darling. I can see your baby's head, your wean's determined to get out into the world. But the bairn needs your help. Needs you to stop fighting it.' He leaned forward. Allie didn't want to think about what he was doing. Just the thought of slimy blood and whatever else was down there was making her stomach churn.

She turned back to face Jenny, whose eyes were rolling back in her head like a frightened horse in a Western. 'I know it's sore,' she said gently. 'But it'll soon be over,

Jenny. And then you'll be holding your wee one in your arms. You'll be a proud mammy, and all this will just be like a bad dream, honest.'

Jenny convulsed suddenly, screaming again, crushing Allie's hand in her grip. 'That's good, Jenny,' Danny gasped. He was sweating as hard as Jenny now. 'Push again.' He waited. 'Now breathe. A deep breath for me. I can see a shoulder. Now push again, darling. You can do this.'

The next twenty minutes passed in a blur of blood and sweat, Jenny's moans, Allie's encouragement, Danny's anxious glances and a chain of cigarettes from the father-to-be. Allie kept repeating the same meaningless phrases. 'You're doing great,' and 'You're a star, Jenny,' and 'Nearly there.' She was aware that other people had formed an audience around them. Then all at once, Danny had a red and purple bundle in his arms and the thin wail of a new-born baby struck a counterpoint to Jenny's groans.

'Well done, you've done amazing,' Allie said.

'You've got a son.' Danny turned to grin at the man behind him, whose knees gave way as he collapsed on to a seat. Tears sprang from his eyes.

'I love you, Jenny,' he cried, his voice thick and hoarse.

'I still fucking hate you,' Jenny sighed. But the rage had gone from her voice.

One of the other passengers produced a towel. Allie kept her face turned towards Jenny, determined to avoid what was going on at the other end. She helped Jenny sit up, inching her along the seat so she could prop herself up against the window. Then Danny passed Jenny the baby, wrapped in the towel, his little face scrunched up against the assault of sights and sounds and sensations.

The father staggered to his feet and pushed through to

Jenny's side. He kneeled down beside them and kissed his son, then the new mother. 'You're incredible, Jenny,' he said. 'I love you. Gonnae marry me?'

Jenny looked down at him, and in the moment, Allie saw a hint of steel behind her exhausted eyes. 'Fuck me, Stevie. If I'd known that was all it would take to get you to ask me, I'd have fell pregnant ages ago.'

Danny leaned over and muttered to Allie, 'Great quote, that's a strapline if ever I heard one.' He registered her surprised expression. 'It's a page lead at the very least, Allie. Maybe even the splash.'

'If it is, it's your story,' she said. 'You saved the day.'

He shook his head. 'It's a woman's story. You know that's what the desk will say.'

He had a point. She was growing accustomed to the twisted logic behind the allocation of stories. It had taken years for women reporters to gain a toehold in national tabloid newsrooms. Eventually it had dawned on the bosses that some stories benefited from what they called 'a woman's touch'. Allie understood perfectly the motivation behind her hiring. That didn't mean she had to collude in it, though. 'You delivered the bloody kid,' she protested.

He looked down ruefully at his bloodstained hands and the streaks on his jumper and trousers. 'Exactly. I've suffered enough. You know the kind of shit I'll get from the guys in the newsroom. It'll be, "Ooh, Matron," like I'm in a Carry On film every time I turn around. Plus they'll want a picture byline of the reporter on the spot and that could screw me up for doing any undercovers. Once I break this story I've got on the go, I'll get the chance to do the big investigative stories. Look, Allie, all you've got to do is say it was some mystery man who refused to give his name.'

'What? And get bawled out by the news desk for coming back with half a story?'

Danny scanned the bystanders and saw the guard keeping a cautious distance from the group of well-wishers round the new family. He stepped across to him. 'I'm a reporter on the *Clarion*,' he began.

The guard took a step back. 'I never did anything wrong,' he said hastily.

'No, pal, nobody's even hinting at that. But it looks like we're hogging the limelight if we do a story about me birthing a baby on a train stuck in a snowdrift. But see if it was to be you in the story? You'd be the hero of the hour. And it's not like you didnae come for help, right?'

The guard looked confused. 'But all these folk saw what really happened.'

'They'll forget all that, they'll just tell all their pals about seeing a baby born on a train. My colleague here' – he pointed to Allie – 'she'll write the story. Jenny and Stevie, they don't care who gets the credit.' She had to admit, his smile was charming.

'I don't know . . . ' The guard was wavering.

'You might even get a commendation or a raise or something.' He turned back to Allie. 'Have you got a camera on you?'

She nodded. 'In my bag.' She always carried her compact Olympus Trip 35 around with her; her first news editor had instructed her not to leave home without it. 'There's never a bloody pic man around when you need one,' he'd said.

'Away and get it,' Danny told her. 'They'll want pix.'